What Reviewers Say About

KIM BALD...

"Her...crisply written action scenes, juxtaposition of plotlines, smart dialogue make this a story the reader will absolutely enjoy and long remember." – **Arlene Germain**, book reviewer for the *Lambda Book Report* and the *Midwest Book Review*

ROSE BEECHAM

"...a mystery writer with a delightful sense of humor, as well as an eye for an interesting array of characters..." – *MegaScene*

"...her characters seem fully capable of walking away from the particulars of whodunit and engaging the reader in other aspects of their lives." – *Lambda Book Report*

"...creates believable characters in compelling situations, with enough humor to provide effective counterpoint to the work of detecting." – *Bay Area Reporter*

JANE FLETCHER

"...a natural gift for rich storytelling and world-building...one of the best fantasy writers at work today." – **Jean Stewart**, author of the *Isis* series

RADCLY*f*FE

"Powerful characters, engrossing plot, and intelligent writing..." – **Cameron Abbott,** author of *To the Edge* and *An Inexpressible State of Grace*

"...well-honed storytelling skills...solid prose and sure-handedness of the narrative..." – **Elizabeth Flynn**, *Lambda Book Report*

"...well-plotted...lovely romance...I couldn't turn the pages fast enough!" – **Ann Bannon**, author of *The Beebo Brinker Chronicles.*

"...a consummate artist in crafting classic romance fiction...her numerous best selling works exemplify the splendor and power of Sapphic passion..." – **Yvette Murray, PhD**, *Reader's Raves*

JUSTICE
IN THE
SHADOWS

by
RADCLYffE

2005

JUSTICE IN THE SHADOWS
© 2004 BY RADCLYFFE. ALL RIGHTS RESERVED.

ISBN 1-933110-03-1

THIS TRADE PAPERBACK ORIGINAL IS PUBLISHED BY
BOLD STROKES BOOKS, INC.,
PHILADELPHIA, PA, USA

FIRST EDITION: MARCH 2004
SECOND EDITION: SEPTEMBER 2004, BOLD STROKES BOOKS, INC.
THIRD PRINTING: MARCH 2005, BOLD STROKES BOOKS, INC.

CREDITS
EXECUTIVE EDITOR: STACIA SEAMAN
PRODUCTION DESIGN: J. BARRE GREYSTONE
COVER PHOTOS: LEE LIGON
COVER DESIGN BY SHERI (GRAPHICARTIST2020@HOTMAIL.COM)

By the Author

Romances

Safe Harbor	Tomorrow's Promise
Beyond the Breakwater	Passion's Bright Fury
Innocent Hearts	Love's Masquerade
Love's Melody Lost	shadowland
Love's Tender Warriors	Fated Love

Honor Series	**Justice Series**
Above All, Honor	A Matter of Trust (prequel)
Honor Bound	Shield of Justice
Love & Honor	In Pursuit of Justice
Honor Guards	Justice in the Shadows

Change Of Pace: *Erotic Interludes*
(A Short Story Collection)

Acknowledgments

The Justice series has given me the opportunity to explore a host of characters whom I find more complex with each writing, while delving into topics that fascinate me on many levels. It's a joy to reap pleasure in myriad ways from a process that in itself affords great personal fulfillment. Writing never fails to reward me, emotionally and intellectually, and weaving the densely woven—at times tangled—threads of this ongoing tale is immensely satisfying.

My thanks go first to Ms. Ann Bannon, who graciously found time in her busy schedule to review the first book in this series and to provide the cover quote. I am humbled to be so honored.

I also wish to thank the many readers who have purchased the earlier works, written to me asking for a sequel, and recommended the series to others. Your encouragement and support spur me on when I think I'll never figure out what's around the next corner for our band of lovers.

Thanks also to Laney Roberts and Stacia Seaman for expert editing, to my beta readers, Athos, Eva, Diane, Denise, JB, and Tomboy, for daily encouragement, and to the members of the online community, most especially the Radlist, for spreading the word.

Lee and I took a midnight drive to the red light district with our digital camera to procure the cover photos, but Sheri, as always, made them art. She never fails to bring my words to life with skill and vision.

I am fortunate to have two grand passions in my life – writing and Lee. Contemplating that, words fail. *Amo te.*

Radclyffe 2004

Dedication

For Lee,
For embracing even the shadows

CHAPTER ONE

D r. Catherine Rawlings awoke, naked, her cheek against her lover's shoulder. They'd slept with the window open in the bedroom of her first-floor apartment, and a faint breeze ruffled the curtains at the window. It was dark. *Five a.m.?*

Soon the alarm would go off, and another day would begin. She loved awakening to the still-new pleasure of Rebecca's body, but even so, she was uneasy, haunted by all that remained unfinished. The last few weeks had been so intense, both personally and professionally, that she'd hardly had time to adjust to the emotional maelstrom.

Despite the reservations of her police detective lover, Rebecca Frye, Catherine had agreed to consult with a joint police and federal task force formed to expose a local child pornography ring. In the process of profiling the perpetrators, she'd become friends with some of the investigators and had also become deeply invested in stopping the abuse of helpless young girls. And in the last twenty-four hours, things had gone terribly wrong. Now one woman lay in a coma, the team had been shattered by jurisdictional rivalries, and the criminals were no closer to being apprehended.

Her last conversation with Rebecca just before they'd fallen into bed, both physically exhausted and emotionally numb, drifted back to her.

"What's going to happen now?"

"I'll be back on regular duty in a day or so, and I'll have new cases to worry about." Rebecca rested her cheek against Catherine's hair and closed her eyes. *"It happens like this in police work. You work your ass off, and then you can't make the case because of a technicality, or you* do *make the case, but the perp plea-bargains it down to nothing."*

"So you're letting this go?" Catherine asked, surprised.

Faintly, Rebecca shook her head. "Clark will pull the plug on this task force—he's probably already made the call. But I'll keep doing what I'm trained to do until we make this right—for Jeff, for Michael, for those young kids."

Jeff Cruz had been Rebecca's partner in the Special Crimes Unit of the Philadelphia Police Department, until he and an undercover detective, Jimmy Hogan, had been murdered three months ago. Their killer was still at large, their murders unsolved.

Michael Lassiter had been struck down the night before the porno sting operation by a hit-and-run driver in a thwarted attempt to kill J.T. Sloan, her lover and the civilian computer consultant on the task force. She lay in the intensive care unit at University Hospital in critical condition.

Jeff, Michael, those nameless teenagers—victims all.

"I'll keep doing what I'm trained to do until we make this right..."

Make it right. That's what Catherine's lover did. Stood for right, sometimes at peril to herself.

Catherine's right hand rested on Rebecca's chest, her fingers motionless against the ridges of scar tissue above Rebecca's left breast. Some of the scars were only days old. She didn't need to trace the outlines to feel each one intimately. She saw them with her eyes open or closed. She saw them in her dreams.

She shivered and pressed closer.

"Catherine?" Detective Sergeant Rebecca Frye kissed the top of Catherine's head, one hand drifting up and down her arm in a slow caress. She was still a bit stunned to find herself in Catherine's bed—in Catherine's life. They'd been together four months, and for a large chunk of that time, she'd been in the hospital recovering from a near-fatal gunshot wound. *Hardly the best way to start a love affair.* "Are you cold?"

"No." Catherine turned her head to press her lips to the skin beneath Rebecca's collarbone. "I love you."

Rebecca caught her breath. "I can't get used to hearing that. It's so...damn good." She held Catherine tighter.

"We'll practice," Catherine murmured. "But I don't want you

to get too used to it."

"No chance." Rebecca felt Catherine shiver again. "Is it last night?"

"What?"

"Whatever it is that's bothering you." Rebecca laced her fingers softly into the thick auburn hair at the base of Catherine's neck, stroking her slowly.

And you wonder why I love you? You, with your cop's instincts and your gentle hands. Catherine took a deep breath and made a conscious effort to shake off the melancholy. "I keep thinking how unfair it all is. You and the others—you worked so hard, put yourselves at risk, and to have it all taken away—God, aren't you angry?"

"You worked just as hard helping us nail down the perp's identity," Rebecca pointed out. "Aren't *you* angry?"

"Yes." Catherine startled herself with the vehemence of the reply. "God, yes. I am *so* angry about Michael being hurt, and Sloan suffering, and Jason putting his life on the line. And you—working around the clock when you're barely out of the hospital. It's just so unjust."

Rebecca laughed quietly, and the sound was harsh with frustration. "I can't think about it that way. Because if I did, I'd turn in my badge...or pick up a bottle again."

"I'm sorry," Catherine said swiftly, realizing that she was just getting a taste of what was Rebecca's daily fare. As a psychiatric consultant to the police force, she'd seen the alcoholism, the broken marriages, the gradual loss of humanity resulting from the stress and frustration of the never-ending violence and senseless brutality that police officers faced regularly. She'd witnessed it clinically and thought she'd understood it. But now that she had experienced the disillusionment and helplessness personally, she felt it as an ache in her bones.

Catherine rose up on one elbow to study her lover's face in the rapidly brightening dawn light. Rebecca looked drawn, and with good reason. She wasn't yet completely recovered physically from the gunshot wounds, and she couldn't be emotionally healed from the loss of her partner or her own near-death, either. Her state of mind, however, was difficult to discern. Like many cops, Rebecca kept her pain and uncertainties to herself.

"You have to deal with this all the time, and I'm not helping, am I?"

"You're wrong." Rebecca drew Catherine down and kissed her mouth, then murmured, "You are the one sane thing in my life."

"You don't know how glad I am that's true." Catherine framed Rebecca's face with her hands, lightly tracing the strong jaw with her fingers, then skimming through the thick blond hair. She thought about the bottle of scotch that Rebecca had purchased only the week before and then poured down the sink without drinking. Searching the deep blue eyes, Catherine tried to see what Rebecca could not share. "Do you still want to drink?"

"Every day." Rebecca's full mouth lifted into a shadow of a grin. "But I'm okay. I promised I'd tell you if I got into trouble, and I meant it."

"Thank you." The words were barely a whisper as Catherine's lips brushed Rebecca's.

"I love you. You don't ever have to thank me." Rebecca kissed her again, then shifted upright, drawing Catherine with her. Encircling her with an arm and softly cupping her breast, Rebecca rested her chin atop Catherine's head and mused out loud. "I *know* Avery Clark and his whole Justice task force ties in somehow with Jeff Cruz and Jimmy Hogan being assassinated. That can't be a convenient coincidence. Clark might *think* he can just pull the plug on this operation and we'll take it lying down, but he's wrong."

Catherine's heart thudded painfully. "What are you going to do?"

"Just dig around a bit." Rebecca was evasive, both out of habit and out of a desire not to alarm her lover. She'd lost more than one lover who couldn't stand the constant worry of being involved with a cop. She didn't intend to let that happen this time. What she felt for Catherine went far beyond anything she had ever known, and the thought of losing her made her stomach churn. "I know Sloan won't walk away from what happened to Michael, and I'd rather keep her busy doing computer checks for me than worry that she's running around grabbing people by the throat."

Remembering the fury in Sloan's face when she had accosted Avery Clark in the hospital, accusing him of being responsible for Michael's injury, Catherine could only agree. "She's in agony, Rebecca. She feels guilty for what happened and helpless to change it. Plus, she's terrified of losing her lover. Until Michael recovers, Sloan's going to be very volatile."

"I'll keep an eye on her," Rebecca promised. *As if anyone could control Sloan.*

"Who's going to keep an eye on you?" Catherine asked, only half teasing. "Watts?"

Rebecca snorted. She thought of the overweight, perpetually rumpled, and generally believed to be washed-up cop she'd been saddled with after Jeff's death. The same cop with whom she'd gone through a door the night before without a second's hesitation and to whom she'd entrusted Catherine's life when she'd thought herself about to die. "Yeah, right."

Catherine merely smiled.

"What are you doing today?" Rebecca turned to stretch lazily against Catherine's body, running both hands up and down her lover's back. When she circled her palm in the small hollow at the base of Catherine's spine, she felt her tense. She pressed harder, insinuating a leg between Catherine's thighs. "Hmm?"

"Back to routine." Catherine's voice was husky and slow. She rested a hand against Rebecca's chest, rubbed her thumb across a nipple. She smiled when Rebecca gasped. "Rounds in the morning, then clinic...ahh, yes, right there...in the afternoon. I thought...that's nice...I'd stop to see...Mmm..." Catherine tilted her head back, her eyes hazy. "Unless you intend to make good on what you've started, Detective..."

"Oh, I do." Rebecca grinned and slid one hand between them, cradling Catherine's breast as she rocked her leg a little higher.

"Thank God." Catherine felt Rebecca's mouth on her neck, felt teeth against her skin, and felt herself grow heavy and wet. "When you touch me..." She lost her thought as fingers closed around her nipple, sending streams of pleasure streaking along her nerve fibers. Her stomach clenched with excitement.

"What?" Rebecca squeezed the hard nub, twisting very gently, her head suddenly light at the sound of a quiet whimper. "When I touch you...what?"

Catherine found Rebecca's eyes, tried to focus on them

through the blur of desire, needing something to prevent her surrender to passion too soon. "You make me...forget...everything. Oh, darling...stop...for a second."

"Too much?" Rebecca murmured, easing her grip on the tense nipple.

"Too good. You'll make me come."

"Didn't you just say..." Rebecca's eyes widened as fingers stole between her thighs, sliding unerringly around the hard ache of her own desire. She felt a tug along her length, and her whole body twitched. "Ohh...Jesus, don't do that unless you want me to go off right away."

"Not right away." Catherine stroked her lightly. "But soon."

Rebecca's brain was already swimming. She drew her fingers down Catherine's abdomen, laced them through the silken hair between her legs, and glanced gently over her clitoris. "You're so beautiful."

"Kiss me while you make me come," Catherine breathed against Rebecca's mouth.

Their lips brushed tenderly, as lightly as a breeze through summer leaves, their fingers echoing the kiss over flesh ripe with promise. A sigh, a quiet moan, the only sounds. A lip sucked gently between careful teeth, the touch of a tongue soothing the tiny bite. A lift of hips, a flood of arousal, a cry cut short by the quick rush of pleasure.

"Catherine," Rebecca whispered. "I love you."

"Please," Catherine moaned. "Don't stop..." *touching me, loving me, needing me...*

When their tongues slid inside warm welcoming hollows, hands followed, until they filled one another, body and soul. They pressed ever closer, muscles straining, hearts thundering, blood racing, climbing for the heavens.

Rebecca groaned, shuddering in Catherine's embrace. "You're making me come."

"Yes, oh yes." Catherine pressed her face hard to Rebecca's chest as she clenched around the fingers curled inside her being, holding her very life with certainty and strength. "I'm coming... with you. Always...you."

❖

Only blocks away, a black-haired woman with violet eyes sat beside the bed of a still figure in a room illuminated only by the otherworldly glow of medical equipment. With impersonal readouts and muted sounds, those machines monitored the fragile essence of her lover's life. Hunched forward, elbows on her knees, unaware of the cramps in her shoulders and thighs, J.T. Sloan held Michael Lassiter's hand tenderly in both of hers. Slowly, carefully, she turned the heavy platinum wedding band on Michael's finger, the mate to the one on her own, and watched with desperate intensity the pale eyelids below delicate brows for signs of awakening. The nurses had washed the blood from Michael's rich blond hair, but Sloan could see it still. See it on Michael's face, in her hair, pooling in the street below her head as she lay so still in the road.

"Michael," Sloan whispered, tears streaking her cheeks. "I'm so sorry, baby. So sorry."

Catherine had sworn that Michael had opened her eyes for just a second the night before, but she hadn't awakened since. The doctors told Sloan that Michael had a closed skull fracture along with a serious concussion and that it was difficult to predict when she might regain full consciousness. They said that head injuries were tricky.

Tricky. Sloan moaned softly, but she didn't realize it.

There's some swelling in the brain. She could wake up in an hour, or a day, or a week. They didn't say *she may never wake up at all,* but that was all that Sloan could hear.

Bowing her head, she brushed Michael's hand back and forth across her cheek, choking on her fear and her guilt. *If I lose you, I'll die.*

No truth had ever been clearer to her.

❖

Six a.m. Quitting time.

The thin blond with the short, spiked hair leaned back in a booth in an all-night diner on the corner of Twelfth and Locust and sighed. All the other girls had gone home, but she'd stayed just a little longer.

Stupid. She's not coming.

It had been a long night and not a particularly profitable one. She could have turned a few more tricks, but she'd turned down most of them. She'd made enough to cover her food for the week doing quick hand jobs in the front seats of the mid-range sedans of the middle-aged suburban husbands who wanted to get off on their way home. But twenty bucks a pop wasn't enough to make the rent. For that kind of money, she'd need to do more than the hand action and the occasional blowjob in dark alleys. She'd have to fuck for it.

And she hadn't been. Not since the night she had seen Anna Marie lying naked on a dirty mattress in a filthy hotel room, looking so frail and helpless. Looking so pathetic, and so very dead. She had gazed at Anna Marie, but she'd seen herself. She wasn't particularly afraid of dying. There were worse things than that. But she hadn't run away from one kind of hell just to end up another kind of victim. Sure, she had a place of her own, and she didn't owe anyone for it. She was a free agent. Dangerous choice to be alone on the streets without a pimp, but she got by. But she was too smart not to know that some night it could be her, and seeing Anna Marie like that had brought it all home. She'd get into the wrong car or walk down the wrong alley, and it would be her, broken and tossed aside.

It almost *had* been her, not so long ago, even after she'd quit giving it up on her back in the rooms-by-the-hour over on Thirteenth. He'd said he just wanted a quick toss and he'd give her fifty bucks if she'd jerk him off just the way he asked for it. Like she didn't always. *Jesus.* He was clean-cut and well spoken and looked like a lawyer, so when he said he was in a hurry and didn't need a room, gesturing with his chin toward an alley at the end of the block, she figured he'd come fast. So she said, *Sure, come on baby, let me take care of that for you.* But when they'd walked so far into the dark narrow space that she couldn't see the street, he pushed her hard against the jagged brick wall and slid his hand up under her skirt. He grabbed her roughly and unzipped with the other hand, and she knew she was in trouble.

It all happened so fast.

She screamed and kicked at his crotch, and he roared and slammed her head into the wall when she tried to run. Then there was a terrible flash of pain in her forehead and blood in her eyes, and he punched her in the stomach and she thought she might die. Then suddenly, he let her go and she slumped down, and through the tears and the blood and the awful pain, she saw—

"Hey, Sandy."

Sandy looked up into Dellon Mitchell's blue eyes, remembering the fierce look the young cop had had on her face that night. The night she'd stood between Sandy and her assailant.

"Hi, rookie. You look like shit."

"Thanks." Mitchell managed a smile, but her eyes were dull with fatigue. "You eat already?"

"Just about to," Sandy lied, because she wanted an excuse to stay. She'd never seen Mitchell like this, so worn and weary. Supercop wasn't in uniform, either, but was wearing a dirt-smeared football jersey and jeans. It was scary to see her looking less than spit-and-polish, or less than strong and sturdy. Sandy did a quick eye scan for signs of injury, fearing she'd been hurt somehow. "You buying?"

"Sure." Mitchell grinned for real this time. "You order for us, okay?"

Reassured, Sandy cocked an eyebrow. "What's with you, anyhow? Something happen?"

"Just a bad night."

"Did you guys go after those Internet pervs?"

Mitchell nodded.

"You get 'em?"

"We got the guy we wanted." Mitchell's voice was harsh with anger. "But the fucking feds took him right out from under us. We came away empty."

"That sucks, Dell," Sandy said vehemently. "So you still don't know where they're filming the skin flicks or where they're getting those kids?"

"Nope." Mitchell tapped her fork on the tabletop despondently. "And now I'm probably gonna get pulled back to a desk somewhere."

"They screwed you over for helping me, didn't they," Sandy said quietly. It wasn't a question.

Mitchell wanted to object, but the last time she'd tried to soft-pedal the truth with Sandy, she'd almost walked out on her. "I'm in trouble for clubbing the guy with my weapon."

"The fucker deserved it."

Mitchell met Sandy's eyes. "Yeah, he did." *And I'd do it again if someone was hurting you.*

"So what now?" Sandy searched Mitchell's blue eyes, looking for truth and afraid she'd find what she was hoping for. More afraid that she wouldn't.

Mitchell's gaze softened, and she almost reached out to touch her. "We have breakfast, then I walk you home. Sound okay?"

Sandy's throat felt oddly tight. "Sure, why not."

Forty-five minutes later, they stood in front of a row house south of Bainbridge where Sandy had a small studio apartment.

"So, I'll see you later," Mitchell said, making no move to leave. She leaned against the rickety wood railing on the small stoop while Sandy pulled a key from the impossibly tiny purse that hung on a long chain around her neck. Her scoop-neck cotton top was too thin and too tight, designed to show off her breasts, and Mitchell noticed.

Sandy looked up and caught Mitchell's gaze moving over her. Men stared at her body all the time, sometimes with fever in their eyes, and their looks left her cold. The appreciative warmth in Mitchell's eyes made her blush. "If they're gonna stick you on a desk somewhere, I guess maybe I *won't* be seeing you."

"That doesn't matter." Mitchell shook her head, her stomach suddenly tight. "I'm not going anywhere."

Sandy didn't believe her. She shrugged.

"Anyhow, I think the psychiatrist doing my eval is on my sid—"

"They're making you see a shrink?" Sandy's voice rose in indignation. "Jesus, Dell."

"It's SOP...uh...standard operating procedure in a disciplinary situation."

"That blows." For the first time, Sandy realized just how bad things were for the rookie because of her. Quickly, unthinkingly, she stepped across the small space and rested her fingers on Mitchell's cheek. "I'm really sorry."

Surprised, Mitchell straightened, her chest unintentionally

brushing Sandy's. "Not your fault. I'd do it again."

Sandy's nipples contracted swiftly at the touch of Mitchell's shirt against her breasts. Startled, she dropped her hand and backed up, wondering if Mitchell had felt it. "Nobody asked you to."

"Yeah, yeah." Mitchell grinned. "I gotta go. *I'll see you.*"

"Whatever," Sandy replied. But, her body still humming, she remained in the doorway watching until Mitchell was out of sight.

CHAPTER TWO

At precisely seven-thirty a.m., Catherine opened her inner office door to the waiting room and motioned for her first patient to enter. She sat down behind her desk, surveyed the young woman sitting opposite her, and frowned. Officer Dellon Mitchell was still in the clothes she had worn the night before during the task force raid.

"Haven't you been to bed?"

"Watts and I had a lot of paperwork to do. By the time we cleaned that up, it was late...early...uh, today already."

"We can reschedule if you—"

"No." Mitchell made an effort to sit up straighter and tried to clear the cloud of exhaustion from her brain. "I need to get this done. With the task force most likely dead, I'm going to be reassigned." She grimaced. "And I want to get back to the street. If I have this thing still hanging over my head, they'll bury me somewhere."

"Have you talked to Rebecca?"

"About what?" Mitchell looked confused.

"Maybe she can help you with this situation."

Mitchell stared at her, then laughed shortly. "It doesn't work that way, Dr. Rawlings. You don't take your troubles to anyone, especially not to a detective like Frye."

Catherine said nothing, realizing a bit belatedly that she didn't want the discussion to focus too sharply on Rebecca. She might become distracted by her patient's impressions of her lover, and what mattered was how Dellon felt—not how she viewed Rebecca.

"She's so...she's what every cop wants to be," Mitchell continued, following her own thoughts. "Always in control, always in command, always so...on top of the job. *She* wouldn't whine to anyone about anything." She looked at Catherine as if that explained everything.

Catherine nodded, thinking briefly of how much it cost her lover to maintain that kind of emotional discipline, day after day. Then she brought her mind back to the weary young officer. "Who *do* you talk to, then?"

"No one."

The words were spoken softly, and for the briefest instant, Mitchell looked away.

"Someone at home?" At the slight shake of the dark head, Catherine asked gently, "Friends? A lover?"

Wary, Mitchell hesitated. "Does this have something to do with my evaluation?"

"No. This just has to do with you." Catherine smiled, aware of what troubled Dellon. "I'll dictate that report the moment we're done and see that it goes to your captain this morning. I'll tell him what I told you the last time you were here—that your actions were appropriate considering the circumstances."

"Then what does the rest of it matter?"

Catherine leaned forward. "You do a difficult and dangerous job, Officer. Sometimes talking about it can make it easier."

A muscle in Mitchell's jaw twitched, and she clamped her teeth down to stop it. She thought about the late-night conversations beneath dim streetlights and the early-morning breakfasts. She thought about the dark alley and the hulking stranger. Maybe if she hadn't been so tired—maybe if Catherine's eyes hadn't been so kind—she would have kept quiet.

"I have a friend."

Catherine waited.

"The woman I told you about...the woman who was in the alley that night. We talk sometimes."

"What's her name?"

"Sandy." Mitchell smiled faintly. "We weren't going to talk shop, but that's changed recently."

"Because of what happened?"

Mitchell shook her head. "Before, I think. Just sorta gradually." Her eyes met Catherine's. "I met her on the job a while back, and then I'd see her on the streets in my sector. She's a prostitute."

Catherine remembered what Dellon had told her about coming upon the woman being assaulted in the alley. *He had one hand around her throat and the other under her skirt. Her thighs were bare, pale, ghostly in the moonlight. I saw her face for the first time then. There was blood on her face...She had been screaming before—shouting, I think—for him to stop. Now she was...whimpering. I was afraid he was going to kill her.*

"That's a dangerous profession as well." Catherine's voice was mild as she watched Dellon's blue eyes darken and turn inward. It amazed her that Dellon had been as restrained as she had been in subduing the assailant. Her mind skittered to an image of Rebecca confronting the man who had held a gun to Catherine's head. The calm in her lover's eyes just before she fired. Forcefully, she pushed the memory away.

"Dangerous?" Mitchell raked a hand through her hair. "Jesus Christ..." She gave Catherine an apologetic look. "Sorry...yeah, I guess you could say that."

"And does that worry you?"

Mitchell met her gaze. "Yeah." She paused. "All the time."

"Have you told her that?"

"Hell, no." Mitchell smiled. "She'd tell me to take a walk and not come back."

"She sounds pretty independent," Catherine observed, noting the tension easing from the tight body and taut features the longer Dellon spoke of her friend. *More than friendship?*

"Hard-headed and short-tempered." Mitchell's voice had softened. "Almost as bad as a cop."

"Almost?"

Mitchell laughed, freely this time. "I guess she'd argue that."

"We're about out of time, Officer. Do you—"

"Could you call me Dell?"

Surprised, Catherine nodded. "Of course. Dell, what are your plans for further sessions?"

"Do I have to say right now?" She hadn't wanted to come at first, had only done it because she'd been forced to. *Now...*

"Just call and let my secretary Joyce know what you decide."

Mitchell stood and held out her hand. "Okay, thanks." They

shook, and she started to turn away, then looked back. "It helps, sometimes. To talk."

"Yes." Catherine's eyes were gentle. "Come back any time, Dell."

❖

Across town, Rebecca walked into the squad room on the third floor of the 18th precinct and threaded her way through the crowded maze of metal desks and haphazardly placed chairs toward her desk in the far left corner. She slowed as she approached, an eyebrow cocked in surprise.

"Somebody die I don't know about?"

William Watts looked up from the *Daily News* as Rebecca slowly lowered herself into a chair, all the while regarding him curiously.

"What? Why?"

Rebecca tilted her chin at him. "The suit."

He looked down, then met her gaze blankly. "I got two."

"Uh-huh." She'd never seen him in anything other than a shiny out-of-style brown one that looked as if he'd picked it up at Goodwill. The one he wore currently was still probably a good ten years out of style, but it was clean and pressed. *Scary.*

She picked up a stack of folders, glanced at them, and tossed them aside. She wasn't interested in old cases, or new ones for that matter. She was interested in only two specific unsolved ones—Jeff Cruz's murder and the attempted murder of J.T. Sloan. They had to be related, because each of them had the smell of an inside job.

"You gonna talk to the Cap this morning?" Watts asked.

"About what?"

"About *what*?" His face contorted in anger. "About the feds stealing our collar. About somebody leaking the information that we were going for a bust last night. About someone arranging to take out a member of our task force—the one really critical person—the cybercop?" He lowered his voice. "Don't let Sloan or McBride know I said that—about them being important. Especially with them being civilians and all."

She was silent for a minute, regarding him thoughtfully. She didn't want another partner. Jeff had been more than that to her;

he'd been her friend. Half the time she didn't even like Watts. Then she stood. "Let's take a ride."

Without a word, he followed her into the hall, down the stairwell, and out into the rear parking lot. The minute he was outside, he lit a cigarette, drawing deeply as he hurried to keep up with Rebecca's long strides. When they reached her red Corvette, she opened the driver's door and gave him a look. Sighing, he dropped the half-finished smoke to the asphalt, scuffed it out, and wedged himself into the front seat.

Rebecca wheeled the car deftly out of the lot and headed for the on-ramp to I-95. A few minutes later, they were rocketing south.

"Who'd you tell about the plans for the raid?" she asked without preamble.

"What? Fuck, nobody." His voice was indignant.

"That leaves Catherine, Mitchell, Sloan, McBride, or Clark." She looked at him, her expression remote. "Which one do you figure for the snitch?"

"Well, we know it ain't the doc," he replied immediately. "And McBride and Sloan are way tight, so it wouldn't be them. The kid? No way would Mitchell talk." He paused. "That kid's got stones. For a girl, she ain't a half-bad cop."

Rebecca stared at him until he fidgeted in his seat.

"Okay. She's a good cop." He watched her eyes. They were hard chips of blue-gray stone. "For a man or...woman."

She grinned and looked back to the road.

"Fuck," he said under his breath. He eased his cramped legs under the low-slung dash. "And I can't figure Clark for torpedoing the bust. He went to all the trouble to set up this joint task force when he could just as well have done it without us." He reconsidered. "Well, he *could* have done it without us, but not as fast. What's your take?"

"I agree." Rebecca's voice was low, flat, the way it got when she was simmering with rage. "It wasn't anyone directly related to the team."

Watts waited for the rest, and the silence grew. Then he whistled, low and long. "Fuck me. You think it might be the captain?"

Rebecca pulled into the passing lane and blew by an eighteen-wheeler. The speedometer tipped ninety and headed right. Watts made a grab for his seat belt.

"There's something you don't know," she said at length. "Trish Marks over in Homicide told me that Captain Henry got with *her* captain behind closed doors, and then she and her partner were pulled off the investigation into Jeff and Jimmy's murders."

"That smells bad."

"Yeah, it does." Rebecca eased up on the gas. There wasn't much traffic, but they were about to cross the Delaware line, and the state boys down there might not be all that friendly to a Philadelphia cop tearing up their highways. "I don't want to think it's him, but..."

"You'd be a puss...ah, a chump to trust him right now." He fingered his cigarettes wistfully, wondering if she'd ever let him smoke in her ride. "But it could be someone higher up in the department."

"Maybe. Or someone with access to department records."

"How?"

"I don't know, but someone pulled all of the CSI evidence reports on Jeff and Jimmy."

"Stole 'em? How in hell did they get past that ball-buster Flanagan?"

"It's a long walk back, Watts. And Dee Flanagan's a friend of mine."

"Yeah, well, I speak the truth." His tone was righteous. Flanagan, the head of the Crime Scene Investigation Unit, was notoriously unfriendly to cops.

Rebecca grinned. "In this case, I agree." She slowed, made a U-turn across the median, and headed back north. "They hacked the reports out of her computer, it seems."

"Huh." He watched the scenery fly by for a few miles, apparently half-asleep. When he spoke, however, his voice was clear. "But *we* have our very own computer whiz kids, and one of 'em's got an ax to grind."

"Uh-huh."

Watts turned in his seat and studied Rebecca's sharply hewn profile. "You're thinking about running a shadow investigation of your own, aren't you? Going after the leak in the department?"

"It all ties together somehow, Watts. I *feel* it. The porn ring, the Justice inquiry, the sex videos, Jimmy Hogan's intel—all of it." She gripped the wheel hard, although her face revealed nothing. "Who knows, this case might even shake loose Zamora and bring down a big piece of the organized crime operation."

"We could get hung out to dry, too."

"Who said anything about *we*?"

He huffed. "We're partners, Sarge. Right?"

Rebecca eyed the shabby cop in the clean blue suit and sighed. Almost too quietly for him to hear, she grunted, "Right."

❖

"The Haldol should be fine for the agitation," Catherine remarked as she signed off on the resident's progress notes. She handed the chart back to him and checked her watch. She had an hour before clinic.

Just outside the intensive care unit, Catherine saw a redheaded woman walking in her direction. Slowing at the woman's nod, Catherine said, "Hello. I'm Catherine Rawlings. We were never properly introduced the night Michael was brought in."

"Sarah Martin." The redhead extended her hand.

Catherine noticed that her creamy skin was dusted with pale freckles and there were faint circles beneath her eyes. The smile was soft and genuine, but her cornflower blue eyes were troubled. "How's Michael?"

"Not awake yet." Sarah glanced briefly at the double steel doors leading into the intensive care unit. "God, what a place."

"Yes. So necessary, but so terrible as well." Catherine remembered what it had been like when Rebecca had been sequestered behind those doors, attached to tubes and machines and surrounded by medical personnel who were kind, but often too busy to notice the terror of those waiting for their loved ones to live or die. She shivered. "How are Sloan and Jason holding up?"

"Jason is at Sloan's. I think he's working on whatever they got from last night's operation." She sighed. "He's crazy about Michael and adores Sloan. It's his way of helping."

"I only met Michael the night of the accident," Catherine said, "but Sloan is wonderful." They stepped out of the path of a lumbering portable x-ray machine being guided effortlessly by a woman so small she was dwarfed by it. "You and Sloan have known each other a long time, I gather."

"We met when we were both stationed in Southeast Asia. Government jobs. God, we were green then." Sarah pushed back her wavy, shoulder-length hair with both hands, her expression pained. "A long story and a long time ago." She glanced at the gray doors again. "I hate this. I can't get her to leave. She's about to collapse."

"I know how she feels," Catherine murmured. At Sarah's look of surprise, she smiled wanly. "Rebecca Frye, my lover, was shot and almost died a few months ago. I was afraid if I left her for a minute, she...I just wanted to be there, as if my presence would make a difference."

"I'm sure it did." Sarah touched Catherine's hand gently. "I'm glad Rebecca's okay."

"Yes, so am I." Catherine wondered just how fine her lover really was, but pushed the worry aside. "I was just about to go check on Michael."

"Good," Sarah said. "If you could talk to Sloan..."

"Of course." Catherine smiled kindly. "You should get some rest, too."

"I'll try. I have patients this afternoon." At Catherine's questioning look, she added, "I'm a doctor of Oriental medicine. The only good thing that came out of my tour in Thailand, except my friendship with Sloan."

"Well, it sounds as if both Sloan and Michael will be in good hands when Michael comes home."

Sarah smiled appreciatively, and the two women parted.

A moment later, Catherine entered the small cubicle where Michael Lassiter lay. Sloan, who was slumped in a chair by the bedside, head back and eyes closed, jerked upright at the soft sound of her entrance. "Hello, Sloan."

"Catherine." Sloan's voice was hoarse, her eyes dark hollows, their normally vibrant violet brushed black with pain.

Catherine lightly touched Sloan's cheek in passing and stepped to the bedside, taking Michael's hand in hers. Leaning down, she said softly, "Good morning, Michael. It's Catherine Rawlings. We met very briefly two nights ago. You're in the hospital, but you're doing very well. Sloan is here."

The only response was the slow, even rise and fall of Michael's chest.

Catherine turned, her heart twisting when she saw the tears on Sloan's cheeks. Crouching down, she placed both hands on Sloan's face, cupping her strong jaw. "You have to get some sleep."

"Do you think she heard you?"

"Yes, I do. And I know she knows you're here." Catherine brushed the jet-black hair off Sloan's forehead. "You cannot let her wake up and find you like this. She'll need all her strength to get well, and worrying about you will not help her do that."

Sloan searched Catherine's eyes, clinging to the certainty she saw there. "I'm afraid to leave. What if..." She looked away, trembling.

"There's an on-call room my residents use on the next floor. Rebecca's slept there more than once. You can shower and get some sleep, and you'll only be five minutes away." Catherine pulled Sloan to her feet and slid her arm around the muscular woman's waist when she swayed. "I'll speak to Michael's nurse and give her the number there. I'll be sure that you're called the second there's any change."

Sloan wanted to protest, but she kept hearing Catherine's words. *Worrying about you will not help her get well.* Carefully, she lowered the steel rail that ran along the side of the bed and leaned down to kiss Michael.

"I'll be right back, baby. I love you so much."

Catherine spoke to the staff, found scrubs for Sloan in the locker room next to the ICU, and walked her up to the residents' room. "No one will bother you here."

"Thanks, Catherine." Sloan passed a trembling hand over her face. "Where's Rebecca? Did she find out anything about the guy we caught last night?"

"God," Catherine murmured. "Not another cop to deal with."

"I'm just a cybercop." Sloan tried for a smile, but her brain was so fried she could barely move a muscle.

"Not much difference that I can see," Catherine grumbled. "You go to bed. I'm sure Rebecca will be by later to fill you in."

"Okay, sure. Thanks."

The minute she was alone, Sloan pulled off the clothes she'd been in for over a day, stepped into a cold shower for two minutes, and then collapsed naked onto the bed. She was instantly asleep.

It seemed like only a minute later when the phone rang.

CHAPTER THREE

Yeah," Sloan croaked groggily.

"This is Dr. Torveau, Ms. Slo—"

"Is she all right?" Sloan pushed herself upright, fumbling on the end of the narrow bed for the clothes Catherine had left her. "Is she..."

"She's stable. She's not awake, but she's starting to show some purposeful movement. It could be any time."

"I'll be right there."

Sloan dropped the phone into the cradle, stood abruptly, and almost toppled over. Her head was spinning, and she was forced to sit again until the dizziness passed. She tried to remember when she'd last eaten and couldn't. Carefully, she pulled on the soft cotton scrubs worn thin by countless washings, then tried standing again. *Better.*

Three minutes later, she was waiting by Michael's bedside once again. The clock in the main ICU read 2:10 p.m. She'd been asleep almost three hours, but it felt like less than one. Fatigue was something she could deal with, if only Michael would wake up.

"Baby, it's me," Sloan whispered, brushing her fingers over Michael's pale cheek. "I love you." She'd said it a thousand times in the last forty hours. It was all she could think to say. It was the only thing that mattered in her life. "I..."

Michael's lids fluttered. Sloan held her breath.

"Michael? Baby?"

Sloan blinked, because she thought she might be dreaming. Blue eyes, the crystal blue of clear ocean water, met hers. She sucked in a sharp breath, then reached trembling fingers for the hand that moved weakly across the crisp white sheets toward hers. She could barely make a sound as she lifted Michael's hand, thrilling to the faint pressure from Michael's fingers returning her grip.

"Hi, baby." Her voice cracked on the words.

"Slo...?"

"Right here." Sloan looked around, wondering if she should call someone. But nothing in the world would get her to move from Michael's side. "You're going to be okay. You're in the hospital, but you're going to be okay."

"You?"

"What, love?" Sloan leaned closer. She was shaking so much she thought her legs might go. "I can't..."

"Are you...all..." Michael swallowed painfully. "...all right?"

"Oh God." Sloan laughed, an edge of wild tears in her voice. "You're here...that's all I need."

"Water?"

"I have to check." Sloan searched in the tangle of lines and wires and tubes until she found the signal button. "It'll just be a minute."

"Head...hurts."

"I know, baby. I'm sorry." Sloan's insides twisted as she remembered the blood and the bone-deep scalp laceration. Now that Michael was awake, Sloan felt her fear rapidly turning to rage. *I'm going to kill the motherfucker who hurt you. I swear to God I am.*

Michael sighed and closed her eyes. Sloan's heart tripped with sudden apprehension. "Michael?"

"She's just asleep," Ali Torveau, the trauma surgeon, said quietly from the doorway. "She'll be in and out like that for a while."

"When can she come home?" Sloan's voice was thin with anxiety.

"Too soon to tell. She could be ready in a day or two, or it might be a few weeks." Torveau put a hand on Sloan's shoulder. "Head injuries are—"

"Yeah, I know. Tricky."

Torveau nodded. "That they are. But she's going to be fine. Her chest x-ray is clearing up and the renal injury is stable. She was lucky."

"Lucky." Sloan glanced back at her lover, so fragile, so

precious. Her rage turned to acid in her guts. "Yeah."

❖

When Rebecca's pager sounded for the third time in less than half an hour, she looked at the readout and grimaced. "I think our time is up. That's the captain's number again."

Watts just grunted.

They'd been cruising around Twelfth and Locust, looking for contacts, hoping to find someone who'd heard some street gossip about the thwarted arrest the previous night. They'd gotten exactly nothing. If the guy had been some kind of player, no one was talking about it.

"You want to come back to the station with me? See what he wants?"

"Might as well," Watts said, hiding his surprise. Frye didn't usually include him in briefings with their superiors. "We ain't getting jack out here."

"I'll come back out later tonight—see if I can shake down some of my sources."

"How 'bout that whore you mentioned the other day?"

Rebecca stiffened and said nothing. Although the description was true, she rarely thought of Sandy as one of the marginal, beaten-down women who sold their bodies with seemingly careless disregard for their own ultimate fate. Sandy wasn't like that, not yet. She was still clear-eyed and spirited, still fighting the forces that colluded to drag her down.

"You said she knew some girls who had made a couple of skin flicks." He watched the muscles in Rebecca's jaw tense and chose his words carefully. "If she could maybe reach out to them, get a line on who contacted them—"

"I'll see if I can put her with someone from Juvie." Rebecca's tone was clipped and short. "Let her look at some pictures. Chances are those girls have been picked up for something by now, and they're in the system. Maybe she can ID them for us."

Watts cleared his throat. "We've got our own pictures she could look at, maybe. Better than Juvie's mug shots. *Recent* pictures."

"What?" Rebecca pulled into the lot behind the one-eight and turned in her seat to regard him with just the faintest hint of suspicion.

"Spell it out. I'm not in the mood for twenty questions."

Looking slightly affronted, he replied, "Didn't Sloan say she was recording that little fuckfest last night? There're two girls right there that we know are involved for sure."

"And a guy," Rebecca said softly. "Jesus, Watts. You're beautiful."

He smothered a smile and pulled out his cigarettes.

"Not in here," Rebecca warned automatically as she unclipped the cell phone from her belt. She doubted that anyone would be in at the converted warehouse on Front Street where Sloan lived and worked, but she tried the main number for starters. A male voice answered on the fourth ring.

"Sloan Security."

"Jason, it's Frye."

"Hey." His voice was flat, tired.

"Any news on Michael?"

"Not yet."

Rebecca pushed aside both her sympathy for Michael and those who loved her as well as her anger at the assault. The best thing she could do was find whoever was behind it. "Do you have Sloan's laptop there? The one she used last night to monitor the live feed of the sex video?"

"Sure. I was just about to call you."

"You have something for us?" Her pulse rate quickened, and she saw Watts sit up straighter beside her, apparently listening intently.

"Maybe."

"Let's hear it. I could use some good news."

"I've put together a decent facsimile of the guy. I was just about to run it through the databases." Jason's tone was animated for the first time. "If we're lucky, I'll get an ID."

"Excellent. How good is the likeness?"

"Average. The cameraman was smart and stayed away from the guy's face. I had to extract the images from several partial views and do a computer simulation to get the composite, but it's good enough for an ID if he's ever been entered anywhere."

"Wait a minute—back up," Rebecca said. "What databases are you talking about?"

"The usual—DMV, NCIC, Armed Forces—"

"Ah, those would be restricted access files, Jason."

Silence.

"Right." Rebecca blew out a breath. "Do it."

"It's working now."

"Good." Rebecca opened her door and stretched a leg down to the curb. "I'll be by..." She glanced at the man in the passenger seat. "*We'll* be back sometime tonight."

"I'll be here."

"Later then," Rebecca said before she ended the call.

Whistling softly, Watts levered himself out of the car and lit a cigarette. He'd barely dropped the match when Rebecca slammed the door, keyed the alarm, and headed toward the back entrance of the station house at a fast clip.

"Where's the fire?" he puffed as he hurried to her side.

"Look—we probably took whoever's running the kiddie porn show by surprise last night. They're going to be tightening up their Internet security ASAP, especially if they know that Justice has one of their mid-level guys." She shouldered through the rear fire door on the first floor and headed toward the elevators. "They could be reorganizing the whole operation, too—changing personnel, switching out the kids, relocating the studio right now."

They were silent as they rode to the third floor in the company of two uniformed officers and a clerk. Once in the hallway leading to the vice squad room, Rebecca continued, "We've got to get as much as we can as fast as we can."

"Well, it ain't gonna do us any good if we have a heart attack or something." He hadn't forgotten that barely a week had passed since Frye had been flat on her back with a collapsed lung, looking like a corpse searching for a grave.

Rebecca gave him the eye. "So quit smoking and try the gym." She thought she heard him mutter "Bite me," but couldn't be sure. She stifled a grin and picked up her pace.

❖

"You want to tell me how you managed to come away empty from an operation that you were supposed to be coordinating, Sergeant?" Captain John Henry's voice was level, but his mahogany face was a shade darker than usual with barely suppressed irritation.

"I was hoping you could tell me, sir." Rebecca's eyes were winter gray and her voice colder still. She stood before her captain's desk, Watts just behind her to the left. Her demeanor was almost casual, but her gaze never left Henry's face.

He stared back until the silence grew ominous. Watts coughed.

"Sit down, Sergeant."

"I'm fine, sir."

"That wasn't a request." Henry hadn't raised his voice, but his formidable shoulders bunched with tension. He looked past his senior detective to the third person in the room. "Step outside, Detective."

"Uh..." Watts glanced at Rebecca, who hadn't moved a muscle. *These two have been heading for a rumble ever since the Cap got Frye's girlfriend mixed up in that serial killer thing. Shit.* He shuffled his feet.

"Go ahead, Watts." Rebecca's voice was soft. Dangerously soft.

Shit. Reluctantly, Watts left.

"Your psych evaluation paperwork is still incomplete." Henry regarded her almost benignly. "I could pull you out of the field and plant you behind a desk until you grew roots."

"Whitaker must have forgotten to send the report," Rebecca replied.

"Nice try, Frye. Whitaker says you have a final meeting before he signs off."

She gritted her teeth. The mandatory psych evaluation she'd had to endure after being shot was the last barrier to getting her full street creds back, and the department shrink wasn't giving an inch. "I guess there was a miscommunication."

"I'm sure." Henry tipped his chin toward the chair. "Now sit your ass down."

Rebecca sat. Despite her concern that Henry might be behind the leak that had led to the attempt on Sloan's life, he was her commanding officer, and he held all the cards.

"Agent Clark called the chief this morning to thank him for

the cooperation of the PPD and to say that the task force was 'on hold' temporarily."

"Until when?"

"Time unknown."

"I don't think Clark will be calling back any time soon. He needed a fast track into the criminal infrastructure in this city, so he used the *joint* task force as a front." Rebecca snorted. "He got what he wanted, and now he's cutting us out of the loop."

"That's SOP for the feds." Henry sighed. "Did you come away with *anything* from the operation?"

"Other than a critically injured civilian?" Rebecca rarely disclosed all the details of her investigations to anyone, even her captain. That kind of secrecy and mild paranoia was typical for police officers. Information and political connections were the currency of law enforcement, and intel was her leverage—on the streets and in the cop shop. "Not much. We know there's a local Internet porn ring streaming live sex videos. The guy Clark snatched from us last night is a part of it."

"Connected to organized crime?" Henry asked almost eagerly. "It would be big if we could tie Zamora and his crew to this."

"Nothing solid." Rebecca watched him for some sign that his interest was more than the simple ambition of a cop wanting to clean up his city and advance his own career at the same time. If he were the mob's inside man, his questions might give him away.

"Have you got anything working on the streets that might pay off?"

"Soft stuff. The 'I maybe heard somebody say something about that' kind of talk." She leaned forward almost imperceptibly. "Look, Captain. If you give me a little room to work this, I know I can break something open. I still have the whole team. Clark was never instrumental—it was the computer jockeys and Watts's legwork that caught us all the leads. We know almost as much as the feds, and they don't have the contacts I do."

He eyed her impassively. "This wouldn't be about you wanting to look for Cruz's killer, would it?"

"No, sir." Rebecca never blinked. "I'm sure Trish Marks and the rest of the homicide team are working that one as hard as they can."

"Uh-huh." His deep voice was soft, almost soothing. He leaned back in his leather chair, the only concession to comfort in the room, and steepled his surprisingly elegant hands in front of his chest. His heavy lids appeared nearly closed. "I have no authority to approve that kind of operation."

Rebecca said nothing. She knew this game.

He tapped his fingers on the arm of the chair. "I think it might take Whitaker another week or so to finish his report. Then the whole recertification package has to get approved. Until that happens, you can't go into the regular rotation."

She furiously analyzed the angles. He was giving her the unofficial green light to keep hunting for the leaders of the porn ring, and anything else she might turn up. But unofficial meant unprotected, too. He was keeping himself out of the loop and therefore unaccountable. She'd be alone, without departmental sanction. If Henry was dirty, this was the perfect way to set her up. Much the way Jimmy Hogan had been set up. A cop working outside was easier to dispose of.

"I'm sure Whitaker will want to see me another time *or two*, yes sir." Regardless, she needed the freedom to pursue the case, and this was the only way she'd get it.

"I'll see that those appointments get scheduled." Henry fixed her with a sharp glance. "You make sure you keep them."

And cover your *ass*. Rebecca stood. "Absolutely."

"Sergeant," the captain added before Rebecca turned away. "I'm sure there's a great deal of paperwork accumulated from the operation with Justice. The commissioner will want in-depth reports. If you need help getting them in order, you can have a man or two to assist."

"Watts," Rebecca said immediately, ignoring the faint look of surprise on Henry's face. She hesitated. The job was risky, professionally and probably physically. There'd already been one assassination attempt. Anyone she chose could be in danger. Firmly, she said, "And the uniform—Mitchell. She's one hell of a clerk."

"Clerk." Henry almost smiled. "I'll see to it."

Rebecca had almost reached the door when she heard the quiet words, "Good luck, Sergeant."

She didn't answer as she stepped through the door and closed it behind her.

❖

Watts waited just outside. "What'd he say?"

"Not here." She walked straight through the squad room and out the door, and she didn't stop until they were once again in the parking lot.

"Jesus Christ." Panting, Watts leaned against the rickety metal railing that ran up one side of the concrete stairs. It creaked ominously under his bulk. "Aren't you supposed to take it easy with your bum lung and all?"

Rebecca breathed just a bit quickly, but she felt none of the pain that had preceded her collapsed lung the week before. "My lungs are fine."

She glanced at her watch. Five-thirty. Six months ago, her workday would have been far from over. She'd be headed back to the Tenderloin in the hopes of finding some of her confidential informants crawling out of bed and hitting the streets for the start of their night. She'd stay out—dropping into the bars, talking, watching, listening—taking the pulse of the city until the night dwindled into dawn. Night after night. That had been her life.

But it wasn't now. Couldn't be now. Now there was Catherine.

"I'll be at Sloan's tonight at nine. Call Jason and Mitchell and tell them to meet us there."

"Mitchell? What is she—"

Rebecca's stare stopped him cold. "I don't intend to explain every little order I give, Watts. Do you want this detail or not? Make up your mind."

He jiggled the change in his pocket and thought about the stack of files on his desk. Cold cases—old cases that had run out of steam. No leads. No suspects. No hope of closure. He could sit on his ass and make phone calls for the next three years and retire with thirty years in. Good pension, good health benefits. Or he could throw in with Frye, who seemed to attract danger like a moth to a flame.

He studied the tall, intense blond woman by his side—a tough street cop whose only agenda was justice. A cop's cop.

"Yeah, I don't have anything cooking right now." He shrugged. "I'll ride along."

"Right." Rebecca turned to leave.

"Where you goin' now?"

Her first impulse was to ignore him. He wasn't her partner; she was just working with him because he had good cop instincts. He didn't need to know anything about her. Not about those things she kept close to her heart. She stopped by the Vette and looked back. "I'm going to the hospital to page Catherine and take her to dinner."

He didn't change his position, but his beard-stubbled lip flickered with a grin.

She wasn't sure, but she thought she heard him mumble something about being domesticated. Just in case, she muttered, "Bite me, Watts," before she slid into the Vette, keyed the ignition, and roared away.

In the rear view mirror, she saw him laughing.

CHAPTER FOUR

Catherine stepped from the elevator and glanced around the hospital lobby. She took a moment, standing still in the midst of the milling crowd, to appreciate her lover from a distance. Rebecca stood with a shoulder against a column, talking on her cell phone. She wore a gray gabardine suit and a plain white shirt, a thin black belt encircling her waist. The shoulder holster was not visible under the carefully tailored jacket, but Catherine knew precisely where it lay along Rebecca's left side, just below her breast. The detective had always been lean, but since the shooting, she'd become noticeably thin. She no longer looked ill, but chiseled and sharp. If possible, Rebecca was even more beautiful now than the first time Catherine had seen her.

She remembered looking up from her desk the night they'd met to see the tall, blond-haired, blue-eyed detective striding toward her with a degree of assuredness that suggested she was rarely intimidated. She remembered, too, that the term *Viking* had flashed through her mind. She'd been instantly captivated by Rebecca's intensity and drive. In the months since, she'd come to love her for so many other reasons—most especially for the sensitivity and tenderness that very few other than Catherine ever saw.

At that moment, Rebecca closed her phone and surveyed the room. When her eyes met Catherine's, she smiled, and her glacial countenance softened for an instant.

Catherine's heart beat rapidly as it always did when Rebecca touched her. Quickly, she made her way through the crowd to Rebecca's side.

"What a surprise." She reached for Rebecca's hand as she kissed her cheek. "I'm so glad to see you."

Rebecca laced her fingers between Catherine's and pulled

her gently out of the path of the steady stream of hospital visitors. "Any chance you can get away for a while?"

"I have a little over two hours before I need to see patients in my office. I just have two scheduled tonight." Catherine tilted her head, searching Rebecca's eyes, appreciating the warmth she found there. "Just what do you have in mind, Detective?"

"I suppose there's no chance we could roll around in the on-call room for a while?" Rebecca took a step closer until her body just touched Catherine's.

Catherine drew a surprised breath and then saw the amusement flickering in her lover's face. "You shouldn't tease me while I'm working, darling."

"I was only partly teasing." Rebecca's voice dropped a register as she traced her fingers over Catherine's forearm. "But if you have to work later, I suppose you should have dinner instead of sex."

"I'd like both," Catherine murmured. "But I think the rolling around part should wait until later."

"That sounds like a plan. Can you leave now?"

Catherine linked her arm through Rebecca's. "Let's go."

❖

Rebecca had parked illegally in front of the hospital, and within minutes they were on the expressway headed west.

"Where are we going?" Catherine asked.

"DeCarlo's."

"You're kidding. On the spur of the moment like this?" Catherine turned in her seat to study Rebecca's face. "Is this a special occasion?"

Rebecca shook her head. "Nope. I just thought you'd like it."

"Oh, I like it." Catherine rested her hand on Rebecca's thigh, softly running her fingers up and down the tight muscles beneath. "Thank you."

"For what?" Rebecca asked curiously as she pulled into the small gravel parking lot adjoining the century-old mansion that housed DeCarlo's restaurant.

"You don't usually stop work this early."

Rebecca blushed. She wasn't used to anyone being able to tell what was going on with her as easily as Catherine did. It wasn't that she minded; it was just that it continued to surprise her. "I'm not done, exactly."

"You're going in later?"

"Can I tell you over dinner?"

"Of course. Does Anthony know we're coming?"

"Uh-huh. I called him from the hospital to make sure he could take us." Rebecca reached for Catherine's hand again as they approached the wide, pillared front porch. "He understands that we're on a tight schedule, too."

As Rebecca had intimated, Anthony DeCarlo met them personally and showed them to their usual table overlooking the manicured rear gardens. At a word from him, a waiter instantly appeared to take their order.

Once they were alone, Rebecca said, "I'll be going back out for a few hours this evening."

"Will you come by the apartment when you're done?" Catherine still found it necessary to ask, uncertain of how much to expect. Although they had shared an intense beginning in the midst of crisis and weathered the trauma of Rebecca's shooting, they had really just begun to negotiate the framework of their relationship.

"Yes, if you don't mind that it might be late." Each time they had this conversation, Rebecca was anxious. Every relationship she'd ever had had suffered and ultimately failed because of who she was. Because of the cop she was. She didn't know how to be any different and didn't think she could. All she could do was pray that she managed to give Catherine enough of what *she* needed to keep her.

At this, Catherine raised an eyebrow. "Rebecca, I know you have to work. I know what you do. You don't need to apologize for that by taking me out to dinner."

"I'm not..." Rebecca fell silent as the waiter brought their first course. "It's not that. Okay, maybe a little, but not totally. I wanted to see you. I...I miss you." She shook her head, amazed. "Jesus, I just saw you this morning, but I miss you."

"I'm sorry." Catherine reached across the table and took Rebecca's hand. "I miss you, too. This is all as new for me as it is for you. I don't want you to feel guilty about being who you are. I love you. And loving you means loving the cop in you. I know that."

Rebecca brought Catherine's hand to her lips and kissed her palm softly. Her throat was tight and suddenly she wasn't hungry at all. Or rather, she was hungry, but it was only for the touch of Catherine's hands upon her skin. "I just want to do everything right."

"Well, you're doing very well so far." Catherine reluctantly drew her hand away, because the heat from Rebecca's fingers was making it difficult for her to think. "Are you working on a new case?"

"Uh..." Swiftly, Rebecca calculated, trying to gauge how much she should say. Trying to guess if what she might reveal could cause a problem.

Across the table, Catherine watched her lover's expression become closed and withdrawn behind the cop's mask. Seeing Rebecca drift away hurt her and produced a quick surge of fear. *This is what would come between them, this secrecy that was Rebecca's second nature*—perhaps even one of her defining characteristics.

The protracted silence called Rebecca from her internal musings, and she looked into Catherine's eyes. What she saw there tore at her heart—uncertainty, but more importantly, acceptance and trust. Precious feelings, every one.

"No, not a new case." She took a deep breath. "Officially, I'm not working on anything. Henry wants me to see Whitaker another time or two before he'll clear me to resume full duty."

"Officially." Catherine's stomach clenched. "And *unofficially?*"

"Unofficially, I've been green-lighted to continue looking into the pornography ring."

"You have to help me here," Catherine said quietly. "You have to tell me what this means."

"It's not all that unusual." Rebecca heard the undertone of anxiety that Catherine had tried to hide, and she wanted to change the subject. She wanted to talk about anything except this. But Catherine was waiting, asking her for the truth. *Jesus. Was it always this hard talking about work with my lovers?*

But Rebecca knew the answer. It had never been this difficult because she'd never shared this part of her life with anyone. She knew she had to now. She didn't understand completely why, but instinctively, she knew in her heart that this was what Catherine needed.

"What it means is that Henry wants me to make this case, but he can't put his name on it in case we run afoul of Justice or some other higher-up along the way. This way, if it works out and we bring down someone big, he'll be able to take credit for the bust and everyone will be happy. If the investigation turns sour, he can say he didn't know anything about it."

"It sounds suspiciously like the kind of hospital politics that Hazel has to deal with all the time," Catherine said, speaking of her friend and department chair, Hazel Holcomb. "The difference is, of course, that no one is likely to shoot at Hazel."

"It won't be that way, Catherine," Rebecca assured her firmly. "We'll be doing a lot of work right from Sloan's with computer traces, just the way we have been doing. You don't need to worry."

"Rebecca, darling," Catherine said softly. "I will try my very best to understand and support you. I truly mean that. But you can't expect me not to worry."

"I promise it will be all right." Rebecca reached for Catherine's hand again. "Try to believe that."

"Will you let me help?"

Rebecca's first impulse was to say no. She hated having Catherine anywhere near an active investigation, because the first time Catherine had consulted on a case, she'd nearly been killed. She forced out the words. "Yes, if you really want to. Chances are we'll need your profiling input."

"Good. I hate what's happened, too."

Rebecca rubbed her face briskly with her free hand. "God, this relationship business is tough."

Catherine laughed, her eyes suddenly sparkling. "I love you, Rebecca Frye."

"What did I do?"

"And that's one of the big reasons why. You give me what I need, just because you're you."

❖

After Rebecca dropped Catherine off at the hospital, she drove twenty blocks south across the river that bisected the city and into a markedly different neighborhood. There the narrow run-down row houses fronted the sidewalks with tiny landings or none at all. Gentrification had not reached that part of Center City, and the poor and the disaffected naturally migrated there. She made one quick stop and then headed north for Old City and the renovated warehouse that housed both Sloan Security's central office and Michael and Sloan's home.

She found street parking and climbed the stairs to the recessed alcove in front of an unmarked door. A small security camera swiveled high in one corner, and she glanced up automatically. The front door lock was disengaged and she walked through into the enormous first-floor garage. Usually Sloan's black Porsche Carrera was housed there, but the vehicle had been totaled during the hit-and-run that had injured Michael. It had been impounded as evidence in the subsequent investigation.

The industrial elevator in the rear was controlled electronically from above, and as she approached, the double doors opened soundlessly. She entered and disembarked a moment later on the third floor into a huge open space divided by simple workstations and filled with electronic equipment, most of which was not yet available on the general market. She made her way to the central console, where she found Jason McBride, Sloan's business associate, studying a computer monitor. When he glanced in her direction, she could tell immediately that he'd been working without sleep for at least two days.

As always, his appearance was impeccable. His blond hair, parted on the side and combed back, was perfectly trimmed. His blended silk trousers and dress shirt were flawlessly pressed. He was astonishingly handsome, with refined features and a resonant tenor voice. There were deep shadows under his brilliant blue eyes, however, and when he spoke, his voice was hoarse with fatigue.

"Hi, Rebecca."

"Jason." She glanced around. "Mitchell and Watts here yet?"

"No," a voice from behind Rebecca answered.

Rebecca turned and saw Sloan walking toward her. The security consultant, who wore her signature blue jeans, white T-shirt, and scuffed brown boots, had apparently just come from the shower. Her hair was still wet. She looked roughly twice as bad as Jason, but Rebecca was happy to see that Sloan's eyes were clearer than they had been in days.

"Sloan. Good to see you." Rebecca held out her hand in greeting. "How's Michael?"

"She was awake for a few minutes this afternoon." Sloan smiled as she shook Rebecca's hand. "I'm going back to the hospital soon, but when Jason said you were coming over, I wanted to be here."

"That's great news about Michael."

"Yeah. It is." Sloan shrugged away the underlying worry that Michael's recovery was *too* good to be true and glanced at Jason's monitor. A series of images that appeared to be faces were rapidly flashing on and off the screen. "So far, no hits on the composite of the guy in the video. We've been working up images of the two girls as well. I'm just about to do a run with them."

Before Rebecca could reply, a small series of pings signaled activity from the perimeter cameras. She turned to her left and glanced at another series of monitors. Watts and Mitchell were displayed climbing the steps to the front door.

"Sector one, disengage," Sloan said quietly, and the front door locks clicked open. "Come ahead, Detective Watts. Officer Mitchell."

Another minute passed, and then Watts and Mitchell joined the group.

"Just like old times," Watts rumbled. He glanced at Sloan with the merest hint of discomfort in his expression. "Uh...how's your girl?"

Sloan smiled softly. "She's better."

"Good. That's good."

"That's great," Mitchell, also in jeans, a black T-shirt, and motorcycle boots, added.

She sidled over to Jason, peered over his shoulder at the computer, and began to talk to him in low tones, questioning him about the mechanics of the image formation. With a note of excitement in her voice, she murmured, "Sweet."

"Mitchell."

Mitchell spun around at the sound of Rebecca's voice. "Yes, ma'am?"

"Talk with you for a minute." Rebecca moved away and Mitchell followed. When they were out of earshot of the rest of the group, Rebecca said, "Sorry I didn't have a chance to brief you earlier. Did Watts fill you in on the way over?"

"The detective said that we'd be following up on the leads we got during the investigation with Justice." She straightened her shoulders. "I want to thank you for requesting m—"

"There's a bit more to it than that, Mitchell." Rebecca studied the young officer's face, noting again that there was something in Mitchell's eyes that said she'd had her share of trouble. "We'll be flying without a net. If we come up empty or turn up something ugly, we could all burn for it."

"Something ugly?" Mitchell queried immediately.

She's quick. Smart, eager, dependable. Detective material. Rebecca hitched a shoulder. "An operation like this could tank your career, and you have promise."

Mitchell almost smiled, but her eyes were dark. "I appreciate you saying that, ma'am, but—"

"Mitchell, Jesus. Can the ma'am."

"Yes, Sergeant. But my *career* is about as sunk as it could get. Before your captain called my watch commander, they had me on a crossing-guard detail." Mitchell shrugged. "But that's not what I really care about. What went down with Clark was way wrong. They fucked us—excuse me, ma'am—and I want to see this through."

"Yeah. They fucked us all right. You're in, Mitchell, as long as you understand the situation."

"Understood, ma—Sergeant."

Rebecca nodded and walked back to Jason. "Can you leave that program running, or do you have to baby-sit it?"

He shook his head. "No. If we get a hit, it will freeze the frame."

"Okay, then, listen up," Rebecca said, getting everyone's attention. "Let's go get some coffee and assess the situation."

They moved to the conference room in the rear, filled coffee cups, and settled around the granite-topped table.

"We've got a week, maybe two tops, to finish what we started with the investigation into the Internet porn ring." Rebecca looked at the people gathered around the table. "I have two primary goals—the first is finding out how and where they're getting the kids, where they're stashing them, and who's behind the video business."

Sloan's right hand tightened into a fist. "What about—"

"The second," Rebecca continued, unperturbed, "is finding out who leaked the intel about the raid last night and ordered the hit on Sloan. When we know that, we'll know who put Michael in the hospital."

"How we gonna work it?" Watts asked.

"From two directions," Rebecca replied. "Sloan and Jason will work the computers ID-ing the players in the porn video. Jason—you need to log on to the chat rooms under some of your aliases and see if there's anything going on there that could lead us to a name. Mitchell—you work that angle, too."

Mitchell nodded, her expression intent.

"Sloan," Rebecca met Sloan's hot eyes, reading the need for action, for retribution, in her purple gaze, "I need you to do some hacking."

"Into where?"

Rebecca hesitated, glancing once at Mitchell. The young officer returned her scrutiny steadily. "Into the PPD."

Watts muttered softly, "Fuck me."

"Someone raided the Crime Scene Investigation Unit's master files and derailed the investigation into the deaths of two police officers. One of those officers was Avery Clark's contact within the department—Jimmy Hogan. The other was my partner." Rebecca blew out a breath. "I'm betting that person was the same one who fingered you for the hit, Sloan."

"Based on what?" Sloan's head pounded and all she could feel was rage. She didn't want justice. She wanted blood.

"Gut feeling."

Sloan searched the cool blue eyes. Not a hint of anything soft in them. "Yeah. Okay. Your call then."

"We need street intel," Watts said into the ensuing silence. "All this computer jerking o—uh, *investigating,* is fine, but we need names, leads, something to chase."

"That's the second wing of our operation. You and I will work that, Watts." She glanced at her watch just as the repetitive ping of the security system sounded once more.

"System—show sector one," Sloan ordered and a monitor mounted on a wall bracket flashed to the landing in front of the main entrance.

Mitchell gasped.

A thin blond in low-riding jeans and a skin-tight top stood staring into the camera. The audio picked up her voice. "I'm here, so you gonna open up or what? Hey, Frye? Jesus."

"That would be my CI," Rebecca remarked flatly. "Better let her in before she starts in on the door."

CHAPTER FIVE

W atts swiveled in his chair to follow the progress of the newest arrival on the monitor. As the image on the screen switched from one security camera to the next, he whistled softly and watched the woman saunter across the garage to the elevator.

"Tasty. Looks like jailbait, though."

"Detective," Rebecca said in a voice so soft it would have been inaudible were it not so deadly. "Be careful what you say about one of mine."

Mitchell, whose eyes were riveted on the monitor as well, stiffened. *One of mine.*

"No offense, Sarge," Watts said in a mollifying tone. "I just meant to say she looks about thirteen and—"

"No further commentary is required." Rebecca watched Sandy's progress as she disembarked on the third floor and looked around in astonishment. Jason rose to go meet her and escort her back to the conference room. "She's on my payroll now and that's all that matters."

"Officially?" Mitchell's voice sounded loud compared to Rebecca's.

Rebecca regarded her solemnly, noting the tension in the young officer's body and the harsh edge to her voice. *So there is something going on with those two.*

She'd seen the two young women together more than once in the Tenderloin, walking together late at night or meeting in the all-night diner. They hadn't been aware of her scrutiny most of the time, but if she had seen them, eventually others would as well. Rebecca saw no need for Mitchell to know the details of her arrangements with a CI; in fact, it was information she rarely disclosed. But Mitchell's eyes were hot and her hands balled into fists, and the only way to defuse the situation was with a reprimand or the truth. "Yes. She's registered."

Since when? Mitchell clamped down on her response. It wasn't her place to question her sergeant. It was just that she had never realized that Sandy was working so closely with Rebecca. Being a registered confidential informant meant that Sandy was listed with the department by name and paid out of department funds on a regular basis. Mitchell had read between the lines earlier when Rebecca had intimated that their investigation might turn up something, or *someone,* dirty in the department. And if that were the case, Sandy's identity was now on file for that person to find. *Jesus, as if being on the streets isn't dangerous enough for her already. Why not just hang a target around her neck?*

She must have made some kind of noise, because Watts jostled her shoulder and muttered, "Take it easy, kid. Just sit back and watch the Sarge work her snitch."

Mitchell managed a nod as Jason walked in with Sandy beside him, but her stomach was in knots.

"Can I get you some coffee or a Coke?" Jason asked.

"How about a beer?"

"I think we've got some Stoudt's. That okay?"

Sandy did a quick scan of the room, hesitating for a millisecond on Mitchell's face before fixing on Rebecca with a defiant stare. "Yeah, sure. Why not."

"Hi, Sandy," Rebecca said before going around the room and introducing each individual. She referred to Watts and Mitchell by rank. She did not give Sandy's last name.

Addressing the group at large, Rebecca explained, "I asked Sandy to come down because I want her to look at last night's live feed. It's possible she might recognize the location, or the girls, or even the guy. We got some sound, too, so maybe a voice will be familiar."

Watts grunted in appreciation. Mitchell said nothing, but her eyes never left Sandy's face.

"I can bring it up on the big screen in the viewing room," Sloan offered.

"Great. So's we can all get a close-up of the guy's pecker."

Watts inclined his head toward Sandy. "Any chance you'll be able to recognize *that*?"

"Depends," Sandy said flatly as she took the can of beer from Jason. "Most of them look pretty much the same, except..." her eyes dropped briefly to Watts's crotch, "some of them are a lot smaller than others."

Watts grinned, not looking the least bit offended.

Mitchell stood quickly, pushing back her chair so hard it nearly tipped over. "Can we just see the video and find out if there's something there?"

"Good idea, Officer." Rebecca gestured toward the door. "Let's get started."

Sandy stayed close to Rebecca's side as the group wended its way through the core of the work area toward another smaller room at the opposite end of the building. She was aware of Dell walking just behind her, but she didn't acknowledge the rookie's presence. *Frye didn't tell me Dell would be here tonight. Jesus, she looks pissed, too.*

In the viewing room, Sloan slid a DVD into a computer. "The original's in our vault. This is a copy, but the quality should be fine."

She pushed a button and immediately images sprang to life on the large screen on one wall. Quickly, everyone took seats as she dimmed the lights. With the exception of Sandy, they'd all seen parts of it before. Jason, Sloan, and Mitchell had spent countless hours trolling the Internet sex chat rooms and bulletin boards, assuming various personae, including young girls and the men who were interested in having sex with them.

Ultimately, Jason, posing as a potential customer willing to pay high fees for live sex sessions broadcast via the Internet, had lured a man known only as LongJohnXXX into a face-to-face meeting. LongJohnXXX was directly connected to the pornography ring they were working to expose. He was the man they had hunted, trapped, and ultimately lost when Avery Clark and his Justice agents had usurped the arrest.

Now they were forced to begin again.

"I want you to look at the girls first," Rebecca said into the silence. "Then we'll go back and you can look at him."

Sandy was oddly silent as she watched the action on the screen. A man in a generic uniform meant to be playing a deliveryman entered a nondescript room in which the only furnishings were a bedroom set of the type sold in discount warehouses, a few lamps, and a chair. The bed was made up with a faded quilt.

"Faked," she muttered.

"What?" Rebecca asked. She pulled her chair close to Sandy, and in the near-dark, they looked as if their shoulders were touching.

"It's a movie set, not a house. You can see there's no ceiling, there in the corner."

Rebecca nodded. "We figure it's some kind of warehouse or abandoned factory. Maybe a garage."

Sandy leaned forward as two girls entered the room. One was Asian and the other Caucasian. Both appeared very young. The man stripped as they feigned surprise and awkward shyness.

"Can you...you know...make this bigger?" Sandy stared fixedly at the screen.

"Which part?" Watts grunted.

"I want to see their faces...their eyes."

"Just a second." Sloan made some adjustments and zoomed in on the Asian girl's face.

Sandy nodded in satisfaction. "She's young, but not quite as young as they want you to think."

"How old?" Rebecca asked intently.

"Fifteen, maybe sixteen. Do they take their clothes off?"

"You think anyone would pay if they didn't?" Watts's previous jocularity had dissipated, replaced by an unusual undertone of anger.

Right on cue, the two girls disrobed and began to caress the man, running their hands over his chest and back, pressing their bodies to his. The dialogue was sparse and typically uninspired, peppered with the liberal use of "Oh yeah, baby" and "Ooh, you're so big." Someone in Sloan's viewing room made a disgusted sound.

All the activity was obviously staged but with enough realism, apparently, to satisfy the viewing market. On the screen, the now-naked thirty-year-old man, a big beefy guy who looked like a college football player gone to fat, stood by the side of the bed while one of the girls performed fellatio on him. Kneeling on the floor next to them, the other girl fondled him while his large hand roamed over her barely perceptible breasts.

"Anything?" Rebecca whispered softly.

"I don't know them," Sandy replied hollowly. Watching the young girls do what she herself did on a nightly basis was harder than she had expected it to be. It was even worse knowing that Dell was watching. Sandy tried not to wonder if Dell was imagining *her* doing those things, using her hands and her mouth on some stranger. She had felt many things about her life on the streets, from anger to emotional numbness, but she had never before been embarrassed. She clung to her rage most of all, because it was the one thing that kept her strong. *Fuck. Why do I care what anyone thinks? Even her.*

"Okay," Rebecca whispered, hearing the discomfort in Sandy's voice. She touched the young blond's hand, once, very lightly, then drew away. "You're doing fine." Over her shoulder, she said to Sloan, "Get us a shot of the guy now."

"It's mostly just gonna be his dick," Watts remarked.

The images blurred, and then a profile of the man's face came into view. Sandy straightened suddenly. "Wait...can you go back?... There..." She pointed at the screen. "On his neck...is that a scar?"

"Sloan?"

"Can't be sure, but Jason can work it up for us later with the imaging software."

"Good girl, Sandy." Rebecca's voice was tight with excitement. "Do you know him?"

"Seen him, maybe," Sandy replied. "I remember something about a guy with a scar on his neck shaped like a...whatdayacallit... a scimitar."

"Is he a john?" Watts asked gruffly.

Sandy flushed, and then was angry at herself for showing even that little bit of emotion in front of these strangers. *So Frye told them I'm a whore. So what.*

"Why don't you shut the fuck up," Mitchell growled as she leaned close to the heavy detective. "She came here to help."

Watts stared, his expression one of shock. He was, for once, left without a comeback.

"Turn it off," Rebecca ordered.

The lights came up and they all stood, blinking, carefully not looking at one another.

"If you can give me pictures of those girls, I can show them around," Sandy offered.

"Jason will get them made up for you tonight," Sloan replied.

Sandy nodded, really looking at Sloan for the first time, slowly taking in the wild dark hair, the amazing eyes, the muscular physique. She looked a bit like an older Dell, except Dell's body was sexier, all wiry and tight and...*Oh man, what is that about!*

"Maybe flashing those pictures around's not so cool," Mitchell said, moving closer to Sandy. She almost reached for her hand, and then stuffed her fists into the pockets of her jeans instead. "You start asking about those girls and somebody might take notice. Somebody you don't *want* to take notice."

"Mitchell," Rebecca warned. *I've got to rein her in before she crosses a line.*

Sensing the warning in Rebecca's voice, Sandy lifted her chin and snapped, "I can take care of myself, rookie. Why don't you just worry about the cop stuff, 'cause it looks to me like you guys haven't been doing such a hot job with that lately."

"We've all got some work to do," Rebecca said sharply. "Jason, you finish running the images through the databases and get a couple of sets of prints for me. Sloan, when you're a little more settled, I'll brief you about that other issue."

"Sure. Fine." Sloan looked at her watch. It was almost eleven, and for the last twenty minutes she'd been unable to concentrate on anything except getting back to Michael. The longer she was away from her bedside, the more anxious she became. "I'll be at the hospital until sometime tomorrow morning. I'll catch up to you then."

Rebecca merely nodded, wanting to suggest that the security consultant get some sleep first, but knowing that it would do no good.

"I'm gonna knock off for the night," Watts said. "But in the morning, I'll start digging into whatever Jimmy Hogan was doing for Justice. Probably won't get anything, but it's gotta be done."

While the others worked out the schedule for the next day, Mitchell and Sandy slowly drifted toward the elevator.

"Come on, I'll walk you home," Mitchell murmured to Sandy. She rested her fingers lightly against Sandy's bare elbow. To her surprise, Sandy didn't pull away, even though the blond hadn't looked at her directly since the lights had come up in the viewing room.

"Sandy," Rebecca called, catching up to them at the elevators. "Let's take a ride."

"Sure," the young woman replied with a sigh, moving her arm away from Mitchell's hand. "It's your dime, Frye."

Outside, Watts went one way and Sandy and Rebecca walked in the other direction to the Corvette. Mitchell stood on the sidewalk, shoulders hunched in the chill night air, and watched them go.

❖

"You did well up there," Rebecca said as she drove south on Front Street, the lights of the Ben Franklin Bridge glowing blue as it towered into the dark night sky just above them.

"I didn't do a thing." Sandy looked out the window. "I told you I don't know them."

"Know anybody who might?"

Sandy shrugged. After another minute, she replied, "Maybe. There are a lot of new girls around. Young ones like those kids in the video. I'll ask."

"What do you mean by 'a lot'?"

"Seems like every few weeks there's a new crop. Mostly in the clubs."

"I didn't think you worked the clubs."

"I don't, but I hang in them."

"What about the guy? You know him, don't you?" Rebecca studied Sandy's face in the light of the passing headlights. Not for the first time she realized how pretty she was. "Sandy?"

"I'm not sure, but I think he used to be a bouncer at Ziggie's."

Rebecca drew a sharp breath, and her pulse rate jumped. Ziggie's was a skin club at Eleventh and Arch that featured nude dancers, and it was mob connected. A guy reputed to be one of Zamora's front men owned it. *Finally, a connection.* "Did you ever dance there?"

"Who, me?" Sandy snorted. "Not hardly. You need tits out to Arizona to shag in there. And you have to blow every bartender in the place." She hesitated, unused to sharing information with the police, even Frye. They'd had an informal relationship for a year or so. Frye would hunt her down, ask her a few questions, drop a few dollars on her. But that afternoon, the detective had shown up at her apartment unexpectedly and made her an offer for something more formal. With a higher price tag attached. More information, more help, for more money. Sandy sighed. "But I know someone who did work there."

"Can you put me with her?"

"I'll see if I can find her."

"Sandy..."

"Yeah, yeah. I said I'd try. Jesus." Sandy pointed to a bar up the block. "You can let me out here."

"Uh-uh. I'm taking you home."

"It's not even midnight!"

"When I stopped by earlier and you agreed to go official with me, you turned in your streetwalking creds."

"I'm not gonna trick." Sandy sounded affronted. "But I need to be out and seen, otherwise people will get suspicious. And suspicious people don't talk. You know that."

Rebecca had the inexplicable desire to tell her no, but she knew the savvy young woman was right. Sandy had to maintain her street contacts or she'd be useless as an informant. Rebecca pulled to the curb. The sidewalk was alive with junkies looking to score, low-level dealers shuffling along murmuring the name of the drug of the hour to every likely buyer passing by, and hookers standing under streetlights or leaning against the front of buildings.

When Sandy reached for the door handle, Rebecca said, "Wait."

Surprised, Sandy turned in her seat. "Now what? Man, you never quit."

"Here," Rebecca said as she pulled her wallet from her back pocket. She extracted five twenties, almost all that she had. "Your first paycheck."

Sandy looked at the bills and smiled wryly. "Five hand jobs. Won't pay the rent."

"I'll see that there's more. And your hands are clean."

"Yeah. Ain't that a thrill."

"One more thing."

"Frye, you're hurting me sitting out here."

Rebecca had already checked and knew that no one was watching them. "A police officer can be suspended, even fired, for fraternizing with a prostitute."

Sandy grew still. "Fraternizing—you mean, even if they're just...like friends?"

"Sometimes 'friends' looks like something else." Rebecca's voice was soft, almost gentle. "Hard to prove otherwise."

"I don't have any cop *friends,* and the only ones I have sex with are the ones who force me." Sandy pushed open the door. "So there isn't anybody who ought to be getting into trouble. Okay?"

"Take this." Rebecca leaned across the seat and held out a cell phone. "We need to stay in touch."

Sandy studied it, then slipped it onto the waistband of her jeans. "Does this mean *we're* goin' steady?"

"It's just business, Sandy."

"Aren't you worried that someone will think we're more than *friends*?"

"I can handle that."

And Dell can't. That's what you're telling me, right, Frye? Sandy turned her back and headed for the bar.

Rebecca watched the thin young blond walk away, knowing that she was putting the girl in danger by employing her as an informant. But the streets would be no kinder to Sandy if she was forced to sell her body to survive. At least this way, she might have a chance. And Rebecca needed the information Sandy could provide. A devil's bargain, perhaps, but one she would have to live with.

CHAPTER SIX

S loan walked quickly through the silent hospital halls, the events and conversations of the last few hours almost forgotten. There was work to be done, she knew, and she wanted to be part of it. *Needed* to be part of it, needed to do *something* to make up for the agony she had brought into Michael's life. But that was for tomorrow. Now, at this moment, there was only Michael.

She'd been gone from Michael's bedside longer than she had since Michael had been injured, and the nearer she drew to the heavy metal doors of the intensive care unit, the greater her sense of foreboding. By the time she pushed through, she was nearly running. When she reached the door of the single cubicle and looked in, she saw only the empty bed with the pristine white sheets neatly made. Her stomach turned over, and her head grew light. Blindly, she stretched out one hand to the doorframe for balance. In her mind, one word echoed over and over. *Michael!*

"I'm so sorry," a nurse said as she quickly approached, an expression of compassion and concern on her face.

Sloan closed her eyes, the roaring in her head making it difficult to make out the words. *Oh God, oh God...what am I going to do?*

"I tried to call you—"

Numbly, Sloan pulled the cell phone from her belt. The battery was dead. She stared at the small, dark-haired woman with the kind eyes.

"...upstairs a half-hour ago."

"What?" Sloan couldn't seem to catch hold of the words that were floating past her. "What did you say?"

"We needed the bed, and she's doing so much better she was just transferred to a regular room."

"She's all right?" The rush of blood into Sloan's head was so abrupt that she developed an instant headache. The pain, however, was a welcome replacement for the numbing terror.

"Her vital signs are great, and she was awake for a few minutes." The nurse smiled. "Take the elevators right outside the door to the fifth floor. 519."

"Thank you." Sloan's voice, hoarse with fatigue, cracked. "Thank you for everything."

She couldn't tolerate the wait for the elevator. Instead, she shouldered through the fire door into the stairwell and took the three flights of stairs at a run. By the time she reached the hallway, she was panting. Quickly scanning the room numbers, she hurried down the far side of a horseshoe-shaped arrangement of hospital rooms until she found 519. Then, unaccountably, she was afraid to go in. She wasn't certain how many more times she could bear to speak Michael's name and get no response. The silence went deeper than sound. Michael's absence from her life left her hollow, like a gourd left out in the desert sun until even the seeds inside had shriveled and crumbled to dust. She rang with emptiness.

Sloan pushed open the door and stepped resolutely inside. *You'll keep saying her name until she opens her eyes and comes back for good.* That's *how many more times.*

There was only one bed, and the lights had been turned down until the objects in the room were mere suggestions of forms. From the darkness came a soft sound, the answer to her prayers.

"Sloan?"

"Hey," Sloan whispered as she approached the bed, her vision blurred with tears. As she blinked them away, her eyes gradually adjusted to the dim light, and she could see Michael propped up against two pillows. The relief of finding her awake was akin to pain, and Sloan's stomach cramped, causing her to bite back a groan. She grasped the hand that Michael lifted, clinging to the warmth. "Aren't you supposed to be sleeping?"

"Haven't I been sleeping for two days already?" Michael's voice sounded stronger than it had when she had awakened twelve hours before. "I think the nurses told me that it's Monday night...or maybe Tuesday morning?"

Sloan leaned over, brushed her lips across Michael's forehead, and then with her free hand stroked her cheek. "It's very early Tuesday morning. How do you feel?"

"Weak. A little confused. I can't remember what happened." Michael's eyes traveled over Sloan's face. "There was an accident, right?"

"Yes." Sloan's heart ached to see Michael's normally vibrant blue eyes clouded with confusion and pain.

"You're not hurt, are you?"

"No, baby," Sloan said, her voice choked. "I'm not hurt. You don't have to worry about anything. You just need to work on getting well."

"You look tired." Michael's eyelids drooped and she forced them open. Smiling tremulously, she said, "In fact, you look terrible. Go home."

Sloan laughed gently and pulled a chair close with one hand. Then she found the latch beneath the bed to lower the rail and leaned forward, one hand on Michael's hip beneath the covers and the other still linked with Michael's. "Usually after two days apart, you think I look fantastic."

"Well, some things about you always look fantastic." Michael sighed. "I'm awfully tired, and I have this headache...it's so hard to think clearly."

"You don't need to think. Just close your eyes and get some sleep."

"Yes," Michael murmured. Then she twitched suddenly and her eyes flew open. "It was a car, wasn't it? A car hit me."

There was an edge of fear to Michael's voice, and Sloan felt a rush of fury like none she had ever known. She had suffered indignities and injustices in her life; she had been jailed by the very people she had sought to serve; she had been betrayed by a lover and abandoned by her friends. But nothing had ever managed to incite her rage the way this assault on the woman she loved had done.

Struggling to keep her voice calm, she said, "You rest now, baby. We'll talk about it in the morning."

As if the effort of remembering were exhausting, Michael sagged against the pillows in acquiescence. "You, too...you go home. Go to sleep."

Sloan stroked Michael's cheek as she slipped into sleep. She would stay, ensuring that no harm would come to her lover that night. Then in the morning, she would seek retribution.

❖

It was just after midnight when Rebecca used the key that Catherine had given her and let herself into the garden apartment in West Philadelphia. A single lamp burned in the living room, casting the space in warm shadow. She snapped it off as she passed by, making her way by memory to the bedroom in the rear. As she walked down the hall, she was surprised to see a light glowing ahead. Slowing at the door, she smiled at Catherine, who was propped up in bed, nude, with a book.

"You're still awake."

"Hi." Catherine placed the book face down on the covers by her side. The window was open, and the cool September breeze wafted through the room. There was just a hint of fall in the air. "You're early."

"Am I?" Rebecca raised an eyebrow as she stripped off her jacket followed by her shoulder holster. She walked to the far side of the bed and placed her weapon in the top drawer of the bedside table, then leaned across the bed and kissed Catherine. "Isn't tomorrow a workday for you?"

"It is. But I just wasn't tired." Savoring the heat of Rebecca's lips, too quickly withdrawn, Catherine sighed with pleasure. *I can't seem to sleep without you.*

"I'm going to take a quick shower. I'll just be a sec." Rebecca was already halfway to the bathroom, unbuttoning her shirt as she walked.

"Hurry back."

The slight hint of invitation in Catherine's voice was enough to make Rebecca's blood surge. She turned and let the shirt slide from her chest, watching Catherine's eyes fall to her breasts. "Don't fall asleep."

"Don't worry, Detective. I won't."

The shower was purely functional, and Rebecca did not linger. Within minutes, she walked back into the bedroom, naked, toweling off as she approached the bed. She stopped abruptly when she observed the intense expression on Catherine's face. "What?"

"You really don't have any idea how beautiful you are, do you?"

Constantly amazed by Catherine's desire, Rebecca blushed. She lowered the towel and held it still bunched in one fist, feeling her lover's gaze travel down the length of her body. By the time Catherine's eyes had returned to hers, Rebecca was breathing quickly. "I get excited just watching you look at me."

Catherine pushed the sheet aside, revealing her own nakedness, and rose to her knees, moving closer to the edge of the bed as she did. She held out one hand and when Rebecca took it, she pulled Rebecca close. Threading her arms around Rebecca's waist, she drew one small tight nipple into her mouth, reveling at the swift gasp from her lover.

Closing her eyes, Rebecca rested her palms on Catherine's shoulder for balance. Her skin was cool, and Catherine's mouth was very warm, and all of her concentration was soon focused on the way that teasing tongue moved over her breast. Her thighs trembled as she leaned forward, forcing Catherine to take more of her into her mouth. "Please...do it harder."

Moaning with satisfaction, Catherine sucked harder, drawing the tight rosette back and forth between her teeth. Her breasts were pressed to Rebecca's thighs, and her own nipples tightened, making her shiver. When Rebecca uttered a small cry and thrust her hips against Catherine's chest, an answering rush of arousal flooded her thighs. Gasping, Catherine tilted her head back and looked up into her lover's face. Rebecca's eyes were nearly closed, the blue gone purple with desire. Her neck was arched, exposed and vulnerable, a pulse racing wildly beneath the skin. Catherine couldn't think; she could only act. Arms still tight around Rebecca's waist, she pulled Rebecca down beside her on the bed and leaned over her.

"I need things from you," Catherine proclaimed. Drawing her hand up the inside of Rebecca's quivering thigh, Catherine found her wet and open and moved inside her, gently but swiftly filling her.

"What...do you need?" Rebecca arched off the bed, groaning as Catherine withdrew, then entered again. With her right hand, she grasped Catherine's wrist, forcing her hand deeper still.

"I need..." Catherine leaned over Rebecca's body as she pressed even further. "...this passion, this life..."

Rebecca's words were strangled. "Take it."

"Yesss." Catherine stroked to the rhythm of Rebecca's heartbeat pulsating around her fingers. "God, what you make me feel."

With tremendous effort, Rebecca turned her head and forced her eyes open. She was close to coming and could barely make out Catherine's face, but she found her eyes, wide and dark with need and desire. There, in the fierce gentleness of Catherine's embrace, Rebecca shed her defenses and lay down her burdens. "Take me."

The impact of her strong lover's trusting surrender swelled Catherine's heart to bursting. With a cry of her own, she brought her mouth to Rebecca's, entering her there also as she thrust faster within. When every muscle in Rebecca's body contracted at once, Catherine brushed her thumb rhythmically across Rebecca's clitoris and catapulted her into orgasm.

"God God, yes yes..." Rebecca moaned, writhing beneath the onslaught of release. Breathless, panting, she finally tugged weakly at Catherine's wrist, stilling her motion. "I'm done...I can't...no more. But stay inside."

Catherine rested her forehead against Rebecca's shoulder, her chest heaving with exertion and arousal. When she felt Rebecca's hands glide down her back to cup her hips, she smiled. "Relax for a minute. Enjoy it."

"Oh, believe me, I'm enjoying it."

Rebecca's strength was slowly returning, and with it, the urgency to claim her lover. Lifting her hips, she pushed upward and turned Catherine beneath her. In another instant, she was kneeling on the floor, her hands under Catherine's thighs, drawing Catherine to her mouth. She found her as she knew she would— ripe and swollen with urgency. It would take little, she knew, to stir Catherine to climax. But she did not want a moment's satisfaction that would flare and burn with little heat; she wanted to savor the essence of their love until it scorched through every cell.

Slowly, carefully, Rebecca explored with her lips and her tongue, soothing and teasing and tormenting until Catherine twisted against the sheets, her legs pressed to Rebecca's shoulders.

"I'm ready. I'm so ready. Please." Catherine's voice was a whisper, her breath broken with need. "There. Oh, Rebecca, there."

Rebecca slid her palms beneath Catherine's hips and lifted her more firmly to her mouth, drawing the last drops of Catherine's desire between her lips. Catherine came as Rebecca inexorably called the passion forth from her soul.

❖

"Ah, God." Rebecca lay on her back with Catherine's head on her shoulder, the sheets pulled up to their waists as they luxuriated in the aftermath of lovemaking. Idly, she ran strands of Catherine's thick auburn hair through her fingers as the tension of the day fell away. Before Catherine, she would have been struggling to sleep at this point. She would have gone to the gym to work out in the middle of the night or stood at the narrow window in her second-floor apartment above a convenience store to watch the street life below. She would have fought the urge to drink; she would have fought the desolation and loneliness in her heart. Now, all she could feel was peace. "I could get used to coming home to that."

"That could be arranged." Catherine's voice was light, almost drowsy, as she brushed her fingertips lightly over Rebecca's breast. She felt Rebecca stiffen and the fingers in her hair grew still. "What?"

"Nothing."

Catherine leaned far enough away that she could see Rebecca's face, which was smooth and expressionless in the moonlight. "Are you afraid that I'm proposing marriage?"

"Are you?"

It was Catherine's turn to grow still. Rebecca had come into her life on a whirlwind of passion in the midst of terror. Before Rebecca, her life had been orderly and predictable and satisfying. She had been alone, and she had sometimes been lonely, but for the most part, she had been content. Rebecca had changed everything. Now, she was bombarded with a constant onslaught of feeling—hungers and desires, both physical and emotional. Rebecca felt as necessary to her life as air and water and food. She craved Rebecca's presence when they were apart, starved for her touch, ached to touch her. If that was not the grand passion she had dreamed of but never quite dared to believe in, such love did not exist in this world.

"Yes," Catherine said softly but quite clearly. "I am."

Rebecca tightened her grip on the woman in her embrace, but said nothing.

When the silence grew too heavy, Catherine spoke again. "Does that frighten you?"

"Yes." Rebecca closed her eyes, waiting for Catherine to draw away. Each day, she found it harder to steel herself to the certainty of loss. Each day, she hoped a little more that this miracle would not end.

"Why?" Catherine moved closer, drawing her thigh across Rebecca's, curling her arm across Rebecca's chest.

"You don't know what you're getting into." There was sorrow in Rebecca's tone. "The job...it...takes something from us."

Catherine lay very still, almost breathless. These were the moments—even more than the exquisite joy of their physical union—these were the moments of connection that she lived for. "What, darling? What does it take?"

"It takes...pieces of our hearts. Tears them out, turns them to stone." Rebecca sighed and pressed her face to Catherine's hair. "I'm afraid there isn't enough left for you."

"Oh no, you're wrong." Catherine's voice was tender and sure. "I don't know everything that drives you to do the work you do. I don't know why you're willing to face such horrors every day or why you're willing to risk your life for strangers. I might never know all the reasons, although I want to." Gently, she slid onto Rebecca's body and braced herself on her elbows, her hands in Rebecca's hair. Holding Rebecca's gaze, she whispered, "But I do know that the reasons begin in your heart. And what's in your heart is why I love you."

Rebecca shuddered, needing so badly to believe. "There are things I've done...things I *do*..." She sighed again. "Tonight I..." Hesitating, she reconsidered. *Maybe there are some things best kept secret.*

"I can hear you thinking."

Laughing, Rebecca shook her head. "Now that's scary." She

sat up a bit and pulled Catherine back down into her arms. "You remember Sandy?"

It was Catherine's turn to grow still. *Sandy. The young woman you were with when your lung collapsed. The woman who looked like she was half in love with you. Is she the woman you see at night when you leave here?*

"Yes," Catherine replied, pleased that her voice was steady. "I remember."

"I did something with her today," Rebecca admitted reluctantly. "Something you might find less than honorable."

"What?" Catherine asked carefully.

"The details aren't really important. The point is, there are things that I do that you might have trouble with."

"In this particular instance, the details matter."

"Why?" Rebecca put a finger under Catherine's chin and studied her face. "You don't think...me and Sandy?" She laughed. "Christ, no."

Catherine blushed. "She's very attractive, and she obviously cares about you."

"Catherine, I love *you*." Rebecca kissed her, lightly at first, then with a sudden surge of passion. When she drew away, she said intently, "There is no one else. Not Sandy. No one."

"I'm not used to feeling jealous," Catherine confided with a touch of embarrassment. "I'm sorry."

"Nothing to be sorry about. I kind of like it. But you don't have to worry." Rebecca shrugged. "Besides, Sandy doesn't like cops, or so she says. She seems pretty damned fond of Mitchell, though."

"Dellon Mitchell?" Catherine couldn't hide her surprise. Then she remembered the conversation with the young officer.

"I have a friend."

"What's her name?"

"Sandy."

"Uh-huh. They're looking pretty tight. I had to warn Sandy off her tonight."

"Why?"

"We talk sometimes."

"If Mitchell gets fingered by someone for being chummy with

a prostitute, it could cost her her badge."

"So you told Sandy to stay away from De...Mitchell?" Catherine asked carefully, aware that Rebecca had no idea that Dell was her patient.

"Just suggested it." Rebecca laughed quietly. "No one tells Sandy anything."

"And that bothers you?"

"What? Oh, no—that's something different. I signed Sandy up as a confidential informant today."

"That means what? You made her relationship with you official, somehow?" Catherine's mind was still on Dell and the effect that Sandy's withdrawal might have on her. Dell clearly had feelings for the girl, and if what Rebecca had intimated was true, those feelings might very well be reciprocated by the young prostitute. Catherine realized with a start that she had only been half listening. "I'm sorry, darling. You're worried about her?"

"I was just saying that getting information to me is always risky. Now she's going to be doing it a lot more regularly." Rebecca drew the sheet up over them and yawned. "It's late. We should get to sleep."

"I'm sorry. I'm fading a bit."

"Mmm." Brushing a kiss on Catherine's lips, Rebecca closed her eyes. "Me, too."

As Catherine began to drift off, she realized that Rebecca had managed to avoid addressing her proposal. Only then did she realize just how much she wanted Rebecca to say yes.

CHAPTER SEVEN

Michael turned carefully at the sound of her door opening. The pain in her head was constant, alternating between a low-level ache hovering at the top of her spine to an all-out cannon barrage that beat against the back of her eyeballs until it hurt to keep her eyelids open. The room lights were turned down low, but even the scant illumination was difficult for her to tolerate.

"Good morning," Ali Torveau said as she approached the bed. "It's good to see you awake."

"Hello," Michael said, her voice betraying her confusion.

"You don't remember me, but I'm Dr. Torveau, the trauma surgeon who's been taking care of you since you came into the hospital."

"I have a few blanks in my memory for the last couple of days. I'm sorry."

Ali shook her head. "There's no need to apologize."

As the surgeon spoke, she glanced over a flow sheet attached to a clipboard in her right hand. Laying that aside, she withdrew her stethoscope from the right-hand pocket of her white lab coat and leaned over the bed. "How does your chest feel? Your ribs are bruised and several are cracked, but they'll be fine eventually."

"It hurts a little when I take a deep breath. Not too bad, though." Michael waited silently as Ali moved the stethoscope over her chest and back.

"You sound pretty good." Ali straightened and slung the stethoscope around her neck. "Now, what about your head?"

Michael grimaced. "That's not doing quite as well. Major headache."

"Any double vision?" Ali produced a penlight and shone it into Michael's eyes, flicking it rapidly from one to the other. When

Michael gasped and turned her head away, the surgeon frowned. "Does that hurt?"

"It feels like you're sticking an ice pick through my eyeball."

"Guess it does hurt, then. We call that photophobia, and it's fairly common after a serious concussion." Anticipating the next question, Ali added compassionately, "It's almost always temporary, but I can't tell you how long it will last. It could be a few days; it could be a few weeks."

"When can I go home?"

"That depends on a number of things." Ali shrugged. "You're improving rapidly, but the major area of concern is your head injury. I've ordered a repeat CT scan for later this morning, although I don't expect it to show anything abnormal."

"And if it's okay?"

"You haven't even been out of bed yet," Ali responded with a small laugh. "Let's take things one day at a time."

Michael glanced toward the closed bathroom door through which the pulse of a shower was faintly audible. "I'd really rather recover at home. I wouldn't even mind hiring a private duty nurse, if you thought I needed that."

"Some reason you're in a hurry to get out of here?" The surgeon realized that her question was rhetorical, but she sensed more than the usual urgency for discharge.

With a sigh, Michael leaned her head back against the pillow. It was difficult for her to concentrate for more than a few moments, and any kind of effort seemed to make the headache worse. "I can rest at home as well as here. And Sloan isn't getting any sleep at all."

"This has been hard on both of you, I know," Ali said sympathetically. "How about if I talk to her—"

"Talk to who about what?" Sloan asked as she entered wearing a fresh pair of scrubs and toweling her hair with the coarse white towel the hospital had provided. She walked directly to the bed, leaned down, and kissed Michael's forehead. "Good morning."

"It is now." Michael smiled, the headache diminishing for an instant. "We were talking about me going home."

"Really!" Sloan spun around to stare at the trauma surgeon,

her eyes glowing with excitement. "So soon? God, that would be great."

"Whoa. Slow down. You two are getting ahead of me here." Ali held up her hands as if to ward off a blow, but she was smiling, too, as she regarded Michael. "Let's see what this morning's CAT scan shows. If that looks good, I'll stop by this afternoon and reevaluate you. Then...we'll see."

"Good enough." Sloan couldn't keep the pleasure from her voice. Just the idea of having Michael at home was enough to ease the constant heaviness in her chest that made it hard for her to take an unfettered breath. "Do you have any idea when you might be back?"

Ali checked her watch. "I've got surgery in just a few minutes. Sometime after two, most likely."

"I'll be here." As the surgeon started for the door, Sloan called softly, "And thanks."

Michael reached for Sloan's hand. "Now, will you go home and get some sleep?"

"I slept last night."

"You are the worst liar."

Sloan managed to look affronted, but after a moment, the corners of her mouth angled into a grin. "Okay. So maybe it was only a minute or two, but I definitely closed my eyes."

"I love you."

The words hit Sloan like a hammer blow. Her knees suddenly weak, she reached blindly behind her for the chair. She didn't even remember sitting; the next thing she was aware of was gasping for breath as tears poured down her cheeks. "Oh God, I'm sorry. I'm so sorry. I love you so much."

"Come here, love," Michael murmured, tugging on Sloan's hand.

Somehow, Sloan managed to get the bed rail down and very carefully stretched out next to Michael, curling on her side and pressing her face close to Michael's on the pillow. "I'm such a mess without you."

"Well, I'm here," Michael soothed, stroking Sloan's face. "And you know I'll never leave you, don't you?"

"I know." Starting to believe that everything was truly going to be all right, Sloan took a shuddering breath, smiled, and rested her fingers against Michael's cheek. "So, how are you really feeling, baby?"

"Better with you next to me. I just want to go home."

"Just as soon as possible. I promise."

"That's fine then." Michael sighed and closed her eyes, murmuring, "Because your promises are as good as gold."

Sloan continued to caress Michael's face as she slipped into sleep. *I promise to take you home soon. And I promise, no matter what, that you'll be safe from now on.*

❖

When Sloan was certain that Michael was asleep, she eased from the bed, found her socks and shoes, and—once dressed—slipped from the room. On her way through the hospital, she stopped at a pay phone and made a call.

A female voice answered on the second ring. "Hello?"

"Sarah? It's Sloan."

"Is Michael all right?"

"She's great. Awake and talking." Sloan felt a sudden wave of anxiety. "I don't think she remembers much, though."

"It will come back to her in time." Sarah's voice was calm and gentle. "In case you hadn't noticed, darlin', it's six-thirty in the morning."

"Huh. Getting late. Is Jason around?"

Sarah laughed. "He's in the study. I'll get him."

A minute later, Jason came on the line. "Hey! Terrific news about Michael."

"Yeah. There's even a chance she'll come home soon." Saying the words made Sloan feel uncharacteristically superstitious, so she quickly moved on. "What are you doing?"

There was a beat of silence, then, "Phishing."

Sloan frowned. Jason was referring to the practice of stealing confidential information from on-line consumers by pretending to be a legitimate business updating the consumer's account. He would send an e-mail claiming that there had been a problem with the billing of an account and warn that if consumers didn't update their billing information, they risked losing their account or being referred to a collection agency.

The message directed consumers to click on a hyperlink in the body of the e-mail to connect to the "Billing Center." When consumers clicked on the link, they landed on a site that looked exactly like the company's legitimate site, but which was, in fact, a front for Jason's tracking program. When consumers entered their name, address, and credit card information, Jason would be able to record it.

There was one problem, and that was the possibility of being traced *back* by a savvy computer user. And Jason was working from home. Sloan asked, "You're casting lines from there?"

"Not exactly. I'm routed through Amsterdam."

"Ah. Okay then." Sloan relaxed, knowing that there was little chance that the electronic trail would lead back to Jason or Sarah. "Learning anything about our friends?"

"Might be."

Sloan caught her breath. "How about we discuss this at the office?"

"Sure. When?"

"I'm on my way."

"Let me make Sarah some breakfast, and then I'll be over." After a second, he added, "You want me to bring you something?"

"No, that's okay. Thanks. Hey, Jase—can you call Frye? Tell her I'm ready to saddle up."

"You sure? With Michael still in the hospital?"

Sloan's violet eyes darkened to black. "All the more reason to go after them."

"I'll tell her where we are. Okay if I get Mitchell, too? I could use some help tracking this information."

"Frye said we could use her. Do it."

"I'm on it."

"See you soon." Sloan hung up, her fatigue magically dissipating. She was ready to hunt.

❖

At seven-thirty, Rebecca settled into a plain office chair in the drab institutional room and nodded perfunctorily to the middle-aged man seated across from her behind a laminated wood desk.

"Good morning, Sergeant," he said.

"Doctor."

"I was a bit surprised to learn that you had scheduled three more sessions with me."

Three? Rebecca was about to say that *she* hadn't scheduled anything, but thought better of it. The less anyone in an official capacity knew about her off-the-record investigation, the better. And the continued counseling, originally mandated as a result of her in-the-line-of-duty shooting, was part of that cover. "Captain Henry was in favor of it. It's his call."

"How are you feeling?"

"Fine."

"I understand that you had a bit of a problem last week."

A bit more than one. Rebecca waited. *Never volunteer anything during an interrogation.* Which was how she viewed therapy. Although she knew that theoretically Rand Whitaker, the police psychologist, was there to help officers who were traumatized from the daily violence they witnessed or stressed from the constant physical danger or addicted to drugs or alcohol, she didn't trust him. He wasn't a cop. Catherine was the only non-cop in her life she really trusted. Sloan and Jason *were* cops in their own way, and Sandy—well, Sandy was unique. Sandy had her own code of ethics. It wasn't one most people would understand, but Rebecca did. Sandy was loyal to her friends and expected nothing from anyone that she hadn't earned. One way or the other.

"...ER with a punctured lung," Whitaker finished.

"Those are confidential files." Rebecca's voice was flat but resonated dangerously.

"The ER treatment summary was forwarded to your central file for insurance purposes and ended up on my desk."

"Convenient."

Casually, Whitaker rocked back in his desk chair and clasped his hands over his stomach. He regarded her benignly. "You weren't this angry last week."

Rebecca folded back the tab of the plastic cover on her lunch-truck coffee. Lifting the container, she asked, "You mind?"

Whitaker shook his head, indicating his own ceramic mug

from which a tendril of steam wafted. "Something happen since you were here last?"

"Isn't *that* in the report?"

"It's always good for you to tell it."

"Nothing out of the ordinary." Rebecca sipped the scalding brew, wondering, not for the first time, how they made it so hot and so tasteless at the same time. *Nothing, that is, if you don't count a murder attempt, a sabotaged arrest, and a torpedoed investigation.*

"You were on some kind of temporary assignment, as I recall. A desk job, wasn't it?"

Whitaker showed no sign of annoyance at Rebecca's obvious reluctance to engage in any kind of dialogue. When she merely nodded once more, he continued unperturbed. "How do things stand with that presently?"

"That assignment is over. I'm in-between now."

"In-between?"

"My paperwork isn't quite in order, and Henry won't assign me to any regular duty because of it."

"Ahh...I see. So *I'm* the sticking point."

"Yes."

"And you're angry with me about the delay in returning you to full duty?"

His tone and expression were mild, but Rebecca had the insistent feeling that she was being very gently psychically probed. There was a faint tingle in her consciousness, as if someone were touching a hot wire to the surface of her brain. It was distinctly unpleasant. She let out a breath. "No, I'm not particularly angry at you. You're only doing your job. But I'm tired of the bureaucracy and the bullshit."

"Don't you think those things are synonymous with city government, to some degree?"

Rebecca couldn't help it. She laughed. "True."

"So why do you persist?"

"What?" Her confusion was genuine.

"In the job. Why keep doing it when there are so many obstacles and, so often, very little reward?"

"Because it's what I do best."

"How do you know if you've never done anything else?"

"I just know." *I feel it. The rightness of it.*

He looked as if he wanted to say more, but he asked instead, "Any other reason?"

"Because without laws and law enforcement, there'd be anarchy."

He raised an eyebrow. "And with them?"

She hesitated, trying to figure his angle. *Where is he headed? What is he searching for?* And then she decided that the truth was the safest course. "Sometimes you get lucky. Sometimes, there's justice."

"How's Dr. Rawlings?"

"She's fine." Rebecca held his gaze, refusing to reveal her surprise at the abrupt change in the direction of the conversation.

"How does she feel about your job?"

"Why does it matter?"

"One major source of stress in a police officer's life is stress at home. Very often, domestic discord stems from the erratic hours or complaints by a spouse of...emotional absence."

A spouse? Clever bastard. But his words hit close to the mark, and Rebecca colored. "I'm not stressed."

"Then you may be the only officer who isn't." Whitaker smiled slightly. "I'm not certain why you're here, Sergeant, but I know it's not because you want to be."

"I was ordered to come."

He shrugged as if to say he knew there was more. "Since you're here, we might as well use the time productively."

"What do you know about Catherine?" she asked abruptly. *Never let the witness lead the discussion. Always take the offensive position.*

Whitaker blinked. "Uh...I know you two met during the serial rape case. I know that you saved her life." A beat passed while he visibly regrouped. "And I suspect that you're lovers."

"Why?" Rebecca's tone was laser sharp.

"You haven't denied a personal relationship, and every time her name comes up, you become defensive. No...not defensive. Protective." He smiled. "Which is what you do, after all, isn't it,

Sergeant? You protect others. Especially those you're responsible for."

"That's the job description."

"Does she mind what you do?"

"Her name does not belong in your report. If you want me to come back for another session, you had best see that it isn't there." *And you want me to come back, don't you? You want something from me.*

"You have my word." He leaned forward. "Is she bothered by your job?"

"We're not going to discuss Catherine Rawlings." Rebecca glanced at her watch. "And it's time for me to go."

"We have another minute or two. Would you quit if she asked you to? Theoretically, of course."

"What difference does that make, *theoretically?*"

"It says a lot about you."

Rebecca stood, pulled down the cuffs on her charcoal blazer, and shrugged her shoulders infinitesimally to adjust her weapon harness. She pointed to the gold shield exposed on the flap of the leather badge case that protruded from her breast pocket. *"That* says all you need to know about me."

"I don't agree, Sergeant," he rejoined softly.

"Your prerogative."

As Rebecca reached for the door, she heard the quiet words from behind her. "You didn't answer my question."

She turned the knob, pushed the door open, and stepped out into the hall. She didn't want him to see her face, because she was afraid he'd realize that she didn't know the answer.

CHAPTER EIGHT

Rebecca walked directly from Whitaker's office to the stairwell at the end of the corridor and climbed one flight to the third floor. Uniforms and plainclothes officers were coming and going at the change of shift, and she nodded to those she knew as she made her way to the vice squad division. As she had come to expect, even though it daily continued to shock her, Watts was already at his desk. As if by some sixth sense, he glanced up from the newspaper to the open doorway just as she stuck her head in. With the tilt of her chin, she motioned him out into the hallway.

"Anything new?" she asked as he leaned against a wall and fired up a smoke.

"There was a message on your desk to call Jason, so I did. The computer cops want us to come over."

"Now?"

"Yep."

"Well, it's not like we have any hot leads to chase. And the less time we spend around here, the better. Let's go."

Twenty minutes later, they were buzzed into Sloan's building, and in the span of another minute, they were upstairs. Jason and Sloan, and—to Rebecca's surprise—Mitchell as well, were all seated at computer stations, cups of coffee on the counters beside them.

"Morning," Rebecca said to the small group. The others returned the greeting; uncharacteristically, Mitchell merely grunted. Glancing at Sloan, Rebecca raised an eyebrow. "How are things at the hospital?"

Despite the creases of fatigue in her forehead and the shadows marring her cheeks, Sloan's eyes were sparkling. "Much better. Thanks."

"Glad to hear it. So, what's up?"

"Jason," Sloan said, swiveling away from the computer screen to face Rebecca, who leaned a hip against a waist-high file cabinet, "go ahead and bring them up to speed."

"I pulled some of the old transcripts from the chat rooms," Jason explained, "especially the ones that LongJohnXXX logged on to frequently. I made a list of all the e-mail addresses of people who used to chat with him on a regular basis, figuring that some of them must be subscribers to the porn videos he was relaying."

"How'd you do that?" Watts asked, still at sea where computers were concerned.

"Sometimes the addresses were available through the member listings of the Internet newsgroups, and other times I had to trace them back through their ISP addresses."

Watts's expression registered something between confusion and constipation. "Yeah yeah. I'm sorry I asked."

Jason smothered a grin. "Unfortunately, the list is long, and there's no way of knowing at this point how many of the individuals are locals. There's also no way to know if they really have anything at all to do with the porn ring."

"But?" Rebecca could hear the excitement in his voice.

"But once I get names and addresses, it shouldn't be that difficult to find out other things about these guys. If they really are guys, that is."

"What?" Watts snorted. "You think there's gonna be a whole lot of broads who like to jack...uh...get their jollies watching that kind of stuff?"

"Remember," Sloan interjected mildly, "a lot of these bulletin boards and chat rooms are just places for people to talk about sex. They aren't necessarily looking to do anything other than find material for their fantasies. And a lot of times, women hide their identities, especially at first, so that every guy on the bulletin board doesn't descend upon them."

"Kinda like in real life, huh?"

"A lot more than you might think." Sloan glanced at Jason. "Go ahead, Jase."

"I can put together profiles, and we can do the same thing we did with LongJohn. Maybe we'll get another hit."

Rebecca looked skeptical. "It's a long shot."

"It's not like we have a lot else going right now," Jason responded, looking not the least bit deterred. "Mitchell can help with the runs, and once we have some probables, I thought Catherine might look at them. She can...sense things. She's a great profiler."

Rebecca opened her mouth to say no, and clamped her jaws tight instead. Catherine had said she wanted to be part of what was happening. The team could use the help, and this seemed safe enough. She rubbed the bridge of her nose where a headache was forming. There seemed to be no way at all that she could keep Catherine away from the investigation.

"Yeah. That's a good idea."

Watts studied her curiously. Under his breath, he said, "You feeling okay, Sarge?"

Rebecca gave him a withering glance. "Bite me, Watts."

Watts looked inordinately pleased.

"Anything new at the cop shop?" Sloan inquired.

"Let's go back to the conference room for a briefing," Rebecca suggested. "I've got some ideas."

Once they were all settled around the table with fresh coffee, everyone waited for Rebecca to speak. Feeling their expectant gazes, Rebecca knew that she had to make a decision now as to how much she would share with the team. Two people present were civilians, one was just a rookie cop, and what she had to say was beyond sensitive. But each of them was willing to walk the high wire without a net in the name of justice. She owed them her trust.

"Sandy gave me a lead last night. It's not much, but she thinks she might have seen the guy in the porn video at this sex club called Ziggie's."

"Whoa, that's choice," Watts exclaimed. "That place is supposed to be mobbed up."

"Right." Rebecca nodded. "It may be another connection to Zamora. More importantly, it might be our way into the sex network in this city."

"Can Sandy work the place?" Sloan asked. "It would be good to have someone on the inside there."

Mitchell's face turned white. "You want her to turn tricks in there for information? Why don't you just shoot her instead? At least that would be quick and painless."

Shocked at the outburst, Sloan jerked around in her seat to stare at Mitchell.

"Officer," Rebecca shot out. "You're out of line."

"I think what Sloan means, kid," Watts interjected hurriedly, "is for Sandy to *talk up* the staff and maybe the clients, see what she can find out, not actually peddle her ass in the back room."

Mitchell blushed and met Sloan's eyes. "Sorry. I guess I jumped the gun."

"It's okay."

"Not a bad thought, Sloan," Rebecca said, "but unfortunately, I think Sandy's too well known in the Tenderloin." Rebecca watched Mitchell as she spoke. The young officer stared straight ahead, her back ramrod stiff, her neck flushed. She was controlling her anger, but just barely. "If Sandy started hanging out at Ziggie's for no good reason, especially if she were talking around, someone would notice."

"Good point."

"She might be able to put me with someone who knows a little bit more, though. I'll meet with her later and see what else I can get."

"What you need is someone undercover," Jason observed mildly. "Sandy's a good source, but she's at risk if she becomes too visible. You need someone who's part of the club scene."

Watts spoke up. "What about getting someone from vice who works undercover?"

"It would mean bringing someone else into the loop," Rebecca mused. "It's an idea, though. Maybe we can put a female cop in Ziggie's."

"To do what?" Jason asked pointedly. "Dance topless? I think most of your detectives would consider that a little beyond the call."

Rebecca smiled. "I agree. But maybe we could have someone ask around, say she's looking for a job, see what we can get that way."

Jason inclined his head in agreement. "That might work. But

it won't help in terms of talking to the other girls or to the johns. And that's where the money's gonna be."

"You're right." Rebecca blew out a frustrated breath. "There's just not enough of us to cover all the bases."

Sloan eyed Jason, watching him work Rebecca. He was good, but so was the detective, and Sloan did not think that Frye would like having been played when she figured out where Jason was leading her. "Do you have something in mind, Jason?"

"I know someone who can get inside."

Of course you do. Jesus, Sarah is going to kill us.

Rebecca shook her head. "I can't bring in another civilian. And I don't want someone on the team I don't know."

"It's not what you think," Jason said.

"You want to explain?"

"Let me set something up for later, and if you're not happy with it, we'll forget the idea."

"Fine. At this point, I'll consider any option." Rebecca drained her cup, stood up, and walked to the coffee machine, her back to the room. The last item of business was the hardest for her to present. Sighing, she filled her mug and walked resolutely back to the table. She looked directly at Sloan. "We need to dig out the leak within the department. That's going to be on you."

Sloan's violet eyes flashed. This was the green light she'd been waiting for. "I need a list of everyone you can think of who might have known about the operation last weekend. Jason and I will need to trace financial records, employment histories, educational background, previous postings—anything that might tie in to Zamora or point to some other criminal activity."

"I know," Rebecca said. "It will take me a while, but I'll get you the names."

Beside her, Watts shot upright in his chair. "Wait a minute. You're going to be naming cops, and most of those cops—maybe *all* of them—are going to be innocent. You can't hang them out to dry."

Rebecca knew it went against the grain. It was contrary to everything that a cop was trained to uphold. *You never turn against your brothers; you never allow anyone outside the brotherhood to break the blue line.* Slowly, Rebecca turned her head and met

Watts's indignant gaze. "In or out, Bill."

It was the first time she had ever used his given name, and Watts recognized it for what it was. She was asking for his support, the kind of support that only a partner could give. He coughed faintly, clearing his throat. "It's going to be a pretty big list. Cops, clerks, people in the DA's office. Judges. Jesus." He ran a hand over his face and spoke directly to Rebecca. "I'll trace the path of the warrant from the DA back to us. You give them the names from inside the department."

"Fine." After a beat, Rebecca said, "Thanks."

"No problem, Sarge."

Rebecca squared her shoulders. "For starters, there's Captain John Henry, commander of the Vice Unit. Elizabeth Adams is the civilian clerk, and she probably handled the paperwork for the warrant. At this stage, I'm unaware of anyone else in the department who might have known about it directly."

"Are you suspicious of either one?" Jason's question was placed mildly, but he knew it was inflammatory by its very nature. He looked away to give Rebecca time to compose her answer. It didn't surprise him, though, when she answered immediately. She was clearly committed to doing whatever it took to ferret out the person responsible for the attempt on Sloan's life.

"I wouldn't be suspicious of Henry if I hadn't been told that he was involved in shutting down the investigation into the recent murder of two cops. If he wasn't part of the cover-up, he was at least aware of it and let it happen." Her tone was bitter. "So that puts him high on the list. Adams I don't know at all, but it's hard to believe it would be her."

"Is there anyone who has access to your field reports or your files or any records that might have had information about what we were doing?" Sloan inquired.

Rebecca started to shake her head, and then stopped abruptly. Her face, usually as smooth and refined as cut stone, hardened even further. "God damn it. I was...injured...earlier this year and out of commission for a while. In order to be reinstated, I had to see the department shrink. He could have picked up something from me."

"That's a stretch," Watts blurted.

Sloan shook her head. "Not necessarily. In all likelihood, he has access to everything Rebecca's been involved with. Also, he probably has unrestricted access to any file he asks for."

"Are you still seeing him?" Jason asked directly, no apology in his voice. This wasn't personal, this was business. Deadly business.

"Yes." Rebecca gave no explanation, because the reasons didn't matter. "Why?"

"I don't know," Jason mused. "I was thinking about a disinformation campaign. Maybe giving the wrong information to some of the people we suspect, just to see what happens."

"It's possible, I guess." Rebecca's expression was unmistakably skeptical. "It seems a little too cloak and dagger for me, though."

Jason and Sloan both smiled.

"Excuse me, ma'am?" another voice interjected.

Rebecca looked at Mitchell and raised an eyebrow. "Officer?"

If possible, Mitchell sat even straighter. "*I* may have inadvertently revealed some information about the operation as well. In...uh...counseling."

"Jesus, kid, you too?" Watts's tone was disgusted. "Is everybody in the goddamned department getting shrunk?"

"You're seeing Whitaker?" For the first time, Rebecca's voice held an edge of excitement. Connections were what made a case— small things that seemed inconsequential at first often turned out to be the key that fit the lock that broke it wide open.

"No, ma'am, not Whitaker. Dr. Rawlings."

Watts sucked in a breath and Rebecca went completely still. The previous night's conversation came back to her. She'd been talking to Catherine about Mitchell and Sandy. *How much does Catherine know?*

"Well, I can guarantee that Catherine is not the source of the leak." Rebecca's voice was cool, even, her hands steady as they rested on the tabletop. Her inner turmoil was known only to herself.

"No, I didn't mean that," Mitchell hastened to add. "But maybe something I said..." She stopped, embarrassed. *Jeez, Frye is never gonna trust me now.*

"What about Catherine's reports, her files?" Sloan stood and walked to the coffeemaker. "She must keep some kind of records, and if there's something in there, someone may have gotten hold of it."

"That should be simple enough to determine." Rebecca tried to keep the edge from her voice, but it was difficult. Anything to do with Catherine threatened her objectivity. "We can ask her."

"I don't think she'll tell you, Sergeant," Mitchell said respectfully.

Rebecca barely managed to swallow her retort. She drew a long breath and settled herself. "No, of course she won't. You're absolutely right, Officer. Dr. Rawlings will not discuss her patients in any way."

"If it would help, I'll give my permission for her to—"

"If that becomes necessary, we may go that route. But let's hold on that for now." Rebecca had been down that road with Catherine before. It was not a trip she wanted to take again. "But I appreciate your offer, Mitchell."

Mitchell colored. "Yes, ma'am."

"Are you still in counseling, too?" Jason asked Mitchell.

Both Mitchell and Rebecca looked uncomfortable at this point. This was one point upon which they were in total agreement. Cops didn't see shrinks.

"No, not exactly. We left it...open."

"I think you should keep going," Jason recommended. He glanced at Rebecca and grinned. "In case we have to use some cloak and dagger stuff."

"It's up to Mitchell," Rebecca said. *It's none of our business.*

"What about getting me direct access to the department's computer system?" Sloan thought the temperature in the room was getting a little heated and figured that a change in direction was warranted. "I can hack in from outside the system, but it's harder to cover my trail. Plus, it would be easier to work from the inside in terms of tracing the path of departmental records."

Rebecca nodded. "I think I can get you in. The CSI chief is mightily pissed off that someone raided her computer and stole the files of an ongoing investigation. I think she'll let you tear her system apart."

"I can work on it on site?"

"Sure. If anyone asks, you're just one of the IT people who came around to upgrade her system. No one will think twice about it."

Sloan looked thoughtful. "You trust her to know what I'll be doing?"

"Yes."

"Good enough."

"When can you start?" Rebecca asked.

Sloan looked at her watch. "I can take a fast look at her system this morning, but I have to be back at the hospital by two." She couldn't hide her smile. "There's an outside chance Michael might be able to come home today."

A chorus of pleased exclamations followed.

"We have to assume that whoever went after Sloan knows about all of us." Rebecca's expression was serious, but her voice completely calm. "That means heads up for everybody. Make sure you're not being followed anywhere, and if something doesn't look right, assume that it's wrong. Sloan, Jason—do you two carry?"

"I'm licensed, but I don't usually carry," Sloan replied. Jason shook his head in the negative as well.

"You might want to consider it. Remember, Sloan, you were the primary target the other night. Whoever's behind this may figure that you no longer pose a threat since we already made our move against the Internet porn ring. Still, you never know."

Sloan thought about the fact that Michael would be upstairs, possibly in a few hours. She nodded, her eyes as flat and dark as onyx. "Understood. Jason and I will ensure that our perimeter here is secure as well."

"Huh," Watts grunted. "I don't see how you could get any more secure."

"There are always ways, Detective."

"Mitchell," Rebecca said as she stood. "I want you here with Jason and Sloan, working up background and tracing down those e-mail addresses. Sloan, I'll call you as soon as I clear things with the CSI chief, and if you've got time, I'll take you over there to meet her." She glanced at her watch. "Let's say we meet back here around five this afternoon. Jason, does that give you enough time to contact your source?"

He nodded. "Plenty of time."

"Watts, you were going to poke around in Jimmy Hogan's files. Go ahead with that."

"Roger, Sarge."

"And I think I'd better pay a visit to Dr. Rawlings."

Ordinarily, Rebecca welcomed any excuse to see Catherine. However, she had a feeling that this particular visit was going to be much more business than pleasure.

CHAPTER NINE

After Rebecca and Watts left, Mitchell glanced at Sloan and Jason with an uncharacteristically uneasy expression.

"Do you think I can take an hour or so of personal time?"

"This isn't One Police Plaza, Dell." Sloan grinned. "You can come and go as you please. No one's punching a time clock here."

"I know there's a lot of work to do, but..." Mitchell colored slightly. "I just need to take care of someth—"

"Go ahead," Jason urged. "There'll be plenty left to chase when you get back."

"Thanks," she said, already up and on her way toward the hallway and the elevator beyond.

Once downstairs, Mitchell walked rapidly the few blocks to the subway station and caught the El train going west. Exiting at Fifteenth, she walked south through neighborhoods that progressively deteriorated the further she went. At Fitzwater, she turned west for half a block until she stood across from a dingy, gray-shingled row house that looked no different than any of the other run-down buildings on the street. Six doorbells were aligned vertically on the right-hand side of the plain wooden door. It was ten-thirty in the morning, and she had a feeling that if she rang, no one was going to answer the doorbell in the upstairs rear apartment.

Fortunately, she knew from experience that the front door was usually unlocked. She crossed the street, took the few stairs to the small porch two at a time, and twisted the plain brass knob. As expected, the windowless door opened into a tiny foyer that was littered with fliers and dead leaves. Despite the bits of trash, the hallway beyond was surprisingly clean, without the usual faint hints of urine and old food that often lingered in buildings such as these. She passed no one on the stairs. On the third floor, there were two doors, and she walked directly to the one with a painted-over metal letter B just above eye level and knocked.

She waited a moment, not expecting an immediate answer, and then knocked again, louder.

"Go away," a grumpy sounding voice called from within.

Grinning, Mitchell rapped briskly. Despite her simmering sense of anger and disquiet, the sound of Sandy's voice and the image it provoked gave her a swift jolt of pleasure.

Another minute passed during which she could make out faint sounds of movement coming from the other side of the door. Then it was opened as far as a security chain would allow, and a flashing blue eye peered out.

"What the fu—Dell!"

"Hiya, Sandy."

The door closed in Mitchell's face, the chain rattled, and the door sprang open again.

Sandy, eyes a bit bleary, looked up and snarled, "It's ten o'clock in the morning, and I've only been asleep for two hours. Go away."

"It's almost eleven. Are you always so cranky when you wake up?" Mitchell asked brightly.

"Only when someone wakes me up when I should still be sleeping." Sandy frowned and cocked a hip against the edge of the door. She wore only a tiny white tank top that barely reached below the swell of her breasts and a pair of pale pink bikini underwear. The pale expanse of her flat abdomen was broken only by the thick silver stud in her navel. "What are you doing here?"

Mitchell tried not to look at the barely covered body, but just the quick glimpse she got before she forced her eyes back to Sandy's face was enough to make her stomach tighten. "Can I talk to you?"

"You okay?" As soon as the words were out, Sandy realized how unusual the feeling was behind them. She'd only ever had a few friends she was close enough with to get concerned about, but worrying about Dell seemed to come naturally. Maybe it was just that she still had dreams about that night in the alley when Dell was on the ground and that huge fucker was kicking the shit out of her. "Well?"

"You going to let me in?"

Sandy stiffened suddenly as if finally coming awake. "You shouldn't be here, Dell. Frye said..." Her voice trailed off and she looked away.

"What? Frye said *what*?" Mitchell took one step inside the room and then caught herself. "Is it okay if I come in?"

"Yeah," Sandy said softly. Then, her voice suddenly stronger, "Jesus, you can't stand out in the hall any longer. Someone's gonna see you."

"Who's to see me? And so what if they do?" Mitchell had never seen Sandy look uncertain about anything. Aggravated. Aggressive. Angry. Yes. But never anxious, like now. "What's the matter?"

"Nothing," Sandy said with a shrug. She crossed the room to the sofa, which had been opened into a small daybed. The pale blue cotton sheets covering it were pulled back, and a single pillow rested in the center.

Mitchell stared at the bed. Then she quickly averted her eyes and looked around the room. She'd never been inside Sandy's apartment before. In fact, she'd never been *alone* inside anywhere with Sandy.

The studio apartment was neat and clean. The furniture, while mismatched for the most part, was old but stylish. The kinds of pieces that could be picked up at decent secondhand stores. There was a large hooked rug on the floor and a few inexpensive reproductions of familiar-looking abstracts on the walls.

"Nice place."

"Thanks." Sandy perched on the edge of the bed, elbows on knees, her chin resting in the palm of one hand. "I'm *really* glad you like my decorating. Now, do you want to tell me why you woke me up?"

"Do you think you could...uh...put some clothes on?"

"I've *got* clothes on, Dell." Sandy saw Dell's eyes flicker down her body, then rapidly fix on some point on the floor between them. She also saw the faint flush rise from the patch of skin visible at the open collar of Dell's white shirt and spread up the young cop's neck. Sandy's heart sped up and a distinct stirring trickled through her stomach. She liked the way Dell looked at her. A lot. She grabbed for her jeans and pulled them on.

Mitchell relaxed and looked around for a place to sit. There wasn't anywhere except the bed, and she wasn't sitting there. She put her hands in her pockets and leaned against the corner of a dresser that stood against one wall. The entire way over to Sandy's, she had been propelled by worry and anger. Now that she was there, inside Sandy's surprisingly warm and cozy apartment, she didn't know what to say.

"What?" Sandy's voice was gentle.

Softly, Mitchell said, "I didn't know you were working for Detective Sergeant Frye."

"I wasn't...not before yesterday. Mostly, she would come around now and then asking about street talk, and I'd help her out." Sandy stood and crossed to the small kitchen on the far side of the room. She opened the refrigerator and pulled out a Coke. "Want one?"

Mitchell shook her head.

"Why do you care?" Sandy pulled the tab and took a deep swallow. Her question held no trace of belligerence, only curiosity. She wondered if Dell had any idea how much she wanted to know the answer to that question—had wanted to know for weeks now what it was that kept Dell coming around. What put that look of fierce concentration in Dell's eyes whenever they roamed over her face?

"It's kind of a dangerous job."

"Which job would that be? Being an official snitch or being a cop?" Sandy walked back to the bed and plopped down. Dell hadn't answered the question. Sandy leaned back, her legs slightly spread, a challenging expression on her face. "You could get hurt, too, rookie."

"There's a difference and you know it." Mitchell tried and failed to keep the aggravation from her voice. *At least I have a gun. And backup. Sometimes, anyhow.*

"Yeah, sure. I suppose you think being a cop is special and being an informant is just one step up from being a stoolie?"

"Oh, for crying out loud, Sandy." Mitchell ran her hands through her hair in exasperation. "I don't want you to get hurt, okay? Is that so hard to understand? Jesus, why are you always such a pain in the ass?"

Sandy jumped up and stalked to within a few inches of Mitchell's surprised face. "I did *not* ask you to worry about me. And I don't need you to take care of me. Okay?"

"Has it occurred to you that you're out there by yourself?" Without thinking, Mitchell put her fingers around Sandy's forearm. "You're totally unprotected."

"I can take care of myself."

"Oh, yeah. You've done a great job with *that* so far."

Sandy jerked her hand away and barely stopped herself from flinging it across Dell's face. "Get out."

"Sandy..." Mitchell's face was white and her eyes huge, the deep blue shadowed with pain. "I'm sorry. I didn't mean that the way you think."

"I *know* what you meant...that I'm just a who—"

"No." Mitchell raised her hand slowly. "No." She brushed a fingertip over the scar on Sandy's forehead. Her voice was pitched low, tight with feeling. "*This* is what I mean. How many more times can you take a beating like this?"

Sandy wanted to pull away, to spew angry words, but she couldn't. Dell's touch was so gentle, her expression so tender, her body so near. Dell was trembling. They both were. Sandy remembered the first time she'd seen Dell, standing guard on the stairs outside the room where Anna Marie's violated body lay growing cold. She remembered intentionally brushing her breasts against Dell's arm in passing, just to rattle the rookie and steel her own nerves for what she knew she would find upstairs.

"Dell..." Sandy murmured, wanting to feel her nipples pressed to the hard warmth of Dell's chest. But unlike that first night, this urge wasn't born of anger or fear; it was born of desire. Heat surged between her thighs, and she gasped as she felt herself grow wet. She stumbled back a step, breaking their tenuous contact.

Mitchell, her hand outstretched, wanted so badly to follow. There was something in Sandy's voice, a hushed yearning that made Mitchell's heart twist and her head roar. She wanted to touch Sandy again, run her thumb over the moist surface of Sandy's slightly parted lips, slide the tip of her finger between them. She wanted the fire she knew was waiting there. "Hey..."

Sandy took another step back. "You should go, Dell." There was no anger in her voice now.

"Can I come back?" Mitchell didn't even know why she was asking, but she had to. "I won't bug you about Frye again."

"Yeah, right." Sandy tried to sound flip, but she was watching Dell's mouth, and that made it hard to concentrate. Dell had a beautiful mouth. Then Frye's voice cut through the haze. *"A police officer can be suspended, even fired, for fraternizing with a prostitute."*

"Look," Sandy said as forcefully as she could. "If you're so worried about me, you should probably not ruin my reputation by hanging around here, okay? Jesus, talk about making people suspicious of me."

"It doesn't have to be here."

"Anywhere is dangerous, especially with me asking around the way I'm doing." Sandy tilted her head, searched frantically for the right words to make Dell go. "Look, I'm Frye's now, okay? I don't want anything to mess that up."

Mitchell straightened as if struck. "You're right. I'm sorry." She reached behind her for the doorknob. "Just watch your back, okay?"

Then she was gone, leaving only the echo of her footsteps in the hall. Sandy listened until she couldn't hear her at all.

"You be careful, too, rookie," she whispered. Her fingers rested lightly on the scarred wooden door in a final caress.

At 11:24, the side door to Catherine's private office closed behind her last client of the morning. The psychiatrist leaned back in the large padded leather chair, closed her eyes, and sighed. She'd been seeing the troubled young student for several months, and she found every session draining. It was often so difficult not to offer advice, but to listen instead, occasionally gently steering the conversation in a direction that might help shine a different light on the problem.

Trying to gather herself for the afternoon ahead, she might actually have fallen asleep if the intercom line on her phone had not rung. She leaned forward, picked up the receiver, and hit the blinking button. "Yes, Joyce."

"Detective Frye is here, Doctor. Your next appointment is scheduled at one, so you have a bit of time."

Suddenly invigorated, Catherine smiled. "Tell her to come in, please."

When Rebecca came through the door a moment later with a brown paper bag in one hand, Catherine was waiting just inside. She placed a hand on Rebecca's shoulder and leaned close to give her a kiss on the mouth. "What a nice surprise."

"I took a chance that I might catch you between sessions. I brought lunch."

"I knew there was a reason that I love you." Catherine reached for Rebecca's hand and led her to the sofa in front of a low coffee table. "Indian?"

"Uh-huh."

"Wonderful. I'm famished." Catherine extracted the various containers from the bag along with the plastic forks and paper napkins and spread them out on the table. After they'd dished out and begun to sample the food, she asked, "Is there another reason that you're here—besides rescuing me from starvation, of course?"

Rebecca hesitated. There were very few things in her life that made her uncomfortable. Being at odds with Catherine was one of them. When they fought, even when they merely couldn't see eye to eye over some issue, it left her feeling disjointed and strangely hollow inside. The simplest solution would be not to bring up topics that she knew would produce friction between them. That had been her modus operandi in each of her previous relationships, and they had all ended disastrously. She supposed that if she truly thought evasion were possible in this instance, she might try it even still. Unfortunately, emotional subterfuge did not work with Catherine Rawlings. And in her heart, Rebecca knew that Catherine deserved more than that from her.

With a sigh, she pushed the container of spinach and cheese aside. "I had a briefing with Sloan and the others this morning. We've been putting together a plan of action."

"Problems?" Catherine continued to eat slowly, suspecting that

Rebecca would not have come by in the middle of the day had things gone smoothly. One of the traits that intrigued and annoyed her most about her intrepid lover was Rebecca's self-sufficiency. Catherine freely admitted that she needed to feel needed, and sometimes she wondered just how much Rebecca really *did* need her.

"We're working on a couple of angles, but one of the critical things that we have to do is find the source of the information leak that led to the attack on Sloan."

"And you suspect someone within your department." Catherine could only imagine how difficult it was for Rebecca to investigate her own people.

"If not there, then somewhere else close to the investigation. Somewhere close to *someone* associated with the investigation."

"And there are a limited number of people who knew the details of what you were planning, right?"

Rebecca nodded. "How well do you know Rand Whitaker?"

Clearly surprised, Catherine sat back, her hand resting gently on Rebecca's thigh. "Only casually. We see each other at local psychiatric meetings and now and then at seminars at the university. I've heard him speak several times on stress-related issues in the workplace. He seems solid enough."

"Do you know anything about him personally? Whether he seems to live beyond his means or if he has a couple of ex-wives and a bunch of kids he has to support?"

"You suspect him of providing information to...whom? Someone who would commit murder?" The incredulity in her voice was unmistakable. "I can't believe it. And how would he have gotten the information? Surely you didn't tell him anything?"

"No, but he works in the department. And I was seeing him in an official capacity. It's possible he could've gotten access to almost anything I was involved with. A phone call to a clerk—it's not like we have much in the way of internal security." Rebecca ran a hand through her hair, frustrated once more by her inability to find a solid lead.

"I suppose anything is possible," Catherine mused, "but I don't know him well enough to speculate."

"I didn't really think that you would, but I had to check." Rebecca turned until she faced Catherine fully, their knees slightly touching. She wanted to take Catherine's hand, but that didn't feel right considering what she was about to say. "Something else came up this morning as well."

"Oh?" Catherine waited, watching Rebecca's eyes. *Now we'll get to the reason why you're here.*

"Dellon Mitchell said that she's been seeing you. For a while, it seems."

Catherine remained silent.

Rebecca forged ahead. "Is there anything that she might have told you that could be accessible to someone outside this office? Anything about the investigation?"

"It would be better if we discussed this after Officer Mitchell gives me a call," Catherine said gently. "I don't feel comfortable discussing this with you until then."

"Catherine," Rebecca said, trying to keep exasperation from her voice. "Mitchell already *told* us she was seeing you for counseling. She knew that I would talk to you when she said it."

"I believe you, of course. But I would still rather discuss with *her* what information she's comfortable with me revealing."

"Déjà vu. Jesus." Rebecca closed her eyes. In a low voice she muttered, "I think it was right about at this point the first time around that I fell in love with you."

Taken completely off guard, Catherine's heart lifted. "Why, Detective Frye, could it be that you're mellowing?"

Ice blue eyes suddenly bored into Catherine's, only to soften instantly. "Sensitivity training."

Catherine laughed out loud and moved closer on the sofa. Rebecca automatically threaded her arm around Catherine's waist, and the psychiatrist rested her head on the detective's shoulder. "I can tell you this. I can't imagine that anyone has been going through my files."

"Did you send periodic reports to the department?"

"No, only a final report just this week."

"What about session notes? Could there have been anything in those?"

"I don't see what." Catherine shook her head. "They're all very cursory. Not detailed at all."

"Do you save them on a computer?"

"Yes," Catherine replied, stiffening slightly. "But surely you don't think—"

"I don't know what to think." Rebecca's tone was harsher than she intended, and she swiftly kissed Catherine's temple in apology. "I'm sorry. I think someone lifted files from one of the police department computers, so anything is possible."

"If it's all right with Officer Mitchell, I'll check my notes and let you know if there's anything in my records remotely connected to what you've been doing."

"Thanks." Rebecca would have liked to have ended the discussion there, but she had one more thing to deal with. "Mitchell said she wasn't sure if she was coming back to see you again."

"We can't discuss this, Rebecca."

Rebecca held up a hand. "Just hear me out. On the off chance that someone is looking at your files, it might be a good idea for Mitchell to continue to see you. At some point, we might need to use that fact to our advantage."

"You mean, have her *pretend* to see me, as part of your investigation?"

"Right," Rebecca said hurriedly.

"No."

Rebecca blew out a long breath. "I knew that felt too easy."

"I have a therapeutic relationship with Officer Mitchell. I can't allow that relationship to be subverted, and it would be, if I saw her under false pretenses."

"Even if she agreed?"

"Even then. The dynamic of our interactions would be permanently altered, and I would no longer be able to function effectively as her therapist."

"But you *would* see her if she wanted you to?"

Catherine drew away and studied Rebecca carefully. "Promise me that you won't order her to do something like you're suggesting."

Rebecca opened her mouth and then closed it again. "I don't think I can do that."

"Well." Catherine stood abruptly and paced back and forth between her desk and the seating area, frown lines furrowed between her brows. Just as precipitously, she stopped and faced

Rebecca. "There are moments when you are quite incapable of appreciating anyone else's work other than your own. Do you realize how frustrating that is?"

"Yes."

"Good. Because this is one of those moments." Catherine walked behind her desk and sat down. "If and when Officer Mitchell returns to this office, I will assume it is under her own free will, with no other agenda. If I discover otherwise, you and I will have a problem."

Completely unexpectedly, Rebecca felt a wave of nausea. She forced herself not to change expression and asked steadily, "What does that mean?"

"It means that I will be very angry with you." Catherine tilted her head and narrowed her gaze. "What did you *think* I meant?"

Rebecca gathered the remains of their meals into the bag and stood. "I'm sorry I had to bring this up in the middle of your workday."

"Rebecca," Catherine said softly. "I love you. That doesn't stop just because you aggravate me."

"I'm glad," Rebecca murmured. "Because I'm probably going to do that more than once before this is over."

"Yes, I suspect that you probably are." As Rebecca reached for the door, Catherine called gently, "I'll see you tonight, darling."

"Yes. Okay." Before Rebecca crossed the threshold, she turned and looked back at the remarkable woman who had changed her life. "I love you, you know."

"Yes. I know." Catherine smiled. "Be careful, Detective."

CHAPTER TEN

"Who's the 'dark angel' in your office there?" Maggie Collins asked the small, wiry, sandy-haired woman in the neatly pressed jeans and dark blue polo shirt.

"Dark angel?" Dee Flanagan glanced fleetingly away from the microscope into which she had been staring with fierce concentration.

"Aye. The handsome one who's been lurking in your office since the middle of the mornin'."

"Ah. Her." As Dee looked back through the eyepiece and adjusted the focus, she said softly in a completely conversational tone, "Do you know how easy it would be for me to commit murder and get away with it?"

The younger woman with the shoulder-length curly red hair, the sea-foam green eyes, and the hint of Ireland in her voice laughed. "Fixin' to do away with me, are you, darlin'?"

Dee, the chief of the Crime Scene Investigation Unit, straightened and turned to face her senior crime scene technician and lover. "Not you, my love." She hitched a shoulder in the direction of the office that was separated from the rest of the long laboratory space by waist-high partitions and glass windows. "The competition."

Maggie's eyes softened the way they often did when she looked at Dee, and she shook her head in mock consternation. "How long will it take before you believe that you have always been and will always be the only one?"

"Don't look at me that way when we're working." Dee's expression was stern but her voice husky. Maggie, fifteen years her junior, had a way of taking her by surprise, and the love in her eyes was hard not to get lost in. The CSI chief cleared her throat. "Her name is Sloan. She's some kind of computer whiz. Frye brought her in earlier this morning."

"I didn't think I recognized her as one of the usual techies. What's she doin' poking around in your computer?"

With a quick glance around to be certain that they were alone, Dee confided, "We're hoping she'll be able to figure out where my files on Jeff Cruz and Jimmy Hogan disappeared to."

"Really." Maggie tilted her head, looking thoughtful. "Are you doin' something you shouldn't be doin', Dee Flanagan?"

"Me?"

Maggie stepped closer, the fingers of her left hand briefly brushing across her lover's right. "If there's some kind of trouble brewin', I don't want you in the mix."

"Somebody raided my files, Mags. Someone invaded my territory." As head of the department, Dee was in the position where she didn't have to do field work, or even bench work for that matter. Nevertheless, she was always present at major crime scenes and often at the most commonplace ones as well. She oversaw the work of her technicians personally, got her feet wet and her hands dirty collecting evidence samples, and was often the last one to leave a scene. She was fiercely close-mouthed about the evidence analysis until she was certain of her facts. Her rigid adherence to protocol and dictum drove cops crazy, but when they had a tough case, it was Dee Flanagan they wanted to work it. She was unshakable in the courtroom, and defense attorneys had long since given up trying to maneuver her into changing an opinion once she had rendered it. "If those bastards thought I would just forget about stolen files, they're bigger fools than I imagined."

Maggie's expression darkened. "Jeff Cruz and Jimmy Hogan were cops, and someone killed them in broad daylight and got clean away. The sort who would do something like that wouldn't think twice about protecting themselves if someone else started poking around. I don't want them comin' after you."

Dee's first impulse was to argue, but she'd heard the faint quaver in Maggie's voice. Maggie had come to America as a child, but not before losing her father and a brother to the ongoing conflicts in Ireland. She'd seen them die in the streets when a bomb exploded, and even two decades later, she still awoke screaming.

"You don't have to worry, my love. I'm sure I fall well below anybody's radar. If anyone is going to draw unwanted attention from this, it's going to be Sloan in there, or Frye."

"Oh, Dee, do you think I don't know you? If there's a fight to be had and it has anything to do with what's yours, you'll be right in the middle of it."

"How come you think you know so much?" Dee's brown eyes softened, and for a brief instant, she wrapped her fingers around Maggie's, squeezing gently.

"Because I'm the one who loves you."

"Don't worry. I promise I'll stay clear of anything that looks like trouble."

Maggie nodded, trusting the sentiment but not believing the words. There were things she had learned on the bloody streets of her childhood, and one was that the nature of a person could not be easily changed. Not even for love. "I'll be getting back to work then, before the boss catches me shirkin'."

Dee watched her walk away, knowing two things. She'd been blessed the day that Maggie Collins had walked into her office looking for a job, and if Rebecca and her friend Sloan discovered who was behind the theft of her files, she wanted to be there when they went after him.

❖

"How's it going?" Dee asked.

Sloan pushed back the tall stool on which she had been perched since midmorning and eyed the CSI chief. She didn't notice the cramped muscles in her lower back or the ache between her shoulder blades. For three hours, she'd been so absorbed in her work that she'd almost been able to ignore the constant undercurrent of anxiety that she'd been living with for days. Almost. Her worry over Michael still skittered over the surface of her consciousness, but the full-blown terror had eased the instant Michael had opened her eyes, and the news that perhaps her lover would be coming home later in the day, had almost banished her fear. Almost.

"Your computer is a dinosaur. I'm surprised it still runs."

"Police issue. You should see what the patrol cars look like." Dee moved through the small space in which every surface was covered with stacks of journals, boxes of crime-scene mockups, files, and reference books. Her office was a cluttered contrast to the pristine, sparkling spaces of her laboratory beyond. "Find anything?"

"Not yet." Sloan managed to smother a smile. Rebecca had warned her before entering the sanctum sanctorum of Dee Flanagan's lab that the CSI chief was notoriously humorless where anything concerning her work was involved. Rebecca's exact words had been, "Don't touch *anything* and try not to piss her off."

Dee sat behind her desk and sipped from the mug of coffee she had carried in with her. "Whoever took the files did it months ago. Do you really think you can find anything now?"

"If you had a body that had been buried for twenty years, would there be anything still there that would help you find the killer?"

"There's *always* something there. The flesh decays, but even as it does, it changes the nature of whatever surrounds it—chemically, physically, biologically. The bones tell their own tale—age of the victim, gender, sometimes even the manner of death. The answer is always there; you just need to know how to read the story."

Sloan nodded. "That's what it's like with a computer, too. Even the best hacker leaves a trail. Just by trying to erase the evidence of their presence, they change *other* things, always leaving some sign of having been there."

"Locard's Exchange Principle," Dee murmured.

"Right. A criminal always leaves evidence of his presence at the scene *and* takes some bit of it away on himself."

Dee regarded Sloan appreciatively. *Not just a pretty face. But then she wouldn't be, not if Frye trusts her.*

Sloan grinned, catching the look. "Forensics is forensics—a computer's just a different kind of crime scene."

"Apparently." Dee leaned forward over the desk, her intelligent eyes alight with excitement. "So—what does the intruder leave behind?"

"Could be any number of things, depending on how your system is set up and how he accessed your hard drive. One of the first places to look is the log files, which are sort of a diary of events. Information is constantly stored automatically by the operating system without you ever being aware of it. An entry is made in a log file whenever a user logs into the system or attempts to log in, or opens a file, or *attempts* to open one, or runs a program, or accesses data in any form. There are also telephone logs which will tell us when attempts were made to dial into the computer from remote access, and usually, with a little creative backtracking, I can get those phone numbers. Once I secure your system, the next thing I'll do is analyze the log files around the time your data disappeared and look for evidence of illegal entry."

"Secure my system?" Dee frowned.

"I want to put some filters and blocks on the system to make it harder to hack into. And I want to expand the log files to gather more data each time the system is accessed."

"No offense, but isn't beefing up the security now a little late? Why waste the time? I got the impression Frye was in a hurry."

Sloan regarded the other woman contemplatively. She didn't know much about her, except that Rebecca had said Flanagan was the best crime scene analyst she had ever seen. The fact that Rebecca trusted the woman enough to reveal to her that she was running an undercover investigation within the police department was enough to make Sloan trust Flanagan as well.

"If someone tampered with your data once, there's no reason to think that he hasn't done it before or since. How often do your cases have something to do with organized crime?"

"Often enough."

"It might be advantageous for *certain people* to access your files and find out just what evidence you had accumulated on a certain case, even if they *couldn't* take a chance on altering it."

"Altering it! Jesus Christ. Just the suggestion that evidence may have been tampered with could overturn dozens of verdicts." Dee stood suddenly, quickly threaded her way through the obstacle path on the floor, and shut her office door. She turned, leaning her back against the closed door, and riveted Sloan with her gaze. "That kind of speculation would be disastrous."

"I'm aware of that," Sloan said quietly. "And I have no intention of combing through hundreds of case files looking for signs of tampering. Hopefully, we'll be able to identify the hacker and then look elsewhere for corroborating evidence to link him to the crimes. That way, we can leave your department out of it completely. But we'd better be sure your system is secure now."

"If you find something that suggests my files have been compromised in any way, I want to know."

Sloan shook her head, appreciating the other woman's integrity, but also recognizing her naïveté. "Look, I've been involved in this kind of thing before, and if that turns out to be the case, it's going to fall on your doorstep. That's not something you want to have happen." *Your career will be over, and you'll be lucky to escape criminal charges. Even then, the civil suits brought by people claiming they were incarcerated unjustly will stretch for fifty years.*

Before Sloan could elaborate, Dee repeated forcefully, "There are people in prison right now because of evidence I presented at trial. There are also a fair number of scumbags walking the streets who got off because my analysis exonerated them. I *have* to know I made the right calls."

"Despite its importance, the crime scene evidence is only one piece of the case presented at trial. The verdict doesn't rest on your testimony alone."

"I don't give a good goddamn about the other pieces of the case. I only care about mine."

"I understand." Sloan glanced at her watch. "I don't have much time today, but I wanted to get a look at your system so that I could get a sense of what I need to do. I'll be back either tonight or tomorrow morning. How do I get in here?"

"I'll give you the combination to the touchpad lock on the morgue admissions bay door. You can walk here from there through the underground corridor. Just follow the red stripe on the floor, and it will lead you right to the lab." As she spoke, Dee walked back to her desk, grabbed a scratch pad, and scrawled some numbers. She handed the slip of paper to Sloan, who took it, folded it, and slid it into the breast pocket of her white button-down-collar shirt.

"Thanks." Sloan closed her black satchel, which held tools and software programs, and stood.

"I'll get you a key to the lab on your way out," Dee said as she opened the door.

"What if someone sees me in here and asks why I'm working after hours?"

Dee grinned, a mischievous look that was twice as charming

for its rarity. "Just tell them I wouldn't let you work in here during the day. You could throw in something about me being a pain in the ass—that will help with the authenticity of your story."

Sloan laughed. "I'll just mention that I touched something, and you threw me out."

"I see that Frye instructed you well."

"She's very thorough."

"She's the best detective I've ever seen." Suddenly serious, Dee said, "She's taking a risk going after the traitor, especially if it's a cop. But it has to be done, and she's the one to do it. Still, they put down two cops without making even a ripple in the pond. She should watch her back."

"Yeah, well, she's not going to be alone. I can promise you that."

Dee was surprised by the sudden harshness in the dark-haired woman's voice, and when she looked into the vivid violet eyes, she saw deadly resolve. She felt a little better knowing that Frye had this tough cybercop on her team. "Good. Because I've finally browbeaten her into following the rules down here. I hate breaking in new cops."

Sloan just grinned as she walked with Dee toward the exit. It was time to put revenge aside. Now it was time for Michael.

❖

When Sloan entered Michael's room shortly before two, she found what appeared to be a party in progress. Michael, looking pale but visibly stronger than just that morning, was seated in a padded hospital chair by the side of the bed, a thin blanket over her knees. A narrow strip of white tape encircled her left wrist where an intravenous line had previously been lodged. Its absence lifted Sloan's spirits almost as much as seeing Michael out of bed.

Sarah crouched beside the chair, her hand on Michael's knee. Ali Torveau leaned against the side of the bed, a plastic folder containing Michael's hospital chart tucked under one arm.

"I'm not late, am I?" Sloan walked directly to Michael, leaned down, and kissed her briefly on the lips. In a quieter voice, she murmured, "Hi, baby."

"Dr. Torveau says I can go home," Michael announced,

gripping Sloan's hand with surprising strength.

Almost afraid to believe it, Sloan glanced at the trauma surgeon. "Today?"

"Right now," Torveau replied even as she held up a hand. "Under certain conditions."

"Anything," Sloan responded quickly.

"Someone, preferably a trained medical professional, needs to stay with her twenty-four hours a day."

"I'm an OMD," Sarah interjected. "I'll stay as long as you think necessary—that is, if Sloan and Michael don't mind me moving in for a bit."

"That would be great, Sarah," Sloan said instantly. "Thanks."

"That sounds good," the surgeon agreed. "It's also very important that I be advised immediately should there be any change *at all* in your symptoms, Michael—that means a worsening headache, visual disturbances, weakness—even temporary, cognitive or expressive difficulties, or seizures."

Sloan felt slightly ill as she listened to the list of potential problems and struggled to keep her expression blank. "How long do we have to worry about something like that happening?"

"Some complications could develop months from now, particularly a seizure disorder, but I think it's reasonable to say that after a week or two, we can all relax."

"Can I work?" Michael asked. "I wouldn't have to leave the house."

"Michael..." At a swift look of warning from Sarah, Sloan clamped her mouth shut and swallowed the protest. All she could see, still, was Michael lying on the ground in a puddle of blood. But Michael didn't know what had happened, and there was no reason to make her afraid now.

Ali raised an eyebrow. "I don't expect you'll feel like working for a week or so. But," she added at the look of dismay on Michael's face, "if it doesn't involve digging ditches or moving heavy furniture, I don't see why you can't try it when you feel up to it."

"Good." Michael smiled wanly. "I already feel like I've lost time that I'm never going to get back. I just want to do something that makes me feel normal again."

"I understand. Just remember, even though you're being

discharged, you're still recovering. Don't expect too much of yourself."

"What about sex?" Michael kept her eyes on the surgeon's face, but a soft sigh of resignation from Sloan's direction was impossible to ignore. Michael merely smiled.

"You *are* feeling better. It's amazing what a normal CT scan will do for some people." Ali laughed. "Usually, my position is if you feel like it, then it's safe to do it. I wouldn't get too vigorous the first time or so, and if you experience a headache as you approach orgasm, slow down. Maybe stop and rest for a while."

"Is making love dangerous after this kind of...accident?" Sloan took Michael's hand, her attention directed at the surgeon.

"Not ordinarily, no. Remember, though, there are fluctuations in blood pressure during sex, and right now, Michael's brain is a little sensitive to sudden changes."

"Don't worry, darling," Michael teased softly, "I wasn't thinking about it for tonight."

"Darn." Sloan grinned and hid her relief. The thought of anything harming Michael, even making love, terrified her.

Sarah laughed. "I'll go pack some things and head over to your place, Sloan."

Sloan gave her a swift peck on the cheek. "Thanks, Sarah. I owe you."

"No, you don't—not for this. You owe me a workout, though. You've been slacking off the last few days." Sarah bumped Sloan playfully on the shoulder as she spoke, but her eyes were serious. *Michael isn't the only one who needs to get back to normal life. I've never seen you look so haunted.*

Ali handed Sloan a card. "My office number. Call and make a follow-up appointment for a week." She sketched a wave and followed Sarah to the door. "I'll take care of the discharge orders now."

Alone, Sloan crouched by Michael's chair. "You sure you're ready? Because you—"

"I want to go home." Michael slipped her fingers into the back of Sloan's hair and stroked her neck. "I want to sleep next to you tonight. I need that."

Sloan closed her eyes. "So do I."

CHAPTER ELEVEN

A re you comfortable? Do you need anything?"
"I'm perfect." Michael, in an oversized Cal Tech T-shirt
of Sloan's and loose pale blue cotton pajama bottoms, sat with her
back propped against several pillows in the corner of the couch in
the living room of the loft she had shared with Sloan for just over
a year. A light throw blanket covered her legs and stretched along
the length of the sofa. She'd been home twenty minutes, and Sloan
hadn't stopped fussing for a second. The headache still throbbed,
but less sharply now, and the pain was more distant, muted by the
pleasure of being home. Michael smiled and held out her hand.
"Come sit beside me, love."

When Sloan kissed Michael's fingers, then moved toward the
opposite end of the couch, Michael protested. "No. Up here with
me."

"There's not enough room."

"There's always been enough room before. We've made love
here more than once. I'm a bit fuzzy but *that* I remember."

You're still so pale. And I can see the pain in your eyes. Sloan
settled carefully onto the far end of the couch, afraid that the mere
motion would somehow hurt Michael. "Dr. Torveau said bed rest,
and we're already cheating by letting you camp out here instead of
in the bedroom. I want you to be able to sleep."

"I will." Michael shifted and patted the leather seat by her
side. "Especially if you lie down here next to me."

Sloan hesitated.

"I'm not going to break." Michael's voice was soothing, her
eyes tender. She couldn't miss the worry in Sloan's face. "Please,
love."

That was all it took. Sloan could no more *not* answer that

call than she could stop her heart from beating. Slowly, she eased herself down until she was on her side facing her lover, her head resting against Michael's shoulder. "Okay?"

"Mmm." Sighing, Michael rested her cheek against the top of Sloan's head and stroked her face. "Wonderful."

For a moment, they were silent, relishing the closeness after the days of separation and fear. Sloan listened to Michael's quiet breathing as her lover's gentle fingers traced her eyebrows, the arch of her cheek, the corner of her mouth. Michael's touch spoke as clearly as any words of devotion and desire. Sloan closed her eyes and reveled in the sensation of being loved.

"Will you tell me what happened?"

Michael's request was delivered so quietly that at first the words did not penetrate Sloan's consciousness. When she finally understood their meaning, she stiffened. She would have drawn away, but Michael's arm tightened around her shoulders.

"Baby, Dr. Torveau said—"

"I hate this. The way I feel—like something is missing." Michael's fingers trembled as she continued to caress Sloan's face. "That hurts almost as much as the headache."

The anguish in her voice was more than Sloan could bear.

"You were hit by a car, out in front of the house." Sloan spoke slowly, carefully, gauging how much to say by the cadence of Michael's breathing. She listened fretfully for any sign that Michael was upset. "It happened Saturday night."

"I can't remember."

Sloan drew away enough to meet Michael's gaze. "You will. It's normal not to be able to remember for a while. It's going to be okay, baby. I promise."

"Was anyone else hurt?"

"No." A muscle in Sloan's jaw bunched and quivered. Pain lanced behind her eyes. "No one else. Just you."

"The other driver?"

"He didn't stop." The words felt like acid in her throat. Sloan's hand clenched into a fist where it rested on her blue-jean-covered thigh. *God damn it. It was supposed to have been me!*

Michael felt her lover tense and saw the white-knuckled fist. "What is it? What aren't you telling me?"

"Michael. Baby." Sloan's voice was nearly pleading. "You just got home. You're supposed to be resting. We can talk about this tomorrow."

"Promise?" Michael drew Sloan's head back to her shoulder and kissed her forehead. She waited until Sloan gradually relaxed in her arms again. "I have to know what happened so that I can put this all behind me. You have to help me with that."

"I will. I promise." Sloan nuzzled her face against Michael's neck, needing to feel the heat of her skin and the rush of blood through the rippling vessels, so vital, so alive. Her voice was hoarse as she whispered, "I love you so much."

"I'm here. Right here." Michael pressed against Sloan's body, drawing solace from her nearness even as she offered Sloan the comfort of her embrace.

"Don't ever go."

"No, love. Never."

❖

Sarah walked from the guest bedroom at the far end of the loft into the living area and discovered the two lovers asleep in one another's arms. She gazed at them, a tender smile on her face, wishing that the peace they shared at that moment could last forever. Unfortunately, the ringing of the phone shattered the silence, and the brief interlude was over. Sarah grabbed it, but not before Sloan stirred, fighting to open her eyes while mumbling with the last vestiges of exhausted sleep. "Who...what?"

"Sloan and Lassiter residence," Sarah said, turning her back to the resting women and trying to speak quietly.

Silence.

"Hello?"

"Sarah?"

"Jasmine?"

"What are you doing there?" the rich contralto voice inquired. "Is something wrong?"

"No, Michael came home from the hospital a little while ago, and I volunteered to stay with her for a few days." Puzzled, Sarah mentally flipped through the calendar in her mind. "Where are you?"

Another beat of silence. "Downstairs."

"Why? You don't have a show tonight, do you?" Sarah glanced over at the couch where Sloan had shifted to a sitting position, leaning with elbows on knees, her head in her hands. She looked weary beyond imagining. Sarah covered the mouthpiece. "Sloan—go back to sleep. It's Jasmine. I'll tell her to call back later."

"Jasmine?" Sloan said the word as if it were foreign to her, then suddenly straightened. "What time is it?"

"Almost five." Sarah held up a finger as she listened. "She's awake now...What? When?...What kind of meeting? With the police?...You'd better come up." She replaced the receiver and stared at Sloan, who gave her an apologetic smile. "We don't want to wake Michael."

Gingerly, Sloan rose, then bent to tuck the blanket around her lover. She crossed to the huge double metal doors, touched the code into the keypad, and the doors slid soundlessly open on well-oiled tracks as the gears hidden within the walls engaged.

Just beyond, a woman who resembled an older version of Sandy stood waiting. Her layered hair was slightly longer and dark where Sandy's was blond, but she was lithe and sensuous like Sandy. Her skin-tight black pants, body-hugging Lycra top, and scarlet silk blouse left open and tied casually at her narrow waist gave her an aura of confident sensuality. Her make-up was understated but artfully applied, subtly accentuating the sweep of arched cheekbones and the curve of her full lips. She might have been a high-priced call girl or a runway model.

"Jesus, you look...great." Sloan was tired, and her defenses were down. She always found Jasmine attractive, but sometimes the intense visceral response actually left her uncomfortable. She understood its involuntary nature, but there were any number of reasons why it troubled her, and the fact that she was happily married and had no desire for any woman but Michael was only one of them. The other was that not only was Jasmine committed as well, she was also a man. A straight man, at that, and Sloan's best friend. Most of the time she was able to balance her affections for Jason and Jasmine, but there were times, like now, when she looked at Jasmine and saw only a beautiful woman.

"Hello, sexy." Jasmine kissed Sloan on the mouth. "You look like roadkill."

"Thanks." Hastily, Sloan cautioned, "Michael's asleep."

Jasmine stepped around her into the room while the doors silently closed. Sarah waited close by, and Jasmine kissed her cheek almost shyly. "Hi."

"Hi yourself," Sarah replied, her tone subdued. Briefly, she touched Jasmine's hand. "New slacks?"

"Mmm. This afternoon."

"Nice." Sarah gestured with her head. "Let's go into the bedroom, and you can tell me where you intend to wear them." She gave Sloan a hard look. "And just what you two are getting yourselves into."

❖

"Did you get anywhere with Jimmy Hogan's files today?" Rebecca asked as she and Watts waited to be buzzed in at Sloan's front door.

Watts flipped his cigarette into the street, where it died in a shower of sparks. "Nowhere to get. The guy was like a ghost. He had no regular contacts in narco, even though he was *supposed* to be a narc. I talked to three or four guys I know there, and they all said the same thing..." The green light on the electronic keypad blinked and he followed Rebecca into the cavernous garage. "He'd leave phone messages about drug buys from time to time...mid-level kinda stuff. Never led to any really big busts. And never any indication that he was closing in on anyone or anything big."

"Yeah," Rebecca said disgustedly as they moved toward the elevator. "*That* kind of intelligence he was probably saving for Avery Clark and Justice."

"Well, we know he was feeding Cruz intel, because the day they got taken out wasn't their first meet."

It was still hard for Rebecca to talk about her previous partner. Harder still for her to believe he was dead. "That was almost always small stuff, too. That chicken house up on North Broad was the biggest thing we got from him, and I'm still not sure he knew what was there when he tipped us."

"Well, Hogan knew *something* that got him killed."

Rebecca stepped into the elevator. "Maybe he didn't *know* he was on to something. Maybe he was trying to get something from Cruz, and not the other way around. *Christ,* I wish Jeff had told me what was going on."

"Hey," a voice called from behind them. "Hold that, will you?"

Rebecca braced the door with a hand and turned. Sandy hurried toward the elevator. At Watts's obvious look of surprise, Rebecca explained quietly, "I don't know what Jason has in mind, but Sandy is our eyes and ears on the street. I figured she'd have the best sense of whether we can put someone undercover where we need to and make it work."

"Jesus, it's not even dark," Sandy complained. "I haven't had breakfast yet."

"Hi, Sandy." Rebecca smothered a smile.

Sandy grunted a greeting and pointedly ignored Watts, who was studying her sheer V-neck blouse and painted-on Capri slacks with interest.

"It's September, ya know. Aren't ya cold?"

"I'm hot-blooded."

"No foolin'."

Her glance was withering. Watts hummed something tuneless and rocked back and forth on his scuffed black wingtips, his hands in his pockets, jiggling change.

When the elevator stopped, Rebecca led the way down the hall to the conference room. Sloan was already there, leaning against a counter with a cup of coffee in her hand. Another woman stood nearby, one hip tilted against the end of the conference table. Mitchell, having arrived just before Rebecca and company, sat on the far side of the table in her usual spot.

"Hey," Sloan said as the group filed in.

"Sloan," Rebecca acknowledged, studying the dark-haired woman at Sloan's side. She was certain they hadn't met, but the stranger seemed familiar nonetheless.

"Yo," Watts said, eyeing the woman, too, as he settled heavily into a seat. Sandy sat beside him, pointedly not looking at Mitchell across from her.

"Jasmine, this is Sergeant Frye, Detective Watts, and Sandy."

As they all nodded, Sloan continued, "Jasmine works at the Troc, and she knows some of the regulars at Ziggie's."

"Uh...doin' what, exactly?" Watts asked, his gaze dropping from Jasmine's face to her breasts and lingering a moment. "The Troc's the kind of club that offers all kinds of *entertainment*."

"I'm a singer," Jasmine replied, her voice whiskey warm.

"That's it?"

"What else did you have in mind?"

Watts glanced at Rebecca, who continued to study Jasmine intently. When the other detective made no comment, he continued, "It wouldn't be such a bad thing if you did some...favors for the customers, now and then. At a place like Ziggie's, that would be... natural. If you were into that, I mean."

"Soliciting sex is illegal, Detective," Jasmine said with a sensuous smile. "You're not suggesting I break the law?"

Watts shifted in his chair, almost as uneasy at Rebecca's silence as he was with the way Jasmine's voice made his blood race. He didn't usually go for hookers, but Jesus, she was something.

Abruptly, Rebecca stood. "Excuse me a moment, Miss..."

"Just Jasmine." She nearly purred the words.

Rebecca smiled, then glanced at the blond beside her. "Sandy?"

Sandy rose, pretending not to notice the hard stare that Dell threw her way, and followed Rebecca to the far end of the room. They stood close together, backs to the others, and looked out the window to the Delaware River a few blocks away.

In a quiet voice, Rebecca asked, "Know her?"

"Uh-uh."

"Seen her around before?"

"Nope, and I'd remember. She's major competition."

"What do you think?"

"She's good. Really, really good." Sandy shrugged. "If she works the streets, she wouldn't do it in our neighborhood anyhow. Not the right clientele."

"Who do you know who could check her out for us?"

Sandy shook her head. "I'm not sure. I know a few trannies, but...she's different. Classy...I don't think she's selling it."

"No, neither do I. Ever seen her in Ziggie's?"

"I don't hang there, I told you that." Sandy shrugged. "Maybe she's just what she says...a singer. The Troc has regular drag shows."

Rebecca sighed. She needed a street contact badly, but she was loathe to trust someone she didn't know, even if Sloan and Jas—"Son of a *bitch.*"

"Huh?" Sandy gazed up at the tall cop and was surprised to see a smile on her face. "What?"

"I can't believe I didn't see it."

Sandy stared as Rebecca turned and walked back to her place at the table.

"Jasmine?" Rebecca asked. Blue eyes rose to hers. A full mouth smiled slowly.

"Yes, Sergeant?" The tone was openly seductive now.

"They know you by name in Ziggie's?"

"Probably. I drop in there now and then with some of the other entertainers from the club."

"Other drag queens?"

"Huh?" Watts straightened in his seat.

Mitchell swiveled on her chair, eyes narrowing as she looked at Jasmine.

Sloan grinned.

"We prefer the term female impersonators." Jasmine tossed her head and moved closer to Sloan. She linked an arm through Sloan's and leaned into her. "Although some of the other performers *are* drag queens, of course."

"Huh? What's she saying?" Watts's voice had gotten louder.

"She's a *he,* you twit," Sandy said disparagingly.

"No." Watts looked at Rebecca, who nodded. He slumped in his chair, shaking his head. "Fuck me."

"How many people know who you are?" Rebecca asked.

Jasmine shrugged, her expression serious. "Not that many. Not in Ziggie's, that's for sure."

"Because that's the flaw in this plan," Rebecca said. "Someone knows Sloan was investigating the porn ring. And if they know about Sloan, then they know about Jason."

Mitchell suddenly gasped. "Oh man...Jason. You're... beautiful."

"What!" Watts exploded.

Sandy giggled, then burst into laughter. "You *rock,* Jasmine."

Watts stared from face to face as if he had suddenly found himself surrounded by alien life forms. Then he half rose from his seat, his palms flat on the table. "Somebody better tell me what the joke is before I do damage here."

Sloan took pity on him. "Jasmine is Jason's stage name, Detective."

"Jason's stage name?" Watts looked as if he had been pole-axed. His head tilted from side to side as his face turned from red to purple. "Jason?"

Jasmine smiled kindly. "Jason isn't here at the moment, Detective. He asked that I stop by to lend you a hand."

Watts sat, placed his hands in his lap, and stared fixedly at the tabletop.

"How friendly are you with the girls in Ziggie's?" Rebecca asked. "Because if there's someone in there who knows about the porn videos, it would be them."

"Nodding acquaintances. Most of the working girls consider us competition and there's little love lost because of it."

"You're not competition," Sandy remarked flatly. "Working girls can't compete with chicks with dicks."

Watts made a strangled sound. Mitchell's eyes glittered as she fixed on Sandy's face.

"*I'm* not selling anything." Jasmine's voice was soft, but edged in steel.

"Too bad—you'd bring in the bucks." Sandy's tone was conversational.

Finally, Jasmine smiled. "Why, thank you, honey."

"What makes you think that you can get what we need in Ziggie's if the girls won't talk to you?" Rebecca asked.

"I might not be able to, but I have friends from the Troc who are very close acquaintances of the dancers at Ziggie's."

"No way," Rebecca said sharply. "No more civilians."

"No, I don't want to use them either, but I was thinking I could put one of us with them. It would be a natural way in, and I'd be close by as backup, too."

Rebecca frowned. "I don't follow. We've already decided we

can't put Sandy in Ziggie's."

"The show at the Troc has both female *and male* impersonators," Jasmine explained. "The drag kings are regulars at Ziggie's. I can put one of us with them."

"A drag...king?" Watts finally found his voice. "A girl pretending to be a guy? Are you kidding? Who?"

Jasmine turned and her gaze fell on Officer Dellon Mitchell.

CHAPTER TWELVE

No," Rebecca said immediately. "Mitchell's not trained for undercover."

"I can do it." Mitchell's voice was quiet and sure.

"Undercover work takes practice, kid," Watts interjected. "You gotta *be* the person twenty-four seven, because if you lose it for just a minute, you'll get made. And then..."

He shrugged his shoulders, and a heavy silence fell around the table.

"Dell would be a sitting duck," Sandy said into the ensuing void. "Nobody's gonna take her for anything but a cop. Jesus, look at her."

"Look at Jasmine," Sloan remarked quietly. "She's *believable,* don't you think?"

"Yeah, but Jasmine is the real deal. And she's probably been doing it for years." Sandy tilted her chin at Mitchell. "You think Supercop can learn to pass as a drag king in a week?"

"Sandy," Mitchell interrupted, her voice low. "Take it easy."

"You're just dumb enough to try it. Fuck, Dell." Sandy slammed back in her chair, muttering something about moronic cops under her breath.

Rebecca glanced sideways at the young blond, contemplating the ferocity in her voice. It surprised her. Sandy rarely displayed any overt signs of attachment. At least not for anyone other than a few of her girlfriends in the life. Rebecca hadn't missed the use of Mitchell's first name, either. *That's just perfect. These two are already way too involved. God damn it. Another complication I don't have time to deal with.*

"There's no point in even discussing it," Rebecca said flatly. "We don't have time to create a good background cover for you,

Mitchell. You can't just one day *appear.* You need a history, a backstory, contacts, people who know you as your alternate persona."

"That's where I come in," Jasmine said, her tone mildly conciliatory. It wasn't her intention to undermine Rebecca's authority, but in this particular situation, she was the expert. "If *I* introduce *him*..." Jasmine glanced at Mitchell. "He has instant credibility." *Do you get it?*

Mitchell's expression was intent, sensing Jasmine's question, hearing Watts's warning. *You gotta* be *the person twenty-four seven, because if you lose it for just a minute, you'll get made. And then...*

"I can do it."

Satisfied, Jasmine continued. "Once he's part of the group at the Troc, that buys him entrance to Ziggie's with no questions asked. It shouldn't take more than a matter of days to establish him as a regular."

"Yeah?" Watts asked belligerently, leaning forward with his forearms crossed on the table, fixing Jasmine with a direct stare for the first time since he realized who she was. "And what about the little matter of Mitchell looking like a guy? *She* don't, even if she does have short hair and not much in the way of tits."

"Oh, I don't know," Sloan said smoothly. "I think she looks like Orlando Bloom."

Jasmine tilted her head, her lips parting appraisingly as she studied a blushing Mitchell. "Mmm, I can see that."

Watts looked at Rebecca. "For Christ sake's, Sarge. This is nuts."

Rebecca shrugged. "Jasmine?"

"Actually, Detective, she doesn't *have* to look like a man. She only has to give the *impression* of one," Jasmine explained calmly. "That's the art of impersonation. Our intent is for her to be a believable drag king, and *that* is almost entirely a matter of projecting a masculine attitude."

"That right?" Watts's expression darkened. "If it's just an *attitude,* then how come you *look* so much like a girl?"

Jasmine smiled sweetly. "Because I am."

"Oh, for fu—"

"Let's assume," Rebecca interjected, sensing that Watts was about to blow a fuse, "that Mitchell can pass..."

"I can." Mitchell met Rebecca's gaze. "Isn't it what we do all the time, Sergeant? Play the game?"

Rebecca studied the unflinching, deep blue eyes. *So you know already? Playing the game—yes, that's what we do. Pretending that the things we see don't affect us, that the fear isn't real, that the violence doesn't touch us. That we aren't bleeding inside.*

"Assuming—" A series of high-pitched beeps interrupted her.

Sloan swiveled to check one of the two monitors mounted in the corner, then stood and walked to a panel on the wall below. Pressing a button, she said, "Good evening, Dr. Rawlings."

On the screen, Catherine smiled back. "Hello."

"Come on up. We're in the east conference room."

"Thank you."

Everyone got up and replenished their coffees, except for Sandy, who murmured something to Jasmine. Jasmine opened the refrigerator and extracted a can of Stoudt's, which she handed to the young woman. A moment later, Catherine appeared.

"I'm sorry," she said upon seeing the group gathered in the conference room. "I didn't mean to interrupt your meeting. I checked at the hospital, and they told me Michael had been discharged. I just thought I'd take a chance on stopping by to see how she's doing."

Sloan smiled. "She was sleeping earlier. But it's good you're here, because Jason and I want to discuss some things with you anyhow."

"Fine." Catherine glanced at Rebecca uncertainly. "Should I wait in the other room?"

"No," Rebecca said. "Please join us."

"Thank you." Turning to Jasmine, she extended her hand. "I'm Catherine Rawlings. We haven't met."

"Jasmine."

Catherine tilted her head, something in the voice tripping a memory. "Or *have* we?"

"It's a long story." Jasmine's eyes sparkled. "I'll tell you some evening, if you let me buy you a drink."

Catherine laughed. "All right then." She reached across the

table and offered her hand to Sandy as well. "Hello. Good to see you again."

Sandy blushed, an almost unheard of event. Carefully, she took Catherine's hand. "Same here."

Once Catherine was seated to Jasmine's left across the table from Watts, Rebecca gave her a capsule summary of the plan and Mitchell's role. Then the detective turned her attention to Jasmine. "Assuming that Mitchell is accepted by your friends at the Troc, how soon could we get her into Ziggie's?"

"Almost immediately. At least a few nights a week, the kings go to Ziggie's or one of the other clubs after the Troc closes. Plus I'm doing a show later this week," Jasmine replied. "A group of us usually go out after to celebrate, while we're still...dressed."

Watts snorted. "To a topless bar?"

Jasmine stiffened, and, for the first time, she looked angry. "Our choices are limited, Detective." She made a conscious effort to lighten her tone. "Besides, it's a good place for the drag kings to practice, since almost all the patrons are men. It's a chance for them to see how well they fit in."

"You might be able to dress Mitchell up right," Watts persisted, "but who's gonna teach her the moves? *You?*"

"Jason can help," Jasmine said. "But you'd be better."

Watts's mouth fell open. He didn't say another word.

"Where do you live, Mitchell?" Rebecca asked.

"Independence Place." Mitchell named one of the expensive high-rises just south of Walnut at Sixth Street, bordering Washington Square Park.

Rebecca shook her head. "No good. We'll need to find you an apartment a little more downscale than that."

"There's a place open in my building," Sandy said quietly.

Before Rebecca could object, Jasmine said, "That might be good. It wouldn't hurt for Mitchell to have a girlfriend, either. Another piece of the picture."

"Not if I'm going to strike up a friendship with one of the dancers in Ziggie's," Mitchell pointed out hastily, carefully not looking in Sandy's direction.

"That isn't necessarily true." Sloan smiled gently. "Ever heard of cheating, Officer?"

Mitchell blushed and Watts snorted.

"Okay," Rebecca said, lightly slapping her palms on the tabletop. "Let's go with this plan for now. Jasmine, you're in charge of getting Mitchell...geared up."

"What's your address, stud?" Jasmine asked. When Mitchell gave it to her, she added, "I'll be over in an hour or so. Why don't you bring Sandy, too? She can be our first audience."

Mitchell looked like she wanted to object, but she just nodded her assent.

Rebecca glanced at Watts, her expression deadly serious. "If they need any help in that regard, do it."

"Right." He bit off the word as if it hurt to say it.

Rebecca turned to Sandy. "What's the situation at your building? Is there a building superintendent who handles renting the apartments?"

"That's a fancy name for the guy, since he doesn't do shit around the place, but yeah."

"Bring Mitchell around. Tell him sh...*he's* a friend of yours who needs a place right away. Cash. I'll take care of getting the money to you tonight."

Mitchell looked even unhappier.

"Sure." Sandy shrugged indifferently.

"And I still need you to find one of those girls who told you about making the sex videos a few months ago. There's a good chance that she's been to the film site."

"I told you before, I won't name names."

"I don't want their names. I just want to talk to one of them."

"Okay," Sandy said reluctantly. "I'll see what I can do."

"Good. You still got the phone?"

"Yeah, yeah."

"Use it." Rebecca surveyed the group. "Let's plan on a nightly briefing here at six. Mitchell, you're dismissed. Sandy..." She hesitated, but had to admit that Jasmine's plan for Mitchell's new persona to have a girlfriend made sense. "Go with her."

"Yes, ma'am," Mitchell said as she stood. Sandy merely sniffed.

Rebecca watched them go, trying not to second-guess her decision. She rubbed the bridge of her nose to fight back a headache, struggling like an apprentice juggler to keep all the twirling plates aloft. "Tomorrow, Jason and Mitchell can keep trolling on the Internet sex sites to solidify the suspect list." For the first time, she met Catherine's eyes. "It will help if you can profile them like you did with LongJohnXXX. Jason will tell you what we're looking for. I'll leave it to you to work out your schedule with him, since I know you have other commitments."

"Will *Jason* be back tomorrow?" Catherine glanced at Jasmine and raised an eyebrow. She'd finally recognized where she knew that voice from. *And those beautiful eyes.*

"He'll be in and out." Jasmine's eyes twinkled as she crossed her legs and spread one arm along the back of Sloan's chair, her fingers lightly brushing Sloan's shoulder. Her blouse tightened across shapely breasts. "I'll see that he calls."

"Of course. Thank you," Catherine said, suddenly aware that she was staring. Aware, too, of the distant pulse of arousal. *Well. That's unexpected.*

Drawing her eyes away, Catherine angled in her seat so that she could focus on Rebecca, who continued to outline the team members' responsibilities. Jasmine's image disappeared as Catherine observed Rebecca doing what she did so well. Her lover's mind was keen, her command presence clear, her determination unwavering. She was starkly beautiful, at once intimidating and exciting. What Catherine felt when she looked at Rebecca went far beyond arousal. It bordered on a nearly indefinable hunger.

Rebecca had turned her attention to Sloan. "You've got the interdepartmental computer traces."

"Right. I'm going back tonight. Less traffic on the network. Fewer people to notice me—either in the flesh or online."

"Tomorrow I should have a list of people in the district attorney's office who were involved with generating the warrant for the Justice bust," Watts offered. "I'll call...Jason with them."

"Good. Sloan, as far as the police officers who could possibly have had anything to do with the leak," Rebecca said with reluctance, "you should probably check out Trish Marks and Charlie Horton, two detectives in Homicide, as well as Captain Henry and Elizabeth Adams. Adams is the civilian clerk who generated the paperwork to go to the district attorney from our end."

"Got it," Sloan said, jotting down the names on one of the ubiquitous yellow legal pads lying around the conference room.

Rebecca pushed back her chair. "Anyone have anything else to add?"

Everyone shook their head. Watts muttered good night and left immediately. Rebecca turned to Catherine.

"Are you going upstairs to visit Michael?"

"I thought I'd say hello if she's awake." Catherine could usually judge Rebecca's mood by the color of her eyes. At the moment, they were the gray of thunderclouds, and Catherine wondered just how much that storm had to do with her own imminent involvement in the investigation. She tried not to make assumptions about such things, knowing only too well how deceiving appearances could be, but such caution was difficult where her lover was concerned. Rebecca's state of mind was so critical to her own comfort, her own life. That dependence on another human being was still new, and still frightening. "What about you?"

"How about I wait here, and then we catch some dinner? I don't imagine Michael's up for a crowd."

"Are you going back to work tonight?" Catherine asked, remembering Rebecca's comment to Sandy about bringing cash by "later."

"Probably. Yes." Turning her back to Jasmine and Sloan, Rebecca added, "If you don't mind too much."

Catherine brushed her fingers along the edge of Rebecca's jaw and smiled. "Not *too* much."

The brief touch sparked heat in Rebecca's stomach, and she sucked in a breath. Voice thick, she murmured, "Don't be too long, okay? You just started something."

"Really?" Catherine appeared to consider the thought. "Then let's order Chinese and take it home. We can eat it in bed."

"I'll make the call."

"I'll be right back."

Rebecca's gaze followed her lover as Catherine left with Sloan and Jasmine. *Home.* Home was very rapidly becoming Catherine's apartment. That idea was starting to feel comfortable. When it wasn't scaring the bejesus out of her.

❖

Sloan peeked around the corner into the bedroom. Michael, her blond hair freshly washed, lay in bed wearing one of Sloan's old cotton shirts that had once been blue but was now faded nearly to white. "Everybody gone?"

"Hello, love. Yes, I'm quite alone." Michael smiled and stretched out a hand. "I missed you."

"Me, too." Sloan crossed the room and settled onto the corner of the bed. "You hungry?"

"Sarah made me some soup earlier. She left the rest on the stove for you. You should have some."

"Sure," Sloan said automatically. She wasn't hungry. In fact, she couldn't remember the last real meal she'd eaten. It had been sometime the day before Michael had left for her meeting in Boston. After that, the hours had disappeared in a blur of motion and terror.

"Sarah told me a little bit about what happened."

Sloan's heart lurched in her chest, and her stomach was instantly queasy. "What do you mean?"

"About the accident."

"Damn it," Sloan burst out, one hand fisting the covers. "It's too soon—"

"It's not her fault. I asked her."

"What happened Saturday night?"

Sarah continued gently toweling Michael's hair. "What can you remember?"

"Not much." Michael, a thick terrycloth towel wrapped around her naked body, leaned back against Sarah for support. "I know there was an accident, and Sloan told me I was hit by a car. She said the driver didn't stop."

"Then you know almost as much as we know." Sarah carefully worked a wide-toothed comb through the long tresses, stopping intermittently to remove the small islands of clotted blood that clung tenaciously to the silken strands.

"I know there's more." Michael closed her eyes, the headache exhausting, just by virtue of its constant presence.

"Sloan will tell you."

Michael started to shake her head, then stopped when the pain escalated. "No. She can't. It kills her to talk about it. I can't stand to see the pain in her eyes."

"God, I know." Sarah's sighed. "Sloan is incapable of hiding her feelings, no matter how hard she tries. If it hurts me to see her hurting, it must be awful for you."

"Yes. Agony." Michael reached for Sarah's hand and held it tightly. "So for both of us, could you help me understand what's happened?"

"You will remember on your own, given enough time."

"It's not the memories I need as much as knowing what's coming. There's a meeting downstairs right now, isn't there?"

"Sloan is an idiot if she thinks she can keep anything from you." Sarah's voice was husky with tenderness.

"She thinks she's protecting me," Michael replied, instantly coming to Sloan's defense. "I love her for that. For that and so many other reasons."

"You know she lives for you, don't you?" Sarah leaned down and kissed the top of Michael's head. "She would never intentionally keep something from you, except to prevent you from being hurt."

"Sarah," Michael said softly, "you needn't tell me how she loves me. She's the heart of my heart."

"Of course she is. I've always known that."

"Then, please, tell me what's happening."

"Do you remember that Jason and Sloan were involved in an investigation with the local police and the Justice Department?"

Michael was silent a long moment. "Something...about the Internet...a pornography ring, right?"

"Yes. Something...ah, God...something went wrong. Someone found out what Sloan and the rest of them were investigating."

The silence stretched longer this time. When Michael spoke, her voice trembled. "So the accident...wasn't an accident?"

"Here, put this on," Sarah directed, holding up the shirt she had pulled from Sloan's closet. She helped Michael stand and finished drying her off. Her expression was carefully blank as she gently patted the soft cotton over the large bruises on Michael's ribs and back. "I should put something on that abrasion on your *hip. Wait a minute." Quickly, blinking back tears, she turned to the medicine cabinet and fumbled about until she found a large tube of antibiotic ointment. Despite her care, Michael winced as Sarah spread the soothing ointment on the raw surface where the skin had been stripped away by her body's impact with the harsh surface of the street. "Sorry."*

"No. That's all right." Michael rested one hand on Sarah's shoulder for balance. "But they couldn't have meant to hurt me, could they? I didn't know anything."

When Sarah met Michael's eyes, her distress was clearly evident.

Tears overflowed onto Michael's cheeks. "Sloan. Of course... they wanted Sloan. Oh, God."

"Hey," Sloan said anxiously, moving nearer on the bed. She brushed her fingers over Michael's cheeks, catching the tears on her fingertips. "Hey, hey, baby. It's all right. It's all right."

"Is someone still trying to hurt you?"

"No! No." Sloan settled on the bed next to Michael and wrapped her arm around her lover's shoulder, forgetting to be careful for the first time since Michael had come home from the hospital. All she wanted was to comfort her. She pressed her lips to Michael's hair, stroking her cheek with her free hand. "Everything is fine. There's nothing for you to worry about."

"You're sure?" Michael pressed close, swallowing a moan when her tender ribs protested. It felt too good to be in Sloan's arms to move away, even to ease the pain.

"Absolutely." Sloan consciously eased her grip, because all she *wanted* to do was hold Michael more tightly. She had been afraid for what felt like forever that she was going to lose her, and now that Michael was close, she wanted her fiercely. It had nothing to do with sex, and everything to do with existence. Michael was her heart.

Michael rested her cheek against Sloan's chest, listening to the rapid rush of breath and the wild pounding of her heart. She had always loved the heat of Sloan's body and the quick rise of her passion, but never more than now. Just knowing that someone had wanted to harm her lover made Michael desperate to keep her safe.

"I can't imagine life without you."

"You'll never have to." Sloan trembled as she tenderly kissed Michael's lips. She kissed her again—gently, carefully—her passion restrained but her devotion unbridled.

CHAPTER THIRTEEN

How come you don't have a car?" Sandy asked as she and Mitchell crossed Market Street going south on Sixth.

"I have a car." Mitchell walked with her hands by her sides for quick access to her weapon, glancing into each darkened doorway that she passed, reflexively always on patrol.

"So where is it?"

"In the garage at my building. I don't drive to work."

"How come?"

Because I can just hear the grief I'd get if I showed up with the Austin Healy. Mitchell shrugged and stepped slightly in front of Sandy as a large man wearing too many layers of clothes and carrying a bundle secured with twine under his arm shuffled toward them. Probably just a street person, but she wanted to be prepared if he made a move in their direction. She kept her eyes on him as she answered. "I like walking."

"You do that a lot, you know," Sandy observed as the vagrant brushed her in passing.

"What?"

"Get ready for trouble, like with that guy just now."

"Habit, I guess." Mitchell slowed. "Does it bother you?"

"No. I kinda like it."

Mitchell smiled. "You hungry? Should we get a pizza or something?"

"How about we go somewhere after Jasmine does her thing with you?"

Does her thing. Mitchell blushed. "Yeah, right. That." She'd almost forgotten. It wouldn't have been bad, really, if Sandy weren't going to be watching. *What if I can't do it? Jeez, what if she laughs?* Her stomach churned. *What if she doesn't like...him?*

"You're crazy for doing this."

"It's my job." Mitchell stared straight ahead, her pace quickening.

"It is not." Sandy grasped Mitchell's wrist and tugged until the rookie looked at her. "You're supposed to be walking a beat, not club crawling and picking up sluts."

"Picking up...oh, come on! You know that what I do while I'm undercover doesn't mean anything. It's just the job."

"Does that include fucking one of them, too?" Sandy's eyes glittered dangerously.

Mitchell stopped dead. She didn't notice that they were standing in the middle of the sidewalk or that pedestrians were forced to step around them. "I am *not* going to fuck anyone. Jesus."

"Why not? Got something against it? Or is it just *girls* you don't want to fuck?" Sandy jutted her jaw and wondered where the hell *that* had come from. *Like I care who she fucks.*

"You're impossible, you know that?" Mitchell raked a hand through her hair in frustration. She couldn't think of a single thing to say that would come out sounding right. *No, I don't fuck girls.* Or better yet, *I don't want to fuck girls.* No, wait...*I know better than to fuck girls.* "Come on. My building's just up here."

Neither of them said anything else until they were inside the high-ceilinged lobby that was lorded over by an officious uniformed attendant at a long security desk. The floors were polished marble, the walls papered with a delicate gold-on-linen filigree pattern above dark wood wainscoting, and the spacious area lit by huge hanging chandeliers.

"Whoa. This really *is* fancy," Sandy observed as she craned her neck to stare up into the far reaches of the atrium.

"Good evening, Officer Mitchell." The guard greeted Mitchell politely even as he stared at Sandy with a look that verged on a leer.

"Hello, Clifford." Mitchell caught his appraising expression—as if Sandy were an offering on a smorgasbord and he was deciding if he'd try a piece. Her pulse jumped, and her vision got a bit hazy.

Sandy's eyes narrowed as he blatantly perused her body

without even bothering to disguise his smirk. She straightened slightly, knowing that the movement would thrust her breasts forward. His gaze flickered for a moment on her face and then dropped down to fix on her nipples.

"Did you lose something—*Clifford*?" She shot him a disdainful look as he realized she was taunting him, and his face reddened. *All the same, fancy suits or not. Screw you, buddy. A look is all you'll ever get.*

Mitchell took Sandy's hand. Gruffly, she said, "The elevator is this way."

"I think I might've just ruined your reputation," Sandy said sarcastically, withdrawing her fingers from Mitchell's grip.

"No. I think you just made it." Mitchell pushed the elevator button, trying to forget the lascivious look on the doorman's face. For a second, she flashed on the night in the alley when the stranger had been molesting Sandy, and she wanted to go back and punch Clifford just for looking at her. *This is no good. She makes me crazy.*

The elevator arrived and they stepped in. They were alone.

"You mad?" Sandy asked.

"No."

"Sure?" Sandy leaned one shoulder against the wall, her hip cocked, a strip of bare skin showing above the waistband of her tight slacks.

"Yeah," Mitchell said hoarsely, her attention riveted to that pale smooth inch of flesh. She wanted to see if it was really as soft as it appeared. She felt hot and a little dizzy.

Mercifully, the elevator glided to a stop and the faint ping penetrated her consciousness just as she reached out to trace a finger along the border where flesh and fabric met. She jerked back as the door opened. "This is it."

Suddenly shy, Sandy hesitated. "You sure about this? You know, if people see you with me..."

Impatiently, almost angrily, Mitchell took Sandy's hand again and pulled her from the elevator. "What do you think, that you have a big sign that says *hooker* around your neck? Let them think whatever the hell they want to think."

"What about your job? That could be a problem, right?"

Mitchell's head snapped around. She stared hard at Sandy. "Who told you that?"

"Nobody."

*Frye said...I'm Frye's now...*Mitchell jammed her key into the lock and twisted viciously. She pushed the door open and waited for Sandy to enter before walking into her apartment and flicking on the light switch to her right. "What did Frye say to you?"

"Nothing."

"Don't lie. Jesus, just don't lie."

Sandy couldn't miss the current of desperate pain in Mitchell's voice. Immediately, she forgot why she had been angry with the young cop for badgering her just seconds before. "Listen, Frye was just looking out for you, okay?"

"I don't need her to *look out* for me, especially not where you're concerned. What did she *say*?" Mitchell took a step forward, and when Sandy flinched, Mitchell jerked back, instantly feeling sick to her stomach. "God, Sandy, do you think I'd hurt you?"

"No." Sandy shook her head. Tentatively, she placed her palm flat against Mitchell's chest, just above her heart. "No, I...I don't think that."

Mitchell stood very still, afraid if she moved Sandy would take her hand away. The heat from Sandy's small hand burned her skin through the fabric of her shirt. She couldn't feel anything except those few square inches of flesh, and in that one single spot, she felt terribly alive.

"I won't," Mitchell whispered. "Never. I swear."

Tremulously, Sandy smiled. She marveled at Mitchell's heart thudding against her palm. She couldn't remember ever feeling anything like that insistent pounding—wild and strong and strangely gentle. *Like Dell.*

"Don't ask me things, and I won't have to lie."

Mitchell took a cautious step forward. Sandy didn't move her hand, but slid it higher up Mitchell's chest, until her fingers touched the skin of her throat.

"That's not how it works." Mitchell's voice was husky, her body taut with tension. She kept her hands at her sides, afraid she might frighten Sandy again.

"How what works?" Sandy asked, unable to look away from

Mitchell's face. *Your eyes get so dark when you're excit—oh God.*

Sandy stumbled back and dropped her hand.

Mitchell leaned toward her, breathing fast, but she did not follow. *What am I doing? I scared you, didn't I? I'm sorry.*

"What did Frye say?" Mitchell's voice was a whisper.

"That...that you could lose your badge if you hung around me."

Mitchell closed her eyes, fighting the fury. Fighting the memory of loss. *Not again. No one will do that to me again.*

"Look, rookie—"

"*No.*" Mitchell didn't raise her voice, but the intensity of that single word punching the air silenced Sandy's protests. "You and me...that has nothing to do with the job. Do you understand?"

"Hey, okay," Sandy hastily agreed, alarmed by the bleak expression on Mitchell's face and the rage in her eyes. She wanted to touch her again, just to ease that unhappiness, but her insides were still on fire from the last touch.

"I mean it. You don't walk away...not because of that."

Sandy stiffened. "Nobody scares me off. *Especially* not a cop."

Mitchell relaxed minutely, the pain and the panic receding. "Glad to hear it. I was starting to think you were getting soft."

"Huh. Not likely."

They smiled at one another.

"You okay?" Sandy finally asked.

Mitchell nodded. "Yeah, you?"

"Sure."

The doorbell rang.

Mitchell drew a deep breath. "Show time."

❖

Catherine pushed up on one elbow and brushed the hair from her face with her free hand. "What is it?"

"Christ, I'm sorry." Rebecca sat up quickly and swung her legs over the side of the bed. Her voice was muffled as she said, "Look, it's not you, okay?"

"I *could* point out that I'm the only one in bed with you, so it most likely *is* me—but I'm too old to waste my time on false pride."

Gently, Catherine rested her hand against Rebecca's bare back. The skin was slick with the heat of their passion, the muscles tight with tension. "And fortunately, we've been together long enough that I believe you. So, if it's not me, what is it?"

"Nothing, it's just..." The detective ran a hand through her hair. *This is how it starts. First she'll be confused, then she'll be hurt, and eventually she'll be angry. This is when it all starts to come apart.* "It's nothing. I guess I'm just tired. Sorry."

"Rebecca," Catherine said as she sat up and slid a leg around each side of Rebecca's body, wrapping her arms around Rebecca's waist from behind at the same time. She rested her chin on top of her lover's shoulder. "We've made love when you were so exhausted you could barely move a muscle. We've made love when you were still recovering from a gunshot wound. Lord, we've made love in places and at times when sane people couldn't conceive of being turned on. This is not about being tired."

"I want you...you know that, don't you?" Rebecca tried but couldn't keep the desperation from her voice. "You know that's not the problem, don't you?"

"Yes, darling. I know." Catherine smiled and kissed Rebecca's ear. "You do an excellent job of making me feel desirable. And I'm not upset because I couldn't give you an orgasm—in fact, I'm not upset at all. But *you* are—and that's what matters right now."

"If you just give me a minute..."

"I'll give you anything you want. But right now, I think what you need—what *we* need—is communication of a different sort for a moment or two."

Without looking around, Rebecca found Catherine's hand where it lay on her stomach and held it. Catherine's breasts were against her back, a soft warm comfort. Maybe, maybe this time, it really would be all right. "It's the case."

"Mmm, I thought as much." Catherine snuggled her cheek against Rebecca's neck. "What's worrying you about it?"

Rebecca heaved a sigh. "Just about every damn thing you can think of. I've got a ragtag team, short on cops and long on civilians—one of whom is a goddamned streetwalker." *And another who's my lover.* "I've got Sloan trying to smoke out an informant within the department—someone who might be mob connected, someone who probably tried to kill her once already. Watts's career, maybe even his pension, is shot to hell if this operation runs afoul of someone with a lot more clout, or connections, than we can handle. I'm putting a rookie cop undercover, with no prep time and barely any backup. *Civilian* backup at that. Jesus, what a mess. I should be taken out and shot."

"Don't even joke." Catherine stiffened, and for the first time, her voice held an edge. The nightmares had only begun to abate, and there were still nights when she woke in a sweat, haunted by images of Rebecca's life bleeding away through her fingers.

"Sorry." Rebecca turned her head, found her lover's eyes. "I'm sorry."

"Lie down with me." Catherine leaned back on the pillows, drawing Rebecca with her. To her surprise, and pleasure, Rebecca acquiesced willingly. Catherine kept her arm around Rebecca's shoulder, toying with the hair at the base of her neck, stroking her softly. "What makes this any different than your usual investigations? Why does this one bother you more?"

"I've put all of my people in harm's way. The only one who is reasonably safe is me."

Catherine's throat tightened, but she kept her voice steady. "You'd be happier, wouldn't you, if you were the only one likely to get hurt?"

"Of course." Perplexity was evident in the detective's voice.

"You're the team leader—the commander. Your burden is every bit as great as theirs." Catherine kissed Rebecca's temple. "Harder in some ways."

"I'd rather..." *take a bullet than have it be one of them.* But she'd been awakened by Catherine's cries more than once, and she wouldn't willingly remind her of that pain. She sighed. "Then this thing with Mitchell—it's risky. And putting her that close to Sandy, in her building even. I must be crazy...the two of them are already too tight."

"Why is that bad?"

"Forgetting the fact that Sandy is a prostitute and that consorting with someone engaged in illegal activity would cost Mitchell her badge, if they get...involved, Mitchell's not going to be able to think about the job. And not thinking about the job could get her killed."

Yes. I know what happens when a police officer develops personal attachments while on the job. When a police officer forsakes judgment for emotion. Catherine was silent, realizing that Rebecca had never mentioned Dell's encounter with the man in the alley, or her subsequent difficulties within the department. Rebecca didn't know the extent of Dell's history with Sandy. She didn't know how deeply Dell already cared.

"You and Watts...you're partners. You care about each other, right?" She took a breath, because it was hard for her to voice the truths she didn't want to acknowledge. "You'd risk your life for him, wouldn't you? Like you did...with me."

"That's different. I'm not sleeping with him."

Catherine laughed faintly. "Well, I am certainly glad to hear that. Do you think De—Mitchell is sleeping with Sandy?"

"Hell, I'm not even sure either of them is gay." Rebecca shrugged, frustrated. "I just *feel* something between them."

"Yes," Catherine agreed. "So do I. But I don't think that's the kind of thing you can order them *not* to feel."

"Probably not. I tried that, and it doesn't seem to be working." She rubbed the ache between her eyes. "Maybe I'm not cut out to command."

"Oh, but you are. And this is why. You care." Catherine kissed her gently. "You're exactly the right person to lead them."

Rebecca turned her face to Catherine's neck and pressed her lips to the soft skin. She followed with her body, rolling over and pulling Catherine beneath her. Resting on her elbows, one thigh between Catherine's, she gazed into the tender, knowing eyes that never failed to welcome her. It took her by surprise, every time, how quickly the comfort of Catherine's gentle strength could transform into wanting.

Feeling the sensuous rise of Catherine's hips and the light brush of nipples against her own, Rebecca forgot everything except the heat rising within. When Catherine stroked her breasts, her abdomen, the swell of her hips, she let herself be carried beyond thought on the tides of their singular desire. Surrendering to the pull of Catherine's mouth and the rush of fingers over her skin, Rebecca closed her eyes as Catherine claimed her, abandoning control as the knowing touch found the places that made her weak, made her gasp, made her cry out with the swift surge of pleasure rising too quickly to crest and break.

"Now there's only you," Rebecca murmured, riding the surge of excitement that gathered deep in her stomach and poured down her thighs, drowning her in pleasure. "Ah, Catherine, you're making me come."

Catherine watched, awestruck, as Rebecca arched above her, braced on trembling arms, shuddering on the brink of orgasm. *So terribly defenseless, so terribly precious.* "I love you."

Rebecca's eyes flickered open, her usually piercing gaze glazed and unfocused. "I need...you. So much."

"I'm here," Catherine whispered, sliding her fingers from the pulsating clitoris, moving lower, inside, taking possession of what was hers. "And here." She thrust deeper, and Rebecca tensed, poised to shatter. "And...here."

As Catherine caught the skin below Rebecca's jaw in her teeth, the sharp edge of pain cut through the deep well of pleasure, and Rebecca lost her tenuous grip on control. "Oh God, don't... go."

Catherine pulled Rebecca into her arms as she came, cradling her while the breath tore from her on a hoarse cry of fulfillment. "I'm here, I'm here," she soothed, over and over until Rebecca relaxed in her embrace.

"Happy now?" Rebecca finally muttered, her voice drowsy with contentment.

"Mmm, I was *happy* before," Catherine murmured, her hand in Rebecca's hair, drawing the thick strands through her fingers. "Now I'm just downright pleased with myself."

"You should be." Rebecca tried to move, and found that she couldn't. Her muscles wouldn't obey her. "Damn. You feel so good, and I still need to go out."

Catherine nodded, loving the way Rebecca sheltered in her arms, so unguarded, so very much hers. "Stay just a while longer?"

"Well." Rebecca eased onto her side, smoothing her palm down Catherine's abdomen. The muscles flickered and danced beneath her fingers. "I suppose I could be persuaded."

"Oh?" Catherine asked thickly, her mind already losing focus. She'd been aroused for so long, and now with Rebecca touching her, the need burst upon her, bright and hard. She ached. "What would it take?"

"Just say please." Rebecca's hand stroked lightly between Catherine's thighs.

"Oh. Please."

CHAPTER FOURTEEN

Sandy sat hunched on the edge of Mitchell's bed, her elbows on her knees, her chin resting in her hands, intently watching Jasmine sorting through the clothes in Mitchell's closet. Mitchell stood across the room, her backside against the front corner of an oak desk, eyeing Jasmine speculatively, her expression a mixture of trepidation and curiosity. Sandy divided her attention between surreptitiously studying Mitchell's bedroom, which was almost as big as her entire apartment, and Mitchell herself. She'd rarely had the opportunity to just look at the young cop, and now, awaiting whatever magic or illusion Jasmine could create, she mused on the outcome.

What would Mitchell look like as a man? She wasn't tall— just a bit above average height and well built. Her shoulders were nicely developed, her hips and thighs toned and tight. That would help. But more than her body, there was her face. Chin and cheekbones boldly sketched by a few strong lines, large, deep-set eyes, a generous mouth. A visage that on a woman was called beautiful, on a man—handsome. Her dark hair, as close to black as hair could be, was just beyond short, and thick. *Combed the right way—yeah, that could work. And of course, she doesn't have to look like a guy; she has to look like a really good drag king. And the best kings usually look* better *than the average guy. Yeah, Dell can do that.*

"What do you think?" Jasmine asked, addressing Sandy as she turned from the closet with a pale blue silk shirt in one hand and a pair of dark trousers and matching jacket in the other. "Maybe add a tie?"

Sandy studied the very nice suit. *Yeah, Dell would look hot in that. She'd look just like the kinda guy who'd own this place, too—like one of those Center City business types who like to get blown on their lunch hour in a back booth at Woody's. And totally out of place at Ziggie's.* She shook her head. "Too uptown. She'll fit in better if she just looks like a boy version of herself."

"What do you mean?" Mitchell asked, uneasy.

"She's right," Jasmine said, casting Sandy an appreciative glance. "We can't just dress you up and expect it to work. You still have to be as naturally *you* as possible." She put the clothes back. "Look. When you see a stranger on a bus or on the street, and you can't immediately tell the gender, what do you look for?"

"Breasts," Sandy said immediately. "Or not."

"Item number one," Jasmine agreed, giving a smile of approval. She perused Mitchell's chest. "We can handle that."

Mitchell blushed and did not look at Sandy.

"Whiskers." Sandy's eyes danced with amusement.

"I am *not* pasting on a fake mustache," Mitchell blurted.

"I agree," Jasmine affirmed. "Too much chance for it to come loose, especially if you're kissing."

Sandy made a faint hissing sound.

"Plus..." Jasmine continued unperturbed, "it's hard to get beards and mustaches to look natural unless you have a lot of practice. We don't have that much time." She nodded to Sandy. "What else?"

Sandy hesitated for just a second. "A cock."

"Yep." Jasmine tilted her head in Mitchell's direction. "Do you by any chance have—"

"No." The word came out sharp and hard. *Christ, I don't even have sex.*

"Let's work on the clothes first, then," Jasmine said, sensing Mitchell's discomfort.

"Can *I* look?" Sandy asked, getting up and crossing the polished hardwood floor to the double-wide closet.

"Sure," Mitchell said, resigned to having little say in the process.

A minute later, Sandy handed Jasmine first a pair of soft, well-worn black leather pants, then a snowy white T-shirt, and finally a pair of scuffed black motorcycle boots with heavy heels and a wide strap across the arch. "Have you got a jacket to go with the rest of this, Dell?"

"Yeah."

"I don't suppose you have a bike, too?"

"Yeah."

Sandy looked at Jasmine. "Well?"

"The guys at the Troc will die of envy." Jasmine laid the clothes on the nearby dresser and turned to Mitchell, her expression suddenly serious. "The first time or two you'll need help wrapping your chest. It's not as simple as it sounds because you don't want the Ace to show under your shirt. Are you okay with me helping you?"

"I...sure." Mitchell shrugged, wondering briefly if it was really Jasmine—or Jason—asking, and then realizing that it didn't matter. She trusted them both. "I do need your help."

"Uh, Jasmine," Sandy asked abruptly, thinking about Mitchell being naked and another girl with her hands on her, "do you...uh... like guys, or girls?"

"Girls." Jasmine gave Sandy an appraising look. *So that's the way it is.* "But I have a *very* steady girlfriend. Mitchell's safe with me."

"Ah, jeez..." Mitchell pulled her shirt from her jeans and began to unbutton it. "Let's just do it."

"I'm gonna get a beer. You got beer, Dell?" Sandy suddenly realized that she didn't want to see Mitchell naked. Or rather, she *did*. A lot. And that was a good reason not to.

"In the fridge. You're not leaving, are you?" Mitchell was relieved that she wasn't going to have to strip down in front of Sandy, but she wanted her to be there. Later.

"Nah. I'll hang out for a while." She walked toward the door and said over her shoulder, "Have fun."

Jasmine opened the small duffle bag she'd carried into the bedroom earlier and extracted a lightweight white cotton Ace wrap. After that, she laid out several other items on the bed, then turned to where Mitchell stood shirtless. Keeping her gaze on Mitchell's face, she approached with the Ace in her hand. "Raise your arms."

Mitchell complied, and Jasmine quickly and expertly wrapped it around Mitchell's chest. She used clear porous tape to smooth down the folds.

"Too tight?"

"No." Mitchell lowered her arms, flexed her shoulders. "Seems okay."

"If you have a problem with it slipping, next time we'll use a little skin adhesive. But I'd rather not, because it itches." She reached for the white T-shirt from the nearby dresser. "Let's see how it lays."

Moving carefully, Mitchell unfolded the shirt.

"Try to forget the Ace. If anything, you've got to expand your movements, not make them smaller. Guys take up a lot of space."

"Like cops." Mitchell smiled and pulled on the T-shirt. "I've had plenty of practice acting like I'm physically bigger than I am."

"I know. That's a big reason why I think this will work—you've already got the walk." Jasmine ran her hand down Mitchell's chest, checking for irregularities or telltale bulges. "Plus, you've got the looks for it. Your face was made for this."

"Like yours?"

Jasmine smiled, surprised. Most people were shy about asking anything about her and Jason, preferring to invent prurient scenarios about who and *why* she was. "I just got lucky with the face. Even if I looked like Vin Diesel, I'd still be wearing a dress."

"Well, I'm glad you look more like Charlize Theron, then."

"Why, thank you, stud." Jasmine took Mitchell's hand and drew her to the bed. "I made a call to one of the boys as soon as the meeting broke up, and he took me on a quick shopping trip. I didn't figure you had any Jockeys."

"Just boxers."

"They won't work. Too loose to secure your drag gear."

"I can see that." Mitchell rubbed the back of her neck as she stared at the *other* items laid out on her bed. If she was going to do it, she needed *all* the equipment, but the array of shapes and sizes was daunting. "Uh...suggestions?"

"Well, I got a few different ones, because I wasn't sure which would be most comfortable for you. You need to wear one big enough to give you a bit of a bulge—that's pretty much required for a drag king. But personally, I don't go for the perpetually hard look. The packing dick is just for show—it won't function, but it won't look like a banana in your pants, either."

Mitchell picked up the pale pink packing dick in its clear plastic envelope and squeezed. It felt real. "No harness with this either, right?"

"Nope. It'll fit right in your Jockeys."

"Well, this one should do, because I'm not gonna need it to work." Mitchell thought about Sandy's accusation earlier. *Does that include fucking one of them, too?*

"Uh—if you're going out with the boys after a show, especially to Ziggie's, you might want the strap-on. Some of the drag kings *do* pick up girls when they're out clubbing. So you might want to at least *look* like you're up for it." Jasmine laughed. "In a manner of speaking."

"Okay. I'll keep them all then." Mitchell kept her face expressionless as she unzipped her jeans and pushed them down over her hips.

Jasmine turned and walked to the floor-to-ceiling windows on the opposite side of the spacious room. Keeping her back to Mitchell, she remarked, "You've got an incredible view of the square from here. Of all of downtown, really."

"Yeah," Mitchell replied as she pulled the leather pants up and settled herself. "Okay."

Jasmine turned. Mitchell stood with hips thrust slightly forward, a thumb hooked over the top of her pants, her fingers splayed across the leather pants, close to but not quite touching the subtle but definite swelling to the right of her fly.

"Well, *Mitch,*" Jasmine said quietly, "I'm having a gender confusion moment."

Mitchell laughed a bit shakily. "Good. So am I."

"Ookaay." Jasmine took a deep breath, wondering briefly how Sarah would feel about a full-out cross-dressing date. Mitchell, just beyond androgynous now, was Eros personified. "Time for the final touches. Bring that chair into the bathroom. I need good light for this."

A minute later, Mitchell sat, automatically sliding a hand up the inside of her thigh to cup her crotch, adjusting for the new position.

"Good move," Jasmine murmured, running her fingers through

Mitchell's thick hair. "Men and drag kings are fond of frequent manual dick checks." She laughed. "Lest it disappear."

"Should be fun on the bike," Mitchell muttered. The unaccustomed pressure between her thighs that escalated intermittently with every small movement was disturbingly arousing. Even more unexpected was the fact that she felt not just physically stimulated, but emotionally excited. Her entire body was tingling, and she couldn't wait for Sandy to see her. *Oh man. What if she doesn't like it? Jesus Christ. What if she does?*

"Are you and Sandy an item?" Jasmine asked as she altered the arch of Mitchell's dark brows with several adept strokes of the eyebrow brush.

Mitchell met Jasmine's eyes in the mirror. "No. Why?"

"Just curious. She's cute."

"Yeah. She is." Mitchell grinned. "Major."

"Uh-huh," Jasmine murmured, switching to a wider brush and picking up a dark shade of toner. As she accentuated the width of Mitchell's naturally strong jaw, she added, "And she's hot for you."

Mitchell twitched. Everywhere.

"Hold still, Mitch." Jasmine worked quickly, efficiently, subtly changing the balance of Mitchell's face with a minimal amount of cosmetics. "You'll be able to do this yourself with just a little practice. Are you paying attention?"

"No." Mitchell worked to steady her breathing. *I'm trying not to think about Sandy.* "You think?"

"If you can't do the make-up, I'm sure Sandy can. I'll run through it with her later." Jasmine dropped a dab of gel into her palm and rubbed her hands together, then massaged it into Mitchell's hair. "Do I think *what,* stud?"

"That Sandy's...you know, interested."

Jasmine laughed. "I thought she was going to relieve me of a few body parts when she figured out I was going to be touching you, sans clothes."

"Yeah?" Mitchell shifted her hips, hoping to ease the faint and distracting throbbing. The conversation was not helping. "Frye warned her off me."

"That's SOP, Mitchell. You know that."

Mitchell stared at Jasmine in the mirror. For just a minute, she'd heard Jason's voice. Jason, who'd been with Sloan at Justice. Jason, who'd walked into a room with an unknown perp, unarmed and without backup. "You think she's right?"

"Frye's a by-the-book cop and an A-one detective. She's also your boss. If she's noticed something going on between you two, you ought to be careful." Jasmine patted Mitchell's cheek. "The rules are there for a reason. If you're gonna break them, make sure you've got a *better* reason, and be smart about it. Which means keep your eyes open when you're with Sandy."

"There's nothing going on."

"Uh-*huh.*" Jasmine walked around from behind the chair and held out her hand, then pulled the nouveau drag king to his feet. She checked Mitch's beard shadow, ran her eyes over the hard muscled chest, let her eyes drop to the prominence of genitalia nestled in soft dark leather. *Nice.* "Do you want there to be?"

"Want what to be?" Mitch was aware of the languid scrutiny, and unexpectedly, he got hard. *If this keeps happening, I'm going to go nuts.*

"Something to be going on between you and Miss Cutie-Pie."

"Yeah." It felt so good to say.

"Well, then, stud," Jasmine said, taking Mitch's hand, "I think you're about to get your chance."

❖

When she heard footsteps, Sandy looked up from the couch where she'd been nursing her second beer and rifling through a magazine about vintage cars. Jasmine walked into the living room with her arm around the waist of...*Oh fuck,* Dell. *Look at you. You are so, so hot.*

"Sandy, this is Mitch."

Watts's words echoed in Sandy's mind. *You gotta* be *the person twenty-four seven, because if you lose it for just a minute, you'll get made. And then...*

She stood, the beer bottle dangling loosely in her grip, taking in the face, the body, the almost-cocky grin. She couldn't stop herself from checking out his equipment, and when her gaze dropped to the leather-clad crotch, he pushed his hips forward just a bit. Sandy bit her lower lip, holding in a small gasp of surprise.

"Hiya, Sandy." Mitch hoped his nervousness didn't show. She hadn't said a word, and he couldn't tell if she liked it or not. *Maybe she doesn't go for drag; maybe she doesn't go for* girls *any way at all. Christ, maybe she's straight. Mayb—*

Well, if he's *my* boyfriend, *time to prove it.* Sandy put the bottle on the coffee table and walked directly to Mitch, not stopping until her breasts nearly touched his chest. Wordlessly, she leaned over, plucked Jasmine's hand from around his waist, took Mitch's arm, and tugged him away a step. Then she stood on her tiptoes and kissed his mouth. Long enough to get him to open his lips, long enough for her tongue to brush his. She felt him along the length of her body, the lean thighs, the flat chest and abdomen, the firm swell of his sex. But it was his lips that held her attention. They were gentle on her mouth, tender and careful in their explorations. *Dell. Always so gentle.*

Mitch's head spun wildly. He had imagined a lot of reactions when Sandy saw him, but not this. His first thought, before the incredible feel of her mouth drove every other thought from his burning brain, was that she was only kissing him because he was a guy. But then he felt her lips urging him to open, firm and certain and free, and somehow Mitch knew that this was not what Sandy did when she was with men. This was something special, just between them. Then he couldn't think at all because his heart was pounding so loudly and his insides were turning over and his legs were shaking too badly to do anything but struggle to stay upright. *And God, can she kiss!*

"So, *boyfriend*," Sandy said calmly after she broke the kiss, "you promised me pizza."

Jasmine laughed, shaking her head in delight and admiration for Sandy's aplomb. "Mitch, love, if that's the way she asks for pizza, you might want to go for Le Bec-Fin next time." She picked up her duffle and headed for the door. "Sandy, call me tomorrow at Sloan's. I want to talk to you about dressing him. Unless you want me to keep doing it."

Sandy didn't take her eyes from Mitch's face. "I'll take care of him."

I just bet you will. Jasmine let herself out, her soft laughter drifting back to them.

"Is it okay?" Mitch asked quietly when they were alone. He still hadn't moved, and neither had Sandy.

"You look great."

"You okay calling me Mitch?"

Sandy shook her head, exasperated. "You *are* Mitch. You have to be, or else you're going to get your Boy Scout ass killed." She took Mitch's hand and squeezed. "You told Frye you could do this, and I'm starting to believe it. So *do* it, rookie."

"Why did you kiss me?"

Sandy smiled a small, secretive smile. "Because you looked a little nervous, and that's not how you need to look. You need to look tough and sure, and I figured a kiss would get you on track." *And because you looked so good I just had to.*

"I'm not nervous now." Mitch's voice was low, husky. He wanted to kiss her again, and this time he wanted to touch her. He'd wanted to touch her for so long.

"Then it worked." Sandy dared a quick peek into Mitch's eyes. They were that dark, dark blue again. Hazy and hot. She liked knowing that look was for her. But she wasn't ready for more. No one had touched her that way, ever. Not with the tenderness of Mitch's mouth and Dell's eyes. "You gonna feed me or not?"

"Yeah." Mitch's throat ached with wanting her, but he'd always known it would be on her terms. It would have to be. She hadn't ended up on the streets because life had been kind to her. He turned away and walked to a coat closet next to the front door. He pulled out his leather jacket, shrugged into it, and then held open a second, softer brown one. "It's getting cold at night now."

Sandy hesitated and then turned to let Mitch slide the coat over her arms. For just a second, she leaned back against him. She felt the quicksilver brush of lips against her neck, and she shivered. "Thanks."

"Come on, *girlfriend,*" Mitch murmured close to Sandy's ear. "Let's go get that pizza."

CHAPTER FIFTEEN

Sloan closed her eyes and rubbed her face wearily. The symbols on the screen had blurred to the point where she knew she'd miss something critical soon. She was alone in the CSI lab, and the quiet colluded with her exhaustion to lull her into torpor. Turning her head, she opened her eyes and focused on the large plain-faced clock on the far wall. Only twelve-forty. She was used to working long hours, and she shouldn't be tired, not at a little after midnight. Except, of course, for the fact that she'd had almost no sleep for four nights running.

She *had* managed a few fitful hours earlier in the evening, curled up with Michael in bed. Until dreams and demons had jolted her awake and she'd almost awakened Michael with her frantic attempts to assure herself that Michael was alive and breathing quietly by her side.

"What's wrong?" Michael murmured drowsily as Sloan's hands coursed rapidly over her body. "Sloan? Love?"

"Nothing," Sloan said hoarsely, breathing hard, forcing herself to lie back against the pillows. Her heart was pounding so hard she was afraid Michael would feel it. "Go back to sleep."

"You're trembling." Michael moved to sit up and then gasped at the sharp lancet of pain that pierced her temple. "God, this rotten headache."

It was the first time Sloan could remember Michael complaining, and she realized that most of the time since Michael had regained consciousness, she'd been taking care of her. Nice, Sloan. Selfish bastard.

"Dr. Torveau gave me a prescription for pain pills for you." Sloan swung her legs over the side of the bed. "I'll get you a glass

of water, and you can take a couple of them."

Michael stopped her with a hand on Sloan's arm. "No. I don't want them. I hate painkillers. They make me so groggy."

"Just this once, okay, baby?" Sloan could see the pain in Michael's eyes. Knowing she hurt made Sloan ill herself. Her stomach churned and her chest ached. Without the slightest bit of guilt, she tried the only ploy that she knew without doubt would work. "Will you do it for me?"

Michael sighed. "All right, just this once—and only if you stay with me and rest. You're worn out, Sloan. I can tell."

"Deal." Sloan kissed her and went to fetch the pills.

When Michael fell back to sleep with her head cushioned on Sloan's shoulder, Sloan lay listening to her lover's even, pain-free breathing until she was certain that the pills were working and that Michael would not awaken. Then she gently eased away from her and slid carefully from their bed. She dressed in the dark and opened by feel the small lockbox built into the closet floor. The weapon she assembled by touch, and that only took a few seconds. Then she clipped the holster to the back of her jeans, settled the automatic into it, and stole quietly from the loft.

"One more scan," Sloan muttered to herself, "then I'll call it quits for the night."

She opened the root directory and searched for the activity log from the time period in question. Data scrolled by, all routine. So routine, in fact, that she almost *did* miss it. A password query, a series of them, and then a password change—followed by file access.

Sloan jolted upright, her attention totally focused, her mind now absolutely clear. Fingers flying over the keyboard, she was quickly immersed in the data stream, functioning on a subconscious level, guided by the intuitive logic leaps that only the master hackers ever attained. She was on the trail of her quarry, and she was close.

❖

Mitch looked around the small, dark, empty apartment. "I'll be fine here tonight."

"Fuck that. You're sleeping at my place." Sandy tugged his arm toward the door. "There's no furniture in here. What are you gonna do, crash on the floor?"

"I'll get a few things tomorrow. I won't need that much."

"Yeah, well, I'm talking about tonight. You are *not* staying here."

Ignoring the fact that he'd never won an argument with Sandy yet, Mitch was too tired to argue. It had been nerve-wracking being out in public with her, even though they had hung out in the Tenderloin around Thirteenth and Arch where just about anything goes. No one had seemed to pay them any attention as they'd walked around, Mitch with his arm around Sandy's waist, Sandy with a thumb hooked over his belt in the back. Despite their apparent anonymity, Mitch had been on constant alert, and the tension had given him a headache. And that was only part of the problem. For three hours, Sandy had been all over him, and it was driving him crazy.

When they got to the pizzeria at Eleventh and Sansom, they ambled to a back booth and took off their jackets. Sandy slid in on Mitch's side, instead of across from him as usual, and leaned against him.

"Help ya?" a heavyset woman on the down side of forty asked in a bored voice a few seconds later.

"A small chee—" Mitch's voice cracked as he felt a hand travel up the inside of his thigh. He made a grab for it under the table, trying to keep his face blank. "Cheese...pizza."

"Drink?" If the waitress saw anything, it apparently wasn't anything new, because she didn't even raise an eyebrow.

"Two beers," Sandy said sweetly as she rubbed her right breast against Mitch's bare arm. The light friction made her nipple harden under the thin cotton, and her smile widened as she heard Mitch gasp.

"Coming right up," the woman said flatly and lumbered away.

"What the fuck are you doing?" Mitch snapped as soon as the waitress was out of earshot.

"Hey, you're my boyfriend, right?" Sandy replied

disingenuously, refusing to let him move her hand from his crotch. "I'm just, you know, acting natural."

"Cut it out." Sandy's fingers were an inch from his cock. It was going to be a big problem if she started fooling with that because he had a feeling she could make him come. Easily. Right there. "Sandy, come on. I'm having a hard time here."

Sandy leaned back and peered into his eyes, serious for an instant. "How come? Is it—you know—uncomfortable?"

Mitch grinned, a frustrated grin. "Yeah, you could say that. And you're not helping."

"You're such a guy," Sandy scoffed. "I'm not even touching it, for Christ's sake."

"But I've been touching you," Mitch said softly. "That's enough."

Sandy's lips formed a soundless oh. She stopped fighting Mitch's restraining hand and moved hers further down his thigh, away from his crotch. "You know, you are maybe the sexiest person I've ever met."

"Is it...just tonight?" Mitch glanced down at the swelling in his crotch, and Sandy followed his gaze.

"No, stupid. It is not just tonight." Sandy rolled her eyes. "It's every night."

Mitch breathed a little easier.

"What? Did you think it's just because of what you've got in your pants?" Sandy's voice was sharp edged and hard. "You think that's what I want?"

"I—" Mitch looked away.

"Oh, man. You are such a blockhead. Like I can't get enough cock if I wanted it." Sandy smiled up at the waitress who stood holding their beers, listening intently now. "Thank you so much."

"Sure, honey." She glanced from Mitch to Sandy, then shrugged and walked away.

Sandy sipped her beer, then regarded Mitch steadily. "It wasn't my idea we start dating. But it's no hardship, okay?"

Mitch saw the smile in her eyes and smiled back. "Same here."

"Good. So act like you're having fun."

Oh. I'm having fun. I'm having a lot more than that. *Mitch put his hand over Sandy's where it rested on his thigh and drew it a little higher. "Anything you say."*

And for the next two hours, Sandy had proceeded to touch him every chance she could. She rubbed her hand up and down his back while they walked, squeezed his butt from time to time, and sidled up to him when they stopped to look in the window of a video store, her pelvis pressed to his hip, her breasts against his arm, her fingers stroking his abdomen just above his pants. When they ended the evening in a neighborhood bar because Sandy had said it would be good for them to be seen together, she'd practically climbed into his lap. All of which had left his nerves shattered and his body screaming for relief.

Much more of *anything* from her, and he was going to come out of his skin.

"Okay, fine," Mitch conceded as they walked down the short dingy hall and into the startling warm oasis of Sandy's apartment. "I'll crash on *your* floor. At least it's clean."

Sandy regarded him steadily. "You can sleep with me."

She turned and pulled out the sleeper bed. It was neatly made up with bright sheets and a blanket. She pulled the covers back and lifted two pillows from a low shelf on the other side.

"I can't." Mitch's voice was low, nearly mournful.

"Why not?"

"Sandy, for God's sake." *Jesus, she never makes anything easy.* "I'm gay."

Sandy's smile when she looked back at the handsome drag king was oddly tender. "No foolin'. So? Can't you be good?"

"Usually." Mitchell blew out a frustrated breath, rubbing at the restraining Ace on her chest. *I want you to touch me so bad. If you're next to me...*"But not tonight. I'm so wound up...I...I just don't think I can."

"Well, I'm not worried." Sandy took a step closer, which in the tiny room brought them within touching distance. "And I'm not scared."

Mitchell's heart tripled-timed. "Well, *I* am."

"Does that hurt?" Sandy asked with concern, pointing to Mitchell's chest. "You've been rubbing it."

"Itches."

Sandy took Mitchell's hand. "Come over here and sit down."

"Sandy..."

"Be quiet, Dell," Sandy said as she put both hands on Mitchell's shoulders and gently forced her down on the edge of the bed. Then she knelt between Mitchell's legs and reached for the bottom of the white T-shirt. Her belly brushed the leather between Mitchell's thighs.

"I'm so turned on," Mitchell confessed in a whisper. "You're making me so nuts, I can't stand it."

"Good."

When Sandy pulled the shirt from her pants, Mitchell closed her eyes and leaned back on her elbows, unable to do anything but surrender. Her stomach was in knots, her skin on fire, her clitoris full and hard and pounding. Whatever this was, whatever this wasn't—no matter what anyone said—she needed it. Needed Sandy's small hands on her, needed that warm mouth...

"Oh Jesus," Mitchell moaned as Sandy leaned forward and kissed her abdomen. "Your lips are so soft."

"Mmm, so's your skin," Sandy murmured, licking a circle around the tight navel. Her breasts rested against Mitchell's fly, and she rubbed them back and forth slowly as she worked her lips over the taut muscles. "You taste good."

The weight of Sandy's body pressing into Mitchell's crotch forced the firm form in her pants harder against her straining flesh. Discomfort became acute stimulation, and her clitoris twitched with warning spasms.

"Wait...wait a second," Mitchell uttered in desperation, one hand cradling Sandy's cheek, the other reaching for the fly of her leathers. "Let me get this out of here."

Sandy grasped her hand and looked up. "Leave it for a little while. It's sexy."

Mitchell blushed and met Sandy's eyes. "It's not...it won't work."

"I don't need it to work, idiot." Sandy pulled the T-shirt over Mitchell's head and reached for the tape holding the Ace wrap in place. "I know who you are, Dell."

Mitchell looked down as Sandy carefully released her breasts, the blond head bent over her naked flesh. With trembling fingers, Mitchell stroked Sandy's cheek, then ran her thumb over the full pink lips. Sandy bit the tip of her thumb, and Mitchell's thighs tightened. When Sandy brushed her fingers over her nipples, Mitchell tensed and cried out. "Oh, that feels so good."

"Yeah," Sandy's breath came faster, her hands shaking as she flattened her palms over the small firm breasts, massaging them gently, then cradling both, her thumbs moving automatically back to the tight pink nipples. Moaning in surprise, she felt herself get wet. She hadn't really expected that. All night, she'd told herself she was just playing with Mitch to get him used to being treated like a guy. But she'd enjoyed it—more than enjoyed it. She hadn't wanted to admit it, but she'd been hot all night. And she wanted Dell now, wanted her the way she hadn't thought herself capable of wanting anyone—not this way—not in her body, in her blood. "Oh yeah, you feel *so* fucking good."

Through eyes gone dim with arousal, Mitchell watched Sandy suck a hard nipple into her mouth, and the sight and sensation drove her close to the edge. She pushed her hips into Sandy, and Sandy thrust back, soft cries escaping her now, too. "Sandy...Sandy...that's gonna make me come."

Sandy lifted her head, laughing wildly, her eyes glittering with exhilaration. "No way, rookie. You'll come when I want you to come."

Lids flickering closed, Mitchell arched her back and lifted her hips. The first tremors of orgasm teased along her spine. "No...I'm com..."

With both hands, Sandy pushed Mitchell back on the bed and quickly shifted away, knowing that the pressure of her body was too much for Mitchell to handle. "Dell," she said firmly, moving from between Mitchell's legs and stretching out beside her. "Come on, Dell, look at me."

Whimpering faintly, dangling on the brink of exploding, Mitchell turned her head and sought Sandy's gaze. "Please, Sandy... please."

"Mmm," Sandy murmured, leaning close, her hand on Mitchell's abdomen now, slowly circling. "You are so sexy when you're hot, you know that? I wanna keep you this way for a while."

"I'm gonna die..." Mitchell ached for the feel of skin against her skin, for Sandy's flesh beneath her hands. She still hadn't touched Sandy, and Sandy had not removed her clothes. "Will you let me touch you?"

She asks? Sandy's eyes grew wide, her lips parting in a combination of surprise and desire. "Oh, Dell—"

They both jerked as a shrill ring pierced the room. Mitchell stiffened as Sandy cursed.

"Motherfucker."

"What is it?" Mitchell asked, her stomach so tight with unrequited need she thought she'd be sick.

"My phone." Sandy's voice was wild.

"Ignore it." Mitchell drew Sandy's hand down to her fly and pressed her fingers to the swelling there. She whimpered; she couldn't help it. "Please."

The sound shrilled again.

"No—it's my *phone*. Jesus Christ." Sandy was having trouble thinking clearly. She was so excited her brain was mush. "*Frye's* phone. That's her calling."

Mitchell went cold. "She *gave* you a *phone?*"

Sandy pulled away, her eyes narrowing as she stared at Mitchell. "Yes, she gave me a phone."

The phone rang a third time and Sandy lunged for her purse. "Yeah, what?" she snapped, trying to sound normal while her entire body was about to melt.

"How you doin', Sandy?"

"Peachy." Sandy glared at Mitchell, who had sat up and was pulling on her T-shirt in quick angry motions.

"Did you get Mitchell squared away?"

"Yeah." Sandy laughed without humor. *Oh yeah, I took care of her all right.* Fuck.

"I have money for you."

"Give it to Mitchell. She put up the rent."

"I will, tomorrow. I have money for you tonight."

Sandy took a long breath. She needed that money to pay her own rent. She followed Mitchell with her eyes as the cop rose a bit unsteadily and walked into the bathroom, slamming the door behind her. "Yeah. Okay."

"Plus I still need the street intel on those filmmakers. You owe me a lead."

"You always want something, don't you, Frye?"

"We have a deal."

"Okay. When?"

"How about right now?"

Sandy panicked. "You can't come up here."

"I wasn't going to." A beat of silence. "What's the matter? You got someone up there with you?"

Oh no, just Dell with a hard-on and pissed as hell. Jesus, she'd probably go for your throat right now. Sandy made a fast decision. "A john."

The bathroom door opened. Mitchell stepped out, her face free of make-up, a small plastic bag she'd found in Sandy's cabinet in her hand. She stuffed the bag with her drag gear into the inside pocket of her motorcycle jacket, her eyes on Sandy.

"That wasn't the deal. You work for me, you don't turn tricks."

"So sue me."

"I could come over and bother your *company.*"

"Look, I'll meet you right now."

Another pause. "Okay. Woody's, in the back room."

Sandy laughed bitterly. "Perfect." She closed the phone and faced Mitchell. "I have to go out."

"She calls and you jump?" Acid burned in her stomach where moments ago it had been desire. "She that good?"

"You're a jerk." Sandy gathered her small purse and headed for the door.

"Take my jacket."

Sandy pulled a tiny royal blue satin zip-up top from the coat tree by her door and slipped it on. When she turned, her face was a mask. "Don't you know by now that they don't buy what they can't see?"

Mitchell paled. "Sandy..."

But she was talking to a closed door.

CHAPTER SIXTEEN

Woody's was a neighborhood bar that had once been almost exclusively gay, but it had gradually morphed into a place where anyone could find their particular flavor of sexual partners. Despite the fact that it was midweek, the place was crowded. It was also noisy and smoky. With only a few minutes until closing, almost everyone was too interested in finishing their last drink or ensuring their latest conquest to notice Sandy.

She quickly threaded her way through the crowd clustered around the bar for last call and walked into the dark recesses at the rear. Frye was seated at a tiny table in the back room. It occurred to Sandy as she approached that Frye and Mitchell dressed a lot alike when they were off duty—tight blue jeans, boots, and leather jackets. Frye was taller and thinner and had a hardness around her eyes that Mitchell didn't have.

Dell will get it, though. She's already got those shadows in her eyes, cop's eyes.

It hurt to think of Mitchell, and she pushed the thought away as she dropped into the seat across from the handsome blond detective. "Funny place for a meeting, unless you're looking to get laid. You looking for some action? 'Cause I'm free now, thanks to you."

Rebecca ignored the taunts. Sandy's anger was one thing she counted on, and she had a feeling it was a big part of what kept Sandy from being swallowed by the street. "You get rid of your *visitor?*"

Oh yeah, I got rid of her all right. Left her high and dry and hurting. She could still feel the heat of Mitchell's anger mingled with the waves of frustration and pain. Despite the ten-block walk, her own body still resonated with arousal. Despondently, she wondered if Mitchell would seek comfort somewhere else that night.

"What do you think? I left him at my place?" Sandy tried not to think about where Mitchell had gone, what she was doing. "You gonna be calling all the time now? It cramps my style."

"You're not supposed to have a *style* any longer, remember?" Rebecca studied the young blond. It was always difficult to tell what was happening with Sandy. There was a wounded look in her eyes, which was rare. She usually hid her feelings much better behind that wall of bravado and sarcasm. *She's not your responsibility, so let it go.* "We can't afford to meet out in the open anymore. The less we're seen together, the better."

"You didn't use to worry about rousting me on the street."

"Things are different now. Before, if anyone noticed, it just looked like I was hassling you, which is what people expect cops to do to prostitutes." Rebecca fell silent until two men squeezed past their table and disappeared into the dark shadows behind them. "But now that we have a *long-term* relationship, it's important that people not put us together. And if you're going around with Mitchell, it's even more important."

Sandy's heart twisted at the sound of Mitchell's name, wondering just how long *their* new relationship—whatever it was—was going to last. "Yeah, well, we don't want to blow her cover."

"No, we don't. Besides, you won't be much use to me if some john takes his fists to you." Every night as she drove the streets, she watched women, some barely in their teens, selling their bodies to survive, knowing there was nothing she could do to change their fates. She tried, and would probably keep trying—scanning the faces, looking for likenesses to the blurred images on the missing persons bulletins, taking those she could convince to leave the life to shelters or women's centers—but it was a never-ending battle doomed to failure. Every day there were more of them. Why Sandy meant more to her than any of the others, she couldn't say. "I have an investment in you, and I expect you to take care of yourself."

"I've managed just fine so far."

"Yeah—that new scar on your forehead is proof of that. Someone beat the living hell out of you, didn't they?"

"It was nothing. I could have handled it even if Dell—" Sandy clamped her jaws shut. *Shit!*

Rebecca's eyes narrowed. "What does Mitchell have to do with it?"

"Nothing."

"Her life is on the line, Sandy. Don't fuck with me, I don't have time." Rebecca's tone was harsh, not with anger, but worry. *What in hell have I missed?*

"I told you, it was noth..." Sandy remembered that night—remembered the fear and the pain. She took a deep breath. "A guy was roughing me up. Dell stopped him."

"Stopped him how?"

"Like cops do—she took the fucker down and arrested him."

"That's it?"

Sandy looked away.

"Sandy, please."

The request startled Sandy. Cops never asked for anything; they just took what they wanted. *But Dell asked.* Will it be all right if I touch you? *And this is about Dell. About keeping her safe.*

"Dell got into trouble for it...because she pulled her gun and got rough or something."

And the pieces tumbled into place. Mitchell on suspension. Mitchell undergoing counseling—mandatory in situations like that. Catherine and Mitchell—Catherine who must have known all about it. *How much hasn't Catherine told me?*

"Okay. Thanks."

Uncomfortable, Sandy shrugged. "So you said you had money for me?"

Rebecca reached into the inside pocket of her jacket, withdrew an envelope, and slid it halfway between them. She kept it covered with her hand. "I need you to find an Asian girl named Lucy."

"Lucy what?"

"No last name—"

"Come on, Frye. Do you how many Asian Lucys there are?"

"She's about sixteen, taller than most Asian girls, and she might work for Angel Rivera."

"Angel's a mean pimp." Sandy's eyes grew hard. "He hooks his girls on smack to keep them working."

"I know that," Rebecca said, her anger barely contained. *And I'd love to put him away, or kick the crap out of him, but he always manages to slip through some crack in the system.* "I want you to stay far away from him. Just talk to some of his girls."

"What did this chick do?"

"I didn't say she *did* anything. I tried showing the picture of the girl from the video around Chinatown. I thought maybe she was a runaway and someone might know her." Rebecca sighed in an unusual show of frustration. Four hours in and out of every bodega and restaurant in a ten-block area and one slim lead to show for it. "No one knew her, but someone said they thought maybe she was a friend of this Lucy."

"That's kinda thin, don't you think?"

"It's what I've got." Rebecca looked at her watch. "It's closing time. We should leave before the lights come up. I need this soon, Sandy."

"Sure, *boss*. Anything you say."

Rebecca slid the envelope across the table, and Sandy automatically covered Rebecca's hand with her own. The detective quickly withdrew, and Sandy palmed the envelope into her purse.

"Where's Mitchell now?" Rebecca asked.

That twist of pain was unexpected, and Sandy jerked involuntarily. To cover her surprise, she laughed harshly. "How should I know? You're the one told me to stay away from her, remember?"

"Things have changed." Rebecca leaned forward intently. "Listen to me. Jasmine can't be with her all the time. None of us can be. She's good, but she doesn't know the streets like you do. I need you to watch her back."

"So what do you want me to do? Move in with her?"

"If you have to."

Sandy stood. "You know something, Frye? You use people."

Rebecca made no reply and Sandy walked away.

You use people.

It wasn't the first time she'd heard it, although not quite as honestly as Sandy put it. Jill had complained that Rebecca put the job first and gave her what was left—which was never enough. Rebecca thought of Catherine, and how much she needed her.

How she so often came to Catherine, weary and drained, and let Catherine comfort her with her body and her tender soul. *I use her, too.*

Rebecca looked at her watch again. *Five minutes till closing. Still time for a fast drink.*

She stood, walked to the bar, and surveyed the rows of bottles lined up on small shelves in front of the mirror. Johnnie Walker Black. A sure remedy for frustration and disappointment. A quick treatment for loneliness and despair. An easy cure for self-loathing.

"What'll you have?"

Rebecca met the bartender's questioning gaze. Her voice was steady but she was trembling inside. "Nothing, thanks. I'm going to go home instead."

He looked at her as if what she had said made perfect sense. "Probably a good idea."

"Yes. It is." She left a five on the bar and held the image of Catherine's face firmly in her mind as she walked away.

❖

Catherine rarely slept deeply when Rebecca was working. She rolled over and opened her eyes, having been roused by a soft noise in the darkened room.

"Rebecca?"

"I'm sorry. I was trying to be quiet." Rebecca padded across the floor and slipped naked into bed. She turned on her side and drew Catherine into her arms, burying her face in the sweet softness of her hair.

"Everything all right?" Catherine snuggled closer, sighing with contentment.

"Mmm. I love you so much."

Catherine heard the faint catch in her lover's voice. "Darling? Did something happen?"

"No."

You use people. It was true, and no amount of rationalization would change it. *Catherine, too.* Rebecca shut her eyes tightly, focusing on the swell of Catherine's breasts against her chest and the firm press of thigh between hers. The skin beneath her hands was so warm, so soft. Gentle lips touched her forehead. She swallowed a groan.

"What is it?"

"Nothing. I'm just beat." Rebecca took a long breath. She wasn't going to burden Catherine with more of her guilt. "It's late, love. We should get some sleep."

Catherine hesitated. She knew there was more. She always knew. Rebecca could hide almost everything from everyone, but her body never lied, and when she lay in Catherine's arms, her secrets were revealed. That was one of the things that Catherine loved about being Rebecca's lover. The raw honesty of the physical intimacy they shared.

"I know you're tired." Catherine kissed her forehead again, then her eyelids, then finally her mouth. She let the kiss linger, felt it deepen, sensing Rebecca drawing strength from their joining, as she herself so often found peace. "We'll talk tomorrow."

"Catherine," Rebecca whispered. *I need you so much. I don't know if I could keep going...*

"What, darling?"

"I...you're the best thing in my life. The most important thing." Rebecca smoothed her fingers over Catherine's cheek, along her neck, and then lowered her head to kiss Catherine's breast just above her heart. "I just want you to know that."

"Oh, Rebecca. I do." Catherine pulled her even closer, wishing desperately that she could ease whatever sorrow tormented her. "Believe me, I do."

"I'm so glad." Rebecca closed her eyes and rested her cheek against Catherine's breast. She finally fell asleep, lulled by the steady comfort of her lover's heartbeat.

Catherine lay awake, stroking Rebecca, wondering what hurt had befallen her while she'd been away, while she'd been doing whatever it was she did alone in the night with so very little to protect her. If she could, Catherine would stand between her and all that had hurt her or *would* hurt her, but such protection was beyond her power to give.

"I love you," Catherine breathed, letting that be enough.

❖

Michael rose carefully. She took a step, switched on the bedside lamp, and then took another step. The headache was there, but much less intense. Her stomach was queasy, an aftereffect of the pain pills. The clock read five-thirty. The side of the bed where Sloan had lain was cold.

She went into the bathroom, splashed cold water on her face, and then looked into the mirror for the first time since the accident. She blinked, drew a shaky breath, blinked again.

Thank God Sarah washed my hair, because the rest of me is a fright.

The left side of her face was bruised from temple to jawline, the skin discolored a purplish-green. Her left upper lid was puffy, the sclera of the eye below bright red with blood. Gingerly, she touched the scalp on the left side of her head. It felt boggy to her touch, and there were crusted stitches buried beneath her hair. She tried to remember what the doctor had told her.

Car accident...skull fracture...broken ribs...bruised kidney.

With horrific clarity, she abruptly recalled the conversation with Sarah. Someone had tried to kill Sloan, and she had been hurt instead.

"My God..."

Michael walked back into the bedroom and surveyed the empty bed, her heart pounding. She picked up the phone from the nightstand and pushed the intercom button for the line into the offices downstairs. It rang...ten...fifteen...twenty times. No answer. She tried Sloan's cell phone. An electronic voice announced she could leave a message.

Her mind was racing as she disconnected, her headache returning full force. She started to dial Sarah's number, and then she remembered.

I'll be right here if you need me.

Michael set the phone down and turned hurriedly toward the hall that led from their bedroom into the greater loft space. The sudden change in direction made her stomach lurch, and she gasped, afraid for a moment that she might vomit. When her system settled, she made her way carefully through the loft to the guest room. She halted at the door.

"Sarah?"

A light came on, and Sarah was instantly by her side.

"Michael? What is it? Are you sick?"

"Where's Sloan?"

"I...what?" Sarah took Michael's hand. "You should go back to bed. You're white as a sheet."

Michael looked beyond Sarah to Jason, who was just tying his sweatpants. He looked worried. She stepped around Sarah, her eyes riveted on Jason's face.

"Where is she, Jason?"

"I don't know. Isn't she here?"

"No. She's not downstairs, and she's not answering her phone."

He looked helplessly at Michael. "She said she was going to check on some data for Rebecca."

"You left her alone?" Michael's voice rose with anger and fear. "What were you *thinking?* Someone tried to *kill* her."

"We're pretty sure that was related to the other case."

"Pretty sure? Pretty sure!" Michael's vision dimmed, and a wave of pain rolled through her head and flooded her consciousness. She swayed and Sarah grabbed her arm.

"Michael. Sit down."

"I'm *fine.*" Nevertheless, Michael allowed Sarah to lead her to the bed. She pressed her fingertips to her temple. "I'm sorry." She lifted anguished eyes to Sarah and Jason, who stood side by side a few feet away, both looking distraught. "Someone tried to kill her and almost killed me instead. Don't you realize what she'll do? God, she'll be crazy."

"Ah, hell," Jason muttered.

"What?" Michael asked sharply.

Jason looked to Sarah for guidance but Michael's voice cut through the air.

"*Tell* me. What?"

"She's working on finding the leak in the department—maybe she found it."

Michael's voice was cold and eerily flat. "And it didn't occur to you that she'd go after the person if she did?"

Jason shrugged helplessly. "I figured she'd call me."

"Find her, Jason," Michael ordered. "You find her right now

and bring her home."

❖

Six a.m. Quitting time.

On autopilot, Sandy trudged up the dark narrow stairwell to the third floor. She unlocked her apartment door, stepped inside, and stared at the woman sitting on the side of her bed. For a moment, neither of them spoke. Then Sandy found her voice.

"What would you do if I came home with a john?"

"I don't know," Mitchell said wearily. "Shoot him?"

"Smart. And if it was Frye?"

Mitchell winced. "Shoot myself, I guess."

Sandy took off her jacket, opened her purse, and took out her cell phone. She pushed a button. "Frye's cut off. You're safe." She crossed the room and sat down beside Mitchell, careful not to touch her. "What are you doing here?"

"I wanted to say I was sorry for being an asshole."

"Okay. You said it."

Mitchell curled her fingers over her knees to hide the shakes. She was so fucking tired. She could have left, gone back to her high-rise. And spent the rest of the night wondering, imagining, where Sandy was and what she was doing. But she couldn't bring herself to leave. She didn't *want* to be anywhere else. She just wanted to make things right.

"I didn't have any right to come down on you for leaving last night. I was...I was a little crazy."

"You were a *lot* crazy if you think Frye and I have anything going on."

"I know. I just..." Mitchell drew a long breath. What could she say? *I was so wild for you to touch me I lost my mind? All I could think about was coming?* "I was wrong. I'm sorry."

When Mitchell started to rise, Sandy put a hand on her thigh, stopping her. "I'm sorry for leaving you in a state. I didn't want to."

Mitchell blushed. "Not your fault."

"Oh, yeah?" Sandy bumped Mitchell's shoulder with hers. "I thought it was."

"I was so hot for you," Mitchell whispered, glancing at Sandy with a half-turn of her head. "I couldn't think straight. I didn't know what the fuck I was saying."

"*Was* hot for me?"

"Am." Mitchell took Sandy's hand, caressed it gently. "Have been for quite a while."

"Same here." Sandy leaned her head on Mitchell's shoulder. "You wanna stay?"

"I have to work today."

"Sleep with me a while first?"

"Yeah. I'd like that."

Silently, they both rose, undressing slowly, watching each other in the breaking dawn light. Sandy lifted the covers and slid under, then held them open for Mitchell. The bed was narrow, and they turned to face one another, their bodies lightly touching. Mitchell rested her hand softly on Sandy's hip. Sandy nestled her face close to Mitchell's on the pillow.

"Is it okay if we just..." Sandy shivered. She'd never been this way with anyone. "Is just sleeping okay for now?"

"It's fine." Mitchell's body was doing the all-over tingle thing again, and she was wet. But that was okay. It was good, great. Perfect. "You're really beautiful, you know."

"Dell," Sandy said gently. "You are such a blockhead."

Carefully, Mitchell inched forward and kissed Sandy, a tender whisper of lips brushing lightly. "I know. But you're still beautiful."

CHAPTER SEVENTEEN

Catherine lifted the phone midway through the second ring. "Hello?...Yes, she's right here." She extended the receiver to Rebecca. "It's Jason."

"Frye," Rebecca croaked. She squinted at the clock and groaned. A little after six.

"Sorry, Rebecca...we can't seem to find Sloan."

Rebecca sat up, instantly alert to the anxiety in Jason's voice. "What have you tried?"

"She's not answering her cell, and she's not downstairs. Look, it's probably nothing, but—"

"I'll make a few calls. Where are you?"

"Sloan and Michael's. I'll head down to the office."

"I'll be over." Rebecca hung up and got out of bed. Catherine slipped out her side and reached for a robe.

"Sorry," Rebecca muttered.

"That's all right. What's the matter?"

"Sloan's in the wind." Rebecca frowned, then picked up the phone and dialed the station house. "Cleary?...Frye. Transfer me to CSI, will you?...I know what time it is. Just do it." She listened to the phone ring and said, "Catherine, why don't you go back to bed. I'll be leaving in just a minute."

"The alarm was about to go off anyhow."

Rebecca held up a finger. "Flanagan? Rebecca Frye...I figured you'd be in early...No...no favor. I just wondered if I left something of mine there yesterday—back in your office. The CD-ROM for the computer game I told you I was going to try...No? No sign of it, huh? Well, if you see it, could you give me a call?...No, no problem. Just getting forgetful, I guess...Yeah, thanks."

"Do you think she's in trouble?" Catherine followed Rebecca

into the bathroom and turned on the shower.

"I don't know," Rebecca said as she stepped under the spray, making room for Catherine to get in beside her. "As far as *I* know, we don't have any hard leads, so I don't see how she could be." She reached for the soap and grimaced. "Of course, I seem to be missing more than a few critical pieces of information these days."

Catherine halted in the process of lathering her hair, sensitive to the nuances of frustration laced with anger in Rebecca's tone. *Ah, we're getting to what was bothering her last night.* "Care to share?"

"Well, for starters, I didn't know that Mitchell was seeing you professionally because of a disciplinary action involving *my* CI." Rebecca tried but failed to keep the resentment from her voice.

"Did Officer Mitchell tell you that?" Catherine asked mildly, leaning her head back to rinse.

"No," Rebecca grunted, reaching for a towel as she climbed from the shower. "Sandy did."

"Really?" Catherine accepted the second towel that Rebecca passed to her. "*She* told you?"

"Not exactly." Rebecca's voice was muffled as she dried her face. Then she draped the towel over the towel bar and faced Catherine. "I put it together from things they both said. I'm a detective, remember?"

Catherine smiled softly. "How could I forget?"

"It would have helped me to know about their involvement, Catherine."

"How?"

Annoyance flickered across Rebecca's features. "Because I might not have been so quick to team them up. Jesus Christ—I practically told Sandy to live with Mitchell in order to protect her cover."

"And knowing that they were friends would have changed that?"

"Maybe. I don't know. That's not the point."

"What is, then?"

"I need to know *everything* about my people!" Rebecca turned her back and placed both hands on the edge of the sink, trying to curb her temper. In a low, restrained voice she continued, "I can't afford to make the wrong decision."

"I couldn't...can't...tell you anything about Officer Mitchell." Catherine raised her hand to stroke the rigid back but caught herself. "I know I don't need to explain that."

"Couldn't you have given me some idea?"

"I'm sorry. No." Catherine did touch her then, a soft glide of fingertips over still-moist skin. "I love you."

Rebecca turned, resting her hips against the counter. "Ah, Christ. I love you, too."

"Is Dellon all right?"

"As far as I know. Jasmine and Sandy are working with her to secure her cover." Rebecca grasped Catherine's hand and pulled her into her arms. They were both still nude, and the rush of excitement that always accompanied the touch of Catherine's body to hers raced along her spine. She sighed. "Now I've got to find Sloan."

"Do you really think she's in trouble?"

"Maybe. I probably shouldn't even be using her, the condition she's in. But I needed her." *You use people.* Rebecca rested her cheek against Catherine's temple and closed her eyes. "I have to go."

"I know. Will you call me? I'm planning to go to Sloan's later this morning to work on the profiles, but if I don't see you there..."

"Yes. As soon as I know anything." Rebecca kissed Catherine's forehead and reluctantly let her go.

Standing in the bathroom door, Catherine pulled on her robe and watched Rebecca dress. Every addition to her armor—the suit, the weapon, the badge—seemed to take Rebecca further from her, and distance, much more than anger, was what frightened her. "Are you still upset with me?"

Rebecca paused, her keys in her hand. "I wasn't angry at you. I was angry with myself." She crossed to Catherine and cupped her chin in one palm, lifting her face. "I understand why you didn't tell me about Mitchell. I want circumstances to be different sometimes, but I never want you to be anyone but you. You're everything I need."

"Rebecca Frye," Catherine murmured, slipping her arms

around the detective's waist. "You know just what I need to hear."

"Do I?" Rebecca kissed Catherine possessively. "I'll call you. I love you."

"Be careful, darling," Catherine whispered as Rebecca strode away. Catherine shivered and pulled her robe tighter about her shoulders. The room seemed smaller and somehow colder with Rebecca's sudden departure. "You're everything *I* need, too."

❖

Jason, unshaven in wrinkled clothes, looked up hopefully as Rebecca walked into the central office area just after eight a.m. "Anything?"

"Nothing." Rebecca had never seen him with a hair out of place, even when he'd been lying on the floor with his hands cuffed behind his back, Mitchell's knee between his shoulder blades. "If she was working in Flanagan's lab last night, there's no sign of it on the computer that I could see. Or anywhere else, for that matter."

"There wouldn't be. Sloan is...well, she's the best." He ran a hand over his face. "I should have realized she'd go after whoever hurt Michael on her own. Michael is...everything to her."

Rebecca understood that. That was what she would do if anyone hurt Catherine. She knew it, in her bones, and she had let Sloan work the case just the same. "It's my fault. Not yours."

"I know her bes—"

He cocked his head, listening to the sound of the elevator descending to the first floor, then to the slow steady whir of the machinery reversing. Together, he and Rebecca watched as the double-wide doors slid soundlessly open.

"Sloan!" Jason's voice was tight with relief.

Sloan's eyes were rimmed with dark shadows, her cheeks gaunt, her clothes beyond creased. Her shoulders sagged, and her step was unsteady.

"You hurt?" Rebecca asked sharply.

Sloan shook her head and sat heavily into the nearest chair. "I got him."

"Where have you been?" Rebecca asked almost too casually.

"Sitting outside his house, waiting for him to come out."

Jesus, God. Rebecca's insides turned to ice. "Who?"

"Captain John William Henry."

Rebecca's face never changed expression, but her stomach heaved. With effort, she kept her voice even. "What did you do?"

Sloan looked at her, her eyes slightly unfocused. "I sat across the street with my gun in my lap, locked and loaded, all night. Knew he'd be out early."

"Oh my God!" Jason jumped to his feet. "Sloan, don't say anything else!"

"What?" Sloan regarded him quizzically. "It's okay, Jase, I—"

"Not another word. I'm calling Jack Goldberg."

Sloan sat up straighter. "I don't need an attorney."

"Are you willing to talk to me without an attorney, Sloan?" Rebecca was quiet, nonthreatening, and she hadn't moved an inch since Sloan arrived.

"No, she isn't," Jason said adamantly.

"I didn't do anything." Sloan leaned her head back and stared at the ceiling. "He came out, he got in his car, he drove away."

Jason sagged in obvious relief.

"That's it?" Rebecca asked.

Sloan nodded.

"You carrying now?"

Again Sloan nodded.

Rebecca walked to her and extended her hand. "Give me your weapon."

Sloan narrowed her eyes.

"Do it, Sloan, for God's sake," Jason snapped.

After a long moment, Sloan complied.

"Jason," Rebecca said, ejecting the clip and putting both it and the automatic into her pocket, "take her upstairs and see that she stays there."

"Wait a minute." Sloan jumped up, her eyes suddenly bright. "I need to run this guy's records, cross-check his—"

"You're done, Sloan. You're off the case."

"You can't do that. This guy is *mine*."

Sloan took one step forward, and Rebecca braced herself. Jason threw himself between them and grabbed both Sloan's arms.

"Take it easy, Sloan," he said hurriedly. "I'll run the checks. Everything there is. I'll get it done."

"Get her out of here, Jason." Rebecca's voice was flat and hard. "Now."

Rebecca remained motionless until Jason and Sloan disappeared into the elevator, Jason with his arm around Sloan's waist. Then she sank into a chair and put her head in her hands. *Captain Henry. And Sloan almost took him out. Christ, how many more ways can I screw up this case?*

❖

Mitchell was awakened by a persistent pulse of pleasure centered in her left breast. She opened her eyes to stare at an unfamiliar ceiling and, in the next second, became aware of the unaccustomed weight of a body lying upon hers. Raising her head, she focused on the blond head bent over her chest and watched Sandy suck her nipple between her lips. A ripple of arousal coursed through her and settled hard between her legs. Her hips jerked, her clitoris grew stiff, and she was instantly wet.

"Ahh, jeez, Sandy." Mitchell's head dropped back, and she closed her eyes again. "What are you doing?"

"I couldn't sleep," Sandy whispered in between alternately licking and sucking the tight nub. "And I couldn't stand to just look any longer."

Eyes still closed, Mitchell trailed her fingers along Sandy's side, brushing the curve of her bare breast. "Feels good. So good."

"Mmm."

Sandy shifted, nestling her own breast in Mitchell's palm. Her voice was soft as she said, "You can touch me now."

Mitchell's breath caught at the sudden gift, amazed by the sensation of Sandy's heart beating under her fingers. "Oh, yeah. You're perfect."

Sandy's laughter registered surprise and disbelief.

Ever so carefully, Mitchell ran her fingertips over the gentle swell of silken skin, thumbing lightly back and forth across the erect nipple. It grew even tighter beneath her fingers, and Sandy made a small mewling sound.

"Okay?" Mitchell asked, opening her eyes and pushing up

against the pillows. Sandy was stretched out on top of her, one thigh between hers.

Sandy nodded, lids half closed, as she rocked slowly against Mitchell's leg. "You can do it...harder."

"You sure?" Mitchell asked, squeezing rhythmically, harder each time.

"It...oh...Dell...I can feel it...all the way down."

Mitchell groaned and captured the other breast in her hand. Sandy arched upward on extended arms, pressing her breasts harder into Mitchell's palms. As Mitchell tugged and rolled her nipples, Sandy began to shiver, her hips moving insistently against Mitchell's thigh.

"Stop," Sandy gasped abruptly. "Dell, stop."

Immediately, Mitchell stilled, her entire body rigid. Her voice was hoarse with tension and arousal. "What? Sandy, what? Did I hurt you?"

Sandy lowered herself against Mitchell's body and pressed her face to Mitchell's neck. She was trembling.

"Hey, hey." Mitchell caressed her lover's back, rocking her gently. "What's wrong?"

"Nothing's wrong," Sandy mumbled, her fingers tracing the curve of Mitchell's jaw. She kissed the side of Mitchell's neck, then the corner of her mouth. "I didn't expect...I didn't think..."

"You didn't expect what?" Mitchell turned her head, and Sandy's lips were there, waiting. She kissed her, and for long moments, she was lost again in the incredible softness of Sandy's lips and the heat of her mouth and the tender, sensuous stroke of her tongue. Mitchell groaned and finally drew away. "God, you can kiss. You make me want to come just kissing you."

Sandy grinned. "Not so fast, rookie."

"So," Mitchell said quietly, working to stay focused through the mists of arousal, "what just happened?"

"Uh...I think you were telling me how good I kissed." Sandy glanced away.

"Sandy? Come on. Help me out here."

Sandy looked back into Mitchell's eyes. She found desire there, and need, and beneath it all, tenderness. "I've never come with anyone touching me before."

Mitchell's eyes darkened; her breath stuttered to a stop. She eased onto her side, keeping Sandy in her arms. Their heads rested close together on the pillow, their breasts and thighs lightly touching. "Do you want to?"

"I almost did a minute ago, and then..." Sandy turned her face away.

Mitchell tapped a finger on Sandy's chin. "And then?"

"I got scared."

"Ah, babe." Mitchell kissed Sandy gently. "I want what *you* want. You tell me."

"I want to touch you." Sandy drew a finger down the center of Mitchell's body, resting her fingers in the dark triangle at the base of her abdomen. "I want to make you come."

Mitchell moaned softly. "That should take about two seconds."

Sandy laughed. "You always so easy?"

"I've been ready since last night. And being close to you like this...I'm wrecked." Mitchell ran her fingers along Sandy's collarbone, then over her breast, stopping just before she reached her nipple. "I want to touch you, too. So much."

"I want you to," Sandy whispered. She found Mitchell's hand, drew it down her own body. She covered Mitchell's fingers with her own and pressed them between her thighs. Her eyes flickered closed, then opened, the pupils wide and dark. "I don't know if I can."

Mitchell felt the heat, felt the hard shape of her desire, felt her tremble. "Anything you say...I'll just stroke you a little, okay?"

"Yes. Yes." Sandy eased her hand away and slipped it between Mitchell's legs, one finger on either side of her clitoris. She squeezed lightly and smiled when Mitchell gasped. When Mitchell mirrored the motion, she moaned. "Nice. Dell...that's so nice."

"Yeah." Mitchell struggled not to come immediately. The hours of wanting the night before, the days and weeks of denying the desire, the incredible wonder of Sandy in her arms—she couldn't contain all the feelings. And Sandy was so good, her touch so sure, that Mitchell just wanted to let go. Had to surrender.

"Dell," Sandy breathed. Touching Mitchell made her so excited, she could barely discern what aroused her the most—

Mitchell's pleasure or her own. Distantly, she was aware of her legs trembling and her hips rocking rhythmically in time to the long smooth strokes of Mitchell's hand. The pressure deep inside was increasing, insistent and so painfully good. "Oh, you just got so hard."

"I'm gonna come," Mitchell gasped. She pressed her forehead to Sandy's, groaning softly as she spasmed in Sandy's palm, shuddering with the swift and merciful release of the tension in her depths. "Sandy. Sandy."

"Oh, yeah." Sandy watched in awe as Mitchell closed her eyes and arched her back, so beautiful. She marveled at the pulsations, alive against her hand. The sharp rise of her own orgasm took her by surprise, and she cried out, every muscle clenching as it struck.

Mitchell, barely able to get her breath, pulled Sandy close and ran her fingers lightly over her clitoris, prolonging the climax. She ached to be inside her, but she held back, waiting until Sandy invited her. "You're beautiful, Sandy. So beautiful."

Beyond words, fearing she would fly apart, Sandy could only cling to Mitchell, whimpering faintly as the waves of pleasure streamed along the pathways of her being. Eventually she became aware of her heartbeat and the amazing lassitude in her body and the harsh sounds of Mitchell's irregular breathing close to her ear. "That was...fuck, I don't know what that was."

"Incredible," Mitchell whispered. "You are incredible."

"I can see why people pay for that."

Mitchell's heart lurched at the words, and then she saw the light in Sandy's eyes. The most beautiful, bright, shining light. A light that could only be happiness. Her throat closed around sudden tears, and she swallowed hard. "I'm available, any time you want."

"Yeah?" She still had her hand between Mitchell's thighs. She pressed the base of the swollen clitoris, then stroked its length.

"Uh-huh." Mitchell's vision got blurry. "No charge."

"Hmm," Sandy murmured thoughtfully, circling faster. "Interesting offer."

Mitchell jerked, moaning softly.

"You're doing that again."

"What?" Mitchell's voice was hoarse, her stomach tight.

"Getting really hard."

"That's 'cause...you're making me come again. Ah...God."

Sandy leaned up on an elbow, grinning. "Yeah?"

"Ye—" Mitchell choked on the word, coming too hard to do anything but fight for air. It went on forever, the contractions so powerful her shoulders came off the bed. When the last ripple of orgasm faded, she fell back, gasping. "Thank you."

Sandy's smile of self-congratulation changed to an expression of astonishment. "Dell, Jesus. You're nuts."

Mitchell tried to focus and finally fixed on Sandy's face. "Why?"

"Because." Sandy leaned near and kissed her. Long and deep and hard. "Because...I *wanted* to be with you."

"Everything was okay?" Mitchell studied Sandy's face with concern.

"Are you gonna ask me if I came?" Sandy's smile took the edge off the sarcasm.

Mitchell blushed. "Uh...I *know* you came. I was gonna ask you if it was good."

Sandy punched her shoulder. "No, idiot. It was terrible. The worst orgasm I ever had. So bad I want to do it again, just to see what all the fuss is about."

"Okay. Now?"

"I thought you had to work."

"I'll be late."

Sandy snuggled into the crook of Mitchell's arm and ran her hand up and down the length of her chest and abdomen. "How come you didn't ask me if I was safe?"

"Because I trust you." Mitchell kissed the wisps of sweat-dampened hair that clung to Sandy's cheek. *And I wanted you so fucking much I didn't care.* That thought scared her more than anything ever had.

"I am. I'm always careful, and I get checked." Sandy felt the muscles in Mitchell's abdomen tense. *And I haven't been fucking, but you don't know that. And you're still here with me. Why? Why are you here, Dell?*

"I'm glad, because I don't want anything to happen to you. If you tell me to use protection, I'll use it. If not, I won't." Mitchell lifted Sandy's chin. "But I'm not gonna stop touching you until you tell me to. No matter what."

"You got a girlfriend, rookie?"

"No."

"How come?"

"I'm holding out for Mitch's girl."

Sandy laughed. "I don't know, Dell. Mitch is fucking *hot*."

"Uh-huh. I noticed you thought so."

"Yeah, I did." Sandy rolled over and straddled Mitchell's hips, rubbing herself against the base of Mitchell's belly. She was still wet and the fleeting friction against her erect clitoris made her groan. "But then, so are you. Big time."

Mitchell reached for Sandy's breasts, gently cupping them as she arched her hips, making Sandy bite her lower lip and close her eyes. "So I've got a chance?"

"We'll see, rookie," Sandy whispered. "We'll see."

CHAPTER EIGHTEEN

The second Sloan walked in the door, Sarah accosted her. "Are you out of your mind?" Sarah stood an inch from Sloan, her face flushed, her voice a lethal whisper. "Michael has been *frantic*. Do you know what that kind of stress can do to her right now? *God damn* it, Sloan."

"Where is she?" So tired she could barely stand, Sloan looked past Sarah to the bedroom. "Is she all right?"

"I just *said* she wasn't." Sarah tried to keep her temper in check, but she'd been so worried for both her friends that her nerves were frayed beyond repair. "She's in the bedroom. I finally got her to at least lie down."

"Sarah," Jason murmured gently. "It's okay."

"No, it's not," Sarah snapped. "I am sick of the two of you taking chances, as if nothing mattered except—"

Michael's voice came softly from across the room. "It's all right, Sarah."

When Sarah whirled in Michael's direction, Sloan took the opportunity to step around her. She crossed quickly to her lover, asking anxiously, "Are you okay?"

Michael rested her palm against Sloan's chest and smiled faintly. "You look awful. Take a shower and go to bed."

"Okay."

Sarah gaped as Sloan disappeared into the bedroom. "Amazing."

"Is she all right?" Michael asked, looking to Jason.

"She's a bit...strung out." He wasn't certain how much to say, but he wasn't going to be the one to tell her where Sloan had spent the night. Or what she'd been contemplating. "I think she needs a break from work for a while."

"I'll see to it." Michael smiled at Sarah. "Don't be too angry with her. You know she'd never intentionally hurt any one of us."

"Ah, hell," Sarah said with a sigh, threading her arm around Jason's waist and leaning into him. With her cheek on his shoulder, she met Michael's gentle gaze. "I know that. But, damn, sometimes she makes me crazy."

Slowly, Michael nodded. "She's not leaving here today, so if you two want to go home—"

"I've got to get back downstairs," Jason interjected, his tone apologetic. "We're about to brief."

"And I'm staying right here for at least a few more days," Sarah said adamantly. "You know damn well as soon as Sloan gets some sleep, she'll be at it again." She looked pointedly at Jason. *"Whatever* it is you two are into this time."

He shrugged sheepishly. "Mostly it's just the ordinary computer sleuthing."

"Mostly, maybe. It's the *other* part that worries me. Let the police take care of the rough stuff this time, okay?"

"That's the plan." He said it because it was true. But sometimes real life just worked out differently.

"Don't expect Sloan any time soon," Michael remarked, turning away. "And thanks, both of you."

❖

When Michael reached the bedroom, she discovered Sloan, naked and still damp, just emerging from the bathroom.

"Come to bed." Michael loosed her robe and slid under the sheets, stretching an arm out across the pillow.

Sloan lay down next to her, rested her cheek on Michael's shoulder, and sighed. "I'm sorry."

"Where were you?"

"Working...I thought I'd be back before you woke up." Sloan kissed Michael's neck. "I didn't mean to worry you."

"You didn't worry me so much," Michael replied, threading her fingers into Sloan's thick, dark hair. "You scared me."

Sloan's stomach clenched. She was so very tired, and her mind wasn't working well. The first few hours that she'd sat in the dark watching Henry's house, she'd had only one thought—*This is the man who hurt Michael. He has to pay for that.*

When she'd first arrived outside his house, it had seemed so clear what she needed to do; but as time passed, she'd become confused and uncertain. She knew Michael wouldn't want her to take matters into her own hands; Frye would know immediately it was her doing if anything happened to the guy; and, as she'd turned the automatic over and over in her hands, she had come to doubt that she could pull the trigger. Had she caught the driver of the vehicle the night Michael had been struck, she would have killed him. Of that she was certain. But sitting alone in the cold dark night, contemplating it, she didn't think she could go through with it.

"I'm really beat, baby," Sloan murmured. "I fucked up last night. I...I'm not thinking right. I haven't been right since you got hurt."

"I know, love." Michael kissed Sloan's forehead. "Everything is going to be all right. I'm going to be all right. So are you."

"I'm so sorry you were scared. I never meant for that to happen." Sloan shuddered. "God, I never meant for any of this to happen."

"Promise me you will not get out of this bed for the rest of the day."

Sloan nodded wearily, curving her arm around Michael's body and pressing close. "I promise. Whatever you want."

"I want you, right here beside me." *Always.*

Sloan didn't reply. She was already asleep.

Michael closed her eyes. The world never felt as right as it did when Sloan was nearby, and right now what they needed in order to heal, above all else, was each other. They were together, and it was a start.

❖

Mitchell stepped off the elevator at Sloan Security and hurried down the hallway toward the sound of voices. She was late. Way late. She thought about Sandy as she'd last seen her, lying naked, asleep in the midst of the tangled sheets. Feeling almost high, Mitchell grinned, knowing that she wouldn't have changed anything about the last few hours.

When she walked into the conference room, her euphoria rapidly dissipated. Watts, Detective Sergeant Frye, and Jason were gathered around the conference table, and surprisingly, Dr. Rawlings was there, too. The atmosphere was grim.

"Sorry I'm late," Mitchell said, her eyes on Rebecca.

Watts gave her a hard stare. "Late night out with the *boys, Officer*?"

"No, sir, I—"

"Did you get settled into the apartment?" Rebecca asked briskly. She didn't have the patience for Watts's heckling at the moment.

"Yes, ma'am, I di—"

"Good. Sit down. We're in the middle of a briefing."

Mitchell sat, her gaze forward. *What the hell has happened? And where is Sloan?*

Rebecca walked to a whiteboard that Jason had exposed by opening sliding panels in the wall at one end of the room. "Sloan thinks she's nailed our leak. I want to be sure, because we're going to have to concentrate all our resources on building a case against him if she's right. We can't afford to do that until we've eliminated all the other possibilities." With a black marker, she wrote Suspects at the top of the blank board and underlined it. "Let's go through them, one by one."

Next she wrote PPD to the far left of the board. Beneath it, she wrote Captain Henry—Special Crimes, Adams—Civilian Clerk-SC, Trish Marks—Homicide, Charlie Horton—Homicide. She looked around the room. "Anyone else from the police department who ought to be on the list?"

Silent shakes of the head and a grunt of disgust from Watts.

"Okay." She moved over an inch and wrote City Hall. "Watts? Want to fill in the players?"

Watts pulled a tattered leather-bound notebook from the inside of his brown suit jacket, flipped it open, and read dispassionately. "Two ADAs handled the warrant for the bust at LongJohn's because the request came in on Saturday at changeover time or some such shit. That would be Margaret Campbell and...uh...George Beecher. The judge was Sally Marchamp."

As he spoke, Rebecca added the names. With one more

shift to her right, she headed the last column under Suspects with Civilians. Beneath that, she wrote Whitaker and Rawlings. When she turned, she met her lover's gaze. Much as she'd expected, Catherine regarded her calmly, but there was a quizzical expression in her eyes.

Rebecca surveyed the room. "Who can we absolutely eliminate? Let's start with the PPD."

Watts cleared his throat. "Marks and Horton. They got assigned the Cruz and Hogan hits on a random rotation. It could have been any two homicide dicks who caught it. They have no other connection to anyone in the case other than that, and I've never heard even the slightest hint that either of them is dirty."

"Neither have I." Rebecca knew that Watts was biased against the leak being a cop, but she tended to agree with him that Marks and Horton were low on the list. "Jason? What do you have?"

Jason spoke from memory. "Mitchell and I have run preliminary data searches on the entire list—at least the easily accessible information. Military and employment histories, arrest records, and basic financials—credit reports, mostly. I don't have the in-depth bank and investment statements yet, but I should within the next twenty-four hours."

"Anything stand out?"

"Marks and Horton don't raise a blip—nothing to suggest they live beyond their means or have ever been anything but ordinary cops. Horton had one reprimand for excessive force in his jacket, Marks had one commendation."

"Jesus H..." Watts blurted. "How'd you get to those records?"

Jason regarded him impassively.

Mitchell flushed, thinking about her own personnel file. She'd never be free of the disciplinary action, even though she'd been cleared. Then she flashed on Sandy and the scar on her forehead from where the guy had struck her, and she no longer cared.

Rebecca drew a line through the names of the two homicide detectives. "Who else can go?"

"Dr. Rawlings," Mitchell said clearly. She glanced briefly at Catherine, who smiled back. "I didn't tell her anything about the detail—only that I was on it. I did not discuss the nature of the operation or the timing of the raid."

"There was nothing in any of my notes or reports that specified what Officer Mitchell was involved in professionally at the time of our sessions," Catherine advised quietly. She had arrived just before the meeting had commenced, and she and Rebecca had not spoken except for a moment when Rebecca had hurriedly informed her that Sloan had returned unharmed. "Even if someone had invaded my private files, there would be nothing to find."

"Fair enough." Rebecca crossed out Catherine's name.

"If I might add," Catherine said steadily, "I've known Rand Whitaker professionally for many years. Although anything is possible, I can't see him being involved in anything nefarious."

"He's got a house in the Hamptons, drives a vintage Ferrari, and owns a huge estate in Merion. He doesn't get all that on what the PPD pays him as a consultant," Jason pointed out. "His lifestyle alone is suspect."

"In addition to that, he's got too many potential avenues of access to information to eliminate him at this point," Rebecca said flatly. "He stays on the list until we get the in-depth financials, at least."

"That seems reasonable." Catherine didn't argue, because she could sense Rebecca's strain. Whatever had happened after they'd parted that morning, it was serious. Rebecca was clearly disturbed, and since this was her area of expertise, Catherine saw no reason to refute her opinion.

"Adams, the clerk, was hired by the department *after* the information from Flanagan's reports went missing. Since we're assuming that the person who set up Sloan is also behind that, she can go," Jason recommended. "Postulating *two* inside sources of our leaks isn't reasonable."

"Agreed. We're down to five, then," Rebecca said to Jason. "You need to run the ADAs and the judge." She took a deep breath. "And we need everything you can get on Captain Henry. As soon as Sloan is able, I want to talk to her."

"I think she's out of commission for the rest of the day."

"Tonight then. I want to know what she's got on Henry and how sound she thinks it is."

"I'll call you the minute she surfaces."

"Fine," Rebecca said, her tone clipped. If Sloan had been a cop under her command, she'd have suspended her. As it was, all she could do was shut her out of the investigation. And doing that was going to be a headache. First, because she knew Sloan would fight her, and second, because as angry as she was at Sloan's stunt the previous night, Rebecca understood her motivations. "She's going to have to give us a solid reason to go after him. He's a ranking officer with a good rep."

Jason took a breath and carefully did not look at Watts. "Henry's credit cards are maxed out, he has a second mortgage on his house, and he's got nothing showing in the way of assets. He's borrowed against his retirement fund as well. Money could be a motive for him to turn."

"A lot of cops sail close to the wind," Watts growled. "The city doesn't exactly pay like the *private* sector."

"Any indication of where his money is going?" Rebecca found the prospect of investigating her commander distasteful, not only because it went against everything she'd been trained to believe in, but also because she respected the man as a cop. Still, cops turned every day. The pay was bad, the thanks almost nonexistent, and temptation everywhere.

"No sign yet." Jason kept his voice level, ignoring Watts's dig. "Gambling, drugs, or a mistress would be the best guesses. Any hint of those?"

Rebecca glanced at Watts, who shook his head. "None that I've ever heard. He's married, has a couple of kids, I think. Always seemed like a straight arrow."

"I'll have more tomorrow," Jason said.

"Make it today. I want you all over that suspect list. I want everything there is on them, ASAP."

"Understood." Jason didn't even bother to mention how hard that would be without Sloan. He didn't think the time was right to remind the detective of that, not after the little standoff the two had had earlier. The first day he'd seen them together, circling each other warily, he'd been reminded of two alpha females claiming their territories. He had a feeling he'd be seeing it again soon.

Rebecca leaned forward at the end of the table, her palms flat on the granite surface, and met each individual's gaze as she spoke.

"Here's the game plan, then. Mitchell, you work with Dr. Rawlings reviewing the Internet porn user profiles. We still need to see if we can get a connection there to someone local. Catherine, can you spare us some time today?"

"I've cleared my schedule for most of the day. I can come back after hours this evening if necessary."

"Thanks." Rebecca held her lover's eyes for an extra second, the hard edge in her blue eyes softening for a heartbeat before she looked away. "I've got a slim lead on one of the girls from LongJohn's video." She explained about the possible connection between the Asian girl in the video and the prostitute named Lucy. "I've got street sources looking for her."

Mitchell stiffened. *Sandy.* She worked to keep her expression neutral. *Okay, so Sandy's the sergeant's CI. I know that. That's Sandy's business.* But it rankled her, and she wasn't sure why. Combing the streets for information for the detective was no more dangerous for Sandy—in fact, probably less so—than prostituting herself. The sergeant wouldn't mistreat her or ask for sexual favors, which Mitchell knew sometimes happened. *But Frye has a hold on her. They have a relationship.* Mitchell stared at the tabletop, realizing she was jealous, and realizing, too, what that meant. *I'm hooked on her.*

"Mitchell, you with us?" Rebecca asked sharply.

Mitchell jerked upright. "Yes, ma'am."

Rebecca gave her a hard stare. "As I was saying, Watts and I will chase the street leads on the Internet porn setup. Where do we stand on the inside action at Ziggie's?"

Jason said, "Jasmine will take Mitch to the Troc tonight. Introduce him around. We should be good to go for him to hit Ziggie's within a day or two."

"Mitch? Who the hell is Mitch?" Watts barked. The mention of Jasmine set his teeth on edge.

"Friend of mine," Mitchell replied evenly, meeting his gaze.

"Oh for fuck's sake." Watts got set to say more but a deadly look from Rebecca had him coughing into his fist instead. He contented himself with a snicker. "Right. *Mitchie.*"

Mitchell straightened in her seat, almost seeming to grow in size. Her alto voice resonated with warning. "That's Mitch. *Not Mitchie.*"

For a second, Watts just stared. Then the corner of his mouth twitched and finally, he grinned. "Okay, kid. Okay. Don't get your... balls...in an uproar."

"Wouldn't think of it, Detective. Sir."

Rebecca rubbed the bridge of her nose. *Christ. The two of them are like kids.* But she recognized the camaraderie beneath the jibes, and that's what made the team work. That's what made someone put their life on the line for you without a second thought. "Do you two think you could give me your full attention, or would that be asking too much?"

"Yes, ma'am," Mitchell replied briskly.

"Sure, Sarge." Watts smothered his smile.

"Fine. We're looking for any information on the guy in the sex video who might work or might *have* worked at Ziggie's, and any information the girls there might have about how the videos are getting made. Who organizes it, who picks the girls, when and where they're shooting the flicks. Anything to point us to a location. Questions?"

No one had any.

"We'll meet here at the usual time tonight. If anyone gets anything before then, I'll expect a call. *No one* makes a move without my say-so."

As the group dispersed, Watts sidled up to Mitchell. In a voice too low for Rebecca to hear, he asked, "So, kid—what's the deal? When you walked in this morning, you had that 'just got laid last night' look."

"Yeah?" Mitchell replied curiously. "How can you recognize it, considering how long it must be since you've looked that way?"

Watts shook his head remorsefully. He had a hard-assed female partner who outranked him, which was bad enough, but now he had a snot-nosed rookie giving him shit. He laughed out loud. Life was good.

CHAPTER NINETEEN

Rebecca slumped into the closest chair and blew out a long breath. "Jesus, what a crew."

"How are you doing?" Catherine pulled her own chair closer and rested her hand on Rebecca's forearm.

"Okay." Rebecca gave her a weary smile. "I feel a bit like I'm walking a tightrope without a net here, which I guess I am." She rubbed her face. "I can't believe it's Henry. Or maybe I just don't *want* to believe it."

"Maybe it isn't?"

Rebecca shrugged. "Sloan seemed convinced, and she's good at what she does. Better than good. I haven't gotten all the details yet. She was in no shape to be questioned. Mostly I wanted to kick her ass, anyhow."

"Ah." Catherine ran her fingers slowly up and down Rebecca's sleeve. "She's all right, though?"

"She's skirting the edge, but she's tough. As long as Michael is okay, I imagine Sloan will get it together." Rebecca raised her hand and captured Catherine's fingers, lacing hers with them. "I hope I'm not as big a pain in the ass as she is."

Catherine lifted their joined hands to her lips and kissed the back of Rebecca's fingers, saying nothing.

"That bad, huh?" Rebecca met Catherine's eyes and grinned ruefully. "Then I am even luckier than I thought that you love me."

"I adore you, and it has nothing to do with luck. Rebecca, darling—you're doing an excellent job with this investigation. Even I can see that much."

"I don't know about that. I've got Sloan going rogue—or *more* rogue, I should say, Watts and Mitchell taking potshots at each other, and Sandy and Mitchell—I don't even want to *know* what." Rebecca leaned back and closed her eyes. "Christ."

"This situation is strained for everyone," Catherine observed. "You've brought together a disparate group of people and asked them to work closely together under severe time constraints, which is a significant undertaking. Add to that the personal challenges— why, just asking William to handle the concept of Jasmine is a feat in itself—"

Rebecca laughed.

"Well," Catherine smiled, too. "You see my point."

"Maybe we need group therapy."

"It's actually not a bad idea, or even a new concept. Many businesses—"

"No way." Rebecca straightened, opened her eyes, and leaned over to kiss Catherine gently. "I love you more than anything in the world, but the last thing I want is to get up close and personal with Bill Watts."

Catherine laughed. "Just a thought. We'll hold it in reserve for extreme circumstances."

"*Very* extreme." Rebecca kissed Catherine again, then drew away with a sigh. "I have to go. Captain Henry paged me just before the briefing. He wants a status report."

Completely serious now, Catherine said, "Rebecca, be careful. If he *is* involved somehow..."

"Don't worry." Rebecca stood, her expression suddenly that of a hunter sensing her quarry. "Besides, it's a chance for me to see if *he's* trying to milk me for the kind of information that would be valuable to someone else."

It's a dangerous game you're playing. Catherine said nothing, because this was the life her lover led, but it frightened her nonetheless. As she watched Rebecca walk away, she wondered if she would ever get used to it.

❖

"So, bring me up to speed, Sergeant."

Rebecca sat in the same chair, in the same office, across from the same man just as she had done a thousand times before. This time, however, she looked at him as she would look at a suspect, with an eye and an ear tuned for the slight word-slip or unguarded expression that would point to guilt or transgression. The dark eyes that gazed back at her were clear and hard and unwavering.

"We have a couple of promising new leads on the pornography ring, but nothing solid yet, sir. We're going at that as we discussed, using both the computer angle and our street sources." She purposefully kept things vague. No names, no particulars as to timing. His reaction was what she was after. *Would he bite?*

Henry studied the chiseled features and sharp eyes. She'd always played her cards close to the vest, even with her superiors. "*Promising.* You wouldn't be trying to snow me, now would you, Sergeant? String me along so that I don't pull the plug on a cold investigation?"

"No, sir, not at all." *Is he fishing now?* "As I said, we're in the process of chasing down a couple of good tips."

"Tips that could get us an arrest?"

"That's my goal, sir."

"Because intelligence gathering is all fine and dandy, Frye, but arrests are what boost the division's stats." Henry leaned back in his chair. "The feds made us look bad. I want to salvage something from that operation. Talk about FUBAR."

Fucked up beyond all repair. Maybe, maybe not. Rebecca's jaw clenched, and she consciously made an effort to relax it. "I was there, sir. I want to finish what I started, too."

"Fine. I can buy you another week or so."

"Thanks."

"You done with Whitaker?"

Not yet. Rebecca shrugged. "*I* think so, but I'll have to keep that last appointment."

"Good."

His tone indicated the discussion was over and Rebecca stood. "Thank you, sir."

"Just remember—I want to know as soon as you're ready to move on something."

"Of course." She regarded him impassively. *Unless, of course, it's you.*

Rebecca turned and walked from the room. The door had not

yet swung closed behind her when Captain Henry reached for the phone.

❖

Catherine passed a stack of transcripts across the table to Mitchell. "I've ranked this first group in order of probability, using the identifiers you initially devised to profile LongJohn."

"Thanks." Mitchell glanced at the clock. They'd been working in near-silence for hours, she at the computer and Catherine at the table nearby. It had been a surprisingly comfortable silence. Jason was in another part of the office, running the suspect checks, or more accurately, hacking into confidential databases that would provide the deep background information they needed.

"So what happens now?" Catherine asked.

"Jason and I will attempt to determine these users' true identities, either by direct back-tracing through ISP addresses and servers or by phishing."

"That sounds like it could take a tremendous amount of time."

"You're right. It's the kind of thing that entire electronic surveillance units spend weeks or months on." Mitchell shrugged, undeterred by the scope of the task. It was *almost* as much fun as being on the streets. "But we have an advantage."

"Oh?"

"We have you."

Catherine blinked, uncharacteristically caught off guard. There was absolutely nothing flirtatious or suggestive in the young officer's tone or expression, but Catherine was acutely aware of the fact that they were working alone for the first time. Although their therapeutic relationship was on hold at the moment, certain boundaries needed to be maintained. Some would have said she shouldn't have been working with Mitchell at all. But life's circumstances often put one in situations that defied the rules, and this was one.

"You mean the profiling I'm doing makes that big a difference?"

"Absolutely," Mitchell said enthusiastically. "You've saved us *days,* maybe weeks. Instead of random searches, we've got targeted subjects. You're like a...a magic bullet."

"Well," Catherine remarked dryly, "that's the first time anything psychological has been given such a dramatic descriptor."

"That's what's so incredible about what we're doing here," Mitchell continued, her eyes bright. "We're like...a multidisciplinary team. We're, hell, we're practically a self-contained mini-division. The detective sergeant should be a captain, with what she's put together here."

Catherine was silent. Mitchell's hero worship was touching, and not without cause. The psychiatrist's thoughts, however, were of her lover, and of the loyalty and respect she commanded simply by example. *Oh, Rebecca. You really were born for this work. No matter the cost to you, or to us, it's what you have to do.*

"Well, then," Catherine finally responded. "We had best keep up our end of things. Where's the next batch? I have a bit more time."

"Jason has them." Mitchell stood, then hesitated. "I, uh...I wanted to say thanks again. For your help with the disciplinary thing."

"You're welcome." Catherine hid her surprise. "But I only helped set the record straight."

"You did more than that. I'm not sure how, but you...helped me realize some things, things about myself." *Like why I felt what I felt in that alley. Like how much Sandy really means to me.* "About what I was...feeling."

"I'm glad."

"Yeah, me, too." Mitchell grinned. "So, I'll get those transcripts."

"I'll get us some more coffee." Catherine looked after the other woman, wondering what had happened to put the new light in her eyes, although she had a very good idea what, or *who,* was the cause. Rebecca, with her cop's instincts, had very likely been right all along. Officer Mitchell looked like she was in love.

❖

"You really think it's him?" Watts asked when Rebecca pulled away from the curb, pointing the Vette south on Tenth.

"I don't know. He's in the right place. It's got to be someone with rank." Rebecca slowed for a stop sign, turned right onto Passyunk Avenue, then drove into the heart of South Philadelphia. "I can't see this being some low-level cop or clerk. It just doesn't play."

"Yeah," Watts agreed dispiritedly. "I have to go with you there. But fuck, a police captain in Zamora's pocket?"

Rebecca cut him a look. "Have you forgotten your history? You think in the Rizzo era there weren't almost as many dirty cops as clean ones in this city?"

"That was thirty years ago." He sighed, remembering the time when Frank Rizzo's political machine in City Hall controlled the police and fire departments, and all three were more than friendly with underworld figures. "But, yeah, I hear you. Man, I hate to think it's him, though. Not like I love the guy or anything, but still..."

"He's one of us."

"Yeah." Watts looked out the window. "Where we goin'?"

"We've got a date with some girls."

His eyebrows raised. His voice sounded hopeful. "Yeah?" At the look from Rebecca, he swallowed his grin. "That cute little whore come through for you?"

"Sandy," Rebecca said very softly. "Her name is Sandy."

The warning note that resonated in her voice made his gonads tighten, pull up, and run for cover. "Okay. So, she's yours now. Got it. Sorry."

"Sandy found us *a* girl. I don't know if it's *the* girl. We're going to buy them breakfast and find out."

"Breakfast? It's almost dinner time."

"Not for them. They probably just got up."

"Workin' girls and a double date. My favorite."

Rebecca ground her teeth and pulled into an angled slot in front of the Melrose Diner.

"You sit. I talk."

"Sure, sure, Sarge."

Once inside the noisy, crowded diner, they spied Sandy and a smooth-faced Asian girl who looked about fifteen seated on one side of a red vinyl-covered booth. The chrome-edged tabletop was original, attested to by the scarred Formica. Sandy and the girl had heavy white ceramic mugs of coffee in front of them. Despite the early fall chill, both young women were underdressed in skimpy tops and bare bellies above the uniform of the day—jeans cut so low that wisps of pubic hair would have peeked out had they not been shaved.

Watts slid in first, then Rebecca. A waitress stopped with a coffeepot in hand and said, "What youse havin'?"

Both girls ordered meals that would have given a truck driver pause. Watts and Rebecca ordered coffee.

"Hiya, Sandy," Rebecca said softly, just a touch of menace in her tone. "This Lucy?"

"Yeah." Sandy sounded sullen and did not look Rebecca in the eye. It was important for Sandy's safety as well as her future credibility that she *not* appear to have a friendly relationship with the police. "So we're here. You promised you'd pay."

"Later. *If* we like what you have to say." Rebecca was impressed that Sandy had gotten the girl to agree to a meet. It helped that Sandy was so well known on the streets. Lucy, if that was really her name, probably trusted Sandy where she might have been suspect of anyone else. But then again, it beat making twenty dollars on her back, trust or no trust. "If we don't, you miss dinner and I'll be dropping around when you least expect it to ruin business for a while."

"Yeah, yeah." Sandy shifted on the seat, clearly unhappy. "So ask, then leave us alone."

The girl with Sandy had kept her eyes on the tabletop the entire time. Rebecca slid Jason's composite of the guy in the sex video into her line of view. "Know him?"

The girl shook her head.

"You sure?"

Head nod.

"Ever *seen* him?" Watts grumbled.

The girl shrugged.

Rebecca's pulse jumped. *Good man.* Rebecca slid a folded twenty across the table and under the photo. "Where?"

"Around the clubs," the girl replied after a pause. She had no accent and her voice was soft, gentle. "He drives."

"Drives?" Rebecca glanced at Sandy, who made an *I don't*

know gesture. "What does that mean?"

"He brings some of the girls to the clubs."

"Some of the dancers?"

Head nod.

"Do they just dance? Or do they hook, too?"

"Maybe."

"Where? Which clubs?"

A shrug.

Rebecca passed another twenty. She didn't think the girl was holding out for more money. She was scared. "Which clubs?"

"I don't know...I haven't seen him in a while. Maybe the Blue Diamond—"

"The place on Delaware Avenue?" Watts asked.

She nodded.

"Where else?"

Shrug. "Ziggie's once. I don't know."

"What's his name?"

Negative head shake.

"Okay," Rebecca said. She passed the photos of the two girls who had been in the video with him. "How about them?"

The young girl stiffened.

Bingo.

"Fifty dollars," Rebecca whispered. *Come on. Help me.*

A trembling finger landed on the Asian girl's photo. "She used to dance at the Blue Di. Maybe she still does."

"Name?"

"I don't know." Her voice was almost transparent now. Her dark hair framed a face both guileless and world-weary. She raised liquid eyes to Rebecca's. "Her stage name was Trudy."

"What about the other one?"

"No."

"No you don't know her?"

"She just said that, Frye," Sandy interjected, sensing Lucy was about to bolt. "Jesus. You got your money's worth. Leave us alone so we can enjoy the food. You and Bluto there kinda spoil the appetite."

The waitress slid two plates heaping with eggs, potatoes, and toast in front of the girls.

Rebecca folded a fifty-dollar bill around her card. As she slid that across the table under the rim of Lucy's plate, she said quietly, "I can take you to a shelter where you can get a new name, a new start."

A head shake. Definite. *No.*

"If your pimp beats you, call me. I'll make sure he never does again."

No response.

"You need help—any kind of help, call me." Rebecca gave Sandy a hard stare. "You—keep your nose clean. And keep your ass out of the alleys."

"Yeah, yeah." Sandy snorted with a *kiss-my-ass* attitude and turned her attention to her breakfast.

Rebecca and Watts left, handing the waitress money for the check on the way out the door.

"Did we just get anything?" Watts asked as he crammed himself into the Vette.

"I don't know," Rebecca mused, heading north out of South Philly toward Sloan's. She looked at Watts speculatively. "Have you ever heard of prostitutes having *escorts*?"

"Nope—pimps might cruise around checking up on their stables, but they don't drive the girls to work."

"Sex videos, Internet porn rings, girls being shuttled around to sex clubs." She shook her head. "What does that sound like to you?"

"Organized?"

"Definitely that and—" Her phone rang, and she pulled it from her belt. "Yeah, Frye...okay, fine...on our way."

"What's up?" Watts asked.

"Sloan's awake, and she wants to talk to me."

"Huh. You gonna chew her ass?"

"The thought has crossed my mind."

"Yeah, I'll bet," he said, laughing. "Can I watch?"

Rebecca eyed him flatly. "Gee, *Bluto,* I don't know about that."

"Goddamned smart-mouthed who—" He caught himself. "She's...uh...*smart,* that kid. She played that well."

"She is, and she did." Her mind, however, was not on how

well Sandy had protected her cover, but on a vague idea that was forming in her mind. She needed something that would connect Jimmy Hogan and Gregor Zamora and a bunch of young girls being ferried around to sex clubs and porn shoots. The picture was there, she just needed a few more pieces. And when she had it, she hoped she'd learn why two cops had died.

CHAPTER TWENTY

At Sloan's, Rebecca rode the elevator up one more flight after Watts departed on the third floor. The doors slid open, and she exited into an entryway lit by matte black metal-encased spots nestled among exposed ventilation ducts, electrical conduits, and pipes. The floor was highly polished random-width oak planking and the walls a muted wash of pale color. Industrial chic, and very well done. She looked for a bell or knocker, saw none, and then, out of habit, looked for the camera. She didn't see it, but knew it had to be there, because as she took one step closer to the massive double steel doors, they parted soundlessly. Sloan waited on the other side.

Rebecca stood still on the threshold, taking stock. The security consultant, dressed in her typical jeans and white shirt, looked nevertheless like a different woman than a few hours before. Her eyes were clear and bore barely a hint of shadow; her stance was relaxed but alert; her grin, a toned-down version of her usual cocky one, was confident.

"Detective."

"Sloan."

"Thanks for coming." Sloan stepped aside with a sweep of her arm, bidding entry. "Please."

Rebecca stepped inside and looked around. As she expected, the design and furnishings were more of the same modern style, softened by thick area rugs and surprisingly placid landscape oil paintings on the walls. What caught her attention almost immediately, however—a presence dominating the room—was the exquisitely beautiful woman seated on the sofa in the central living area. Her classically elegant features were scarcely marred by the bruises and obvious swelling. There was pain swimming

RADCLY*f*FE

in her deep blue eyes, though, and it hurt Rebecca on some basic, instinctual level to see it.

"Detective Sergeant Frye—my partner, Michael Lassiter."

"Rebecca," Rebecca said, walking forward to offer her hand. "Hello."

"I'm so happy to meet you," Michael said, smiling into the arctic blue eyes. The gaze meeting hers did not feel cold, however, merely careful.

"I'm glad to see that you're better," Rebecca replied.

"Yes, thank you." Michael glanced at Sloan, who stood quietly to one side. "It was my idea that you come upstairs. I wanted to meet you, and although I'm improved, I wasn't up to the elevator ride, even for a short distance. I hope you don't mind."

"Not at all." Rebecca smiled. "Is there something I can help you with?"

"Other than keeping my impetuous lover out of harm's way?" Michael ignored a slight groan from Sloan's direction, smiling softly. "You can accept an invitation from Sloan and me for you and Catherine to join us for dinner when I'm a bit more worthy of company."

"I'd be delighted to accept for both of us." Rebecca was surprised to realize that she'd have a hard time denying this woman anything. Even in obvious pain, she exuded a quiet grace. Purposefully, Rebecca reminded herself of her duty. "As to Sloan, that's another story. She's a little independent."

Michael nodded carefully, finding that small movements didn't seem to bother her headache as much. "I won't argue. I won't even mention extenuating circumstances of which you're well aware. So, I'm going to leave you two to sort that out."

Sloan moved forward quickly to help Michael rise. Slipping an arm around her lover's waist, subtly supporting her, she glanced at Rebecca. "I'll be right back."

"Of course."

Rebecca crossed to the opposite wall of floor-to-ceiling windows and took in the view. She was idly following the lights of a barge on the river when Sloan rejoined her. She waited for Sloan to make the first move. It wasn't what she expected.

"Sorry if that put you on the spot," Sloan said quietly. "Michael is having trouble remembering things, and—"

"You don't need to explain. She's..." Rebecca struggled for the word and came up short. "She's very...lovely."

"Yes." Sloan's voice was thick, her throat tight.

"And very perceptive." Rebecca's face was inscrutable as she continued to look out. "It would have been a smart move on your part, though, to have me meet her. If you *had* thought of it."

"Oh?" Sloan asked, intrigued. She would have preferred to keep Michael far away from anything having to do with this case—or any case—but Michael had said it would help to fill in the blanks in her memory if she could put faces to the people who populated their world. "Why?"

Rebecca turned her head, met Sloan's gaze. "Seeing her like that...it makes *me* want to put a gun to someone's head." Before Sloan could reply, Rebecca added, "But I won't."

"Neither will I."

"I don't know that." Rebecca leaned a shoulder against one of the thick metal beams that supported the glass sections, her eyes hard. "And if I can't trust you, I can't have you on the team."

"You need me." It wasn't said arrogantly, because they both knew it was fact.

"Jason can do the work." Rebecca would not be blackmailed into making a decision that could compromise her entire operation. Nor would she knowingly put one of her people into a situation they couldn't handle. And Sloan was a loose cannon.

Sloan shook her head. "He's good. He's very, very good. But he can't do what I can do. Ask him."

"You're too close to this one. I knew it from the beginning, and I let it slide. That was *my* mistake." Rebecca fixed Sloan with an unyielding stare. "But *you* blew it last night. You should have called me as soo—"

"I know. I was wrong. I apologize."

Rebecca nodded slightly, accepting the apology. "The fact remains, I don't know that you won't decide the investigation is moving too slowly and take matters into your own hands."

"I won't." Sloan's face tightened and a muscle in her jaw jumped. "I won't because it would hurt Michael."

Rebecca considered the power of that statement. Considered

what she had seen of Sloan's condition when Michael had been injured. Considered the effect that love—no, not just love, bone-deep need—had had on her own life since meeting Catherine. She blew out a breath. "Your word on it?"

"Yes. Absolutely."

"Watts will be deeply disappointed."

Sloan raised an eyebrow. "Oh?"

"He was hoping for a royal ass-chewing."

"You can always fake it," Sloan suggested with a laugh.

"Nah. He'd enjoy it too much." Rebecca grew serious. "I need a full report."

"Let me say goodbye to Michael, and we can head downstairs. It's going to be a long night."

"Yes." Rebecca rubbed her face, thinking about all she needed to do. Thinking about Catherine and another night she would not be with her. "I thought it would be."

❖

When Rebecca and Sloan walked into the conference room together, three sets of curious eyes fixed on them.

Sloan winked at Jason, who wisely pretended not to notice.

Watts craned his neck and examined Sloan from head to toe. "I don't see any bite marks."

"They're there," Sloan said quietly in passing.

Watts smiled, satisfied.

Mitchell decided silence was the safest move on her part.

"Where's Dr. Rawlings?" Rebecca asked.

"She had patients," Mitchell replied.

Rebecca glanced at her watch and grimaced. It was later than she'd thought, and now she'd missed the opportunity to have a quick dinner with Catherine. Automatically, she pushed the disappointment aside and settled into a chair at the head of the table. "Okay, Sloan. It's your show."

"I found a back door in Flanagan's computer," she said. "In simple terms, that's a secret way into a system unknown to the user. Depending on the level of access, the intruder can remove, alter, or delete files. This user had root access."

Jason gave a small grunt of surprise.

"That's good?" Watts asked sharply, hating the way these discussions left him feeling like a rookie again.

Sloan shook her head. "That's bad. At least for the person whose system has been compromised. It means that the intruder can do just about anything to the data and then alter the logs to make it impossible to see what he, or she, has done."

"Cover his trail," Watts commented.

"Exactly."

"And you identified this intruder?" Rebecca asked.

Sloan nodded. "Like I said before, it's impossible to totally erase the electronic trail, but most people would not have found it. I almost didn't." She met Rebecca's gaze. "I tracked the log-on data back to Henry."

"That's pretty sophisticated stuff," Mitchell said quietly.

The comment hung in the air, but the unspoken *for a police detective* was clear to all.

"Does he fit for the rest of it?" Sloan asked. She looked around the room and saw the silent assent.

"What about someone hacking *his* user identity to set up the back door?" Jason postulated.

Sloan shrugged, looking skeptical. "You know how hard *that* would be. We'd be theorizing an even greater level of computer sophistication. And why?"

"To set him up?" Mitchell suggested.

"In case of what? I'm sure the hacker never expected anyone to be looking for this kind of thing."

"I agree," Rebecca said. "The PPD is just starting to establish an electronic surveillance unit. We don't have anyone that I know of who could do what Sloan's done, so our UNSUB must feel pretty safe."

"Do we have anyone *else* who fits for this?" asked Sloan.

Jason shook his head. "*None* of the people who made our short list, including Henry, have the ability to do it, on the surface at least. Two attorneys, a judge, a cop, and a psychologist. I've pulled their college transcripts. No one had any special computer training at all."

"Assuming that the inside source had help, then, the simplest explanation is that Henry gave someone who *did* know how to do it access to hack into the system."

"But you can't prove that from what you have," Rebecca stated.

"Not yet," Sloan admitted. "I need to go back tonight. I need to look at what Henry's been doing. With the information I have, I can easily access his files."

"Do it," Rebecca said immediately. "In the meantime, we work the other angles we discussed this morning. Sandy nabbed us a solid lead—a dancer who might be our video girl. Watts and I will look for her." She turned to Mitchell. "I need you in those clubs as soon as possible. We're looking for information on an escort service that might be transporting girls to the clubs—to perform, to hook, we're not sure. That and any word you can get for us on the video shoots."

"Yes, ma'am."

Rebecca looked at Jason. "What kind of cover story are you going to use?"

"There's a big drag scene in DC. A place called Club Chaos on Dupont Circle is the heart of the drag king scene, and Jasmine performed with some of them there a couple of times." Jason looked at Mitchell. "I thought we could put Mitch out as having been a bouncer at the club. That way, he won't be expected to perform."

Watts looked a little red in the face, but he said nothing.

"I can handle that," Mitchell said. "I'm good at busting drunks."

That drew a laugh, and Rebecca stood. "Okay. Anything breaks, I want to know." She purposefully did not look at Sloan. "Anything." Then she turned to Watts. "I need a couple of hours, then let's cruise the clubs down on Delaware."

"Sure, Sarge." He heaved himself to his feet. "Sounds like my kinda night duty."

❖

Mitchell, sweating and swearing under her breath, humped the mattress up another few stairs. She looked out from under the leading edge, which was balanced on her back, at the open-toed, stack-heeled shoes and skin-tight black slacks of someone standing on the third floor landing. *Nice toes.* Craning her neck, she looked up the length of the very sexy body into laughing eyes. *Totally nice everything.* Her legs got shaky, and it wasn't from the effort of carrying the mattress.

"Hiya, Sandy."

"Hi, Dell. Whatcha doin'?"

"Moving in."

Sandy eased down a step on the narrow staircase, grabbed one side of the mattress, and lifted. "Is this it?"

"It's a start."

"Uh-huh."

Together they dragged it the rest of the way down the dim hall and dumped it unceremoniously into the middle of the empty living room of Dell's studio apartment.

"This is pathetic," Sandy observed, wrinkling her nose in distaste.

"I get a hot plate in here—it will be fine." Mitchell didn't care where she slept. She'd bedded down in worse places. Besides, she wasn't looking at the peeling paint, or the dust bunnies the size of bowling balls, or the questionable growth along the edge of the decades-old icebox. She couldn't look anywhere but at Sandy, so bright eyed and fresh and oh-so-hotsexykissable...Mitchell jerked at the warm touch on her hand.

"Uh-huh." Sandy took Mitchell's arm and tugged. "Come on. You can shower at my place."

"I gotta go to work."

"So do I. Come *on.*"

Once inside the apartment, Sandy closed the door and put both arms around Mitchell's waist beneath her leather jacket. "I thought you'd *never* show up."

Then Sandy pressed full-body against the startled cop and kissed her, taking her time, working her way over the surface of Mitchell's lips before slipping her tongue between them and exploring the inside. By the time she was inside Mitchell's mouth, sucking slowly on her tongue, Mitchell had walked them across the room to the sofa, and they fell onto it in a jumble of arms and legs. Mitchell groaned as Sandy's hand slid up the inside of her leg and cupped her through the jeans. Sandy moaned as fingers found her nipple through the thin material of her top.

"Sandy," Mitchell gasped, pulling her head back, trying to clear the haze of lust that pulsed with the rhythm of the hand squeezing fitfully between her thighs. Tried to hold on to some tiny bit of control. "Jesus, you're making me crazy with that."

"Yeah. Me, too. Do something about it, will ya?"

*Do something about it, will ya? Do something...*Something inside snapped. Mitchell stood abruptly on shaking legs, stripped off her jacket, and threw it behind her. Then she reached down for the bottom of Sandy's top, curled her fingers in the thin fabric, and dragged it up and off. Swiftly, she knelt before the sofa and, with one arm around Sandy's waist, pulled the startled young woman toward her, forcing Sandy to spread her legs to accommodate Mitchell's body. Tight between Sandy's open thighs, Mitchell leaned forward and put her mouth to Sandy's breast, closing around the nipple with her teeth as she caught and squeezed the other between her fingers.

Sandy gave a startled cry, drove her fingers into Mitchell's hair, and pressed her breast harder to Mitchell's mouth. "Oh my God. *Dell.*"

Mitchell was on fire. All day, the memory of being with Sandy— her smell, the softness of her skin, her surprised cries of pleasure— had simmered just below the surface of her consciousness. All day she'd wanted her, and now, now she couldn't touch her enough. She slid the arm that encircled Sandy's waist lower and pulled Sandy's hips even closer against her body. Her own hips rocked steadily, aching for contact, but she didn't want to give up the pleasure of Sandy's breast in her mouth.

"Dell," Sandy gasped, tugging at Mitchell's hair. "Dell, take your shirt off. Come on, baby...let me feel your skin."

With her lips still around Sandy's nipple, sucking the hard knot of flesh relentlessly, Mitchell began tearing at her clothes, pulling her shirt from her jeans, fumbling at her fly. Sandy's hands joined hers and finally she had to release Sandy's breast long enough to lean back and remove her shirt. In the next instant, Sandy's hands were on her, running over her breasts and abdomen, pushing below the edge of her jeans. Everywhere, everywhere she burned.

"Sandy." Shivering with need, Mitchell looked up into Sandy's eyes. "I want to taste you. Please...is it okay?"

Sandy's eyes widened. Her hands trembled as she framed Mitchell's face. "You have...such a fabulous mouth."

"Lie back," Mitchell said, her voice suddenly gentle. "Let me undress you."

"You first," Sandy murmured, her palms flat against Mitchell's belly, pushing down inside the waistband of her jeans. "Off...off... take these off."

Still kneeling, Mitchell worked the denim down, groaning as Sandy's hands moved lower as her body was bared. "Do not...go there," she warned as she stood to kick off boots and jeans. Despite her warning, she couldn't help thrusting against Sandy's palm. The pressure against her engorged clitoris made her head light. She pulled away, her stomach board-hard with arousal.

"Hey!" Sandy protested.

Mitchell grinned, put her hands lightly on Sandy's shoulders, and pushed her back so that she reclined with her legs over the edge of the sofa. "Be patient."

"Screw you, rookie."

But there wasn't much threat behind the words, and the fingers that trailed down Mitchell's arms shook. Carefully, Mitchell slid the tight black slacks down and off, then drew her fingertips up the inside of Sandy's legs, slowing as she reached the apex, resting her palms on the soft skin high on the inside of smooth thighs. Slowly, she lifted her eyes. Sandy, heavy-lidded and breathing quickly, was propped on her elbows, watching her.

"Okay?" Mitchell's voice was hoarse.

Sandy nodded, placing one hand behind Mitchell's neck. "Uh-huh. Better even."

Mitchell let Sandy guide her head down, closing her eyes as she immersed herself in the warm, wet welcome. The first kiss drew a sound of surprised pleasure, the next a long sigh, and when she carefully traced the delicate folds and firm prominences with her tongue, a sob of joy. Sandy's fingers on the back of her head pulled her closer, and Mitchell took the tender clitoris between her lips. As she played the nerve bundle with her tongue, she unconsciously lowered one hand to stroke herself, desperately seeking relief from the pressure pounding between her thighs.

"Ohh," Sandy gasped, jerking nearly upright, both hands

on Mitchell's head now, holding her close, just holding on. She watched Mitchell pleasure her and felt the orgasm coming fast. "Dell...Dell, I'm gonna come."

Mitchell swiftly forgot her own needs, bringing both hands beneath Sandy's hips, holding her fast as she carried her higher. Breath suspended, she followed the rise and fall of Sandy's hips, timed her strokes to the pulse beating between her lips, and thrilled to the sensation of her lover climaxing in her mouth. She didn't stop the gentle ministrations until Sandy, moaning softly, pushed her away.

"Stop." Sandy shuddered. "I'm gonna freakin' explode or something."

Pleasantly exhausted, Mitchell rested her cheek against Sandy's leg. "That's nice."

Sandy grabbed a handful of Mitchell's hair and tugged weakly. "C'mere." She leaned back, swung her legs onto the sofa, and guided Mitchell down on top of her. She edged one leg between Mitchell's thighs. "Oh, you're really wet."

"Yeah. You make me so hot." Mitchell turned her face to Sandy's neck and kissed her. She wanted to come, but she never wanted the excitement to end, so she held very still, holding back. "You feel so good."

Sandy put her mouth to Mitchell's ear and whispered, "Come on my leg."

The words shot through Mitchell like a bolt of lightening, triggering her nerve endings, everything going off at once. Her control shattered, and she came with a shout.

"That's it, baby, that's it," Sandy soothed, stroking the length of Mitchell's back. "You're so sexy, Dell. God."

"You kill me," Mitchell mumbled.

"Mmm. I like that." Sandy tightened her hold, feeling at once incredibly strong and incredibly vulnerable. Mitchell did scary things to her.

But when Mitchell sighed, "Yeah, me, too," all Sandy really felt was happy.

CHAPTER TWENTY-ONE

"W ill you stop fidgeting?"
"It tickles."

"Aww." Sandy drew the brush along Mitch's jaw. "I bet you didn't give Jasmine a hard time."

"Jasmine wasn't standing between my legs." Mitch shifted on the stool, and Sandy pushed closer, making Mitch gasp. Maybe it had been a bad idea to get *fully* dressed before this part. He still wasn't used to accommodating the extra equipment, and Sandy seemed to delight in leaning into just the right spot to make him squirm.

"Good thing," Sandy muttered. "She's way too hot."

"Not interested."

"Shut up, Mitch. You'll ruin my line." Sandy switched to a pencil and widened the already dark brows. "So, where you goin'?"

Mitch hesitated, suddenly uncertain how much to disclose. Somehow, work and Sandy had gotten all tangled together.

"What?" Sandy grew still. Her voice cold, she said, "I'm good enough to fuck but not enough to trust, is that it?"

For once, Mitch anticipated Sandy's quick withdrawal and grabbed her around the waist just as she tried to move away. "Will you just wait a minute? Jesus, Sandy." He took a deep breath. "I'm not used to having a girlfriend, okay? I never talk about work to anyone, so it feels weird."

"You sure that's it?" Sandy relented a little, relaxing in the circle of his arms, surprised by the honesty she couldn't discount. She looked into his eyes, *Dell's* eyes, the eyes that no amount of make-up or drag gear could change. They were soft, deep, tender. Sandy sighed. "Okay, okay. Sorry."

"S'okay." Mitch loosened his grip but still kept his arms lightly around her waist. "You smell good."

"Don't change the subject." But her voice had softened, and she leaned over to kiss him quickly. "So—where you goin'?"

"Jasmine is taking me to the Troc. Depending on how things go, I might go out clubbing with some of the kings later. The sooner the better, Frye says."

"Frye." Sandy snorted. "What a major pain in the butt." Her tone, however, was quietly affectionate.

"You saw her earlier, huh?"

It was Sandy's turn to hesitate. For some reason she couldn't quite figure, Mitchell had a bug up about Frye. And because she wasn't sure why, she didn't know how much to say.

"What? You can't tell me?" Mitch's voice deepened with anger.

"What difference does it make?" Sandy countered. "You *know* about the CI thing, so you know I see her."

"See her. See her, like *talk* see her, right?"

Sandy burst out laughing, pushing playfully into Mitch's body with hers. "You don't think Frye and I are screwing, do you?"

Mitch blushed. "Well, no, but..."

"But what, Mitch? She's never laid a hand on me, even when I offered."

"What?"

"It was a long time ago. I was trying to get her off my back, and I...well, you know...tried to buy her off."

Mitch rested his forehead between Sandy's breasts and closed his eyes. *You asked, asshole.* He felt Sandy's fingers tentatively stroke the back of his neck.

"You mad?" Sandy asked.

"No."

"Sure?"

More than anything else the slight tremor of uncertainty in Sandy's voice cleared his head. He hated it when she was scared. He much preferred her pissed off. "No, it's fine. I understand."

"Even if I wanted to screw her, which I *don't,* idiot, she's seriously hooked up with that doctor."

Mitch raised his head. "Huh?"

"Duh." Sandy kissed him again. "You are so clueless. The shrink...Rawlings."

"How do you know *that*?" Mitch's stomach dropped. *The sergeant and Dr. Rawlings? Oh man, what have I said to Dr. Rawlings about Frye?*

Oblivious to Mitch's shock, Sandy shrugged. "Because Frye was here the night she had a...relapse thing...and I had to call Rawlings. Believe me, they're together."

Frye was here? In your apartment? And she and Dr. Rawlings... oh, fuck. Mitch groaned and put his cheek back on Sandy's breast. "Shoot me."

"Uh-uh, baby. Not until I get you into bed." Sandy reached down and gently squeezed Mitch's crotch. "Just make sure you don't spend it anywhere else tonight."

Mitch got wet and hard. *Shit.* "If I don't get out of here soon, I'm gonna *spend it* right here."

"Mmm. I can do fast."

"I *can't*."

"Liar." Sandy reached down between his legs again.

"Not right *now,* anyhow." Mitch grabbed her hand. "Will you give me a break?"

Sandy laughed again. "No freakin' way." She kissed him, seriously this time, until she felt him start to rock against her, then she stepped back. "See ya later then, stud."

"Jeez, you're a tease."

"Mmm, you complainin'?" What he didn't know was how bad off *she* was. She wanted to lick his neck. She wanted to kiss him until he was ready to come in his pants, and then she wanted to reach inside his pants and find him and Dell all mixed up together. *I'm gonna make myself nuts in another minute, 'cause we don't have time.*

"You hear me complaining?" Mitch murmured, sliding off the stool and pulling her close. He brushed his lips over the edge of her ear. "I'm sorry I can't stay. Man, I want to."

"Sure. So go already, since you're no good for anything else right now." She kissed him one last time to soften the words.

"I'll be good later."

"Promises, promises." But she was smiling as he walked out the door.

❖

"All set?"

"Fine." Jasmine, in figure-hugging deep red slacks, a scoop top, and a short, shiny, black vinyl jacket, had both arms around Mitch's waist, holding on from behind on the motorcycle. "Sandy did a fabulous job. You look great. Are you ready?"

"As I'm ever gonna be."

Jasmine laid her cheek against the worn leather. "Then let's go, hot stuff."

Mitch kick started the bike and pulled into traffic. It was after midnight and the streets were fairly empty. It took less than twenty minutes to ride cross-town to the Troc. He found curbside parking and shut off the engine.

"Nice ride," Jasmine commented as she slid one leg over the seat and stood up.

"Yeah." Mitch took a deep breath and dismounted. *Time to go to work.*

"You okay on the background stuff we reviewed?" Jasmine hooked a hand around his forearm as they walked.

"Uh-huh. I did some web surfing today to look at some of the drag king troupes, too." Mitch shrugged. "I'll be okay."

"I'll be with you tonight, and we'll just hang out. Tomorrow I'm performing, though, so you'll be on your own for a while then."

"I can handle it."

Jasmine slid her arm around Mitch's waist as they reached the door of the club. "I have no doubt."

Immediately inside the door, a burly guy in a tight black T-shirt and black jeans stood with arms folded across his massive chest.

"Hi, Ronnie."

"Hi, Jas." He leaned over and delicately kissed her cheek. "You look gorgeous."

"Thank you." She smiled. "Ronnie, this is Mitch."

He held out his hand. "Yo."

"Hey," Mitch said, shaking the huge hand, which was firm but surprisingly gentle. It was larger and darker inside the club than Mitch had expected, and he blinked rapidly, trying to get his bearings.

"Is Kennie here?" Jasmine asked.

"Sure. He's in the back with a few of the other guys."

Jasmine took Mitch's hand. "Thanks."

"Bye, beautiful."

"Ronnie the bouncer?" Mitch asked as they wended their way through the tables, about half of which were occupied with small groups, couples, and the occasional lone drinker.

"One of them. He also owns a piece of the place." Jasmine held aside a heavy black curtain strung across an archway to one side of an elevated stage. "The dressing rooms are back here. A small lounge, too. That's probably where the guys are."

Mitch took a deep breath. *Show time.*

The lounge was a paneled, low-ceilinged space with a sofa, a couple of overstuffed chairs, a coffee table and a pool table. Two drag kings stood, cue sticks in hand, intently studying the lie of the balls on the faded green felt. A third sat with his booted feet propped up on the table, watching the game, a beer bottle in one hand. All three were dressed in jeans, T-shirts, and boots, and all had the smooth-faced, androgynous features of the drag kings Mitch had seen on the Internet. One had a small trim mustache that looked real, one had convincing sideburns, and all of them were flat chested.

Mitch couldn't help a quick glance at their crotches, wondering how he measured up. *Nothing too obvious. Guess I'm okay there.*

The seated guy rose as they walked around the pool table toward him. He was Mitch's height and a few pounds heavier with a small tattoo, a kanji symbol from the looks of it, low on the side of his neck.

"Jasmine! Hey, didn't expect to see you tonight."

Jasmine dipped her head and kissed him on the mouth. "Hi, Kennie." She tugged Mitch forward. "Ken, this is Mitch. Mitch, Ken Dewar, the troupe leader of the Front Street Kings."

"Hey," Ken said, extending his hand.

The drag king with the mustache snorted. "Yeah, make him

sound important, why don't ya."

"Aww," Jasmine soothed. "We all know how special *you* are, Dino."

"Uh-huh." He grinned. "Hiya, I'm Dino."

"Mitch." Mitch shook hands all around. The third guy Mitch recognized from the Front Street Kings' website. Phil E. Pride.

"Mitch just moved up here from DC. I thought you guys could show him around."

Ken lifted a shoulder and looked Mitch over. "You perform, Mitch?"

Mitch shook his head. "Nope. No talent. At least not on stage."

That drew a laugh.

"What brings you up here?"

"A girl."

Ken raised an eyebrow and glanced at Jasmine.

"Oh, not me, Ken." Jasmine smiled sweetly. "You know I adore every one of you, but you're all way too much man for me..." Everyone laughed. "Besides, I'm allowed to flirt...*a little*...but I am oh so already taken."

"I keep hoping," Ken said.

"I'm going to go talk to some of the girls," Jasmine said. She squeezed Mitch's arm. "I'll see you later, stud."

"Okay."

Mitch took the seat opposite Ken in one of the lumpy chairs and leaned forward, his elbows on his knees. "I haven't been here very long, and I'm trying to get a sense of the scene. It's tough, you know...on your own."

"Most kings hang here, because of our shows. There's seven of us in the troupe, and maybe that many regulars who aren't performers." Ken reached for his beer. "You looking for a job?"

"I could use one. I've got a straight day gig, but it doesn't pay much." Mitch grinned. "Like I said, I'm not looking to perform. I used to be a bouncer, and I can do almost anything around a bar."

"They're always looking for bar backs. Ask Ronnie—did you meet him?"

"Yeah. On the way in."

Ken propped his feet up back on the coffee table. "So—you're friends with Jasmine."

"Yep." Mitch waited, sensing Ken considering that fact.

"You interested in the club scene or is the thing with your girl serious?"

"It's serious," Mitch replied. "But I'm not married."

And just like that, he was in.

❖

Sloan looked up from the monitor when the lights in the main lab came on. It was three a.m. She was rapidly considering her options—excuses, evasion, escape—when a redhead with sea-green eyes stuck her head through the doorway of Flanagan's office, making her potential choices moot.

"Hello," Sloan said.

"You'd be Rebecca's friend, I take it."

"Yes." Sloan saw no point in denying the truth.

"You keep odd hours." The redhead approached. "I'm Maggie Collins, one of the CSIs."

Sloan held out her hand. "J.T. Sloan."

Maggie quirked a brow. "Jefferson? Jeremiah?...Jezebel?"

Laughing, Sloan shook her head. "Just Sloan."

"Well, then, *Just* Sloan," Maggie said with a smile, "this place is going to be hopping in about five minutes. There's been a big pileup on the Schuylkill, and we've got two teams working the crash site. Flanagan will be here shortly."

"I can't leave right now."

There was something in the dark edges of Sloan's violet eyes that gave Maggie pause. After a moment's deliberation, she turned, walked into the other room, and pulled her blue CSI nylon windbreaker off the back of her chair. Returning, she held it out. "Put this on, then, and stay in here. Everyone will be too busy jumping to Flanagan's tune to pay you much mind."

Sloan smiled at the affection in the other woman's voice. "Thanks."

"Should I ask what you're doin'?"

"I'm digging for worms."

"Ah, sure you are." Maggie hesitated. "What Rebecca's doin', that's not my business. But Flanagan, now...she is."

Sloan studied the calm, steady eyes. "There's nothing here to hurt her."

Maggie nodded. "Good huntin', then."

"Thanks," Sloan muttered under her breath. Her fingers returned to the keyboard; her mind engaged the data. She'd found the worm all right. Now what she needed was to discover who'd buried it.

❖

"We have to stop meeting like this," Catherine whispered as arms came around her from behind in the dark. She shifted to make room for her lover in bed.

"I'm sorry." Rebecca nuzzled Catherine's neck, sighing with fatigue and discouragement. "I tried to reach you earlier, and Joyce said you were still in session. Then I got busy and didn't get another chance."

Catherine pushed her hips back into the curve of Rebecca's body and pulled Rebecca's hand between her breasts. She murmured contentedly when Rebecca shifted a palm down to cradle her breast. "It's okay. I missed you, though."

"Me, too." Rebecca felt Catherine's nipple harden against the curve of her hand. It felt so good.

"Any progress?"

"Not much." Rebecca kissed the warm spot below Catherine's ear. "Something's gotta break soon, though. I can feel it."

"Mmm. Good."

"It's not always like this."

Catherine placed her hand over the hand that held her breast and pressed lightly. "I'm not complaining."

"I know. Thank you."

"No need for thanks, but..."

Rebecca stiffened, expecting recriminations, but forced herself not to jump to conclusions. "But?"

"I would really, really like it if you could make it home one of these nights early enough to make love with me when I'm not half asleep." Catherine rolled her hips into Rebecca's pelvis. "I'm so much better then."

"Hmm..." Rebecca rubbed her fingers over Catherine's nipple.

"Does that mean you're too tired now?"

Catherine turned on her back and drew Rebecca on top of her. "Did I say that?"

❖

"What did you say your name was?"

"Sandy." Sandy turned her back on the guy at the end of the bar who was giving her the once-over and faced Trudy, the thin Asian girl from the video. "Lucy said maybe you could put me with this movie guy to make some fast cash. I...you know...need some quick medical assistance."

Trudy looked away. "Lucy sent you?"

"Not exactly." Sandy swiveled on her seat as a hand stroked her shoulder. It was the guy from the end of the bar. "Buzz off, will ya?"

"What'sa matter, honey? You too *busy* or somethin'?"

The guy moved his hand lower, brushing the side of her breast.

Sandy's eyes narrowed and, without moving anything but her arm, she slid a hand up the inside of his leg and closed her hand around his balls. Then she squeezed, gently. "Well..."

He smiled.

She kept squeezing.

His smile turned to surprise, and then his eyes suddenly widened in shock. "Jesus," he whispered desperately. "Let go."

"I'm trying to have a conversation here."

"Okay, okay." His knees buckled, and he grabbed the edge of the bar. "Ah, Christ...please."

His eyes started to tear; satisfied, Sandy released her hold. "Goodbye now."

"Bitch," he croaked, but his voice lacked any venom.

The girl with Sandy watched the stranger limp carefully away. "Aren't you afraid he'll be waiting outside for you?"

Sandy shrugged. "Most of the time they're too drunk by then to do anything. But I'll go out the back just in case." She checked once more over her shoulder, saw him ease carefully onto a bar stool, and turned her attention back to Trudy. "Lucy just told me you'd done this video gig. No details. So—can you fix me up?"

"I don't know." Trudy fiddled with her hair. "I'm not a regular, you know? I filled in when some other girl got sick or something. They usually use their own girls in these movies."

"You mean actresses?"

"Not hardly." Trudy snorted. "Foreign girls, dancers and hookers mostly. I was working the same club with some of them, and that's how I got that one job."

"So can you put me with one of them?"

"Maybe. I don't know."

"Look, if you do, I'll split the money with you."

Trudy's eyes widened. "No way."

Sandy nodded. "It'd be worth it to me. I'm tired of blowing slimeballs like that guy over there for small change."

"Yeah, you got that right." Trudy picked at a nail. After a minute, she said, "I'll ask around."

"Hey, thanks." Sandy tried not to look as happy as she felt. *I earned my money tonight, Frye.* "So let me give you my number, 'kay?"

When she left the bar on Delaware, it was almost four in the morning. Ordinarily, she would have gone over to the strip on Locust and tricked for another two hours in the dark alleys or front seats of parked cars. Tonight she headed home, hoping that Mitch, or Dell, would be there waiting.

CHAPTER TWENTY-TWO

Rebecca groaned and reached for the phone. "Frye."
"It's Sloan. I have to talk to you."
"What time is it?"
"Five."
"How important?"
"Very."
"Ah, Christ. Okay." Rebecca sat up and pushed the sheets aside. "Your place?"
"That'll work. I'll wake Jason."
"You need the rest of the team?"
"It can wait till later."
"Am I gonna like this?"
"Maybe."
Catherine waited until Rebecca put down the phone. Voice fuzzy with sleep, she asked, "Everything okay?"
"Sloan has something."
"Call me later." She burrowed back into the pillow.
Rebecca smiled, walked around to Catherine's side of the bed, and leaned down to kiss her cheek. Lips close to her lover's ear, she whispered, "What's the matter? Something tire you out last night?"
"Mmm." Eyes closed, Catherine smiled at the memory. "Something."

❖

Mitch stood uncertainly before the door to 3B, listening intently for any sound from the other side.
"Sandy?" he called softly, tapping very gently. He waited a minute, then turned to go down the hall to his own apartment. The

door behind him opened.

"Hey."

Mitch spun around, heart racing. "Hi."

"Where ya goin'?"

"I didn't want to wake you."

"Why not?"

"Well, you know...it's late...early...whatever."

Sandy wore only a pair of dark string-bikini underwear and a tank top. She leaned a shoulder against the doorframe, her eyes moving slowly over Mitch's body. He looked even better than she'd remembered in his black T-shirt and leathers. "So, you wanna come in?"

Mitch nodded, trying not to look as hungry for her as he felt. "Yeah."

"How was your night?" She didn't move.

"Long." He moved to the opposite side of the threshold and stretched an arm up along the frame, tilting his body toward hers but not touching her. An inch separated them, and he could feel her heat across the chasm, penetrating his clothes, soaking into his skin. His insides twisted he wanted her so bad.

"Did you go out with the boys?" Sandy asked casually as she lazily drew her fingers across her bare abdomen.

"Uh-huh." Mitch's throat was dry, his eyes riveted on the slow caress. "We...uh...hit a few places."

"Did you score?" This time there was a slight edge to the question.

Softly, Mitch replied, "Not yet."

Sandy reached out, curled her fingers around the waistband of his pants, and yanked him into the room. "Smart answer."

She swung the door closed and then pushed him back against it with the weight of her body glued to his. She wrapped her arms around his neck, pressed her mouth to his, and rubbed the tiny square of black fabric covering her groin over the swelling in his crotch. Her tongue was in his mouth, and as she sucked on his, she moved against him until she was so wet she could feel the dampness on her thighs.

"I've been so hot for you," she breathed against his neck. "So...crazy hot."

Mitch cupped Sandy's butt and held her as she rode him, letting her have...take...do...whatever she wanted. She was going to make him come pretty soon just from the pressure of her thrusting hips, but he figured she knew that, because he couldn't help groaning with pleasure and need.

"Unzip your fly," Sandy gasped, pulling his T-shirt from his pants.

She raked her nails down his abdomen, her thighs braced against his. Then she pulled her tank top off as he opened his pants for her. She looked down, saw the full white Jockeys. She looked up and met questioning blue eyes, so filled with longing it made her heart ache. Gently, she took Mitch's hands and brought them to her breasts. Moaning softly, she closed her eyes and bit her lip as the first touch of his fingers against her hard nipples sent pleasure streaking deep into her core.

"Oh," Sandy moaned, straddling a rock-hard thigh and sliding her slick skin over the cool leather. "You make me want to come so bad."

"Sandy," Mitch whispered, "I want—oh, God..." He leaned his head back against the door and fought to stay standing as Sandy reached into his pants. He felt the force of her fingers on the outside of his underwear, gripping him in her palm and slowly, rhythmically squeezing.

"Can you feel that?" Sandy murmured. "Baby?"

"Yes," Mitchell groaned as the insistent pressure massaged her clitoris.

"Enough to come?" Sandy watched the muscles in Mitchell's neck strain and a pulse race erratically the length of her throat.

"Oh, yeah...Sandy..." Mitchell gave a small cry as Sandy removed her hand and the tantalizing pressure disappeared. "Please...I'm almost there."

"Next time," Sandy reached beneath everything inside Mitchell's briefs until she found skin, then slid a finger on either side of Mitchell's hard clitoris, "wear your working gear."

Mitchell couldn't answer. Sandy's fingers, tugging and stroking her quivering, poised-to-explode flesh, were quickly bringing her to orgasm. With her last bit of will, she pushed her hand down Sandy's belly and inside her bikinis.

"Oh," Sandy cried in surprise, instantly ready to come. "Dell... Dell, put your hand inside me. Oh—hurry, baby."

Shuddering, Mitchell climaxed as she slipped gently inside Sandy's warm depths. Hips bucking, she wrapped her free arm around Sandy's waist and held them both upright as Sandy buried her face in the curve of Mitchell's neck, clinging to her and crying out her pleasure, over and over.

In the midst of her orgasm, Sandy instinctively followed the lift of Mitchell's hips and entered her, pushing Mitchell to yet another, deeper, climax.

"Oh God, Sandy," Mitchell moaned, "you're so good...so good."

"I felt you come," Sandy whispered in awe, trembling as the last waves of her own orgasm faded. She moved her fingers carefully and sensed tender muscles ripple in response. "Oh my God...Dell."

Mitchell swallowed, trying to speak. Finally, "You'll make me come again if you do that."

"Yeah?" Sandy asked weakly, finding it hard to stand. Leaning into Mitchell for support, she tested the theory and smiled as Mitchell jerked and moaned softly. "How long can you go?"

Mitchell rested her cheek on the top of Sandy's head, shivering. "Don't know...first time for this."

"Yeah?" Sandy kissed Mitchell's neck, enormously pleased. "Good."

"I gotta...lie down soon," Mitchell gasped. "And you gotta stop."

"Mmm." Sandy lifted her hips into Mitchell's palm. "You're still inside me."

Mitchell smiled, eyes closed. "Yeah."

"I like it."

There was a note of wonder in Sandy's voice that made Mitchell's heart turn over. "I'm crazy about you, you know."

"Dell." Sandy rested her palm against Mitchell's cheek and stroked her gently. Carefully, she withdrew her fingers from between Mitchell's thighs and immediately wanted to return. "You're such a sap."

Mitchell smiled. She loved the way Sandy caressed her

face and curled into her, so soft and warm. "I'm gonna come out, okay?"

"Uh-huh," Sandy murmured, lifting her hips away, feeling Mitchell slowly leave her. "That was so...so..."

"Yeah. It was." Mitchell sighed and opened her eyes. She looked down into Sandy's sated face and kissed her gently. "You ready for bed?"

"Mmm. Okay."

"I should shower," Mitchell said tiredly. "I smell like a fucking barroom."

"I don't care," Sandy replied, taking Mitchell's hand and pulling her toward the open sofa bed. "Shower later. I want to go to sleep with you naked next to me, and you just wiped me out."

"Me?" Mitchell laughed. "Jesus, *you* were the one who jumped *me*."

Sandy smirked. "I did, didn't I?"

As they undressed, Mitchell laid her drag gear aside and asked quietly, "Did you mean what you said earlier, about Mitch wearing the working gear?"

Naked, Sandy crawled into bed. She watched Mitchell remove the chest wrap. "You have great tits, you know?"

Mitchell blushed. "Thanks."

"I get turned on looking at you with no clothes on."

"Sandy, jeez. Don't you ever get enough?" But Mitchell was grinning as she slid into bed. She turned on her side, drew a finger down the center of Sandy's chest, and cupped her breast. Sandy's nipple hardened immediately. "You are so incredibly sexy," she breathed in awe.

"You make me incredibly hot. *Mitch* makes me hot, too," Sandy said quietly, edging her leg between Mitchell's thighs. "Oh, baby, you're still *so* wet."

"No foolin'." Mitchell kissed the tip of Sandy's chin. "About Mitch—"

"I like playing with him. I like watching your eyes when I feel him up."

The image hit hard and Mitchell jerked, her clitoris stiffening. "Oh, man...here I go again."

Sandy laughed. "So, yeah, I wouldn't mind if Mitch was

packing a working dick."

"Have you ever, you know...done it with one?"

"Uh-uh." Sandy shook her head. "You?"

"Uh-uh." Mitchell drew a deep breath. "But I wouldn't mind... sometime."

Sandy put her hand between Mitchell's legs and held her gently. Sighing, she closed her eyes and snuggled her cheek against Mitchell's shoulder. Drowsily she murmured, "Between you, me, and Mitch, we oughta be able to figure it out."

"Most likely." Mitchell nodded, holding her tight. "Good night, honey."

"Good night, baby."

❖

Sheltered in the warm curve of Mitchell's body, Sandy awoke to the sensation of fingers softly stroking her cheek. She lay unmoving, her head tucked beneath Mitchell's chin, unused to the strange experience of being next to someone and not being afraid. Lightly, she brushed her palm over Mitchell's chest. "How come you're not sleeping?"

"Couldn't," Mitchell whispered, nuzzling Sandy's hair. "Sorry."

"S'okay." Sandy pressed closer, one leg and an arm draped across Mitchell's body. "Something wrong?"

Mitchell shook her head.

Sandy nudged her with her chin. "Dell..."

"I'm worried about you working for Frye."

Sandy tensed. "Would you rather I gave blowjobs instead?"

"No." Mitchell continued to stroke her. "I'd rather you worked at...McDonald's."

"Oh, puh-leeze." Sandy closed her eyes, her heart racing, waiting for what she knew was coming next. *You're thinking about what I do when I'm not with you, aren't you? I'm going to lose you, aren't I, rookie?*

"I know, I know." Mitchell kissed the top of the blond head resting on her shoulder. "I'm just so nuts about you, I can't stand the idea that you might get hurt."

"Jesus, Dell. You're a cop. Ever think *you* might get hurt, and that *I* might not like that?"

"That's different."

"Oh yeah?" Sandy snorted, but felt a bit of the panic ease. Mitchell was still holding her, still touching her gently, her voice still lazy and warm. She hadn't gone away. "Why is it different? Because you're so big and strong and I'm just a girl?"

Mitchell laughed. "No, honey. Because I'm twice your size and I have a gun."

"Big deal." Sandy tilted her head and kissed Mitchell's jaw. "Besides, if I work for Frye, I don't have to hook regularly."

"Now there's a devil's bargain," Mitchell said darkly.

"It's the one I made," Sandy said quietly.

"I *know*. And it scares me."

"You ever had a girlfriend before, rookie?"

A minute passed.

"Once."

"You love her?"

"Yes." Mitchell ran her hand over Sandy's shoulder. "Sandy—"

"She leave you?"

"Not exactly...sort of." Mitchell sighed. "That has nothing to do with this."

"Every place we've been...everything we've done, or had done to us...has to do with this." Sandy pushed up on her elbow and stared fixedly into Mitchell's eyes. "The way things are is the way things are. I want you, Dell." She searched Mitchell's face. "So, you stayin' or what?"

Mitchell pulled Sandy on top of her, wrapped her arms around her, and held her tightly. "Fuck, yes, I'm staying."

"Good." Sandy finally started to relax, the sick fear that had gripped her deep inside gradually relenting. "So do you think maybe you could shut up so we could get some sleep?"

"What, you're not horny?" Mitchell smoothed her palm down Sandy's back and over her buttocks.

"I'm saving myself."

"For what?" Mitchell bit Sandy's earlobe. "Huh?"

"The right girl."

Mitchell laughed, and this time when she closed her eyes,

Sandy's heart beating next to hers, she slept.

❖

"I fucked up in more ways than one the other night," Sloan announced.

Jason and Rebecca sat facing her in the conference room, fresh cups of coffee in their hands.

"How so?" Rebecca asked, sipping the scalding brew. She was tired. Her chest ached. She knew she was running on less than full power—that she'd never quite gotten her strength back after the shooting—but she didn't see that she could do anything about that now.

"I missed something."

Jason sat up straight. "On the back-trace to Henry?"

"No," Sloan sighed, "on the back door itself."

"What, there isn't one?" Rebecca asked sharply. Her fatigue coupled with her lack of expertise in a critical area of the investigation made her very short on patience.

"Oh, there *is* one." Sloan grimaced. "In fact, the whole department's system is so wormy it looks like swiss cheese." She shook her head. "Man, I pity whoever's gonna be running your electronic surveillance unit, because the first order of business will have to be cleaning up your own house—and it's a mess."

"Just give me the bottom line," Rebecca snapped. "It is it Henry or not?"

"I don't think so."

"Christ." Rebecca wasn't sure whether to be relieved or to tear Sloan's head off. "God damn it, how could you have made that kind of mistake? Jesus, we could have blown this whole case!"

"Sergeant," Jason interrupted quietly, "maybe we should hear her out?"

Rebecca spun in his direction, but just before she let loose with another string of invectives, she caught sight of the shadows under his eyes. Then she took a good look at Sloan, who'd been up all night. Again. The cybersleuth looked worn out, although she was making an attempt to stand tall. "Ah, *hell*." She leaned back and shrugged her shoulders, forcing herself to settle down. "Make it simple, but make me understand."

"Networks, especially big ones like the ones that link municipal services, have all kinds of things going on internally. Maintenance functions, if you will, run in the background constantly. A lot of it happens automatically—preprogrammed updates and the like." Sloan waited, gauging Rebecca's reactions. At a nod from the detective, she continued. "There have to be avenues for that work—that information—to travel to individual computers, and the way that happens is via file transfer ports, or entryways."

"Okay," Rebecca said. "I got it."

"Those ports are always open and provide a way into a network—*if* you know how to access them. In essence, they're also huge potential highways for hackers. That's how the Blaster and Sobig worms spread so fast." Sloan glanced at Jason. "We get around that way a lot, too."

Jason nodded grimly.

"So," Sloan continued, "all someone has to do is bring in an infected computer, connect it to the system, and launch the worm. Some worms don't even have to be attached to e-mail or any kind of file, so the user never even suspects. Just—boom—information will start pouring back to the source computer, or anywhere else the hacker programs it to go. Want a password? No problem. Want to read someone else's mail? Have a seat. Want root access to alter or erase entire files? Tougher, but with a good code writer creating the worm, possible."

"And that's what happened?" Rebecca asked.

Sloan nodded. "Someone inserted a worm into the system at the PPD, and it's infected any number of computers. I missed it the first time, because it's a tiny bit of code piggybacked onto a huge file, and when I saw that log-in hack, I went off in another direction. Henry's computer *is* one that was hit, which is how his password was usurped. I don't know how many others there are, but there could be any number."

"You're sure it's not Henry?"

"I couldn't find anything in his files to suggest he's wrong." Sloan shrugged. "And my guess is that he's just a fall guy. But *someone* is able to read and possibly even modify just about every bit of data in the entire system."

Rebecca rubbed her face, drank more coffee, and digested the information. The thought made her stomach heave. Entire cases were built on lab reports, witness accounts, and other information stored in the system. Personnel files, home addresses, health records—the list was endless. *And Sandy's name is in there now, too. All spelled out and officially listed as my CI.* "This is bad."

Sloan and Jason were silent.

"So, we're nowhere?" Rebecca looked from one to the other, working to beat back the hopeless feeling. She'd been at this point before in an investigation. Hell, she'd been stalled for half a year on the death of her own partner. She still had only one recourse, and that was to keep doing the job.

"No, we're definitely somewhere." Sloan's eyes lit up. "I know where the worm came from."

Jason whistled. "You *have* been busy."

"I screwed up the other night." Sloan's eyes were hard, her voice like granite. Thinking about what she had almost done based upon an oversight, no matter how understandable, made her stomach churn. "That could have cost us all."

"Who?" Rebecca's heart raced. *Name. Just give me a name.*

"Not who, yet," Sloan advised. "But I've got where. It came from a computer in the district attorney's office."

"A name," Rebecca said quietly. "I need a name."

Sloan and Jason spoke in unison. "We'll get you one."

CHAPTER TWENTY-THREE

"W hat's that?" Sandy mumbled, pulling the thin blanket over her head and burrowing deeper into Mitchell's side.

"Huh?" Mitchell grunted. "What?"

"That noise."

Mitchell lifted her head and looked around the room. Her pants and boots were by the bed, her shirt inside out on the coffee table, her gym bag with extra clothes and her— "Shit!" She jumped from the bed and almost fell over Sandy's platform sandals. "My beeper."

"Mmph." Sandy rolled over, her back to the room and Mitchell, who sat down on the edge of the sofa bed and punched numbers into the phone.

"Mitchell," she said after a few seconds. "Uh-huh. Okay... sure." She put the phone down and stood up, dizzy with fatigue and hunger. She looked for a clock and couldn't see one. "I gotta go."

"Where?" Sandy's voice was muffled by the pillow over her head.

"Sloan's."

"Now?"

"First I gotta shower. I smell like I spent the night in the drunk tank."

Sandy stumbled into the bathroom in Mitchell's wake and crowded into the tiny shower stall with her. Eyes closed, she put her arms around Mitchell from behind and rested her cheek against her back. "Fuck, Dell, you worked all night."

"Yeah," Mitchell muttered as she let the spray hit her in the face. The water was still cold and the warmth of Sandy's body felt good against hers. "That was Jason. He needs help with something."

"Frye there?" Sandy asked, reaching around Mitchell to the small basket that hung from the showerhead to extract a bottle of shampoo.

"Dunno." Mitchell doused her whole head in the lukewarm water. "Why?"

"I wanna talk to her."

"You got something?" Mitchell asked, waking up quickly now.

Sandy stood with her head back, eyes closed, desultorily working up the lather in her short blond hair. "Maybe."

"You didn't say anything last night."

"We were fucking, remember?" Sandy yawned and edged Mitchell aside to stand under the water.

"Yeah." Mitchell grabbed her around the waist and kissed her neck. "I recall it was spectacular."

"It was." Suds-free, Sandy threw her arms around Mitchell's neck and kissed her, rubbing her wet skin against Mitchell's. "Mmm, that's so nice."

Mitchell tightened her hold, running her tongue over Sandy's lips and into her mouth. Somehow they ended up against the wall, legs entwined, bucking and groaning and groping each other. Mitchell yanked her head back, panting. "Honey, I don't have time!"

"What?" Sandy gasped unbelievingly. She grabbed Mitchell's hand and tugged it between her own thighs. "You don't have a minute? Feel me." She rocked against Mitchell's palm. "Come on, baby. Touch me."

Time lost all meaning as Mitchell eased her fingers into the heat and promise of her lover's desire. "You're so beautiful," she whispered, slowly pushing deeper into the welcoming folds.

Sandy arched her back and threaded her fingers into Mitchell's hair, claiming her mouth with bruising intensity as the sensation of being filled spread though her belly. Never, never had anything—anyone—touched her like this. Being this connected, even more than the sharp and simple pleasure of release, was why she wanted Mitchell so fiercely, constantly, without end. "You make me feel so alive," she whimpered, her hips beginning to lift with the first ripple of orgasm.

"I love you," Mitchell whispered, her thumb caressing the undersurface of Sandy's clitoris as she steadily stroked in and out, one deep thrust after another. "God. I love you."

Stomach taut, legs trembling, Sandy came, filled with the sound and fury of Mitchell's passion. Sobbing faintly, she held on to the one solid thing in her world, helpless to do anything but surrender to the desire she both needed and feared. Slowly, the rolling contractions stopped and she could breathe again. "I'm... like...addicted to you or something. I can't stop wanting you to do that to me."

"What?" Mitchell murmured. "Make you come?"

"Uh-uh," Sandy replied, cupping Mitchell's breast and toying with her nipple. "Making me come out of my mind."

"Sandy, honey." Mitchell laughed shakily, easing Sandy out of the stream of water and backing away. "I have to go."

"What about you?"

"I'm fine."

"You are?"

Sandy looked just a little worried, and Mitchell shook her head. "No, I'm stone hard, and I'd probably come if you touched me for ten seconds, but—"

"But work's more important?" There was more than a bit of ire in Sandy's voice. "Right?"

"No, I just can't come while imagining Frye's face if I show up any later."

"Oh." Sandy reached for a towel. "I can see that. So let's go already. Jeez."

"You're coming with me?"

"I said I wanted to talk to Frye," Sandy replied while hunting under the sink for an extra toothbrush. She handed it to Mitchell. "Here."

"You got a lead on something?" Mitchell asked around a mouthful of toothpaste. When Sandy didn't answer, she stopped brushing. "You're not gonna tell me, are you?"

Sandy shook her head.

Mitchell tossed her toothbrush on the counter and stalked into the next room. She kicked her gym bag into the corner, then, after a second, retrieved it and yanked out fresh jeans and a plaid button-up shirt. Turning, she found Sandy leaning in the bathroom doorway, naked, watching her with an unreadable expression on her face. Mitchell pulled on her jeans and snatched up the shirt.

"What?"

"You think because we're screwing that gives you some rights?"

"*Yes.*" Mitchell stopped buttoning her shirt. "No. I don't know. Maybe."

"Did you mean what you said in there, or was that just sex talk?"

Mitchell stared at her, for a moment angry enough to consider not answering. Then she remembered waking with the softness of Sandy's body curled into hers and the stubborn angle of Sandy's jaw when she was set on doing something and the million other ways that Sandy made her heart turn over, and she forgot why she was angry. "I meant it."

"Say it again."

Mitchell took a step toward her, and Sandy held up one hand, stopping her. "No—from over there. Not when you have your hands on me, or you're horny and looking to get laid."

"I love you."

"I'm a hooker, Dell. And you're a cop."

Mitchell never hesitated. "I love you, Sandy."

"God, you make me nuts." Sandy shook her head. "I'm still not gonna tell you what I have to tell Frye. First of all, I can't—she and I have a deal. *Second* of all," she said firmly when she saw Mitchell open her mouth, "Frye would chew you up and spit you out in itty-bitty pieces. You want that?"

"I hate secrets."

"What, you tell me everything?"

"No, but..." Mitchell's voice broke. "I want to."

There was some long-ago hurt in Mitchell's voice, some unhealed wound in her eyes, and Sandy came to her from across the room in the space between two heartbeats. Unmindful of her still-damp skin, she pressed against Mitchell, tilting her head to meet Mitchell's eyes. "I love you." Quickly, she covered Mitchell's mouth to stop the next words. "That's about us." She replaced her fingers with her mouth and kissed her swiftly. "This thing with Frye, that's business. Remember a long time ago, we said we wouldn't talk shop?"

"I remember." Mitchell's chest was tight. *God, I want you.*

"Well, I guess we can't go back." She kissed Mitchell lightly again. "But we gotta keep things separate, okay?"

"I'll try," Mitchell whispered. She didn't want to let go, but she had to. "Say it again."

"I love you...you blockhead." Sandy laughed. "Now lemme get dressed, rookie. We're late."

❖

When Mitchell got off the elevator with Sandy, the first person she saw was Jason in his usual place, busy with a computer scan of some kind. On the other side of the room, Frye and Watts stood in front of the windows, deep in conversation. Mitchell looked around, her heart racing.

"Where's Sloan?" she asked when Jason swiveled around in his chair to greet them.

"Rebecca sent her to bed."

"Lucky her," Sandy grumbled, squinting in the bright sunlight. "Jesus, it's not even noon and we—"

Mitchell coughed and Jason grinned.

"Just get to sleep, did we?" Jason asked archly.

"Who said anything about sleeping?" Sandy tossed back.

"Sandy," Mitchell groaned.

Jason sighed. "Sorry, you two, but I need help. Frye wants these backgrounds done yesterday, and I can't run them all myself."

"Have we got someone hot?" The excitement was evident in Mitchell's voice as she took the seat at the next console.

"I gotta go talk to Frye," Sandy announced as she walked away.

Jason and Mitchell mumbled goodbyes, then Jason confided, *"Three* someones—Sloan traced a worm back to the DA's office, so we're looking at the two ADAs and the judge for being our inside person."

"When did this break?"

Jason filled her in, and a minute later, they were plotting the quickest route to the information they needed.

"What about the porn user profiles I was working on?" Mitchell asked as she worked her way through a series of links that opened George Beecher's most recent federal income tax return.

"Launch the phish programs, but let the active traces go for now," Jason said. "This is the best lead we have."

"Okay."

"How did Mitch do last night?"

Mitchell glanced across the room to where Sandy stood talking to Frye. "Depends on how you look at it."

Jason glanced over and raised an eyebrow. "Things looked pretty good with Kennie and the others."

"That was fine. It was later." Mitchell stared straight ahead at the monitor. Data scrolled by, and she watched it, automatically shifting through the figures. "This is between us, right?"

"Who don't you want to know? Rebecca or Sandy?"

"Neither of them—for different reasons."

"Dell, if you're having trouble—"

Mitchell turned to him, her eyes focused and sharp. "I'm *okay.* It's just that I didn't expect it to be so...intense."

"What? Being undercover, or the drag, or the club scene?"

"The drag is no problem. It's fine." Mitchell opened another window, clicked through to another site, and started a second scan. *Maybe too good.*

"This is kind of our home away from home, after the Troc," Ken explained as the four of them piled out of his 1968 Camaro. *"We just mostly come here to relax and have a few drinks."*

Mitch's heart sped up. The flickering blue neon sign above the black windowless door read Ziggie's.

"Dance club?"

"Yeah," Ken said, falling into step as Dino and Phil led the way. "Dance club, sex club, probably a little bit of everything club." He shrugged. "Nobody keeps score, nobody asks questions, and nobody cares who you screw or how you do it."

"That's a switch."

Mitch followed the others into another cavernous dark room that looked a lot like the Troc except there were two elevated stages instead of one and they were in the center of the room. The stages were separated from the rest of the space by a low brass railing, and small tables were arranged around all sides. Four nearly nude girls, none of whom could have been more than eighteen, danced two to a stage in small cones of harsh light directed from spots suspended from the ceiling. They were topless and wore minuscule swatches of fabric that covered their sex, but just barely.

Men sat at the tables in the darkened room and watched the girls writhe in a parody of sex, occasionally placing money in their G-strings. A bar ran the length of the room along one wall, and most of those stools were occupied as well. Other girls, some of whom dressed and looked a lot like Sandy, leaned against the men, talking and drinking.

"This place isn't gay, like the Troc," Ken explained as the four of them took seats around one of the tables along the rail. "We like to come here, well, you know..."

"Yeah," Mitch guessed. "To be guys."

"In a manner of speaking," Dino remarked. "It's a good chance to perfect our drag and, well, just to push the envelope a little."

"The girls," Mitch said, indicating the dancers moving suggestively a few feet from his face. "Do they know?"

"That we're kings?" Phil asked.

Mitch nodded.

"Sure, but they don't mind. They know we don't come here to hit on them."

"In fact," Dino added, "I get the feeling that they'd rather it be us slipping bills into their panties than some of the johns in here." He nudged Ken playfully. "Of course, then there's King Stud here. The girls all seem to want to fuck him, even when he isn't doing anything but sitting still, drinking a beer."

"Yeah?" Mitch remarked, genuinely curious. "How come?"

Ken shrugged. "Because I'm good with tools."

They all laughed, ordered beers, and traded stories about the Troc, their shows, and the drag scene. Mitch tried to keep up with the conversation while surreptitiously studying the layout, the clientele, and the employees. From what he could see, it looked like a run-of-the-mill club. The commodities were sex and liquor.

The dancers seemed to be of legal age and didn't seem particularly unhappy, even if they did seem in danger of dying of boredom. He nursed his beer and settled back in his seat, watching his fellow kings flirt with the girls who brought their drinks.

Around three, the scene changed subtly.

The four dancers on the stage disappeared one by one, and four new girls appeared. They were completely nude, however. And they were younger. A lot younger. Mitch looked around the room. Many of the men who had been present previously were gone.

"Where'd everybody go?" Mitch asked.

"It's after hours," Ken explained. "Private club now. You gotta have a membership. We do, 'cause we do shows here every once in while. Jasmine and some of the girls from the Troc, too."

"Oh. I got it." Mitch tried not to seem too interested, but he was sweating. Not a good time for nerves. He wanted to see what the setup was like in the back. Where the girls came in. Who might be with them. "Listen, I gotta hit the head. Uh..."

"Use the men's room. The stalls have doors."

"Okay. Thanks."

He took his time making his way through the bar. A blinking red sign above a dark recess said Bath oo s. He headed that way. As he passed the end of the bar, a hand caught his arm, and he stopped. A tall, thin, pale-faced blond sat on the stool, dark eye shadow making huge deep-set eyes seem even darker. She looked young, younger even than Sandy, maybe, but with the dim light and heavy make-up, it was impossible for Mitch to tell. Her mouth was full, her lips shiny with artfully applied color. She wore skin-tight satiny slacks, green in the half-light, but they could have been blue. Her lace top was nearly transparent, and the blush of areolas and tight nipples accented high, firm breasts.

"You are new?"

"First time," Mitch replied, trying to place her accent. Russian? Czech? No idea.

They were nearly in the dark in the rear of the bar, and the closest customer was half a dozen stools away, eyes glued to the stage. The bartender was cleaning glasses at the far end. The girl drew Mitch near with her eyes and with her slim fingers curled around his wrist.

"You would like a dance?"

Her leg brushed his thigh. Her other hand stroked down his chest, lingering where his black T-shirt disappeared into his pants. A finger traced the inside of his waistband.

"What's your name?" Mitch asked, edging back a fraction. Her perfume smelled earthy and rich.

"Irina."

"Pretty." Mitch glanced down, watched red-tipped fingers drift up and down along his fly.

"What's your name, new boy?"

"Mitch." He caught his breath as her palm lightly cupped him.

"A private dance. In the booth." She bent forward and the very tops of her nipples were visible. "You would enjoy. Mitch."

"How much?" He worked at ignoring the slowly increasing pressure between his legs as she leaned closer to him.

She laughed. Her laughter was light. "I did not say you would pay."

"Sorry, I—" He stiffened as the hand between his thighs began a subtle up-and-down movement. He could feel the slow stimulating friction, and he felt himself respond. Felt the sudden rush of blood, the electric pulse of nerve endings, the hot arousal seeping from his swiftly swelling flesh. "You keep that up and I won't need the dance," was all he could think to say as he moved her hand onto his thigh.

"Hey!" a male voice interrupted. "You're gonna be late for your entrance. Come on."

Mitch backed away as a heavyset, dark-haired man in a two-piece suit took Irina's arm.

"Let's go."

Irina murmured something to the stranger in a language Mitch didn't understand and brushed against Mitch as she got down from the stool. "Next time, yes?"

"Yes," Mitch replied quickly as he watched her walk away, her arm firmly in the grip of the interloper. Alone, Mitch sagged against the bar, stomach seizing with the unexpected arousal. Oh man, what just happened?

He tried to tell himself he'd just been caught by surprise, that it didn't mean anything, that next time it wouldn't happen. He didn't want it to happen. But what if it did?

"Dell."

Mitchell swallowed, forcing back the sensations that accompanied the memories.

"Dell," Jason repeated. "What happened?"

"Nothing," she said quickly. "We went to Ziggie's, which is just what we'd hoped for."

"And?"

"Too soon to tell." Mitchell forced a grin. "But I'm set to go out again tonight after your show."

Jason studied her intently, then looked at the group across the room. Watts was talking, and Rebecca was shaking her head in a vehement negative motion. He kept his voice low. "Did you sleep with someone? Is that it?"

"No!" Mitchell glanced at Sandy. "But what if...what if something happens, and I have to do...something?"

"Like sex?"

Mitchell nodded.

"No one expects you to do anything you don't want to do." He leaned forward, patted her thigh. "Draw a line, Dell. Whatever you can live with."

"What if I can't?" she asked miserably. "Jesus, Jase—I got turned on from just a little hand action."

He tried to stifle a smile. "Dell, were you enjoying it?"

"Hell, no. I was ready to jump out of my skin."

"So, you didn't go looking for it to happen, right?" At her swift negative head-shake, he shrugged. "So what's the problem? It's okay if you responded, it happens. Jasmine practically implodes every time she dances with Sloan."

Mitchell's brows rose. "Does Sarah know?"

"She knows." He smiled tenderly. "She doesn't mind as long as that's all it is."

"I think Sandy might kill me."

He laughed. "I think you're right. Maybe Mitch had better keep that kind of thing just between us boys." He looked up. "Speaking of Sandy, here comes the team."

"Time to talk," Rebecca announced. "Sandy has a proposition."

Mitchell rose, a question on her lips, but Sandy walked by without looking in her direction.

CHAPTER TWENTY-FOUR

W e got a real break when Sandy found Trudy," Rebecca said. "Finally, we've got a direct link to the porn ring, at least the part making the videos. Now we need to work this angle as hard as we can."

As Rebecca outlined the newest plan, Mitchell clamped her jaws tightly together and stared straight ahead. Beneath the table, her hands were balled into tight fists on her thighs and bile churned in her gut. She couldn't believe what she was hearing. Letting Sandy work a sting on the guys who were running the live sex videos? Frye and Watts couldn't possibly think that would work. Sandy was good. Okay, Sandy was *very* good. But she was still an amateur, a novice, where this kind of undercover operation was concerned. It would be like sending a cadet into the front lines of a skirmish. It was crazy. And Mitchell was scared. Scared right down to her toes. *If something happens to her...*

"The first meet will most likely just be for a talk," Rebecca continued. "Hopefully we'll get a location and a time for the video shoot from that."

"What about a wire?" Watts interjected. "It wouldn't hurt to have this guy on tape setting up the job when it comes time to get him to roll on the higher-ups."

"Not a bad idea." Rebecca looked to Sandy. "What do you think?"

Sandy shrugged. "Depends on how big it is, and where I need to put it." Watts sniggered, and she gave him a cutting look. "I don't, you know, wear a whole lot of clothes most of the time. It would look funny if I was all of a sudden covered up."

"We can have the tech people put together a small thigh unit," Rebecca said.

Mitchell couldn't stand it any longer. "What's the point of her wearing a wire if we can't monitor what's going on? There's no way anyone is going to be able to cover this meet." She finally looked at Sandy. "You'll be out there on your own."

Before Rebecca could reply, Sandy spoke. "Look, we don't even know for sure that this Trudy chick is going to come through on this. *If* she puts me in touch with the guy who's lining up girls for the videos, it's just going to be a look-see. He'll want to check out the goods. I don't *need* anybody following me around on this."

"You're wrong—"

"Officer," Rebecca said quietly. She wasn't entirely happy with the idea herself, although Sandy's suggestion had merit. They hadn't had any luck tracking the origin of the video feeds from the data Sloan had downloaded the night of the bust. None of their street contacts had turned up anything of value. Sandy had been the only one able to get even close to the operation. *She'd* been able to find Trudy when no one else had because people would talk to her. She was part of the scene. She was part of the life.

Rebecca had resisted the proposal at first, but Watts had pushed for it. She never liked putting her people into dangerous situations, and although on the surface it seemed that the risk was low, the fact remained that Mitchell's assessment was accurate. In all likelihood, if and when Trudy actually *did* contact Sandy, it would be for an immediate meeting. Which meant that they would have no advance notice and no time to put a surveillance team into place. Sandy would be alone.

On the other hand, every time Sandy met with *anyone* for information, there was always the possibility that word would get around or someone would become suspicious. What Sandy did was dangerous. She knew it, Rebecca knew it, and they both accepted it as part of the job. Officer Mitchell, however, appeared to be having difficulty with Sandy's new role. Rebecca watched the internal struggle play itself out in Mitchell's eyes, and she was afraid that Mitchell's training would not prevail. Before the young officer could say something that Rebecca would not be able to overlook, she softly said, "This is a command decision. If you're having problems working on this team, I can have you reassigned."

"No, ma'am," Mitchell said, biting off the words. "No

problem."

"Good." Rebecca worked her shoulders to ease some of the tension, then she looked at Sandy. "If Trudy or anyone else contacts you, I want you to at least try to postpone the meet until you can call me. Watts will fit you out with a wire—"

"Uh-uh. No freakin' way is *he* doing it."

"Aw, I can't believe *you'd* say no to a little fun." Watts grinned. "Believe me, you'd like it."

"I don't think your heart could take it."

"As long as I live long enough to slip it up—"

"Shut up, Watts." Mitchell said the words quietly, calmly, as she turned in her seat to face him.

He stared at her in surprise. There was something cold and lethal in her expression.

"Dell—" Sandy's voice was soft, gentle.

"Mitchell, you're dismissed. Wait in the other room." Rebecca didn't even spare a glance in Mitchell's direction. Instead, she turned to Jason. "Bring me up to speed on the background checks."

As Jason began his report, Mitchell stood abruptly and walked from the room.

❖

"Let's go, Officer." Rebecca turned and headed for the elevator.

Mitchell rose from the chair where she had been sitting motionless for thirty interminable minutes and followed into the elevator without a word. When they reached street level, Rebecca turned right and began walking toward the river. Mitchell fell into step.

"We have a problem," Rebecca said flatly as they crossed Front Street at Market.

Mitchell said nothing. She knew what was coming. Another disciplinary action. And this time it would mean the end of her career. Again. She put her hands in the pockets of her leather jacket, hoping that Frye had not seen them shaking.

"What's going on with you and Sandy?" It was none of her business, and Rebecca knew it. But Mitchell was her business, and so was Mitchell's future in the police department.

"I'm in love with her." Mitchell couldn't see any point in lying. Not any longer.

"That's just terrific." Rebecca sighed. Silently, she led the way onto the concrete footbridge that arched over Delaware Avenue to Penn's Landing, climbed to the top, and stopped. Leaning her elbows on the waist-high railing, she watched the cars stream by on the street thirty feet below. Mitchell stood beside her, an expression on her face that Rebecca had never seen before. She looked beaten.

"What if I ordered you to choose between Sandy and the job?"

"I'd quit."

"Christ," Rebecca muttered. She turned her back to the wall, leaned a hip against the stone, and faced Mitchell. "You've got the makings of an exemplary officer in almost every way—you're intelligent, dedicated, trustworthy." She didn't add brave, but she believed it.

"Thank you, Sergeant."

"Don't thank me. I'm not done yet."

"Yes, ma'am."

"But you've got a very serious weakness, Officer Mitchell. Your temper. You were insubordinate back there, and it's not the first time. I've let it slide before, but I can't do that now."

"I understand, ma'am." *Jesus, just tell me I'm out. Just say it.*

"I don't think you do." Rebecca watched Mitchell carefully. Beaten, maybe, but not defeated. "Ordinarily, a little bit of temper isn't a bad thing. You need that fire burning inside to face danger without flinching. Do you understand?"

Mitchell thought about going down the alley in the dark, in the rain, alone, barely able to see an inch in front of her face. Knowing that whoever was waiting was probably bigger, probably stronger, and probably armed. But she'd heard a woman scream, and that had made her angry. It was the anger as much as her sense of duty that had carried her into that alley. Softly, she answered, "Yes, ma'am. I understand."

"But a fire you can't control will eat you up, and something's eating you up now."

Mitchell said nothing. Her insides rolled, and for a minute, she feared she might vomit.

"You need to take yourself off the team if you can't deal with what Sandy is doing."

"Aren't I off already?" Mitchell looked at Rebecca, confusion in her eyes.

"That depends. I can't tell you who to sleep with. I can't tell you who to love." Rebecca looked past Mitchell to a ship that slowly made its way into the port of Philadelphia. The sun glinted off the hundreds of steel containers loaded on its deck that would soon be off-loaded, their contents shipped by rail and truck up and down the East Coast. She thought about Catherine, and how having Catherine in her life had made her a better cop because her own fires consumed less of her now. "I *can* tell you that if you can't give her up, you're going to have to learn to live with who she is." Rebecca turned her gaze back to Mitchell's face. "And what she does."

"Sandy said something like that to me this morning."

A smile flickered across Rebecca's mouth. "Sandy is very smart."

"I'm trying."

"Not hard enough."

Mitchell nodded.

"You need to sort this out, in a hurry. I can't order you to, but I think maybe you need to talk to Dr. Rawlings."

Mitchell regarded Rebecca steadily. "I don't want that kind of thing in my file."

"I understand. You'd have to discuss that with her."

"I know about her and you."

Rebecca's eyes hardened. "No, Mitchell. You don't. But if you don't want to see Dr. Rawlings, then find someone else. Because this is your last chance."

"I trust her."

"Then I guess you'll need to ask her about anything that... bothers you."

"Did it bother *you,* when she helped get Blake? When she went into the park wearing a wire?" Mitchell had to ask, even though she knew she was out of line. She couldn't find a place to put her feelings, and she didn't think she could handle them alone.

She knew the details of that case, at least what had gone into the files. Everyone did. It had been a spectacular sequence of events that everyone in the department had talked about for months. But that wasn't what she wanted to know. She wanted, no *needed,* to know if there was some way to live with the fear that gnawed at her when she thought about Sandy alone somewhere and hurt.

Rebecca's blue eyes darkened. Everything in her nature directed her to keep silent. She was Mitchell's superior, not her friend. More than that, she was a cop, and cops never admitted to having second thoughts or doubts or fear. She'd had that credo drummed into her since childhood, and she'd learned to handle her fears and doubts by burying them in a haze of alcohol. Until someone had put her up against a wall and said to her what she was saying to Mitchell now. She took a deep, slow breath and let it out softly.

"I was so scared I thought I'd lose my mind."

"But you handled it."

Not very well. Rebecca shrugged. "No choice. It was my job. And Dr. Rawlings wouldn't have it any other way."

"I want to be on this team more than anything in my life, except being with Sa—"

"I got that the *first* time, Mitchell. Stop telling me things I don't want to know about."

"Yes, ma'am." Mitchell straightened. "I'll talk to Dr. Rawlings."

"Your business." Rebecca held Mitchell's eyes. "You lose it one more time and you're gone. I'll put it in your file, and they'll bury you somewhere until you quit from sheer boredom."

"Yes, ma'am."

Rebecca nodded and turned back toward Old City. "Let's go. Jason says he has work for you."

"Sergeant?"

Rebecca looked over her shoulder, a question in her eyes.

"Why are you giving me this chance?"

Because you're a good cop. Because someone did it for me. Because I recognize the pain in your eyes. Rebecca lifted a shoulder. "Just think of it as a little friendly advice from your Rabbi."

Mitchell's heart lurched, and she felt sick again. Good sick.

Happy sick. She tried not to smile, but it was a struggle. Every rookie hoped for a Rabbi—an older, experienced cop to take them under their wing, to sponsor them behind the scenes with the higher-ups. If you wanted to advance in rank, you needed a Rabbi who could help pave the way. Mitchell couldn't believe that Rebecca Frye had just taken her on. Frye had just made her hers. "Thank you, Sergeant. I hope I—"

"I already said don't thank me, Mitchell. Just get me a lead, will you?"

"Yes, ma'am. I'm on it."

❖

At the corner of Front and Arch, Rebecca spied the thin blond in the short leather skirt, shiny black faux-motorcycle jacket, and calf-high, stack-heeled boots lounging against a light pole. Her face betrayed nothing but ennui, but her eyes were alive and riveted on Mitchell's face. Rebecca sighed and glanced sideways at Mitchell. The officer's expression was just as nonchalant as that of the woman who watched her, but her gaze was hungry.

"Christ." Rebecca pulled her keys from her blazer pocket and stopped by her car. "Five minutes, Mitchell, and then get your ass back upstairs."

In a rare breach of protocol, Mitchell forgot to reply as she hurried over to Sandy. She barely heard the Vette revving in the background or the engine roar as Rebecca pulled away.

"Hi," Mitchell said quietly, reaching for Sandy's hand. Their fingers entwined and she held their joined hands between their bodies, out of sight of casual observers.

"You okay?" Sandy asked.

"Yeah." Mitchell grinned sheepishly. "I'm missing a few pieces of my anatomy, but, yeah."

"I'm sorry, Dell." Sandy searched Mitchell's eyes, looking for the real wounds. "I'm really sorry."

"Why? It wasn't your fault."

"It was." Sandy looked down at their hands, then into Mitchell's face again. "If I'd told you this morning when you asked me what I had to tell Frye, you wouldn't have been caught by surprise."

"Uh-huh." Mitchell laughed softly. "Then we could have had

a big fight at *your* place, and you would have been pissed off, and I would have been *really* late. And Frye would *still* have chewed me out."

"Don't blow smoke at me, Dell." Sandy slid her hand from Mitchell's and eased away. "You know it's not the same thing."

"Look, I got hot upstairs and mouthed off to Watts. That's what Frye was on me about."

Sandy looked away, remembering the pain in her girlfriend's eyes when Frye had come down on her at the briefing. She remembered, too, Frye's warning about what any kind of relationship with Sandy could do to Mitchell's career. "You know, rookie, I can't afford to cross Frye on this deal. If hanging around with you is going to screw it up, maybe we better coo—"

"Don't..." Mitchell's voice broke and she swallowed hard. "Don't do this to me, Sandy. Please."

Sandy had never imagined that someone else's pain could hurt so much. She looked at Mitchell beseechingly. "Dell, I...I don't know what to do."

"Just don't leave me, okay?" Mitchell caught Sandy's hand. "I need you."

"You're nuts." Sandy's heart hurt, hearing the words. Hurt in a good way, like something inside of her that had lain cold and buried for longer than she could recall was coming to life. "I don't want to need you."

"That's okay. You don't have to." Mitchell smiled sadly. "I always knew you were the tough one."

Sandy brushed her fingers down Mitchell's chest. "I said I didn't *want* to...I didn't say I *don't*."

"I love you," Mitchell whispered, raising Sandy's hand to her lips. She closed her eyes and rubbed Sandy's fingers against her cheek. "It feels so right to say that."

"Jeez, will you *cool* it." Sandy jerked her hand away and looked around nervously. "What if Watts or someone sees us."

Mitchell shrugged. "Won't matter now. I told Frye about us."

Sandy gaped. "You *what*?"

"I told her I was crazy in love with you, and if she wanted to fire me, to go ahead."

"Oh, man." Sandy hooked her fingers around Mitchell's belt

and dragged her to relative privacy under the overhang of the nearest building. Then she put her arms around Mitchell's neck and kissed her until they were both breathless. Leaning into Mitchell's body, she muttered, "I want to rip your clothes off and do...things to you."

"Okay."

"Go. To. Work. Dell." Sandy kissed the grinning young cop again and backed away a step. "Do you think you could...call me... later? Just so I know, you know, where you are?"

"I thought maybe I'd see you tonight before I have to go to the Troc with Jasmine." Mitchell put her hands in her pockets and tried to sound casual. "We could maybe have dinner. Say seven? I could come by your place and we'll go out."

Sandy cocked her head quizzically. "Like a date?"

"Yeah. Like a date."

"Even though we're...you know, already...sleeping together?"

Mitchell nodded. "I thought maybe *that* part could happen later."

"Dinner sounds good." Sandy leaned in, kissed Mitchell quickly, and turned to walk away. "I'll have to think about the other part."

Laughing, Mitchell watched until Sandy turned the corner, thinking how hot she looked in that leather skirt.

CHAPTER TWENTY-FIVE

Sloan savored the warm breath against the back of her neck and the soft hand caressing her abdomen. It was twilight and very quiet in the bedroom. Michael lay pressed against her, one arm encircling Sloan's waist. The soft swell of breasts against her back and the whisper of gentle lips on her skin were the most precious sensations she'd ever experienced. The terrible fear that had filled her chest for endless hours disintegrated like ice in the sunlight and flowed from her on a healing river of tears.

"Sloan. Darling?" Michael tightened her hold, sensing the subtle shift in Sloan's breathing. "Oh, no, my love, don't cry."

"I'm okay," Sloan rasped quickly, lifting a hand to brush away the moisture. "Just happy."

"Why the tears, then?"

"It feels so good to have you back."

"It's so good to *be* back." Michael kissed the soft spot below Sloan's ear. "Roll over so I can see you."

Sloan complied, keeping Michael's hand pressed to her abdomen. She turned her head on the pillow to study her lover, who lay on her side, smiling tenderly. "How's your head, baby?"

"In this position it seems fine. Almost no headache at all."

"That's good." The relief that coursed through Sloan was swift and sharp.

"Mmm. How are you?"

"How should I be?" Sloan smiled. "I've spent the day in bed with you. I'm perfect."

"*You*," Michael whispered, "are a very smooth operator, J.T. Sloan." She kissed the tip of Sloan's shoulder. "But I hardly think I've been a stimulating companion."

"Ah, you never know." As always, the sight and scent of

Michael so near had stirred Sloan's passion, but it was the bright, pain-free light in her lover's eyes that made her ache with gratitude and desire. "Have you been awake long?"

"A while." Michael freed her hand from beneath Sloan's and slowly drew her fingers over Sloan's breasts, flicking over her tight nipples before drifting down her abdomen. "I didn't want to wake you."

"You're waking me now," Sloan murmured as Michael brushed her fingertips lightly through the soft hair nestled at the base of her abdomen. Desire turned to a desperate ache, and she shivered. "Michael..."

Michael laughed quietly and traced one fingertip along the valley between belly and thigh.

"Michael, we can't," Sloan warned, edging her hips away.

"Don't make me have to follow you, darling," Michael cautioned. "I seem to do best if I stay in one place. You don't want to give me a headache, do you?"

Sloan sighed and grew still. "That's blackmail."

"Is it?" Michael sounded surprised, and then she laughed again. "All right. So I've been found out."

"We should wait."

She lowered her mouth to Sloan's shoulder again and bit softly, increasing the pressure until Sloan twitched and groaned. "Wait for what, darling?"

"Until you're better."

"I *am* better," Michael insisted, placing her palm gently between Sloan's thighs, her fingers resting against slick, ready flesh.

"I won't be able to come." Sloan drew a sharp breath as a fingertip circled her clitoris. Her head swam with need. "I'll be worried about you the whole time."

"Oh, this is serious." Michael's voice held a hint of playfulness. "All right. You are not required to come. You merely need to submit to my attentions."

"Michael," Sloan said in exasperation, trying desperately to ignore the rush of heat into the engorged prominence beneath Michael's hand. She thirsted for Michael's touch, hungered to touch *her.* But the memory of fear rode hard on her heart, and she fought the desire. "Why are you doing this?"

"Because I've missed you." Michael's tone was serious now, almost wistful. "Because I need to be connected to you. Sloan, I need *you* back, too."

Sloan's heart turned over in her chest, and she was lost. Lost as she was each time the enormity of Michael's love washed over her. "Oh God." Carefully, she turned to face her lover, opening to her. "Anything you want. You know that."

"I love you." Michael smiled tenderly. "I just want to touch you. I want feel your heart beat beneath my fingers. I want to feel your passion flow for me. I want to hear your breath break just for me—"

"I think you could talk me into coming," Sloan murmured, very gently caressing Michael's face, her neck, her jaw.

"I might like to try." Michael kissed the fingers that trembled across her mouth while she kept up her slow steady motion between Sloan's thighs. "But tonight I want you to come on my skin, in my hand."

"Promise me," Sloan implored, her pupils dilating with the surge of arousal mounting beneath Michael's teasing fingers, "that...ah, God...that..."

"What, darling?" Michael watched Sloan's lids slowly close as she pressed the length of her clitoris. "What?"

Sloan forced her eyes open. "That you'll stop if..." Her hips jerked and she gasped. "If it hurts...you...anywhere."

"Sloan," Michael soothed, her own heart beating furiously. "Touching you could never hurt me."

"I want to touch you," Sloan whispered.

"Not this time." Michael slipped lower, moaning softly at the rush of liquid heat that rose to meet her, soaking her hand.

"Michael?" Sloan asked, suddenly anxious.

"I'm all right," Michael soothed. "Relax, darling. Let me have you."

"I love you."

Michael smiled. "Then let me watch you come."

Sloan rested her forehead on Michael's, her hand gently cupping Michael's breast. She kept her eyes on her lover, but she couldn't see. Love, desire, and need colluded to make her blind.

Michael's presence, alive and beautiful and loving, was more exciting even than her exquisite touch. It was too much for Sloan to hold.

"I'm...going to...come soon."

"Yes," Michael murmured thickly. "I can feel it. You're so full, so hard now. So beautiful."

Sloan's hips lifted, and her legs grew rigid in the tangled sheets. A small cry of surprise and wonder escaped her. "Ohh... there..."

"Yes. Yes, my love." Michael held as still as she could, letting Sloan move in her palm, drawing the orgasm out along the surface of her skin. As the pleasure peaked, she massaged the spot inside that she knew would push Sloan to come again, a deep and clenching climax that forced Sloan to arch back, stomach jerking with the pounding pulsations. "Yes, that's right...that's right, darling. Come for me."

Gasping, Sloan slumped down to the bed, her limbs boneless, her chest heaving. "I'm...out of practice."

Michael laughed, a husky sensuous purr of satisfaction. "I'll have to rectify that."

Sloan grasped the hand that moved indolently over skin so sensitive she quivered at the slightest touch. "Not all in one night or I'll never survive."

"Mmm, but you're *so* much fun to play with."

"Are you all right?" Sloan asked worriedly as her senses returned from the stratosphere and she could think again. "Headache? Stomach okay?"

"I'm fine. Everything is working just fine."

Sloan raised a dark brow. "Everything?"

Michael smiled softly, drawing a finger lightly up the inside of her thigh, then touching the moist tip to Sloan's lips. "Everything."

"God, baby." Sloan felt as if she'd been fisted in the gut. Hoarsely, she moaned, "Kill me, why don't you?"

"Oh, I don't think so." Michael moved closer, carefully, and rested her head on Sloan's shoulder, drawing lazy circles on Sloan's belly with her fingers. "What are your plans for tonight?"

Sloan nuzzled Michael's ear, then lightly bit the lobe. "I

should head downstairs. I left things up in the air this morning."

"Mmm. When Rebecca sent you to bed."

"Yeah." Sloan was still pissed about that, but she had to admit that she felt better than she had since the accident. Memories of that night ambushed her, and she closed her eyes, hoping to chase away the nightmare images. "I love you."

Michael felt the sudden tension in the muscles beneath her cheek. "I'm all right."

"I know."

"Then believe it."

Sloan kissed her temple. "I'll try."

"Good." Michael waited until Sloan relaxed again. "Promise me something."

"Anything."

"When you find out who caused the accident, let Rebecca handle it."

Sloan went rigid. "Has someone said—"

"No one had to." Michael lifted her chin and kissed the undersurface of Sloan's jaw. "I know you."

"Michael—"

"Promise."

There was nothing she could do. There was nothing in her, nothing she was, that Michael didn't own. "I promise."

"Thank you." Michael kissed her again. "I know what that took."

"You don't know how much I love you."

Softly, Michael smiled. "Oh yes, darling, I do. You always make me know."

"Will you sleep?"

"If you stay with me a little while longer." Michael closed her eyes, content in knowing that they were both healing now.

"Yes." Sloan drifted, stroking Michael's arm, and felt the pain slip away on the rhythmic tide of Michael's peaceful breathing.

❖

Catherine stretched and sighed. "God, I love sex in the afternoon."

"It's not afternoon," Rebecca pointed out, leaning up on an

elbow and indulging herself in looking at Catherine nude.

"It was when we started." Catherine turned her head and caught the gleam in Rebecca's eye. "What?"

"You're incredible."

Catherine smiled. "I'm not sure I know how to take that, but thank you." She turned, running her hand along Rebecca's side and over her hip. "You're pretty damn good yourself."

"Wonder what Joyce thinks." Rebecca grinned.

"About how good you are? Nothing, I hope."

"About where you disappeared to."

"I hardly disappeared," Catherine politely demurred. "I merely took some...personal time...before my evening sessions."

"Like you usually do."

"All right. So I *never* do." Catherine drew Rebecca's hand to her breast. "It's a habit I might consider cultivating."

Rebecca's eyes darkened, and she brought her mouth to the stiff nipple as she gently squeezed Catherine's breast. Catherine's hands in her hair pulled her face away. Surprised, Rebecca looked up. "What?"

"I have to go to work soon. Don't get me started again."

"We never finished."

"Yes, we did." Catherine laughed. "Several times, but who's counting."

Rebecca laughed, too, and pulled Catherine into her arms as she leaned back. She stroked her lover's hair, aware of a strange new emotion. Contentment. "I'll be late tonight."

"Has something happened?" Catherine asked carefully. She wanted to say, *Don't go out. Stay here. Let me close my eyes knowing you're safe. Let me fall asleep in your arms.*

"Not yet, but soon. Mitchell is going out undercover again, and I want to be nearby. I can't leave her out there alone. She's a kid."

"Do you trust her?"

"Yes. But she's still wet behind the ears. And, Jesus, she's a hothead." Rebecca laughed quietly. "I thought I was going to have to sit her down today. But she's got spine, and she doesn't back away from the truth."

Two qualities Catherine knew mattered a great deal to her

lover. "Be careful, hmm?"

"What, with Mitchell?" Rebecca asked, thinking about all she had said, almost without meaning to, when she and the young cop had talked.

"No, my sweet detective, *you*."

"Oh." Rebecca kissed her. "Of course."

"I know you always take good care of all your people."

Rebecca sighed. "Earlier today, I more or less ordered Mitchell to see you."

"See me? Professionally?" Catherine stirred, then leaned away to watch Rebecca's face. When her lover nodded, she asked, "Why?"

"She's carrying something around in her that needs healing. I figured you could help."

For a minute, Catherine was speechless. "Ordering someone to undergo therapy isn't usually the best way to start that process." Her tone was mild, but her eyes were deeply serious.

"Maybe not, but she's about to fuck up her career. I gave her a choice."

"Me or what—traffic patrol?"

"Something like that." Rebecca grinned again.

Catherine sighed. "Rebecca, darling—"

"It's not as bad as it sounds. I said she could see anyone she wants, and that whether she did or not was up to her. I wouldn't check up on her." Rebecca brushed her fingers over Catherine's cheek. "Okay?"

"It seems it's a done deal."

"Probably." Rebecca shrugged. "Oh, and she said she *knows* about us."

"Ah. Well." Catherine curled back into Rebecca's body. "Grist for the mill."

"Huh?"

"It's a therapy saying. Anything that comes up in therapy, even if it's personally difficult for the therapist or a challenge to the client-therapist relationship, is an avenue for potential benefit if handled correctly."

Rebecca gave that some thought. "I'd rather be shot."

For the first time since the shooting, Catherine found herself laughing when Rebecca said it. She rolled onto her lover and kissed her, a kiss that soon deepened and grew hungry. "Oh dear," she gasped.

"Uh-huh," Rebecca muttered, wrapping her arms around Catherine and turning until she was on top. "Oh dear, indeed."

❖

"Aren't you hungry?" Sandy asked.

"What?" Mitchell looked up from her barely touched dinner. "Oh, yeah. I am." She picked up her chopsticks, then set them down with a sigh. "Not really."

Sandy tipped back her beer bottle and drained it. "So. What's up?"

Mitchell shrugged. "Nothing."

They had sat by silent agreement on the same side of the table in the booth at Chen's. For most of the meal, Sandy had kept one hand on Mitchell, stroking the tight denim over her lean thigh. Now, Sandy nudged her girlfriend's shoulder with hers. "Dell. Come on."

Mitchell met Sandy's inquiring gaze with worried blue eyes. "Look, will you just please promise not to go off to some meeting with this porno guy without checking in? Just do that?"

"Ah, jeez, Dell. Not that again."

"What if something happens, and we don't know where you are?"

Sandy put her hand back on Mitchell's leg and leaned close. "Nothing's going to happen. Trudy will take me to meet the guy. I'll say, Oh yes, I'd love to take off my clothes and suck your dick, and then he'll say, Great, I'll pick you up at such and such a time, blah blah blah. Then you and Frye and Bluto will kick his ass."

Mitchell smiled despite the unease that was burning holes in her gut. "Bluto?"

"Yeah, well—you know who."

"I can't imagine."

"I'm a big girl, rookie. Don't worry."

"You're not used to being undercov—"

"Oh, and you are?" Sandy huffed.

"That's differe—"

"Dell," Sandy said quietly. "Do you think I like getting into cars and giving some jumpy accountant or sweating redneck a hand job?"

Mitchell's jaw tightened. "No."

"You're right. But *they* think I love it." Sandy looked away, then met Mitchell's eyes directly. "I spend most of my life acting."

"Why do you do it?" There was no accusation in Mitchell's voice, only a desire to understand.

"Simple. For the money." Sandy shrugged. "I made a lot before...look, we said we wouldn't—"

"Before what?"

Sandy hesitated. "Before I stopped screwing for it. The quick and easy stuff doesn't pay as well."

"When? When did you stop?"

"Right after Anna Marie was...killed."

Mitchell reached beneath the table and squeezed Sandy's hand. "I'm sorry. About your friend. Not about the other, though."

"Yeah. Me, too."

"So," Mitchell said softly, playing with Sandy's fingers. "Will you just *try*, really try to call Frye if anything goes down. I...I can't take thinking about you getting hurt again."

"Okay, baby, okay." Sandy leaned into Mitchell and kissed her, her hand sliding to Mitchell's stomach and then around her waist. As her tongue met Mitchell's, she whimpered faintly and half climbed into Mitchell's lap.

"Home," Mitchell gasped when Sandy finally broke the kiss. "Home—we gotta go home."

Breathing hard, Sandy rubbed her hand over Mitchell's middle, then down the front of her jeans. "Yeah? To do what?"

Mitchell fumbled for her wallet, her hands shaking. "Take off our clothes, roll around—you know."

"Oh, okay." Sandy tugged lightly on Mitchell's waistband, grinning at the hazy need in Mitchell's eyes. "Then we can dress *Mitch*."

"Oh, Jesus," Mitchell moaned.

Laughing, Sandy tugged her from the booth by the hand. "Come on, rookie. You got business to tend to."

CHAPTER TWENTY-SIX

Chen's House of Jade was ten blocks from Sandy's apartment. The motorcycle ride was short but still long enough for Sandy to drive Mitchell nearly out of her mind. The instant Sandy climbed onto the back of the bike, she wrapped one arm around Mitchell's middle and slid the other hand between Mitchell's legs. With Sandy rhythmically squeezing her through the tight denim stretched across her crotch, Mitchell had no choice but to keep both hands on the bike. Since her mind was half gone, she needed the other half—and every ounce of her physical stamina—to keep the machine upright and on the road. Which left her completely at the mercy of Sandy's wandering hands.

They tumbled off the bike in front of the row house and staggered up the stairs, their arms around one another's waists. Once in the stairwell, Sandy plastered her body against Mitchell's and pinned her to the wall.

Mitchell groaned. Sandy had a way of pressing the edge of her hip between Mitchell's legs, hitting just the right spot to send the blood draining from Mitchell's brain to directly between her thighs. That, combined with Sandy's warm hands beneath her shirt, all over her breasts, was driving her swiftly insane.

"Sandy...ah, God...not until we get upstairs." In self-defense, Mitchell grabbed Sandy's shoulders and pushed her away. "Jesus, anybody could walk in."

"Even if they do, all they'll do is look." Sandy made a grab for Mitchell's crotch.

"Well, I don't want them looking at *you*," Mitchell snapped, her temper fraying as her stomach churned with arousal. She grabbed Sandy's hand and pulled her up the stairs. By the time they reached the third-floor landing, they were bouncing off the walls—first one of them, then the other—stopping to touch and fondle and kiss in a frenzy of need.

Somehow, Sandy got the key in the lock with Mitchell's mouth still glued to hers, and they fell through the doorway into her apartment. In the next second, Mitchell had her up against the door.

"You make me crazy. You make me so fucking crazy." Mitchell felt as if something inside of her was going to explode. She wanted Sandy, craved her, desperately needed her. Unexpectedly, miraculously, Sandy had managed to reach through all the bullshit in Mitchell's life and had touched the critical core, the place where she lived and dreamed and, sometimes, was terribly afraid. Sandy was tough and brave and gentle and sweet, and Mitchell had been so lonely for so long.

Sandy's hands were in her hair—yanking her head down, kissing her, plunging into her mouth, demanding and fierce. Mitchell shoved her hips into Sandy's, and Sandy shoved back, their passion clashing in frantic, furious thrusts. Moaning, Mitchell brought her mouth to Sandy's neck and caught the tender skin in her teeth as she slid her hand beneath the edge of the short leather skirt, gliding up the silky thigh, cupping the sliver of thin fabric soaked with desire.

"Oh yeah," Mitchell groaned. "Oh yeah."

Sandy dug her fingers into Mitchell's shoulders and rocked against her hand, making small broken sounds of pleasure.

Mitchell couldn't get enough. Thighs spread wide on either side of Sandy's legs, she brought the other hand beneath the skirt, bunching it high on Sandy's small waist as she poised to enter her. And then, in an instant of shattering clarity, she saw it again.

He had one hand around her throat and the other under her skirt. Her thighs were bare, pale, ghostly in the moonlight...there was blood on her face...

Gasping, Mitchell stumbled away. "Oh my God. Oh...Jesus."

Stunned, Sandy stared in confusion. Breathing hard, barely able to speak, she croaked, "What? Dell, what?"

Mitchell looked down at her hands, appalled, then back at

Sandy. "I'm sorry...so sorry. Did I hurt you?"

"What are you talking about? Hurt me?" Sandy reached out with a trembling hand. "No. No, *never.*"

"I had you pushed against the wall...I was about to push *inside* you. Just like...Jesus, Sandy..." Her eyes were wounded, suffering, tormented. "Just like *him.*"

"You are not like him." Sandy's voice was steady and hard as steel. "You will never be like him, like *them.*" She tilted her head, narrowed her eyes. "You've been holding back with me, haven't you, Dell? You've been being *careful.*" She said the word like an insult.

"I...no, I..." Mitchell couldn't think. Her body wasn't her own, and her mind was in shambles. "Sandy, I love you."

"Then love me, Dell. I don't need you to protect me." With her eyes riveted to Mitchell's, Sandy slipped out of the black jacket, dropped it on the floor, and in one fluid motion, removed her top. Then she was nude except for her minuscule black leather skirt and black heels. Her voice was heavy, dark, commanding. "You want something, Dell? You come and get it."

Before her next heartbeat, Mitchell was on her knees at Sandy's feet, pushing up the leather skirt with both hands. With a startled cry, Sandy braced herself against the door with her palms flat against the wood.

Mitchell didn't ask permission or even wonder if it was all right. In one seamless movement, she slid her fingers beneath the sheer black silk, pushed it aside, and took Sandy into her mouth. She heard Sandy cry out and felt fingers drive into her hair again, but she was oblivious to everything except the scent of desire and the taste of excitement and the pulsing feverish urgency of Sandy's body.

"Dell, Dell, Dell..." Sandy chanted wildly as she felt herself coming, unable to stop the onslaught of pleasure. Light-headed, trembling, she leaned her head back as colors flared behind her closed lids and heat flashed along her spine. "Oh, baby, you're making me come so hard..."

With Sandy's clitoris throbbing beneath her lips, Mitchell entered her, full and hard and deep. She sucked her, tormented her with her teeth, and nearly lifted her from the floor with the force of her thrusts. She didn't stop, might never have stopped, if Sandy hadn't finally collapsed, bent double over her body.

Panting, still in the throes of blind lust, Mitchell fell back on her heels and caught Sandy in her arms as they both tumbled to the bare wood floor. Mitchell managed to cushion Sandy's fall and gathered her close. "Okay?" Fighting for breath, she repeated urgently, "Honey, you okay?"

Sandy's only response was to press her fingers to Mitchell's mouth.

Mitchell kissed her forehead, her closed lids, her mouth, rocking her gently. A minute before she'd wanted only to take her, claim her, own her, and now she felt a tenderness so profound she ached with an entirely different kind of desire. She wanted to protect her, shelter her, keep her from harm. Always. "You turn me inside out."

Sandy's head lolled back in the curve of Mitchell's arm, and she lazily opened her eyes, a satisfied smile on her face. "Yeah? You're pretty amazing when you don't hold back, you know."

Mitchell ducked her head, shrugging. "I've never been...like that before."

"Must be the company." Sandy nuzzled Mitchell's breast through the thin cotton T-shirt, finding the small erect nipple and tweaking it with her teeth. She murmured appreciatively when Mitchell gasped. "I like you when you're crazy."

"Is that why you're always trying to get me that way?"

"Mmm," Sandy murmured as she brought her hand between Mitchell's thighs, rubbing her gently. "No. I do it because I like you to make me come."

Mitchell laughed out loud. "All you have to do is ask—but I like it when you do it, no matter what the reason." Gently, she grasped Sandy's wrist and moved her hand from between her legs.

"Hey!" Sandy pulled away from Mitchell's breast and gave her a hard stare. "What's *that* about?"

"I came already...when I was inside you."

Sandy's eyes grew huge, and her mouth opened soundlessly. After a second, she shook her head and burrowed into Mitchell's shoulder with both arms wrapped tightly around her. "You better be for real, rookie."

"I am," Mitchell whispered. "I promise."

❖

"Mitch? *Mitch,* you okay?"

Mitch blinked and focused on the bare breasts two feet in front of his face. Quickly, he averted his gaze and turned to Jasmine. "Yeah. Fine."

"I have a feeling she'd like you to look a little more interested." Jasmine studied the drag king with some concern. "You seem a little bit out of it."

"Just tired." It was after three in the morning, and he hadn't had much sleep the night before. Knockdown, drag-out sex with Sandy had pretty much taken everything he had left. After Jasmine's show at the Troc, Jasmine and all the kings had gone barhopping. Ziggie's was their last stop. By then, Mitch was bleary eyed with fatigue.

"You need to be sharp," Jasmine said as she leaned close and rested her hand on Mitch's thigh. With her lips close to Mitch's ear and her hand roaming over his leg, anyone watching would have thought they were lovers, which was just what she intended. "You lose focus, you'll be in trouble."

Mitch tilted his chin and kissed the corner of Jasmine's mouth. Then he moved his lips along her jaw and murmured, "I got it. I faded out a little, but I'm okay now. Thanks."

Jasmine nuzzled Mitch's neck. "Frye will have my ass if anything happens to you."

"Mine, too, if there was anything left of it." Mitch blew softly in Jasmine's ear. "You can probably take your hand off my dick now."

Jasmine laughed and settled back in her seat. "I never get to play with any of the boys."

Phil, sitting to her left, heard the remark and immediately replied, "You can play with me any time you want."

Laughing, Mitch stood and stretched, then pulled a dollar from the pocket of his leather pants, reached out, and tucked it into the barely-there red G-string of the woman dancing just in front of him.

"You coming back, hot stuff?" she purred as she swiveled her hips suggestively.

"I will if you'll still be here."

As she moved away, she tossed a look over her shoulder in his direction. "I'll be back...and I'll be ready."

"I'll be waiting." Mitch glanced at the other kings and Jasmine. "I'm gonna grab another beer."

I need to get someone to talk to me, not just flirt with me. I need to make something happen.

❖

"There're so many things wrong with this picture, I don't even know where to start." Rebecca balanced her third cup of coffee since midnight on her knee and gave Watts a wordless stare.

He returned her gaze with righteous indignation. "I'm a D-two, and I'm sitting on my ass out here in the cold while a wet-behind-the-ears rookie is inside where it's nice and warm."

"You'd look..." Rebecca shuddered, "out of place in leather pants. So you're with me out here in the cold, and if you want to make detective-three, you'll act happy to be along."

Watts snorted, his good sense having vanished with the last ten-degree temperature drop. "And another thing—I'm freezing my nuts off while the kid with the fake johnson gets to watch the girls hump those shiny steel poles. Probably can't even get a decent hard-on."

Rebecca rubbed at the blistering headache that pounded between her eyes. "I don't want to hear about your ass or your nuts or any other part of your anatomy, freezing or otherwise. I just want you to sit there and shut up. We're on surveillance here, not *Entertainment Tonight*."

"At least *I'd* be able to appreciate all the bare tits getting thrown around in there," he grumbled. "So, can I smoke? It's a department ride."

"No," Rebecca replied for the fifth time in an hour. She lifted her coffee cup, halted with it halfway to her face, and squinted at two figures approaching from the far end of the block. Softly she said, "Uh-oh. What's this?"

❖

"So," Mitch said casually to the bartender when he passed him the beer, "Irina here tonight?"

"Who's asking?"

"The name's Mitch."

The thick-necked, heavily muscled bartender took his time looking Mitch up and down. Then he laughed. "I don't think you've got what she's looking for."

"She seemed to like it fine last night."

His dark brows furrowed, and he swiped his damp towel over the polished surface of the bar in annoyance. "It's not my job to keep track of the girls. I haven't seen her tonight, okay?"

"Is she usually here?" Mitch persisted.

"Look, *fella*," he said with disdainful emphasis, "if you want somebody to ride your rod, just offer any of the girls up on the stage twenty bucks. They don't care what it's made of as long as your cash is green."

"I was looking forward to Irina doing that."

"If she and her girls ain't here by now, they ain't coming. I guess you'll just have to go home and jerk off."

Mitch's pulse picked up. "Other girls? You mean besides the ones here already?" He knew he was pushing, but there was something he was missing, something about Irina that he should understand, but didn't.

The bartender seemed not to have heard, his attention focused on something across the room. Mitch turned in that direction, and his racing heart stuttered to a stop while his stomach convulsed with shock. A pretty Asian girl wended her way between the tables, followed closely by Sandy.

For an instant, Sandy looked in Mitch's direction, and when their eyes met, there was nothing in Sandy's expression to suggest that she had ever seen Mitch before in her life.

❖

"What did you say this guy's name was?"

"I didn't." Trudy shrugged. "I don't think he ever said. He's got some kind of accent...I don't know what. Italian. Russian.

Something like that."

"Huh. Look, I'm gonna get a drink. You want something?"

"Nah." Trudy sat at one of the tables opposite the kings and Jasmine. "He should be here soon."

Sandy sauntered to the bar and edged a hip up onto a stool six seats down from where Mitch still leaned his back against the bar. The bartender took his time approaching, and when he got within earshot, she said, "Would it be too much trouble for you to get me a beer?"

"Would it be too much trouble for you to suck my dick?"

"Not if the price is right."

He laughed. "You think in a place like this I have to pay for it?"

"If I told you what I think, I might not get my beer." Sandy lifted a shoulder, a slow easy smile on her face. "And I'm very thirsty."

Still laughing, he pulled a bottle of Budweiser from the cold case beneath the bar, popped the top, and slid it to her. "Four bucks."

Sandy pulled a bill from a slit pocket beneath the waistband of her crotch-high red skirt. Her shoes were the same deep red, and she wore a black satin top with spaghetti-string straps.

"Give me five minutes in the back room, and you can keep your money." As he spoke, his eyes dipped to her breasts and fixed on the outline of tight nipples stretching the shiny material.

"You wouldn't last a minute, but it's still not worth my time." She pushed the bill across the bar.

As he snorted and picked up the money, Sandy hefted the bottle and turned in Mitch's direction. Their eyes met, and Sandy nodded, then turned and walked away.

❖

"What do you think?" Watts asked.

"I think there's going to be a meet right now," Rebecca said sharply. "Christ almighty. We've got three people in there, and we're deaf and blind out here. There's no way we're going to know what's going on."

"She should have waited, God damn it." Furious, Watts

regarded the windowless door of the sex club. "We were supposed to get her the wire tomorrow."

"She gets the call, she goes. Sandy knows the game." Rebecca's stomach writhed with apprehension, but her voice was cool, her face expressionless. "Jasmine and Mitch will keep an eye on her while she's inside."

"Right—a flaming fruit civilian and a rookie whose head is harder than her dick."

"They'll stand up," Rebecca murmured, recognizing Watts's insults for what they were—concern. Gaze nailed to the door, she willed Sandy to walk back through it. *Come on, sweetheart. Bring him out to us.*

"You want I should call for backup?"

"For what? Right now all we've got is a CI looking for information." Rebecca shook her head, then, with more confidence than she felt, said, "We'll tail them when they leave—find his *studio.*"

"This don't smell right."

I know.

❖

A few minutes later, Mitch watched from the bar as a muscular, dark-haired man in a surprisingly expensive-looking suit entered from the rear of the room. The newcomer stopped at the far corner of the stage where two women continued to gyrate and casually, but thoroughly, surveyed the room. After his perusal of the bar's occupants, the man walked to Sandy's table and sat down.

It was the guy from the video. There was no way for Mitch to get close enough to hear the conversation. All he could do was watch helplessly as the man leaned forward and put his fingers beneath Sandy's chin, then turned her head from one side to the other. Acid burned a hole in Mitch's stomach, and when the stranger ran a thick index finger down the side of Sandy's neck and then between her breasts, Mitch's vision blurred with a combination of rage and sick terror.

Do the job. He forced himself to walk casually back to his seat. As he sat, he slid an arm around Jasmine's shoulders. "You see them?"

"Yes." Jasmine snuggled beneath Mitch's arm, keeping her voice low. Mitch's body vibrated with tension. "Take it easy. Nothing's going to happen in here."

"I'm not worried about *in here*."

"Rebecca's outside."

Mitch stiffened as Sandy, Trudy, and the man rose. "They're gonna go out the back door. Frye won't see them leave."

"Mitch," Jasmine warned as Mitch stood. "What—"

"I'll take my bike down the alley next door and come around on the street behind the bar. I should be able to pick them up from there. Tell Frye."

"Wait for backup."

But Mitch was already halfway to the door, and he was not turning back. He was not going to let Sandy disappear into the night.

CHAPTER TWENTY-SEVEN

Oh fuck me, now what is *this* action?" Watts stiffened as he watched the figure emerge from the club on the run.

Wordlessly, Rebecca keyed the ignition in the unmarked police vehicle the instant she recognized Mitchell race toward the big Harley parked at the curb. The young cop swung a leg over the motorcycle, started the engine with one swift, hard leg kick, and wheeled the motorcycle down the alley next to the building that housed the bar. In less than five seconds, she had disappeared from sight.

"Back door," Rebecca grunted as she pulled the car into the street.

"Hold it a minute!" Watts turned in his seat with some difficulty and reached behind to release the lock on the rear door when Rebecca hit the brakes.

The door swung open and Jasmine tumbled in, breathless. "Thanks. They're on their way...out the...rear exit."

"How many?" Rebecca gunned the engine, which responded lethargically, and silently cursed the fact that she didn't have her Vette. Unfortunately, a red Corvette made a poor surveillance vehicle.

"I only saw Sandy, Trudy, and one male—the guy from the video."

"Did you see the vehicle?"

"No."

God damn it. Rebecca gritted her teeth, knowing that they'd been caught unprepared. But they were in it now, and she couldn't leave Sandy out there alone. She turned right through a red light at the corner and accelerated down the block to a narrow street that ran parallel to the one fronting Ziggie's. "What the hell is Mitchell doing?"

"Following them," Jasmine reported grimly.

"Jesus Christ." Slowing, Rebecca edged the vehicle into what was little more than a wide alley. Most of the buildings that backed up to it were dark. "Watts—you see anything?"

"Nothing. It's too goddamned—"

"There!" Jasmine pointed through the windshield as she leaned forward over the front seat. "At the other end of the alley—I think I saw taillights."

Since she had no choice, Rebecca eased the car down the alley, weaving deftly between dumpsters and piles of loose boxes and trash. When she reached the far end, she looked to her left and saw the motorcycle just disappearing around the corner. With a screech of tires, she rocketed the sedan in that direction.

At almost four in the morning, there was very little traffic in North Philadelphia. Since she hadn't seen the target vehicle, she was forced to follow the motorcycle, hoping that Mitchell could manage to keep the suspect in sight. She followed the motorcycle as closely as she dared, using the few cars that were on the road for cover.

"Jesus H. Christ on a crutch," Watts muttered. "I hope to hell that rookie doesn't give himself...herself...ah, fuck...the *tail* away. If these guys think they've been made, they'll do those girls and dump them somewhere."

Since Watts was right, Rebecca said nothing, her jaws clamped tight and her unblinking eyes fixed hard on the road in front of her. As they turned onto a dark street of mostly abandoned buildings and empty lots, she was surprised when Mitchell accelerated fast and disappeared, the red taillight of the motorcycle fading like a candle extinguished in the wind.

"What just happened?" Jasmine's voice was tight with anxiety.

"Let's hope that was a signal," Rebecca murmured as she pulled to the curb behind a broken-down car that sat tireless on rusted rims. She looked in all directions and saw no sign of life. There were half a dozen vehicles parked along both sides of the street, but no one on foot and no lights in any of the buildings.

"What do you think?" Watts asked as the seconds ticked by

and the silence in the car grew heavy.

"We wait."

Five minutes passed.

Six.

No one spoke.

Seven.

Rebecca tilted her head, concentrating on a faint rumble in the distance. It could have been thunder, but the sky was clear, and it was too late in the season for that kind of storm.

Eight.

She glanced in the rearview mirror. There were no streetlights and little moon, and the view behind her was shrouded in gloom. As she watched, a ghostlike form emerged from the shadows.

Nine.

Watts glanced over his shoulder. "Son of a bitch."

Driving without lights, Mitchell slid the big motorcycle in behind the surveillance sedan and cut the engine. Keeping low, she came alongside the vehicle and tapped on Watts's door.

"Where are they?" Watts asked as he opened the door to find Mitchell crouched beside the car.

"Fourth building down from the end of the street on the right. Warehouse of some kind. I don't know what floor they're on. He parked the SUV in a service alley beside it." She worked hard to keep her voice steady. The entire time she'd been following the Explorer, she'd been thinking about Sandy in there, knowing what would happen to both girls if she blew it. "I was afraid he'd made me when he slowed down, so I had to get out of there. I didn't want to come back right away in case they were listening for the bike."

"Okay," Rebecca said briskly. "Watts, call for two black-and-whites for backup. We'll take one unit in with us and put another on the vehicle in the alley."

"You want me to put out a Code 30?"

"Uh-uh. If we call for officer assistance, we'll have twenty cars here and no way to coordinate. I want to go in fast and quiet. No advance warning. Surprise is our only advantage."

"You want to take him now?" Watts asked flatly.

"We have him ID-ed from the video. We know he's in there with at least one minor and violating local, state, and federal laws.

I'd say we have probable cause."

"If they're broadcasting live, we're gonna tip off everyone who's watching."

"It's not the usual night or time for a live feed." She glanced at Mitchell, whose eyes were riveted on her face. "Besides, if we don't move on this now, Sandy and Trudy are going to have to go through with the video."

Watts's face hardened. "Then let's bust up his party."

As Watts reached for the radio to call it in, Rebecca turned to Jasmine. "Stay here. Once we've secured the place, I'll want you to come in and take a look at the computer setup. I don't want to run the risk of losing whatever data is there."

"I can handle a weapon, Sergeant." She smiled. "Although if I had known this was going to happen tonight, I wouldn't have worn these heels."

Rebecca laughed, her tension dissipating as she prepared for the operation. "I have a feeling you'd be just fine, heels or no heels, but I'd rather keep you out of that kind of action."

"What about me?" Mitchell asked.

"I don't want you seen by the suspect. It would blow your cover, and we may still have work for Mitch."

Mitchell's eyes blazed. "Sandy's in there."

"I know exactly who's in there, Officer, and I'm ordering you to stay clear."

"Black-and-whites are on the way, Sarge. Five minutes." Watts leaned toward Rebecca and said quietly, "You gotta get a vest on, Sarge. Christ, you're not even cleared for street duty. And if the doc finds ou—"

"In a minute." Rebecca was still studying Mitchell's face, judging whether the officer would hold. She liked what she saw. "Okay. Back up the uniforms in the alley, Officer. But I want you to stay out of sight unless absolutely necessary. Am I clear?"

"Yes, ma'am. Thank you."

"Don't thank me. Just do the job."

❖

It was cold in the cavernous warehouse. Colder than Sandy had expected, and things were moving a lot faster than she'd anticipated, too. She'd hoped during the disorienting ride through the unfamiliar part of town that Mitch and Frye would be close behind. That somehow they would end this.

But they weren't there, and it had begun.

Sandy tried to get a good look at the second guy—the one who'd been waiting inside and who was now monitoring the equipment and adjusting the lights. She wanted to be able to describe him for Frye. It was difficult to see him because Victor—at least that's what he'd *said* his name was—was blocking her view. Plus the other guy was moving around in the shadows outside the area lit by the bright spotlights. She was pretty sure she could tell Frye where this place was, although she'd never been in this part of the city before.

"Try looking like you're enjoying this, honey," Victor whispered with his mouth close to her ear. He glanced down. "Your friend is."

She hadn't thought it would go down this way, but there she was, and she didn't have much choice but to go through with it. Sandy turned her face away from his and focused on some distant point. She'd been there a thousand times before, and she knew she wouldn't feel his hands or the weight of his body. She wouldn't hear his voice, or his breathing, or the words he would whisper when he thought he owned her. She would be gone; inside her head, inside her heart, he would be nothing...

The sound of splintering wood, pounding footsteps, and hoarse shouts jerked Sandy back to the present. When Victor rolled away cursing, Sandy gripped Trudy and pulled her roughly to the floor beside the bed.

"Keep your head down," Sandy cried, and curled around the terrified girl.

❖

Against Watts's objections, Rebecca went through the door first, with him and two uniformed officers right behind her. She took in the big room in one sweeping glance. The studio setup was right in the middle and brightly lit. Same bed, same backdrop, same pathetic props. Same *star,* except this time the woman he had his hands on was Sandy, and Rebecca wanted to drop him in his tracks. Her blood was burning, but her mind was crystal clear.

She shouted *police* and never stopped running until she had her weapon in his face and her knee in his crotch. Then she flipped him onto his stomach and slapped on the restraints.

"The other guy's headed out the back," one of the uniforms yelled and ran after him.

"Watts, cover this guy." Rebecca got quickly to her feet and glanced at Sandy. *You okay?*

Sandy nodded, her face pale but her eyes clear. She smiled weakly. *Glad ya made it.*

"And keep your eye on these two," Rebecca ordered for the suspect's benefit as she headed after the uniforms to join in the pursuit.

Sandy wanted to ask where Dell was, but she wasn't supposed to know these cops. She wasn't supposed to *be* anything other than a hooker making some quick money in a skin flick. But the question was in her eyes as she looked at Watts. He was looking at the guy on the floor like he wanted to kick him. Or worse.

Watts kept one eye on the prisoner as he shrugged out of his jacket. With one hand, he held it out in Sandy's direction, keeping his gaze averted. "Cover up. You'll freeze your tits off."

"What, you seen enough now?" But Sandy took the garment and pulled it on as Trudy scrambled to find their clothes. She was shivering, and it wasn't just because there was no heat. She didn't think she'd be warm again until she could see Dell. It took Dell's eyes, Dell's hands, to touch the places in her that were cold.

"If you're *real* good, sweet piece," Watts said so the scumbag on the floor could hear, "I'll let you show me some more later."

"Blow me," Sandy snapped.

"Aw, honey," Watts finally looked in her direction, glad to see that she was semiclothed and to hear that the tremor had left her voice, "that's my line."

❖

The alley was dark and the bricks against Mitchell's back were rough and cold. When the side door banged open and a large dark figure hurtled through, Mitchell had one quick flash of that other alley, that other night, and then her adrenaline started pumping and all she saw was the patrol officers tackle the perp. He was big and strong, and he didn't go easy. Both uniforms were on him, and still he writhed and twisted and kicked. The alley reverberated with shouts, grunts, and curses. Frye had said for her to stay clear unless needed, and it looked like she was.

Mitchell sprinted toward the action from her spot just inside the mouth of the alley where Frye had positioned her. She was three feet away from the thrashing snarl of arms and legs when she saw the glint of steel. The suspect pulled a blade from his boot and swung it in a flashing arc toward the back of the female officer who had him pinned. Mitchell dove.

"Knife!" she shouted while still in midair.

The blade caught her in the left thigh before the second officer grabbed the suspect's arm and efficiently snapped it. For the first few seconds, the wound didn't hurt at all, and then the pain rose up like a wave of fire and took her breath away. She rolled away, grabbed for the shank buried in her thigh, and reflexively pulled it out. It took all her willpower to clamp down on the scream that threatened to erupt from her. *Oh fuck, fuck! God. It hurts.*

From somewhere close, she heard shouts and then a steady deep voice that seemed to penetrate the pandemonium with calm strength. Pulling in air, Mitchell tried to get to her feet. Instead, her stomach heaved, and she choked back the bile that surged through her chest. She groaned and tried again to sit up.

"Stay put, Mitchell," Rebecca said sharply as she bent down. "Where did he get you?"

"Leg...ah, jeez...it...hurts."

"Let me get a look."

"I'm...okay, Sergeant," Mitchell gasped, coughing. "I think... it's just a...nick."

"We'll let the doctors decide."

"Sandy...is she okay? Did he—"

"She's fine. He never touched her." *At least that's the story unless she tells you different.*

"Tell her...I'm all right."

"You can tell her yourself in a little while." Rebecca observed the pool of blood beneath Mitchell's leg and her stomach roiled. There looked to be a lot of it. She yanked off her jacket and wrapped the sleeve tightly around Mitchell's thigh, then pulled out her cell phone and called for an ambulance. Kneeling, she put one hand on Mitchell's head and with the other applied steady pressure over the leaking wound in the younger woman's thigh. "We'll get you squared away ASAP. You just take it easy."

"Sergeant," Mitchell muttered, for some reason having trouble focusing on Rebecca's face, even though it was quite near. "I... didn't mean...to blow my cover."

"You didn't, Mitchell," Rebecca said grimly. Mitchell's skin was clammy. "Don't worry."

"Ser...geant," Mitchell whispered urgently.

Rebecca leaned over, trying to hear the faint words. When she finally made them out, she laughed softly and brushed the hair from Mitchell's eyes. "I'll take care of it."

She glanced around. As instructed, the two uniforms had already taken the prisoner out to their patrol car, and she and her wounded officer were alone in the alley. *Jesus, I just hope that Watts doesn't come out right now.*

Then she reached down and unzipped Mitch's pants.

❖

Catherine jerked awake at the first ring of the phone, her heart pounding. Her eyes flew to the clock. 5:44.

She knew instantly that she was alone, and she knew with absolute certainty what the call was about. *Oh my God. No!*

"Dr. Rawlings."

"Catherine, I'm fine," Rebecca said immediately.

The relief was swift and sweet, but short-lived. "What is it?"

"Mitchell's on the way to University. Knife wound. I can't leave the scene..."

"I'm on my way," Catherine said at once as she pushed back the covers and rose. "Are you truly all right?"

"Yes, I'm fine. I'm waiting for Flanagan's team and for Sloan to get here. Then I'll be over."

"All right, darling," Catherine said quietly as she moved about gathering her clothes. "I'll handle things."

"Look, Catherine..." There was a beat of silence. "Watts is bringing Sandy in, too...her and another girl. They, uh...shit...they need to be examined...for forensic evidence."

Catherine closed her eyes. "Of course. I'll call a friend of mine in GYN to do it."

"Thanks. Can you bring them some clothes, too? We'll need theirs."

"I can't guarantee the fit, but I'll find something."

"I'm sorry—"

"No," Catherine said sharply. Too sharply, she knew, but the fear had not quite abated. "I *want* to do this."

"I'll be there soon." Another pause. "Catherine, take good care of Mitchell."

"Like she was my own."

"I love you. I gotta run."

The phone went dead.

I love you.

CHAPTER TWENTY-EIGHT

Interesting team you've got here, Frye," Dee Flanagan said as she stood just inside the warehouse door, hands on hips, surveying what was now *her* crime scene. Her blue-jacketed CSI techs were busy photographing the studio, diagramming the layout, and collecting and cataloging evidence. To her left, an astonishingly sexy woman in clothes that should rightfully only be worn between the hours of midnight and five a.m. sat conferring with Sloan before a bank of video monitors, computer screens, and other electronic equipment.

Following Flanagan's gaze, Rebecca smiled briefly. Once the initial furor had settled, she'd asked Jasmine if she wanted to go home and change, but she'd merely said, "Not until we get this system locked down."

Rebecca shrugged. "Unconventional, perhaps, but unparalleled."

"I'm going to assume they have some kind of departmental sanction and let them do whatever they need to do." Flanagan fixed Rebecca with a hard stare. "But all of the evidence in this room, forensic or electronic, is my responsibility now."

"There's a video disk of the...activity...tonight," Rebecca said quietly. She thought of Sandy and Trudy and, remembering the sight of the man on the bed with them, fury spiked in her gut. "The material is of a sensitive nature. I don't want anyone in the department to see it."

"I'll secure it myself."

Rebecca nodded. "Thanks. I have to get to headquarters to supervise the arrests, contact the DA's office, and set up for interrogation. I've also got a wounded officer—"

"I don't need you here anymore, Frye. In fact, the fewer cops hanging around, the better. You just get in the way, bother my people, and trample evidence." Flanagan lifted a shoulder in casual disregard of Frye's rank and position. "I'll keep an eye on things here."

Because she trusted Flanagan as she trusted almost no one else in the department, with the exception of Watts, and because she needed to see for herself that Mitchell was all right, Rebecca acquiesced. "Okay. As soon as Sloan is satisfied that the electronic data is secure, you can take anything out of here that you need to."

Again, Flanagan nodded, her eyes everywhere at once, ensuring that everything was being handled appropriately. "If there's something that Sloan thinks might need...ah...special treatment, I'll sign for it to preserve the chain of evidence."

"Good enough. I appreciate the help."

"Looks like you made a big score tonight, Frye. Nice going."

It was true, but it wasn't everything she wanted. They had a piece of the puzzle, and they were likely to get media-worthy arrests from it. But she didn't yet have the source of the leak within the department, and she didn't have Jeff Cruz and Jimmy Hogan's killer. She didn't have Michael's assailant. They'd made a start, but the job was far from finished.

"What I've got is an officer in the hospital." Rebecca sighed and rubbed her forehead. "Hell. Thanks for covering me here, Dee."

"Go take care of business, Detective." Flanagan patted Rebecca's back and walked off to chastise a tech for failing to blue-light the sheets on the bed for bodily fluids before bagging them.

Rebecca crossed to where her colleagues were working and leaned down to speak confidentially. "I need to leave. I want to square things away at the station and then get over to the hospital."

Sloan looked up, her eyes intensely focused. "We've got hours of work here. With luck, we'll be able to access the server information and link directly to the mid-level distributors like LongJohnXXX. We just broadcast a message to everyone receiving the feeds from here that the system is temporarily down for maintenance. Hopefully no one will suspect it's been breached and start dumping data at the other end."

"Good. I spoke with the CSI chief. You're green-lighted to do whatever you need to do with this equipment and data, but make sure that everything is documented."

"Of course," Sloan said smoothly. *As much as they need to know.*

Rebecca clapped Sloan on the shoulder. "Thanks."

"Will you call us about Dell?" Jasmine asked.

"As soon as I hear anything."

❖

"Look, I don't need to be examined by any gynecologist. The guy didn't leave anything on or *in* me," Sandy said hotly. "And believe me, *I'd* know."

"It's just routine. You tell the doctor whatever you want, and he'll decide what needs to be done." Watts pulled the unmarked surveillance sedan into the turnaround in front of the emergency department at University Hospital. "But it's important for the case, okay?"

Sandy eyed him suspiciously. He hadn't looked at her once since they'd gotten into the car, and he hadn't insulted her, made any lewd comments, or been the least bit suggestive. Something was wrong. There was only one thing she could think of that he would keep from her. Her stomach cramped.

"Where's Dell?"

"The operation is still ongoing," Watts replied stiffly. "Let's just get you taken care of—"

"I'm not going anywhere until you tell me where Dell is." Sandy's heart was racing, and now her stomach threatened to heave. "Now, or I walk."

To emphasize her point, she pushed the car door open and climbed out. She'd given Watts back his jacket and stood in the early-morning chill in just her scant blouse and skirt, but it wasn't the cold that made her shake. She was more scared than she had been in a long, long time.

"Jesus H. Christ." Watts looked pointedly into in the backseat and said to Trudy, "You. Stay put." Then he got out, slammed his door, and faced Sandy across the hood of the car. "Look, she said she'd call you as soon as she could."

"I want to talk to her right now. Get her on the phone." The longer he stalled, the more frightened she became. *Oh, baby, what's happened? Where are you?*

"Fuck me." Watts rubbed his face with both hands, wondering what he'd done to deserve this ass-end of the detail. "Okay, just take it easy, okay? She got a little dinged up, and she's in the ER being looked—hey!"

He stared after Sandy's retreating back as she raced toward the emergency room entrance. In the next second, he yanked open the car door. The girl inside regarded him disdainfully. "You. Let's go."

He took Trudy's arm carefully and led her rapidly toward the ER. Frye would have his balls if he lost either of them. Come to think of it, she'd probably have his balls anyway. Then he'd fit right in with the rest of the team. *Wonderful.*

❖

Catherine heard the commotion before she could make out the words beneath the shouts. She stepped outside the curtain just in time to witness Sandy rush headlong down the corridor with an irate emergency technician close on her heels and shouting.

"Hey, you! I told you—you can't come back here."

The technician outweighed Sandy by a hundred pounds and clearly intended to throttle her once he caught her, and she was almost in his grasp.

"It's all right," Catherine said as she reached out and caught Sandy's arm, then stepped between Sandy and her pursuer. "She's with me."

The technician gave Catherine a mistrustful stare before his eyes flicked to the ID badge hanging around her neck on a red lanyard. Although he looked as if he wanted to argue, he merely grunted in annoyance and stalked off.

"Are you hurt?" Catherine asked immediately, noting the wild look in Sandy's eyes. She also remembered Rebecca's statement that Sandy and another girl needed to be evaluated. "Have you seen Dr. Valeria?"

Sandy shook her head vehemently. Then she took a deep breath and seemed to control herself by sheer force of will. "Is Dell here?"

"Right inside," Catherine replied with a tilt of her head toward the curtain. "The surgeon just left to review some of her tests."

"Is she—" Sandy's voice broke. "Is she going to be okay?"

Catherine felt the shiver that coursed through the slender frame and saw the terror swim below the surface of her blue eyes. "Yes. Didn't they tell you anything?"

Sandy shook her head, afraid to speak.

"Oh, I'm so sorry. She's been injured...a knife wound to the thigh, but she's stable."

"Can I see her?"

The question was asked with such wistfulness that Catherine's heart ached. "I don't see why not." She took Sandy's hand and with the other reached to pull the curtain aside. "Just for a minute, and then you need to be checked out, too. Deal?"

Sandy nodded in agreement. She'd do anything, as long as they let her see for herself that Dell was not going to leave her.

"She's going to be fine," Catherine emphasized as Sandy brushed past her.

"Sure," Sandy said flatly. *Like anyone would tell me the truth.*

It was worse than she expected.

Mitchell lay on a stretcher, eyes closed, with intravenous lines running into both arms. And she was white. Not pale. White. Sandy's heart sank.

A gentle hand touched her shoulder.

"She's been sedated. She lost a little blood, but her vital signs are stable. She *will* be all right."

Sandy searched Catherine's eyes. Warm, caring, honest. And something else in their depths, too—understanding. *She knows about us.* And the acceptance she saw in Catherine's gaze, more than anything else, calmed her fears. "Thanks."

"You can go talk to her." Catherine stepped back. "I'll be right outside."

Slowly, Sandy walked to the head of the stretcher. She touched her fingers to Mitchell's cheek. "Dell? Baby?"

Mitchell's lids flickered open, her pupils wide and unfocused.

"Hey, rookie," Sandy whispered softly.

Mitchell's lips twitched. "Hiya, Sandy." She blinked, her vision cleared, and she focused on Sandy's face. Sandy smiled, but her eyes looked scared. "It's okay."

"You hurting?" Sandy's lip trembled and she caught it in her teeth. She stroked her hand over Mitchell's hair.

"Not so much. They gave me stuff." Mitchell raised her hand and grasped Sandy's weakly. "You? We get there in time? He didn't—"

"No," Sandy said quickly. "Nothing happened. You did good, baby."

Mitchell sighed. "I love you."

The tears came. Sandy couldn't remember the last time she hadn't been able to stop the tears. But it was all too big, too much to hold inside. Letting Mitchell into her life, loving her, the terrible fear of losing her. She turned her face away to hide the anguish, but she had nowhere else to go. Everything that mattered was in that room.

"Honey," Mitchell said soothingly. "Don't...jeez, couldn't you...yell at me for being too slow or something?"

Sandy sniffed. Smiled tremulously. "Were you?"

"Maybe a little. But Frye put me *way* back in the alley...I had to run a long way." Mitchell struggled to keep her eyes open, but the drugs were winning. "Don't worry, 'kay? I'll be...outta here soon."

"Yeah, I know." Sandy leaned close and kissed her. "I love you, Dell."

Mitchell closed her eyes. "You go home. Don't worry."

It was terrifying to watch her slip away. Sandy brushed her lips over Mitchell's ear. "I'll just wait for you."

The curtain moved and Sandy looked up, instantly on guard. A dark-haired, dark-eyed woman in navy scrubs stepped in and raised a quizzical eyebrow in Sandy's direction before her eyes moved automatically to the monitor above Mitchell's bed.

"Hi. I'm Dr. Torveau, the trauma surgeon."

"Hi," Sandy replied warily.

"Are you family or...?" Torveau saw the young girl tremble and try to hide it behind a belligerent expression. "You want to sit down?"

Sandy shook her head. She wasn't sure what to say. She didn't want to get Mitchell into trouble by revealing their relationship. With enormous relief, she watched Catherine step through the separation in the heavy white curtain that enclosed them.

"How are things looking?" Catherine asked of Torveau. She smiled at Sandy. "Sandy's a very close friend of Dell's. You've met, I see."

"Uh-huh. Just now," Torveau replied. "The arteriogram shows the knife nicked a branch of the femoral artery in the thigh, which is why she lost so much blood so fast. It's stopped now, but the conservative approach is for me to take a look at the vessel and repair the laceration."

Sandy looked rapidly from Catherine to Torveau. "But you can fix it?"

"Oh, you bet." Torveau smiled. "Piece of cake."

"And she'll be okay?"

"Should be. There's very little muscle damage, because it was an in-and-out stab wound. Missed the nerve by an inch."

"All the way okay?" Sandy persisted.

Dr. Torveau tilted her head and studied Sandy seriously. The young blond still had one hand on the patient's head and the other curled around the patient's. *Tough and scared to death.* "I can't tell you she won't have a problem, but I don't anticipate any. A week or so of limited activity and then she should be fine. Sore, but fine. Okay?"

Sandy nodded. "So...you gonna fix it now?"

Torveau laughed. "Right now. As soon as she gives consent. You want me to call you when I'm done?"

"I want to wait." Sandy glanced at Catherine, wondering if Frye would have a fit, worrying about Mitchell's job. Worrying about Mitch's cover.

Catherine watched the uncertainty cloud Sandy's face. "Ali, why don't you page me when you're out of the OR. I'll take Sandy to the cafeteria for some breakfast."

"Sounds like a plan." Torveau met Sandy's uneasy eyes. "I'll look after her."

It was so hard to let go of Dell's hand, but finally Sandy did.

"Okay. Sure." She started to walk toward Catherine, then stopped and turned to the surgeon. "Thanks."

"You don't have to thank me," Torveau said softly.

Once outside in the bustling corridor, Catherine halted. "You need to talk to the gynecologist. I think your friend Trudy is already finished."

Sandy sighed. "The guy never got off. I told Bluto that already."

"Detective Watts?" Catherine bit back a grin.

"Uh-huh."

"Well," Catherine couldn't help the smile, "I'm very happy to hear that you're all right. How about you just talk to Dr. Valeria so she can make out an official report? I have some clothes for you to change into, as well. Old ones of mine—I expect you'll swim in them, but they'll be warm."

"How'd you know..." Sandy stopped. "Frye."

"She called me before you arrived, yes." *And every half-hour since.*

"Okay, fine. I'll *talk* to this doctor."

"Thank you."

Sandy regarded the elegant woman in the heather-green suit, the same warm color as her eyes, and suddenly wanted to lean her head on Catherine's shoulder. Instead, she straightened her own. "So where do I go?"

"Would you like company?"

"Yeah," Sandy said slowly. "Yeah, I would."

❖

A little after nine a.m., Rebecca found her lover and her confidential informant tucked away in the corner of the hospital cafeteria. Catherine looked beautiful, and just seeing her eased the ball of tension she'd been carrying in her chest. Sandy looked worn out, but unexpectedly cute in Catherine's University Med sweatshirt and baggy jeans. For the first time since Rebecca had known her, she looked like any ordinary teenager.

Until she looked up and Rebecca saw her eyes. A lifetime of hurt flickered in them for an instant and then was quickly hidden.

"Hi," Rebecca said as she slid into the free seat.

"Hi." Sandy watched Catherine out of the corner of her eye.

"Hello, Detective," Catherine said in a tone that was almost a caress. She quickly took in her lover's rumpled shirt, which was uncharacteristically untucked. Of more concern were the deep shadows beneath her eyes and the faint tremor in the hand that held the paper coffee cup. "Have you had breakfast?"

Rebecca lifted a shoulder. "Not yet. How's Mitchell?"

"We're still waiting. It's been a little over an hour, so I expect we'll hear any time now."

"I have to get back to the station soon."

"Right away?" Catherine couldn't hide her concern. Less than two weeks before, she'd been the one waiting in the ER while Rebecca underwent emergency treatment. She very much did not want to experience that again.

"Sloan's still at the warehouse, and Jason's back at the office coordinating the data," Rebecca went on, sipping her coffee. "Between what they got from the computers on site and the IDs we've been collecting the last few weeks, we're going to have a list of names by midday. I need to arrange warrants and put together a couple of strike teams to hit these guys all at once."

"Today?"

"Mmm." Rebecca sighed tiredly and leaned back in her chair. "Have to. If we wait, they're going to get wind of the bust, and they'll all rabbit."

Catherine turned to Sandy. "Would you excuse us for just a few minutes?"

"Sure," Sandy replied, getting to her feet with a grin. *Frye's gonna get her ass chewed. Wow.*

When Sandy was out of earshot, Catherine leaned forward and put her hand on Rebecca's arm. "You're in no shape to lead a strike team. You've been up all night, and you just went back to full du—"

"You're right."

"I beg your pardon?"

Rebecca linked her fingers with Catherine's. "I said, you're right. I'm not going to."

"Oh. Well."

"But I still need to organize it. I need to get Watts to walk the warrants through, and I need to brief the teams, and I need to be in the surveillance van timing the arrests." She sighed again. "And I need to brief with Captain Henry—an hour ago, but I've been putting that off."

"You won't be...going through any doors today?"

Rebecca shook her head.

"I won't ask about last night." *Because I already know. Sandy was inside, one of your own. Of course you went through first.*

"Okay." Rebecca ran her thumb over the top of Catherine's warm hand. "Thanks."

"Where's your jacket?"

"I had to throw it away." Rebecca looked around for Sandy. "Mitchell's blood was all over it. She saved a cop's life tonight, Catherine."

Catherine smiled fondly. "She's just your kind of cop, isn't she, my love?"

"Yeah." Rebecca grinned. "Yeah, she is."

CHAPTER TWENTY-NINE

Mitchell swam up through dark heavy waters, struggling against the unseen hand that threatened to pull her ever deeper. Her chest ached, hungry for air, and distantly, pain broke over her like angry surf. Gasping, she opened her eyes.

"Take it easy," Rebecca said gently, resting her palm lightly against Mitchell's shoulder. "You're okay. You're in the recovery room."

"Sergeant," Mitchell said hoarsely, struggling to focus. "Where's...Sandy?"

"Waiting outside with Catherine. *I* had to pull some strings to get in here." Rebecca smiled, pleased to see that Mitchell's eyes were clearing rapidly. "You'll be able to see her in a bit."

"What's happening...with the case?"

Rebecca grinned. "In about two hours, we're going to kick some major ass."

Mitchell groaned.

"Are you hurting? You need me to get the nurse?"

"No. I can't believe...I'm going to miss this." She tried to raise her head but was still too weak.

"Unfortunately, your ass-kicking leg is temporarily out of commission, Officer." Rebecca squeezed Mitchell's shoulder.

"Is it bad?"

"Nah. The surgeon said you'd be back on your feet in no time."

"Back on the team?"

"I don't know that there will be a team after today," Rebecca said quietly. "But I'll see that you get credit for your part in the operation."

"I don't care...about that."

"I do." Rebecca straightened. "Anybody you need me to call? Family?"

"No."

"I've got to go. I'll be back later."

"Sergeant?"

Rebecca raised an eyebrow.

"Kick some butt for me."

The corner of Rebecca's mouth lifted into a feral grin. "You can count on it."

❖

When Mitchell next awoke, the pain was bearable, and her overwhelming sensation was one of hunger. She started to sit up and found that she couldn't. When, undaunted, she tried again, a small hand gently pressed her down.

"You're supposed to lie still."

"Like I've got a choice." Mitchell turned her head on the pillow and smiled at Sandy. "Hi, honey."

"Hi, baby."

"Am I supposed to starve to death, too?"

Sandy grinned. "They didn't mention that part." It was so good to hear Mitchell's voice that she felt tears threaten again. That was crazy. She waited until she was sure her voice was steady. "You okay?"

Mitchell gave the question some thought. She felt weak, and her leg felt like she'd been kicked by a horse. But the pain was tolerable. "Yeah, I think so. You?"

"Yeah."

"You look cute."

"Huh?" Sandy glanced down at the too-big sweatshirt and the shapeless jeans and then snorted. "Oh yeah, terrific. Did something happen to your head, too?"

"My head's just fine." She reached out and caught Sandy's hand. "What time is it?"

"Afternoon sometime."

"You ought to go home. You look beat."

"You're kind of bossy for someone who's flat on her back."

Mitchell grinned faintly. "I kind of thought you liked me that way."

"I like you every way." Sandy leaned over and kissed Mitchell gently on the mouth. She straightened quickly at the sound of a discreet cough behind her. She turned, her expression defensive.

"Sorry," Dr. Torveau said. "Should've knocked."

"S'okay."

The surgeon walked to the opposite side of the bed and nodded to Mitchell. "How are you feeling?"

"Not bad. How am I?"

"You're good. You've got a partial laceration of a pretty big artery in your leg, but it's repaired. No permanent damage."

Briefly, Mitchell closed her eyes. When she opened them, they were bright and focused. "When can I go home?"

Torveau sighed. "Taking care of cops is so much fun." After a moment's consideration, she continued, "You'll need some instruction with crutch walking, and that can't happen until tomorrow. If the wound looks okay then, you should be good to go."

"Thanks."

"You won't be walking on that leg for a week," Torveau cautioned, "so you're going to need some help at home."

"I'll be fi—"

"I'll help," Sandy said with finality.

"Good enough. I'll see you in the morning."

Once the surgeon had gone, Mitchell asked, "Can you help me sit up?"

Sandy carefully worked the bed controls and positioned pillows until Mitchell was upright. "Okay?"

"Perfect." Her leg was throbbing, but Mitchell managed a grin. "Maybe you should get one of those hot little nurse's outfits—you know, the ones with the tight, short, see-through white dresses?"

Sandy regarded Mitchell thoughtfully. "Blow me, rookie."

"Okay." Mitchell caught Sandy's hand and brought it to her lips. She kissed her knuckles gently. "You're the boss."

The worry and fear of the past hours slipped away like mist on the sunrise. Leaning down, Sandy kissed Mitchell again. When she drew her mouth away, she whispered, "You know, you're pretty smart for a cop."

❖

Sloan looked up at the sound of the elevator's soft whir, perplexed because she hadn't buzzed anyone in. Looking over her shoulder, she gasped in surprise, then jumped to her feet. "Michael!"

Dressed in a white silk T-shirt and loose cotton slacks, Michael smiled and walked slowly into the office. "I realized that if I was ever going to see you, I would have to track you down."

"Jesus," Sloan cried anxiously, grabbing an office chair and wheeling it in Michael's direction. "Sit. You shouldn't be down here."

"Hi, Jason," Michael called as she settled into the plush leather. From across the room, he raised his hand and waved a greeting while she eyed her lover critically. "You didn't come home last night, and I didn't see you for breakfast, and you didn't call all day."

"What time is it?"

"Five in the afternoon." Michael's tone was aggrieved.

"Oh." Sloan grinned sheepishly. "Sorry."

Laughing, Michael relented. "Don't apologize. I just missed you. How are things going?"

"I'll know better as soon as we hear from Rebecca. We got her the names of half a dozen Internet porn distributors and ten times that many customers. The operation is going down now and is likely to take a few hours. Depending on how the sweep plays out, it could be big."

"I'm proud of you," Michael said softly.

Sloan pulled another chair near, sat, and took both of Michael's hands in hers. "It wasn't just me. It was the whole team."

"Yes, but you're the only one I'm in love with." Michael streaked her fingers through Sloan's hair. "Will you promise to come to bed later?"

"It'll be late, probably." Sloan caught Michael's hand and kissed the palm.

"I don't have any plans."

"How are you feeling?"

"As if I'm going to get bedsores if I sleep any longer." Michael laughed. "Better. The headache comes and goes, but at least once in a while, it *does* go."

"Thank God," Sloan whispered.

"Are things almost wrapped up here, then?"

Sloan looked away.

"Sloan?"

"Last night, while everyone else was out chasing around the city and breaking down doors, I was back here breaking down a few doors of my own." She met Michael's eyes solemnly, wishing there were some things she *didn't* have to remind her about. "We know that someone downtown leaked the details of the task force operation. When they tried to stop me, they hurt you instead."

"I know. But *you* know that wasn't your fault." Michael saw the resistance and the guilt in her lover's eyes. "Darling, look at me."

Reluctantly, Sloan complied.

"I need you to tell me that you will let that go."

"I'm close to finding out who." A muscle jumped along the edge of Sloan's jaw. "I've narrowed it down to two people. When I get the name...I'll give it to Rebecca."

"I believe you. I do." Michael rested her hand against Sloan's cheek. "Now tell me that you'll stop blaming yourself for what happened to me."

"I can't." Sloan's voice was agonized.

Michael sighed, slid her fingers to the back of Sloan's neck, and pulled her close. With her mouth a breath away from Sloan's, she murmured, "There are countless reasons why I love you. But I fell in love with you for the way you love me." She kissed her, a slow, lingering, possessive kiss. "Just try, for me."

Sloan rested her forehead against Michael's, nodding slowly. "Anything. Always."

❖

At a little after nine p.m., Watts walked into Sloan's office carrying a magnum of champagne. Rebecca followed, a tired smile on her face.

"Well?" Jason asked, rising rapidly to his feet.

"Sixty-four arrests," Watts bellowed. "Including five who

have been under surveillance by the OC division for the last six months because of suspected ties to Zamora."

Sloan handed around plastic cups. "Outstanding."

"You'll be able to hear all about it on the ten o'clock news," Watts continued exuberantly as he poured champagne. "Sarge?"

Rebecca shook her head, then glanced at Sloan. "Any coffee?"

"In the back. I'll get it."

"Why don't we all head back there, and we'll see where things are," Rebecca suggested.

The group trooped back to the conference room and settled around the table.

"The Sarge looks really good on camera. The brass are practically creaming over her." Watts refilled his cup happily. "And rumor has it—"

Rebecca coughed. "Okay, Watts, okay."

He grinned at her.

"Everyone did fine," she said, looking at each of them in turn. "We did what the joint task force should have done—we broke the back of the Internet porn ring."

It *was* a victory, and it felt good. She knew, though, that such triumphs were short-lived, and the beast would rise again. That's what police work was—a series of battles in a war that was never won. She had learned to take satisfaction in each small success, but there were days when she wearied. She squared her shoulders. "But we're not done yet. We've got days of interrogation in front of us. Those porn distributors are all hard-core professionals, and they're not about to roll easily, if at all. Plus, we still don't have a handle on where the girls are coming from."

"What do you mean?" Jason asked.

"This operation was too big and too well organized to rely on casual street pick-ups like last night. I think we'll find that our man Victor was just doing a little business on the side, which is why he hustled Sandy and Trudy over there so fast. I'm willing to bet there are still girls out there being exploited by the guys who set up this deal, if not for other videos, then for good old-fashioned cash money."

"Yeah," Watts agreed. "And we still need to plug our leak."

He glanced at Rebecca. "In a manner of speaking."

She just nodded. "Sloan? Anything on that?"

Sloan hesitated then blew out a breath. "I've got two very good possibles as the identity of our traitor." She stood, too restless to sit. "Margaret Campbell, age twenty-nine, joined the DA's office three years ago. Single, one child."

"Divorced?" Watts asked, suddenly serious.

Sloan shook her head. "Never married."

"A woman," Rebecca mused. "In the middle of a porn operation?"

"She doesn't have to be part of the porn network itself," Sloan pointed out. "She just needs to be tied to whoever is *behind* the pornography racket."

"And is she?"

"Counselor Campbell used to dance in a strip club in Manhattan. Since it was during the time she was a law student at NYU, I'd guess she did it to pay the rent."

"How the hell did you find that?" Watts blurted.

Sloan lifted a shoulder. "There are no secrets, not if you know where to look. She didn't come from money, but she had no school debts—or very few. The tuition money didn't come from scholarships, either. How do women make money that doesn't show up on their tax returns or credit reports?"

"So," Watts said, "you figure what...she got into trouble while working the wrong side of the street and owes someone now?"

"Could be." Sloan leaned against the counter and jammed her hands into her pockets. "Zamora or someone in his organization could be squeezing her."

"Or she could have discovered that serving justice doesn't pay very well," Watts remarked.

"Money's the oldest motive in the world."

"Anything else that doesn't look kosher?" Rebecca asked. She'd worked with Campbell a few times. Tough and competent. But she didn't know her. And she'd learned not to trust anyone she didn't know. "Like big cases she lost that might have been mobbed up?"

"None that I found, but I haven't exhausted the search."

"And the other one?" Rebecca asked.

"The other ADA—George Beecher." Sloan rolled her shoulders and swallowed the rest of her champagne. "On the surface, he doesn't fit our profile at all. Thirty-two, been with the DA's office four years. Ivy Leaguer, comes from old money, owns a condo on the waterfront—which he can afford."

"So why do you like him?"

"When he was twenty, Counselor Beecher was charged with raping a co-ed at a fraternity party."

Watts straightened abruptly. "Charged—but no conviction?"

"Charges dropped. Could be the victim recanted, could be she was paid off, could be she just didn't want to go through the indignity and humiliation of a trial." Sloan's features hardened. "Justice is not necessarily kind."

"Then his record should have been expunged," Watts pointed out. "You're fucking scary."

Sloan just smiled. "Like I said—he's clean on the surface, but that little bit of history puts him on my list."

"So what now?" Rebecca persisted.

Sloan looked at Jason. "Time estimate?"

"Depends on if we get lucky. A few days, could be a few weeks."

She turned to Rebecca. "We have to...access...the home and work computers of both subjects, look at phone records—including mobiles—dig out every bit of electronic data available, *and* do it without alerting whoever launched that worm in the first place."

"And *we'd* have to tail them," Watts added. "You know there have to be face-to-faces at some point."

Rebecca rose and walked to the windows, surveying the familiar view. She was surprised at how hard it was to say what she had to say next. The group behind her was silent. At last she turned.

"I don't see how I can sell it," she said, her face devoid of expression. "We've got suspicions and conjecture and gut feelings, but no hard evidence. And our bust tonight has made my captain very happy because we salvaged something out of that federal FUBAR. *He's* made the brass happy because the numbers look great. *City Hall* is happy because we made the national news. Everybody's happy—end of story."

"But the case isn't finished," Watts complained.

"That's the way *we* see it—but to the powers that be, it's all wrapped up with a nice little bow."

"Well," Sloan said calmly. "We all know how politics work. It was a pleasure working with you, Sergeant. You, too, Watts."

Rebecca regarded Sloan thoughtfully, then said to Jason and Watts, "You want to give us a minute?"

Watts picked up the champagne bottle and gestured to Jason. "Come on, I'll buy you a drink." He cocked his head as Jason rose. "Although I kinda wish you were wearing that little red number."

Jason's perfect eyebrow arched. "And you think *Sloan* is scary?"

As the two men left, Rebecca walked over to Sloan. "You're not going to let it go, are you?"

"Would you, if it had been Catherine?"

Rebecca's eyes narrowed. "I'm a cop."

"Your point is?"

"God damn it, Sloan—"

"I promised Michael that if I found the person responsible, I'd tell you." Sloan held Rebecca's frustrated gaze. "I don't lie to her."

"You'll be putting yourself and Jason and probably Michael and Sarah at risk—"

"I can take care of them."

"Not alone."

Sloan's jaw tightened. "I appreciate your concern."

"Don't go rogue on this, Sloan."

"Then figure out how to sell it to your captain, Sergeant."

❖

"I thought I heard you come in," Catherine said, sitting on the arm of the overstuffed chair and threading her arm around Rebecca's shoulders.

"Sorry. I thought you were asleep."

"Are you coming to bed? It's late, darling, and you're exhausted."

Rebecca leaned her head against Catherine's shoulder, rubbing her cheek over the soft silk of the ivory camisole. "I'm still keyed up, I guess."

"You looked very calm on TV," Catherine murmured, rubbing the tense muscles at the base of her lover's neck. "In fact, you looked fabulous."

"Oh, I bet." Rebecca laughed at the suggestive tone in Catherine's voice and some of the knots in her stomach began to unwind. "I had to borrow a jacket from one of the guys."

"I didn't think that was your usual style, but I'm sure no one else noticed."

"God, you feel good." Rebecca closed her eyes, lulled by the gentle hands and the sweet seductive fragrance of Catherine's skin.

"So do you." Catherine reminded herself that Rebecca had been working for nearly two days straight, but her body didn't seem to be listening. She slid her fingers beneath the collar of her lover's shirt and stroked the skin above her left breast.

Rebecca groaned, feeling the familiar ache settle between her thighs. "I need to shower."

"And then you need to sleep." Catherine's voice was breathy with desire.

"I will," Rebecca promised, pulling Catherine into her lap. As she kissed her, she slipped her fingers beneath the sheer material and cupped Catherine's breast. She moaned in appreciation as the nipple hardened instantly against her palm. "Later."

Catherine wrapped her arms around Rebecca's shoulders and fisted the hair at the back of her neck, losing herself in the pleasure of Rebecca's mouth. When she felt Rebecca's hand drift lower, across her abdomen and under the edge of her silk pajama bottoms, she stopped the questing hand with her own. Gasping, she warned, "If you start, you'll have to finish. You know I can't hold back when you do that."

"I was *planning* on finishing," Rebecca growled, brushing her fingers over the inside of Catherine's thigh. "Ah God, you're wet."

"Then go shower and come to bed," Catherine said urgently. She pushed away and stood on trembling legs. "Because I want you to finish with me."

Rebecca's eyes darkened, and she rose quickly, all thoughts of fatigue, of frustration, of powerlessness gone. Now, there was only Catherine.

CHAPTER THIRTY

R ebecca. Rebecca, darling, it's time to get up."
Groaning, Rebecca turned onto her back, opened her eyes, and blinked against the light, which seemed awfully bright even though the lamp on the dresser was turned down low. It took her a second to focus on Catherine, who stood beside the bed in a two-piece deep plum-colored silk suit, the jacket of which was buttoned over apparently very little.

"Nice."

"What?" Catherine asked, perplexed.

"The jacket."

Catherine glanced down and blushed, noting where Rebecca's gaze was fixed. "This is my going-to-work suit. It is *not* supposed to be seductive."

"Sorry, but it is."

"To you, maybe," Catherine commented with a laugh.

"Not maybe—definitely. Any chance you could come back to bed?"

"None." Catherine leaned over and kissed her, then stepped back out of touching range. She didn't trust her lover, or herself. "Besides, I thought I'd taken care of that particular urge of yours not too long ago."

"You did, spectacularly, but that was last night. Today's a brand-new day." Rebecca sat up against the pillows, carelessly unconcerned about her nakedness as the sheet fell away. "What time is it?"

"Seven." Catherine's eyes flickered over the scar so very close to Rebecca's heart and her own heart missed a beat. *God, it was so close.*

"How come you're up and I'm not?"

Catherine forced a smile. "Because I need to leave for work, and you need to sleep."

Rebecca patted a spot on the bed next to her. "Stay for just a minute."

"Mmm—okay, but you're not allowed to touch." Catherine sat on the edge of the bed and crossed her legs, her skirt sliding to mid-thigh.

"I'm not very good with authority figures." To prove her point, Rebecca leaned forward and kissed the cleft between Catherine's breasts. "Or..." Rebecca ran her finger under the hem of the skirt, "orders."

Deftly, Catherine captured Rebecca's fingers and moved them. "I'm in doctor mode and therefore immune to your charms."

"So this is what happens to romance when we live together, huh?" Rebecca's eyes were dancing.

"We're not living together," Catherine said softly, her eyes searching Rebecca's face.

"I seem to remember you asking." Rebecca's blue eyes were serious now.

"I did. Yes." Catherine traced her fingers along Rebecca's jaw and down her neck. "And I sincerely doubt that seeing you like this *more* often would dampen my ardor."

"Oh, yeah?" Rebecca's voice was husky.

"I can assure you, my love, that fifty years from now I'll look at you and want you just as much as ever."

"Those seem like pretty good terms to me."

"I want you to be sure." Catherine's voice was gentle, her smile wistful.

Rebecca leaned forward, her hands framing Catherine's face, her thumbs brushing the elegant cheeks. Her mouth was very near to Catherine's when she murmured, "I'm certain that I could never love anyone more and that I will never stop loving you."

Catherine's lips curved into a smile against Rebecca's mouth. "Those seem like the perfect terms to me."

❖

"Well, well, well," Captain Henry said with undisguised delight. "The detective of the hour. Sit down, Sergeant...or should

I be the first to say, *Lieutenant?*"

"Sir?" Rebecca sat in the familiar chair and crossed her trousered legs.

"You're not going to be able to refuse the promotion this time, Frye. I've already had a call from the chief who said he speaks for the commissioner, and they both want your promotion made effective immediately. The department needs good officers, and you've earned this."

The department wants to be able to point to a few women *of rank, come election time.* Rebecca chose her words carefully. She wasn't entirely certain she wanted a promotion, especially not if it meant she'd be riding a desk at One Police Plaza. But perhaps she could play this to her advantage.

"I'm a street cop, Captain. I don't want to sit in an office and push paper." She held his gaze. "There's still work to be done on the case my team's been investigating."

He waved a hand dismissively. "Organized Crime is going to work with the DA firming up the cases against the distributors. They've all lawyered up at this point anyhow, so there's nothing that you need to do there. The paperwork on the individual arrests can be handled by some of the detective-ones and our clerks." He leaned forward and folded his hands on his desk. "Look, Sergeant, I'm expected to deliver you to the promotion ceremony in person. The press department is ready to announce it. Don't jam me up on this."

"I wasn't talking about tying up last night's loose ends, sir. I was talking about the other aspects of my investigation which are still open—including the source of an inside leak that fingered Sloan and maybe Jimmy and Jeff."

His eyes narrowed. "Those are serious allegations, Sergeant."

"Yes sir, I'm aware of that." She played her final card. "You might be interested to know, Captain, that whoever's been pilfering files and leaking the details of confidential police operations made things look like *you* were the source of the leak."

His mahogany features darkened dangerously, and he said stiffly, "How?"

"Computer intrusions that track back to you. It's complicated—

I'd need Sloan to lay it all out for you."

"Why am I just hearing about this now?"

"Because until very recently, I didn't have enough facts to bring them to you." She didn't see any reason that he needed to know everything that she knew, or *when* she knew it. Or that for a while she had seriously suspected that he was guilty.

"And now you do?"

"Nearly the whole package. With the right team, I can give you a direct link to Zamora—the same person who's responsible for setting up Jimmy Hogan and Jeff Cruz. We're close, Captain." *And while I'm at it, I'm going to find out where Zamora's people are getting the girls to keep his sex businesses running.*

He studied her contemplatively, and Rebecca knew that he was figuring his angles just as she was working hers. She wondered what the price would be.

"Let's say, hypothetically, I approved a special high-profile case unit within our division, with you as the lead, reporting directly to me. You'd accept the promotion?" He tried to read her response, but saw only the cool blue gaze. The chief had already floated the idea to him, but Frye didn't need to know that. Or why the offer was on the table.

"I get to choose my own people, and," she added quickly, "I want official department recognition for my civilian consultants." *If I can talk Sloan into doing anything* official.

He leaned back, a shadow of a smile on his face. "We might be able to work something out. Of course, there might be a few conditions."

She waited, because there always were—and it was his move.

Henry picked up the phone and punched an extension. "Send him in."

Rebecca turned her head at the sound of the door opening behind her and met the opaque gaze of Avery Clark, the Department of Justice agent who had headed the defunct joint task force and who had usurped the evidence *and* the arrest that belonged to her team.

"Congratulations, Detective Sergeant. Very nice job," Clark said with apparent sincerity.

Rebecca inclined her head slightly.

"I'd like to know how you identified the suspects so quickly.

Commendable."

"You can read my report for the details."

"I'm sure it will be quite illuminating." He took the seat next to hers and nodded to Captain Henry.

"Agent Clark contacted me last night about the scope of your investigation, Sergeant. He said he was impressed."

"I'm flattered," Rebecca said sarcastically.

Clark turned in his seat to face Rebecca. "You made a dent in Zamora's organization, and I'm willing to bet that you've got more leads cooking. We're very interested at Justice in what you might be pursuing."

"I don't work for the Justice Department."

"I lost a man, too, Sergeant."

"And if my team had been allowed to work the evidence from the *last* arrest, we'd be closer to knowing who's responsible."

"But you're still close, aren't you?" he asked softly.

Rebecca said nothing.

"I'm not asking for joint jurisdiction," Clark continued. "I'm asking for cooperation and a sharing of intelligence."

Rebecca grimaced. "I think you've already proven that *sharing* is not high on your list."

"Sergeant," Henry said blandly, "I think that the chief would look favorably upon the development of a major crime unit that interfaced with a federal unit. It's got selling power."

So that's the deal breaker. If I want to keep the team together, I'm going to have to play ball with the feds. A muscle in Rebecca's jaw tightened. "Watts gets promoted to detective third grade, and Mitchell gets her shield."

"I think we can manage that, *Lieutenant.*"

Clark stood, as did Rebecca. He held out his hand. "Let me be the first to congratulate you, Lieutenant. I'm sure we'll be in touch soon."

"I'm sure." She shook the offered hand and turned to Henry. "Thank you, Captain."

"Lieutenant." He watched her walk out, pleased with the morning's work.

❖

When Rebecca stepped into the squad room, Watts jumped up

and hurried over to her.

"Well? What's the word?"

"Not here, Watts. Let's take a ride." She kept walking, waving her thanks to the frequent calls of congratulations from other detectives.

"Oh for Christ's sake," Watts puffed, "just tell me...are the rumors true? Is it Lieutenant now?"

"You always believe everything you hear, Watts?" Rebecca hit the door to the stairwell and started down. From behind her, she heard a long whistle and then a small hoot of pleasure that had her smiling despite herself.

"So where we going, Loo?" Watts hurried to catch up to her on the stairs.

Striding into the parking lot, she said, "We're going to the hospital to see how Mitchell's doing." She pulled open the driver's door of the Vette and slid in. As she started the engine, Watts dropped into the seat beside her. "Then we're going to Sloan's to brief the rest of the team."

He caught his breath sharply. "The rest of the team? Officially?"

"Yep." She gunned the Vette out of the parking lot and grinned. "We're going to be on our own, more or less. HPC—High Profile Crimes Unit." She'd tell him the bad news about Clark after he'd had a chance to enjoy this a little.

"Oh man, that is sweet." He fumbled in the inside pocket of his jacket for his cigarettes, a broad smile on his face.

"Yeah, it is," Rebecca said softly, allowing herself a brief moment of pleasure as she imagined telling Catherine about the promotion. Then she glanced over at her partner, who was just about to strike a match. "Even D-threes don't smoke in my ride, Watts."

"Sure, Loo," he said with satisfaction, pocketing his smokes. "You're the boss." An instant later, he gaped at her and sputtered, *"D-three?"*

Detective Lieutenant Rebecca Frye merely smiled. Her mind was already focused on the hunt to come.

The End

About the Author

Radclyffe is a member of the Golden Crown Literary Society, Pink Ink, the Romance Writers of America, and a two-time recipient of the Alice B. award for lesbian fiction. She has written numerous best-selling lesbian romances (*Safe Harbor* and its sequel *Beyond the Breakwater, Innocent Hearts, Love's Melody Lost, Love's Tender Warriors, Tomorrow's Promise, Passion's Bright Fury, Love's Masquerade, shadowland,* and *Fated Love*), two romance/intrigue series: the Honor series *(Above All, Honor, Honor Bound, Love & Honor,* and *Honor Guards*) and the Justice series (*Shield of Justice,* the prequel *A Matter of Trust, In Pursuit of Justice,* and *Justice in the Shadows)*, as well as an erotica collection: *Change of Pace – Erotic Interludes.*

She lives with her partner, Lee, in Philadelphia, PA where she both writes and practices surgery full-time. She is also the president of Bold Strokes Books, a lesbian publishing company.

Her upcoming works include: *Justice Served* (June 2005); *Stolen Moments: Erotic Interludes 2*, ed. with Stacia Seaman (September 2005), and *Honor Reclaimed* (December 2005)

Look for information about these works at www.radfic.com and www.boldstrokesbooks.com.

Other Books Available From
Bold Strokes Books

Course of Action by Gun Brooke. Actress Carolyn Black desperately wants the starring role in an upcoming film produced by Annelie Peterson, a wealthy publisher with a mysterious past. How far is Carolyn prepared to go for the dream part of a lifetime? And just how far will Annelie bend her principles in the name of desire? (1-933110-22-8)

Rangers at Roadsend by Jane Fletcher. After nine years in the Rangers, dealing with thugs and wild predators, Sergeant Chip Coppelli has learned to spot trouble coming, and that is exactly what she sees in her new recruit, Katryn Nagata. But even so, Chip was not expecting murder. The Celaeno series. (1-933110-28-7)

Justice Served by Radclyffe. The hunt for an informant in the ranks draws Lieutenant Rebecca Frye, her lover Dr. Catherine Rawlings, and Officer Dellon Mitchell into a deadly game of hide-and-seek with an underworld kingpin who traffics in human souls. (1-933110-15-5)

Distant Shores, Silent Thunder by Radclyffe. Ex-lovers, would-be lovers, and old rivals find their paths unwillingly entwined when Doctors KT O'Bannon and Tory King— and the women who love them—are forced to examine the boundaries of love, friendship, and the ties that transcend time. (1-933110-08-2)

Hunter's Pursuit by Kim Baldwin. A raging blizzard, a remote mountain hideaway, and more than one killer-for hire set a scene for disaster-or desire-when reluctant assassin Katarzyna Demetrious rescues a stranger and unwittingly exposes her heart. (1-933110-09-0)

The Walls of Westernfort by Jane Fletcher. All Temple Guard Natasha Ionadis wants is to serve the Goddess, and she volunteers eagerly for a dangerous mission to infiltrate a band of rebels. But once away from the temple, the issues are no longer so simple, especially in light of her attraction to one of the rebels. Is it too late to work out what she really wants from life?
(1-933110-24-4)

Change Of Pace: *Erotic Interludes* by Radclyffe. Twenty-five hot-wired encounters guaranteed to spark more than just your imagination. Erotica as you've always dreamed of it.
(1-933110-07-4)

Fated Love by Radclyffe. Amidst the chaos and drama of a busy emergency room, two women must contend not only with the fragile nature of life, but also with the mysteries of the heart and the irresistible forces of fate. (1-933110-05-8)

Justice in the Shadows by Radclyffe. In a shadow world of secrets, lies, and hidden agendas, Detective Sergeant Rebecca Frye and her lover, Dr. Catherine Rawlings, join forces once again in the elusive search for justice. (1-933110-03-1)

shadowland by Radclyffe. In a world on the far edge of desire, two women are drawn together by power, passion, and dark pleasures. An erotic romance. (1-933110-11-2)

Love's Masquerade by Radclyffe. Plunged into the often indistinguishable realms of fiction, fantasy, and hidden desires, Auden Frost discovers a shifting landscape that will force her to question everything she has believed to be true about herself and the nature of love. (1-933110-14-7)

Beyond the Breakwater by Radclyffe. One Province-town summer three women learn the true meaning of love, friendship, and family. Second in the Provincetown Tales. (1-933110-06-6)

Tomorrow's Promise by Radclyffe. One timeless summer, two very different women discover the power of passion to heal and the promise of hope that only love can bestow. (1-933110-12-0)

Love's Tender Warriors by Radclyffe. Two women who have accepted loneliness as a way of life learn that love is worth fighting for and a battle they cannot afford to lose. (1-933110-02-3)

Love's Melody Lost by Radclyffe. A secretive artist with a haunted past and a young woman escaping a life that proved to be a lie find their destinies entwined. (1-933110-00-7)

Safe Harbor by Radclyffe. A mysterious newcomer, a reclusive doctor, and a troubled gay teenager learn about love, friendship, and trust during one tumultuous summer in Provincetown. First in the Provincetown Tales. (1-933110-13-9)

Above All, Honor by Radclyffe. The first in the Honor series introduces single-minded Secret Service Agent Cameron Roberts and the woman she is sworn to protect—Blair Powell, the daughter of the president of the United States. First in the Honor series. (1-933110-04-X)

Love & Honor by Radclyffe. The president's daughter and her security chief are faced with difficult choices as they battle a tangled web of Washington intrigue for...love and honor. Third in the Honor series. (1-933110-10-4)

Honor Guards by Radclyffe. In a journey that begins on the streets of Paris's Left Bank and culminates in a wild flight for their lives, the president's daughter and those who are sworn to protect her wage a desperate struggle for survival. Fourth in the Honor series. (1-933110-01-5)